PRAISE FOR BE

CW01391228

"*I'm obsessed with Ben Alderson!* .... *perfect romantasy package, with delectable banter, swoony romance, original world-building, and plot twists that will have you wondering who to trust. Go read this immediately.*"
Nisha J. Tuli, international bestselling author of
Trial of the Sun Queen

"*A war brewing between human and fae, the sweetest romance, and the most gut-wrenching betrayals...what more could a romantasy lover ask for? Ben Alderson is a master of building deeply layered worlds.* A Betrayal of Storms *is rich, fast-paced, and packed with deceptions and plot twists that kept me from sleep. Ben delivers once again in the romantasy arena.*"
Stacey McEwan, bestselling author of The Glacian Trilogy

"*Featuring exhilarating highs, heartbreaking lows, and an impeccable sense of tension, the* Realm of Fey *series immerses readers in a high-stakes world of political intrigue and twisty betrayals – and delivers a delicious romance for the ages complete with some absolutely searing heat.*"
Laura R. Samotin, author of *The Sins On Their Bones*

"*Ben Alderson's* A Betrayal of Storms *is everything romantasy lovers will adore - a world full of magic and mystery, lush romance, a beguiling main character and a devilishly charming love interest. Readers will tear through the pages and then beg for more by the end.*"
Halli Starling, author of *Coup de Coeur*

Ben Alderson

A GAME OF MONSTERS

REALM OF FEY BOOK FOUR

AR

ANGRY
ROBOT

ANGRY ROBOT
An imprint of Watkins Media Ltd

Unit 11, Shepperton House
89 Shepperton Road
London N1 3DF
UK

angryrobotbooks.com
twitter.com/angryrobotbooks
A little bird

An Angry Robot paperback original, 2025

Copyright © Ben Alderson, 2025

Cover by Sarah O'Flaherty
Edited by Eleanor Teasdale and Shona Kinsella
Set in Meridien

All rights reserved. Ben Alderson asserts the moral right to be identified as the author of this work. A catalogue record for this book is available from the British Library.

This novel is entirely a work of fiction. Names, characters, places, and incidents are the products of the author's imagination or are used fictitiously. Any resemblance to actual events, locales, organizations or persons, living or dead, is entirely coincidental.

Sales of this book without a front cover may be unauthorized. If this book is coverless, it may have been reported to the publisher as "unsold and destroyed" and neither the author nor the publisher may have received payment for it.

Angry Robot and the Angry Robot icon are registered trademarks of Watkins Media Ltd.

ISBN 978 1 91599 880 4
Ebook ISBN 978 1 91599 881 1

Printed and bound in the United Kingdom by CPI Group (UK) Ltd, Croydon CR0 4YY.

The manufacturer's authorised representative in the EU for product safety is eu-comply OÜ - Pärnu mnt 139b-14, 11317 Tallinn, Estonia, hello@eucompliancepartner.com; www.eucompliancepartner.com

9 8 7 6 5 4 3 2 1

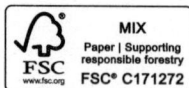

MIX
Paper | Supporting responsible forestry
FSC
www.fsc.org
FSC® C171272

Elise Kova, for inspiring me, guiding me and encouraging me.
I would not be writing these stories without your influence.

CHAPTER 1

Duncan Rackley was dying, and it was all my fault. That was a truth which haunted me day and night, never leaving the edges of my mind. And as I left Imeria Castle behind, I couldn't stop thinking about my duty and how, if I continued to ignore it, the fate of the world – the peace it believed it had finally achieved – was under threat.

I tugged down at the hood of my cloak as the harsh winter winds embraced me. My mare, a beautiful black steed with a velvet coat glittering like obsidian, battled through the downpour of sleet and snow, undeterred and unbothered. Snowflakes as big as my hand obscured the view, leaving gentle kisses against my ice-cold skin. Although my waxed jacket kept the material from becoming sodden, I still felt the chill of my court deep in my bones.

Ice and blood, one and the same. And yet, I felt like a stranger to it. Undeserving and unwanted, human but not. Fey but not. A king in name but nothing more.

Lost to the storm around me, I was no different than the snowflakes that fell: helpless to do anything but exist in the stream of wind that guided me along, waiting for my inevitable downfall.

Life in the wake of saving the world should've been a cause for happiness and joy. At least that was the case for everyone else. For me, I knew the truth. When we destroyed Duwar's gate and its keys, supposedly locking the demon within its eternal prison, the truth was Duwar had escaped in a new prison. The flesh of the man I loved. His bones were a cage hosting the demon, his skin a shield to hide the dark truth from the world. My burden was to know this damning truth and find a solution to it, all whilst the world around me delighted in an era of peace it'd not seen in a long time.

I could hear the town of Berrow before I saw it. The streets were alive with chatter and noise, the delightful call of full homes and streets bustling with my people. *My* people, as if I could claim them, as if I deserved them. But I buried those thoughts as Silvia, my mare, trotted onto Berrow's main street, leaving my horrors and worries behind.

Although I hated to see my people's misplaced love for me, today, I forced myself to face them. In the months that had passed since our battle at Rinholm Castle I'd kept myself secluded in the ruins of my castle, with no desire to mingle with a world which I put under threat with every passing hour. But today, I had a purpose for my visit to Berrow, and for that I'd have to leave behind my self-loathing, if only for an hour.

"King Robin," a fey called from his stall at the side of the road. He was bundled up in fur and thick materials, his pale face almost completely concealed by a knotting of scarfs, all beside two beady black eyes and rosy cheeks as red as apples. For a moment I thought of Jesibel – my friend who had survived Aldrick's treatment but had survived... changed. Like Jesibel, this fey was one of those we freed from the Below: the underground prison beneath Lockinge Castle. I'd promised to return him home, and I'd fulfilled that promise. And yet, he was safer in Lockinge Castle's prison than he was here with me.

Because there was a demon lurking in my shadow.

"How do you fair, my king?" he asked after I didn't reply to his initial greeting. My subtle nod clearly wasn't sufficient as a hello, *or* a farewell. "Could I offer you a warm cider for your travels, a gift of my thanks for everything you have done for us?"

I smiled down at him, unable to formulate words. Truthfully, I wanted nothing more than to take the drink, down it and demand another. Alcohol was ideal at numbing the mind and its anxieties. But it was best the town didn't see the man they called king getting drunk, considering they hadn't seen me in weeks.

Drinking myself into a stupor was something I'd do when I returned to Imeria. Drowning my worries, hoping the sharp spirits would dull the reality of horror I hid inside of me – and the walls of my castle.

"Thanks for your offer." I watched as his expression faltered, obvious upset creasing his forehead into a map of lines. "But maybe next time?"

The peddler nodded, wafting a steaming mug of warmed ale to tempt me one final time. "It's made from the recent harvest at my orchard. Something that wouldn't have been possible without your funding and aid."

I smiled, because it was the least I could do. "I'm glad to hear you've had success, and really, I do appreciate the offer."

A king may not need to explain himself to his people, but old Robin was an over explainer, so I couldn't help but offer one final excuse in hope of dampening the man's clear offence. "I have a meeting with someone very important, best I don't stumble over my words during the conversation."

"Aye, Your Majesty. I understand, thank you for stopping."

I squeezed my feet into Silvia's side, urging her ahead, not wanting to see the disappointment glaze over the kind man's eyes. "Always."

The deeper I travelled into Berrow, the less I could fathom just how much it had changed in the past few months. The once-empty town was now overspilling with life. Fey and humans dwelled beside one another, occupying homes glowing with lit hearths and alive with the song that was joy. The streets had been cleared of debris, ruins of buildings either completely rebuilt or still under construction. If there was anything that could distract me, it was seeing the success of rebuilding Icethorn as the grand place it had once been. Silver linings and all.

Being here, surrounded by it, I found it hard to imagine there was remaining tension between Wychwood and Durmain – the human and the fey realm. Or the internal conflicts in the Oakstorm Court.

A world once divided had been brought together; or at least that was the illusion I had neatly woven.

If only they knew the truth.

I left Silvia with the stable master, who promised her carrots and oats. I thanked him, careful not to allow room for further conversation. Silence was easier to navigate these days. It was what I was used to... unless my advisor, Eroan, came to visit.

Even more vendors had been set up on either side of the street. I smelled cinnamon dusted on baked goods, salted meats roasted over fires and the sharp-tang of harsh cheese mixed with sweet fruits. I would've given anything to join them, to delight in their wares and laugh alongside them. But I had something I needed to do – *items* to collect before I returned home to the demon I hid within its walls.

For the umpteenth time, I mentally ran through my short list.

Iron. Gardineum extract. Books. News from the world beyond my cold castle walls.

Before I knew it, my feet had taken me to my first destination. I scrunched my gloved hands up, starring at the town hall as though it was my greatest enemy. I knew who waited inside and had spent weeks doing what I could to stay away from him, even if that was far from what I wanted to do.

It took courage to step inside, leaving the comfort of the street. But I did it because I had no other choice.

The town hall had been one of the most damaged places in Berrow, so much so I didn't even notice that Berrow had one when I first visited with Erix after escaping a gryvern attack. It'd been excavated from beneath rubble and snow. Once nothing more than a shell – a skeleton of rotting wood and rooms full of snow and ice – it now stood tall, thanks to the supplies my allies in the Cedarfall Court had sent to aid in the rebuilding effort. A month, that was all it took for it to be rebuilt as the heart of Berrow. Dark, oiled beams held up an impressive curved ceiling. The treated wooden panels that made up the exterior and interior walls had been treated with fire, making them impenetrable to the cold and further decay.

I lifted white knuckles and knocked on the door. Not a beat later, they swung open to reveal two soldiers standing vigil on the other side. Both wore the black and grey tones of my court, their silver cloaks stitched with the Icethorn symbol: a sword pointing north through a mountain range.

They bowed the second they saw me, removing their helmets out of respect. I caught the flash of pride in their colourless eyes, round-tipped ears, the twitch of leathery wings unfolding beyond slits in their charcoal-grey cloaks.

Gryvern – or at least they had once been. Now, with the gradual return of their humanity thanks to the death of their sire, Doran Oakstorm, and the claim of their new master, these gryvern were the only soldiers I had to call upon. They were gifted to me by the one who controlled them – the man whose door I had finally knocked upon in my desperation.

"I'm here to speak with" – I took a deep breath, forcing the final word out – "Erix."

The two gryvern spared each other a glance. Their grey-tinged skin reflected the light from the many burning sconces that lined the walls of the corridor at their backs. "We didn't receive word of your arrival, King Icethorn," one of them said.

"We apologise for not being better prepared to welcome you," the other added, looking behind me in search of something that wasn't there. "Did you not arrive with a guard?"

I rolled my shoulders back, feigning the fake smile that I'd perfected, and regretting how easy it was to lie. "We are in an era of peace, the first of its kind in generations, perhaps longer. There is nothing that can threaten me here, not anymore."

It was a point no one could argue with, and yet both the gryvern gave me a look as if they could see right through my lies. "Precaution is still wise, King Icethorn."

"No need for that," I said, waving them off, adorning the mask of the unbothered, cold-hearted king I'd become. "And I didn't send word ahead because this is somewhat of an impromptu visit."

"We understand, although Erix will not be pleased," the gryvern replied, his voice almost sounding forced out of a throat full of stones. "The world may be saved, but you are still the king, and new threats can replace the old. Please, send for us next time, and we will escort you, as previously agreed."

As previously agreed.

No. It was never agreed that I'd need full-time shadows. Erix had attempted to offer it, but my refusal had been clear and that had not wavered since my last meeting with him. Even now I still could hear the sharp tone I'd used the last time I'd been in a room with him, his wild panicked eyes and frantic demands. As if he still believed there was something to fear in the world, and yet when I looked him dead in the eyes and asked him what, he never gave me an answer.

Because he didn't want to, or he couldn't, I wasn't sure.

Our argument had pained me at the time, and the memory weighed on me even now. The gaping maw of time had simmered between us since, drawing us apart just like with all of my friends and allies.

But I had good reasons not to have shadows. I had secrets that required the dark to hide in.

I swallowed down the sudden spike of sickness. If I hadn't cultivated such a rigid control over myself, I would've doubled over and spilled the contents of my stomach across the gryvern's recently polished greaves. "A short journey from Imeria to Berrow will hardly allow room for danger. After all," – I forced a smile – "we're in an era of peace, as I've said. The days of danger are far behind us."

I hardly convinced myself, let alone them.

The air around me seemed to grow heavier suddenly, and I wasn't the only one to notice. The gryvern guards parted before me, just in time for a new voice to join the fray.

"It's with that mindset that you'll find yourself harmed one of these days, *little bird*."

I looked from the soldiers to the corridor behind them. Parting from the shadows, with arms clasped behind his back and chin held high, was the man I'd been avoiding since our last encounter, even though he was the very person I needed in this moment.

He was the person I had needed since returning with Duncan from the Elmdew Court.

Erix. The man I once called my personal guard, my lover. The man who was used as a puppet and killed my father. The man who had proved himself to me, over and over. The man who had vowed that I was his duty, and his pleasure. Erix who'd sworn himself to me, and I'd discarded him the first moment I could.

Perhaps he hated me for how I treated him the last time we saw each other, but if only he knew that I did it to protect him.

I'd do *anything* to protect him.

Erix looked more like the fey I had met for the first time in the Hunter's camp than he had at any time since his unwilling transformation. His skin had reclaimed its sun-kissed hue, no longer a drab grey but sparkling like gold. Bright silver eyes bore into me from where he stood, tall and straight-backed, his entire focus pinned to where I stood. Erix tensed in every manner of the word; his jaw tightened as he drank me in. It was shadowed with a light beard that matched the short-shorn cut of his hair. It was impossible to not admire the structure of his bones, even if I wanted to look away, I couldn't.

He – like his gryvern beside me – had his wings on display outside of his armoured outfit. Half fey, half monster – and yet from the way he looked at me, I couldn't help but remember that he was completely and entirely mine if only

I accepted it. Whether or not he was beside me these days, he still had my best interests at heart.

He always would.

Eroan reminded me as much, every week, when he told me Erix had asked after me during our two-man council meetings. Erix's incessant requests for an audience with me, which I declined every week.

I just wasn't prepared to accept it. Not because I didn't want to, but because I had to protect him.

"Erix," I said in greeting, his name awkward in my mouth. "How – how are you?"

"Surprised, to say the least," he replied, stopping just shy of *his* soldiers – I could pretend they were mine, but it was Erix they ultimately followed. "But the important question is, how are *you*?"

It was such an awkward conversation, as if we were strangers catching up. Which was exactly what we were now: strangers made by my hand.

"I'm fine," I lied. "And you?"

"As I've already answered when you asked me the first time, I'm surprised." He stepped aside and gestured for me to follow him. "I trust you haven't journeyed all this way to reiterate how you don't need me as your personal guard, or have you changed your mind since you dismissed me?"

I opened my mouth and then closed it again. Pathetic, like a fish out of water. Taking a deep breath in, hoping to clear the cobwebs of my anxiety, I ended up sounding like a petulant child. "I didn't dismiss you."

"No?" Erix scoffed, silver eyes trailing me from head to boot. I lowered my hood, feeling as exposed as a person standing in a ray of sunlight in a darkened room. "Not in a manner of speaking. But making me Lord of Berrow, knowing the responsibility that would come with it, is certainly a back-handed way of dismissing me from the service I should be completing."

I stopped stock-still, forcing Erix to do the same. "We've had this conversation, and I'm not willing to open it again."

Erix scoffed. "I thought as much. So, have you come to inquire into my first couple of months as a lord, and see that I'm not abusing my power?"

I picked up my pace again, falling into step with Erix. "I gave you this position because I trusted that 'abusing power' was not ever going to be an issue when it comes to you. There was no one better for the job," I replied.

"Then what brings you to my door?"

"Believe it or not, I've not come all this way to argue again."

Erix huffed a laugh, finally drawing his eyes off me. "Of course you haven't."

"Iron," I said, plain and simple, needing this conversation not to draw on for too long. "Eroan told me your gryvern–"

"*Your* gryvern, Robin. They follow you, as I do; we're your loyal subjects."

I hated the serious bite in Erix's tone, how his words struck as true as the steel at his waist.

"Yes, well," I continued, clearing my throat in hopes that would make me sound more confident with my strange request. "Eroan informed me that they've recently confiscated three carts worth of iron from the Hunters' encampment on the border of Wychwood and Durmain. I've come to see the stores."

"I'm sorry," Erix said. "But you've come too late. The iron has already been dealt with. It was best not to keep such a material close to so many fey. I haven't got anything left to show you."

Dealt with meant it had been taken north of Berrow, to the lake known as the Sleeping Depths, and dumped into its waters, never to be claimed by another again. Which was exactly not what I needed here, considering I had a purpose for a material that removed a fey's power.

A purpose currently festering inside my castle walls.

"What about the labradorite stores?" I added, fumbling for something – anything – that would help me keep my secrets. If Erix dwelled too long on why I was interested in the iron, it would not end well.

One look into Erix's eyes, and apparently, I had failed before I even began.

Erix narrowed his gaze on me. "As agreed with Cassial and his Nephilim, all labradorite stores are being shipped to Lockinge before they make the journey to Irobel. I haven't seen any in weeks. Reports from Cedarfall, Oakstorm and Elmdew are all the same. The borders have been torn down, we are no longer a land of four courts, but a united realm. Just as you desired."

"Good," I said, nodding whilst a cold shiver trailed down my arms like the kiss of ice. "That's good news."

Was it?

It wasn't new information to me, but I was still struggling with the idea that Erix had no iron. I waited for him to ask me why I needed the one thing that could render me powerless: my weakness.

The truth was that iron was no longer the thing that made me weak.

"If you are in need, though I cannot fathom for what for, I could send a request to our allies and ask for a store of labradorite back?" Erix asked. I couldn't help but feel like he was testing me.

"No, no need." Silence stretched between us, so heavy I rushed to bring an end to our interaction. "Well, that's all I came here to inquire. I see Berrow is thriving, which I thank you for. Erix, your work here is... really impressive, but there's no reason for me to waste any more of your time," I said, turning on my heel, the ache inside my chest impossible to control now.

I needed iron. *Lots* of it. The minimal store I had back in Imeria Castle was working as I required it to, but if I was to keep Berrow, Icethorn, Wychwood – everything and everyone – safe, I needed a *lot* more, and soon.

A hand reached out and stopped me before I could walk back to the main doors. "Will I be seeing you in Lockinge for the events Cassial is hosting?"

I'd been made aware that the Nephilim had been hard at work at repairing relations between the humans and the fey. There were talks of a wedding or some other grand event to be hosted, but for whom had yet to be agreed. Regardless, I had no plans to leave Icethorn. Not because I didn't want to run away from what lingered here, but because I couldn't risk taking my eyes off it.

I shook myself free. "No. I don't believe so. Jesibel needs me, and I don't like the idea of uprooting her from her new life. Think it's best I stay behind."

It wasn't entirely a lie. Jesibel had cemented a new life with me, and I didn't want to leave her. But she was a great cover for the real reason I could not leave Imeria. It was enough to stop Erix, or anyone else, asking more questions.

I took a step away, creating distance when Erix called after me. "Robin, wait."

The power he held over me hadn't waned in the weeks we'd been apart. This time he didn't need to stop me with the grasp of a hand, the use of my name was enough. After we'd returned to Imeria with Duncan, I'd put Erix in charge of Berrow as its lord, knowing full well it was the only way I could distract him enough so that he wouldn't discover the truth.

He'd been right, of course, when he'd made the accusation.

"Yes, Erix?" I replied, without turning to face him. I faced the closed doors ahead, the gryvern at its sides doing everything in their power to disappear into the shadows. Altar knew I wished for the same – to disappear.

"How is Duncan these days?" Erix asked the one question that could break me. "It has been a while since… since I last saw him. Believe it or not, I care to know he is faring well."

It was a question that I knew would come, but I wasn't prepared for it. "I will pass on your well-wishes, Erix. He'll be glad to receive them, I'm sure."

"That hasn't answered my question, Robin. And you know it."

I swallowed the bile burning my throat. My heart cantered in my chest, my anxiety close to spilling out physically. "Duncan is getting better each and every day."

It was a lie. No doubt Erix could sniff it on me.

"The people of Icethorn haven't seen in him a long while. And those very people are talking. As Lord of Berrow, may I make a request that the next time you visit, you should both come–"

"I have Eroan to council me on the whispers of my people," I snapped, too late to bite down on my tongue.

Erix followed my remark with silence. It was so tense between us that a knife could cut through it. I wanted to fill the void, to scream and shout and fill the space with the same chaotic noise that haunted my mind.

But it was Erix who spoke next. "Is it a crime to worry about our king and his consort?"

I rolled my shoulders back, taking a moment to put on the mask I imagined a king was expected to wear in an era of joy and peace. "I'm fine, Erix. Imeria is occupying me. Eroan is keeping me up to date on matters."

Erix silenced me with a glance of his softened silver eyes.

"That wasn't why I asked, little bird."

I swallowed the stone in my throat at the use of his nickname for me. There was so much I wanted to say to him, to explain. But, as I told Erix when we last spoke, when he was ready to tell me the truth of what he saw in Duwar's realm, I too would share mine.

"Please, next time you obtain stores of iron, send word to me. That's an order, from your king."

Erix bowed his head, without taking his eyes off me. "I will do as you order, but when the time comes, I will ask why you are in such sudden need for iron, Robin."

This was his way of giving me extra time to come up with a lie that was actually convincing, proving that he knew something was amiss.

"I didn't realise a king needs to explain himself to his lords," I said, hating every ounce of sharpness to my tone.

"A king doesn't, but a friend does." Erix won with his reply. "I'm hoping the final dregs of Hunters have been dealt with, but if I catch word of any, you will be the first to know. This peace has been earned, and we *all* deserve to enjoy it."

I couldn't help but feel as though the comment was aimed at me in a specific way.

"Goodbye for now, Erix," I said, drawing an end to any more conversation.

He looked beyond me, to the gryvern lurking in the shadows of the corridor.

"Maren, would you kindly see King Icethorn back to Imeria?" Erix commanded, voice as steel as the glow of his eyes. "I do prefer our king doesn't walk around so exposed to the elements."

"There is no need for that, I can assure you," I said, but Erix silenced me with a raised hand.

"It's either Maren or me. You choose. You may be king, Robin. But you made me Lord of Berrow for a reason. When in the borders of Berrow, you are my responsibility just as the lowest-born fey is. That was your mistake, because it puts anyone inside the town under my jurisdiction and protection. My land, my rules."

"Land that I can quickly take away from you," I snapped back.

"Which you'll never do, because the moment I'm free of this responsibility, I'll be right back by your side, as your personal guard." Erix forced a smile. He'd won *again*, and from the mischievous glint in his eyes, he knew it. "Now, Maren. If you would kindly see that Robin is guarded at all times, until he leaves Berrow's boundaries."

"Certainly, my lord," Maren replied, before opening the door, taking my lack of response as confirmation of my defeat. But in truth, I used the time to lock eyes with Erix again. My next question was risky, but I had to ask it. "Why the need for guards, Erix? Do you feel as though there are still threats against me that I should be aware of?"

It was his turn to be shocked into silence. I refused to look away, careful not to miss a single nuance of his reaction that would give away the truth of what thoughts he harboured.

Erix had been the one to enter Duwar's gate, going after Duncan, who'd been taken inside. He'd refrained from talking about what happened during the minutes they were inside Duwar's realm. To me, his silence was incriminating. He knew something had happened, but would not tell me what. That was the root of our contention.

"Robin." Erix took a step toward me but stopped himself from getting too close. "For as long as I live, I will always worry about you. You deserve to enjoy the new world more than anyone I know. Stop hiding in the ruins of your castle, and live. Unless you're the one who feels as though threats still linger, you need to come out of hiding. *Live.*"

Live… as if it was that easy. Every day I was just trying to survive beneath my new, haunting burden.

I had asked Erix once before about what he experienced with Duncan in Duwar's realm, and he'd looked me in the eyes and lied. He'd told me nothing had happened, that he'd found Duncan and gotten him out to safety.

That didn't explain the scars down Duncan's chest. It also didn't explain how every time Duncan stood before a mirror, it was Duwar I saw. Either Erix really didn't know, or he was lying.

I knew which it was.

The proof that something happened was currently chained and bound by iron to a bed, in Imeria castle, drugged daily with Gardineum, dying slowly because of the parasite inside of him.

"Maren, I have a few more errands to run before leaving Berrow," I said, turning my attention to the soldier. Her leathery wings twitched at the use of her name, likely calling to the more human side of her than the monster her affliction from Doran Oakstorm had caused. "I'd like to visit the apothecary next. The library after that. Can you escort me there please?"

"Certainly, Your Majesty."

I cringed at the title, knowing I didn't deserve it. "But once those errands are complete, and we reach Berrow's borders, you *will* leave me. As Erix said, I may be his responsibility on the land I gave him, but beyond the border, I'm the one who gives the commands."

Maren bowed, but shot a glance to Erix, who must've nodded in agreement. "I will do as you command, Your Majesty."

"Robin will do," I said, gesturing to the door so we could get out of here.

"Are you in need for more Gardineum then?" Erix questioned.

The reply was thick in my throat. "Pardon?"

"What with the visit to the apothecary, I can only imagine that's what you are going for. Eroan mentioned you still aren't sleeping well a few weeks back. I just didn't realise you still needed the drug to help?"

I felt hot so suddenly, it was as if my blood was Cedarfall rather than Icethorn. "It seems that Eroan needs reminding that gossiping about his king is a punishable offence." I sounded frigid, just like the element I controlled, hard as ice and as unwelcoming as a winter storm.

"He's worried about you. Is that worthy of punishment now too?" Erix asked as I stepped back out onto Berrow's main street. "Overuse of Gardineum can be harmful, not only to your mind but to your body. Although, I'm sure this is nothing Duncan hasn't already said to you before."

The Gardineum isn't for me.

"It sounds like Eroan isn't the only one who's worried." I shot Erix a final look, silently pleading for him to *finally* tell me the truth so we could shatter this barrier between us.

"I just want you to enjoy the life you sacrificed everything to have." Erix ran a hand over his chin, fingers tracing the curve of jawline just as I once had. "Just because you dismissed me, doesn't change what you are. My duty and my–"

"Erix, I'm fine."

That was just it. Everything I'd sacrificed up until this point had been for nothing. Because the life he believed we had, this new world, was all but an illusion balancing on the edge of a knife.

A knife I held.

And all it would take was for someone to come and look for Duncan to discover why.

Three of the four keys to the demon-god Duwar's realm had been destroyed, forever closing off our world from his. But the problem was, Duwar wasn't there like everyone believed. The demon-god was here, in our world, in Wychwood, a stone's throw away from Berrow itself.

Duwar was Duncan, or Duncan was Duwar. I didn't know which way round things were. And deep down I believed Erix held answers as to how this transfer between man and demon had happened. Until he was prepared to share, I would deal with this alone. Now was not the time to bring up our last argument when so many others were listening in.

But his inability to be honest with me had led to me grasping at straws. Letters sent to Rafaela went unanswered, books I scoured through for stories on the demon-god who'd seemingly been wiped from our history told me nothing.

"Goodbye, Erix," I said again, turning my back on him for the last time.

"Wait!" Erix shouted, drawing the attention of the full street of people.

I released a sigh of relief, convincing myself the truth was finally about to come out, that this burden no longer had to be mine to bear alone. But Erix didn't say anything further before extending a cream envelope with a red-gold wax seal.

"This came for you this morning. I was going to give it to Eroan for your next briefing, but I thought I'd do it now. I think it's the most recent developments from Cassial about his planned celebration."

"Thanks," I said, taking the envelope from him, brushing my fingers against his hand. He was so warm, just as I remembered. Against the chill of the street, the falling snow and brisk winds, I craved nothing more than the warmth he could offer – the comfort. "Now, is that all you have to say?"

He withdrew his hand, putting it at his side and flexing his fingers in regret. Or was it disgust? "It is."

Erix turned and left me. The turmoil inside my body seeped out into the world, encouraging the winter weather to intensify. By the time Maren escorted me to the apothecary, I could hardly see an inch in front of my face. The vendors had closed down their stalls and raced back home to see out the storm of my making.

All the while, the storm I raged within would never calm. Not now, not tomorrow – not whilst I secretly harboured a demon-god of destruction and chaos in my bed, in the body of the man I loved.

This was the life we got after we saved the world from a demon-god. A lie. Where captured fey returned to the Icethorn Court, reclaimed their homes and rebuilt lives in the dawn of a new world – all without knowing that it would come tumbling down if I didn't find a solution.

I wished, with every fibre of my being, that I could join them. But my world, my life, was left in tatters in my wake. My secrets threatened this very town, court, world – both human and fey.

I collected the bag of dried Gardineum flower, visited the library to find no new tomes had been found or donated about Wychwood's history, no new stories that could help me understand Duwar. Then I left Berrow, my list of errands barely touched.

Maren did as she was asked, leaving me at the border, not following me any closer to Imeria Castle. Although, from a distance, I certainly felt her eyes trailing me.

Pulling on the reins, I guided Silvia toward my castle's stables, which had recently been rebuilt outside the half-ruined castle of Imeria. It was a project Eroan kept me informed on, alongside the other rapid changes in the Icethorn Court. He was the only person I allowed to visit me in the ruins of Imeria Castle. He came once a week, with scrolls full of news. Without him, I wouldn't have known what was happening in the outside world. How the other fey courts were coping after the death of Aldrick – the Hand – and the destruction of Duwar's gate.

Eroan kept me in touch with reality, while mine was crumbling around me like the ruins of the castle I inhabited.

I hadn't left the confines of Imeria in almost two months, but today had been different. Eroan had visited me earlier that morning and made mention of a camp of Hunters that had been found on the eastern edge of Icethorn land. I'd sat and listened, fighting to keep my face neutral of my horror as he told me about how the Hunters had claimed an old fey settlement, setting up a base for themselves.

The Hand may've been dead, but the poison he left behind would take time to suffocate and shrivel. The Nephilim in Durmain were helping with that, but still more Hunters kept popping up like weeds.

Eroan had been pleased when he confirmed the Hunters been dealt with, the followers of the Hand carted off to Lockinge to await trial by the Nephilim. But that didn't settle me. Knowledge that they would be punished was not the pleasing news I wanted to hear.

It was what Erix's – *my* soldiers – found and collected that had me climbing onto Silvia's back and heading into the town.

Iron. But returning to Imeria empty handed was terrible. Each inch closer to my horror, and I had to think of more ways to get iron.

I needed it, but I had to be careful with how clear I made that need to others. I couldn't tell Eroan why without inciting more questions. If that meant I would have to go looking for more iron myself, I would do that. No matter the threat, considering the one I dealt with was more real and dangerous in my eyes.

Iron to keep Duncan powerless.

Gardineum to force him into a sleeping state, all to keep him safe from himself.

I stood before Imeria castle, wishing I could turn away. Run away. All around me, life bloomed. The parts of the castle that had fallen during the Draeic's attack had been engulfed in life – vines, bright flowers of verdant, purple and yellow – creeping over the ruins.

"This is what my power can offer you," Duncan had said when we returned to Imeria, attempting to trick me into trusting the demon inside of him. But no matter how weak I'd become, I wouldn't listen. But that didn't mean Duncan's words didn't echo in my mind every time I saw what Duwar's power did to my castle. The life it offered, before I wrapped his body in iron and poisoned his mind with Gardineum.

"Believe me, Robin." Duncan had pleaded as I wrapped his body in chains. *"You need to listen to me."*

My reply repeated in my mind. *"No. This is a trick. You're playing with me, Duwar. This has nothing to do with listening to Duncan, but listening to you. But I won't fall for it. Not like Aldrick did. I know what you're doing, and I refuse to play."*

"Then I will die," Duncan had cried. *"You'll kill me, is that what you want?"*

There was nothing I could've said back to him. Because Duncan *was* dying. I saw him deteriorate every day. Slowly, as Duwar poisoned him, and there was nothing I could do to save him. Except there was something. I could accept Duwar's continuous offer. Something that was becoming harder and harder to ignore.

CHAPTER 2

I melted into the silk sheets, luxuriating as Duncan eased two fingers into my arse, all whilst Erix simultaneously twisted his tongue around my nipple. My back arched, my breath heavy with lust. There were so many hands, mouths, gazes, tongues and attentions. Duncan drew his forest-green gaze down over me, whilst Erix looked up from his devouring with eyes the hue of a newly forged blade. I couldn't begin to focus on who was doing what to my body, as the tide of pleasure swept me away.

I was a feast for them. A banquet. A sweet piece of fruit for these two men to take bites out of, sucking the juices of enjoyment from my core. And I would willingly let them.

Both of them could take me, have me, touch me, kiss me.

I reached down to Erix, my arms slow and heavy. As my fingers touched his chin, his pale leathery wings twitch from anticipation. With a guiding hand, I tilted his head up, bringing him away from my raised nipple. I didn't need to look at it to see the swollen pink peak and lightly bruised skin around it.

"Erix," I breathed, desperate and needy. "My Erix."

"Yes, little bird?" he replied.

Duncan continued his tender movement inside of me, his two calloused fingers stretching me, preparing me. He watched as I shared the moment with my royal guard, smiling with acceptance and equal enjoyment.

I didn't want to say the words building inside of me, but I had to. "I – I know you're not real."

Like the shattering of glass thrown against a wall, the atmosphere changed. It always did, although this was the longest I'd ever allowed the dream to go on for.

"Yes, he is *real. At least it can be if you only ask," Duncan sang, removing himself from my entrance, then shifting positions until he was sitting behind me. Too fluid, too easy. My head rested in his lap. My Hunter propping up my head, my guard leaning over my leg, holding them down.*

This isn't real.

"Say the word, my love," Duncan continued, brushing damp strands of hair from my forehead. "Give me what I need, and you will have access to everything you have ever desired."

"Liar." I pinched my eyes closed, trying to regain composure.

"You know I do not lie to you, darling. Now, give me what I want."

"No." I snapped, tears falling down my cheeks. "I won't."

Duwar was getting desperate. Using my weakness to make me equally desperate as well. Poisoning my dreams had become their favourite tactic, and I was quickly weakening to it.

The dreamscape shifted frantically. Both men held me down on the bed with firm hands. The silk sheets had transformed to slithering vipers, wrapping around my limbs and keeping me from moving.

"Don't you want me, Robin?" Erix asked, his voice drawn out and sad. "When you came for me today, I saw it in your eyes. You called for me, so I came."

I refused to answer, not that I needed to. Duncan answered for me. Except the voice was not the deep rasp I'd fallen in love with, but the shadow-shuddering tone of the demon inside of him. "Robin does *want you, Erix. You occupy his mind. Desires, needs, wants... everything I could give him if he only accepted my–"*

I bolted upright in the reading chair, the knitted blanket falling over my knees and spreading across the floor at my feet. It wasn't the type of waking that was slow and steady. My consciousness had kicked me out of the nightmare, lungs breathless, my body clammy with sweat. And yet, as I stared at the far side of the room, where the single bed waited, my body could still feel those phantom hands on it. My fingers lifted subconsciously to my chest, testing the tender nipple beneath my loose tunic, delighting *and* hating how real it felt.

"Another one of your nightmares, darling?" The question came from a hoarse voice from the direction of the bed. It was weak, pained almost, as if each word hurt to speak aloud.

I lifted my gaze and locked eyes with the man before me. Or what was left of the man I had known. A shell of a person, close to death and yet clinging on.

Duncan Rackley.

Every day it was becoming harder to recognise him. Once-bright green eyes had leached of the colour, leaving behind pale pools. Dark shadows hung beneath those eyes, his face sunken and pale. The scar off his eye looked angry and sore, like a fresh wound, instead of one that had been inflicted years before I'd ever met him.

"Sorry," I gasped, rubbing a hand over my mouth. "I didn't realise I'd fallen asleep." I stretched my arms out, feigning some normalcy when nothing about my life was normal. "You should've woken me up."

"I like to see you sleeping," Duncan said, weak smile tickling at the corners of his cracked mouth. "You need to rest as well as I do. Maybe even more so."

"That's a logic I could argue," I replied, hands trembling in my lap. "How are you feeling today?"

"Tired," Duncan announced, monotone, forcing a smile that never reached his eyes. "Fucking exhausted, actually."

The numb ache in my back told me I'd been out for longer than I had wanted. I don't even remember when I had closed my eyes. One moment I'd taken my seat, waiting for Duncan to wake for his morning dosage of Gardineum, then in the next moment I was being devoured by two men in my dreams.

I'd learned that it was better not to speak of the dreams to Duncan. It would either upset him, or lure the demon out... that was if Duwar wasn't already the one I was speaking to.

I stood from my chair, throwing myself into action instead of dwelling on the dream... nightmare.

"You need to eat something," I said, sweeping my eyes over the cold bowl of oats I'd made last night. The full pitcher of water was beside it. "It will give you some energy and–"

"I'm not hungry," Duncan interrupted.

"You say that every morning, and yet you *still* need to eat."

Duncan didn't refuse me again, not as I began our haunting routine. I shut my mind off from emotions and charged forwards with what I had to do. Spoon-feeding Duncan whilst his eyes never left me, lifting the cup to his lips to wash down the cold gruel. Sometimes he resisted, vomiting up the mouthfuls or fighting against me. But other times, like today, he let me do it until the bowl and pitcher were empty.

It was hard to know if he was in control because Duwar was weak, or if he was in control because Duwar wanted me to *think* he was himself, just to control me in return.

I cleaned the corners of his mouth with a rag, my hand trembling.

"When will this end?" Duncan asked, voice hoarse like stone against stone. "How long will this punishment continue?"

"Soon," I replied. "I hope."

"I – I can't hold on for much longer, Robin." Tears filled his eyes, pleading cracking his tone. "Every day I try and every day I continue to fail."

"You are doing your best." My eyes flickered to his, unable to hold his intense gaze for longer than a few seconds. "I'm–"

"You're *killing* me."

I shook my head, knuckles white as I clasped onto the rag. "No, Duncan. I'm trying to save you. I'm – I'm doing everything I can to save you."

"You hate me, that is why? You want me to suffer."

Panic flared in me, white hot. "I love you, Duncan."

"Then why do you treat me like I'm your enemy?"

I refused to cry, refused to give the demon puppet-master exactly what it wanted. "*Duwar* is your enemy, not me."

Tears loosed from Duncan's yellow-stained eyes – of anger or sympathy, I couldn't tell. "I hear Duwar… I see endless possibilities. You know, it shows me a beautiful world. It promises me what could be if only you–"

"Duwar lies," I snapped. "It's trying to trick you, weaken you. Duncan." I choked on his name as emotion crawled up my throat. "You must continue to fight its influence. For me. Do it for me."

Duncan closed his eyes, pinching them shut until his entire forehead creased with deep grooves. "I'm so tired, darling."

So am I.

"Here, this will help for the time being." I paced to the side of the bed, careful not to trip over the web of iron chains holding Duncan down. There were so many chains over him, screwed into the floorboards, entrapping him like a butterfly on a corkboard. The iron kept his fey-given magic muted, while the weight of the metal kept him from getting out of bed. Every couple of days I treated the sore spots the pressure created, but the more wounds I cared for, the more would show up.

But I couldn't remove the chains. This was exactly the purpose I needed the iron for: imprisoning Duncan's human body, rendering him powerless and weak. Keeping him safe… *from* himself.

My heart ached as it always did when I saw him in this state. It went against everything I wanted to do for Duncan. I loved him, so much that I couldn't let him hurt himself, or anyone else.

I was keeping him safe from being hurt by the world outside this room, if they knew what had become of him.

"The Gardineum I've got is fresh this time. It will be easier for you to take it today, and slightly sweeter."

"Please, Robin. No." Duncan cried, rolling his head to the side of his worn pillow, as much as his bindings allowed. "No. No. Not... not today. I need a break. I need space for my mind to fucking work."

I silently refused him, continuing my actions without pause as if I didn't hear him.

If he wouldn't drink the Gardineum, which today I knew he would fight against, then there was another option I could proceed with. Even though he refused the drug most days, no matter how I stewed it into tea and tried to make it pleasant to take, I still knew it always ended with me injecting it straight into his bloodstream.

Duncan watched me reach for the syringe in the leather bag, the glass vial swirling with the iridescent liquid Gardineum. His fate clear as day. Doing this was the only way I could keep him unconscious, his mind closed off to the demon inside of him. At least that was what I reiterated to myself to calm my guilt.

It didn't work, it never would.

Weakened by his tired eyes, I gagged on a sob, releasing my grip on my strength. "I *must* do this. You know I must, Duncan. But I swear to you it will not be for much longer." I gritted my teeth, reigning in my emotions. "I will find a solution."

It had been Duncan who once begged this very act of me. In the few and far between moments when he was in control, he knew what I had to do to keep us all safe. But sometimes, when Duwar's presence was louder inside of him, and more demanding, he would resist. Like today.

It was hard to know who I looked at swaddled amongst the bedsheets.

Later, when I'd leave his room, I would allow myself to break. But not in front of him. *Never* in front of him. Showing weakness to Duncan wasn't my worry – it was the demon that was always searching for something to use against me.

Hence the dreams. Nightmares conjured to taunt me, to wear me down. But the one Duwar had just offered me seemed stronger than before. Perhaps seeing Erix yesterday had opened old wounds, revealed how I really felt – how I could still feel his kiss across my chest, his hands around my wrists.

Nightmares, Duncan called them, and yet they felt completely different.

If only Duwar had worked out that there was nothing more he could use against me. The demon-god had taken my heart, my home, my life, and left me surrounded by ruin.

I pushed on the syringe, squirting out a little liquid from the needle, ensuring there were no air bubbles that would enter Duncan's bloodstream and kill him.

"Robin, please. Don't do this to me. I beg you." Duncan continued to thrash in his bed, screaming bloody murder as I leaned over and brought the tip to his neck. His free hands grappled with me, trying to stop me, but despite the demon inside of him, his physical body was weak.

I couldn't bring myself to strap his arms down. I worried if I made him completely immobile, he'd wake one day thirsty or hungry and be unable to help himself. But it was becoming more and more difficult to convince myself to allow him a little freedom.

Duncan's neck was bruised, black and blue. As were his arms, the inside of his thigh and every place where I'd injected him. I'd rotate what vein I'd administer the injection depending on his cooperation. Today, I needed somewhere quick and accessible.

His neck would do.

The vein I'd entered was raised and sore, with barely days between to heal properly.

This was torture. For him, as well as me. Duncan was crying like a child, until his struggling suddenly ceased. Tears continued to trace down his cheeks, soaking the pillow. But something was different, like the feral part of him had been severed. His eyes locked with mine. Although he no longer spoke, the plea in his stare was louder than any screaming or shouting could've been.

"It's me, darling." He bored his gaze into me, plea evident in every line in his face. "I promise you, it's me. You think I'm trying to trick you into believing me, but I'm not."

Still, I couldn't know which reaction was his and which was the demon trying to control me. I could trust nothing when it came to him.

"Duwar is corrupting you, Duncan," I replied as I emptied the Gardineum into his bloodstream with ease. "You know it, as do I. Everything I'm doing is because you told me to do so. Do you remember?"

"I do." There was something detached about his reply, a signal to who was really controlling this conversation. "I regret the day those requests left my lips."

On the bedside table was a handheld mirror. It was the only one I'd kept with me – every other mirror in Imeria had been destroyed. I hadn't seen my own reflection in so long I was forgetting what I looked like.

I reached for it, holding the glass aloft so it caught the profile of Duncan's reflection. I held my breath, scared of what I would find in the mirror's surface. Would it be him, my Duncan, or the monster using him as a vessel – a puppet?

I didn't need to look properly to see the flash of brimstone and fire. The glowing red eyes and horns of a devil. It was more common than not that I saw the demon and not the man I loved in his reflection. Proving my worries right, justifying my terrible actions against Duncan – or what was left of him.

This calmness, this person conversing with me was *not* Duncan at all.

I dropped the mirror, hands shaking as urgency propelled me. "Nice try, Duwar. You almost had me."

Duncan's sobs stopped, then he smiled up at me, flashing teeth behind cracked lips. "Why do you continue to punish me when I can give you everything you've ever dreamed about, Robin Icethorn?"

Ignoring the demon's taunt, I looked deep into Duncan's eyes and hoped he could hear me. "I'm sorry, Duncan." I sank my teeth into my lower lip until I tasted blood. My hand barely shook anymore. "For all of this."

"But are you?" Duwar asked with a stolen voice. "Are you *really* sorry? Or is that just something you keep telling yourself to make your refusal of my offer worth it? Is your apology a way of you justifying this torture when there is no need for it?"

I kept myself still, not pausing for a second as I withdrew the emptied syringe. "I'm sorry that I'm not strong enough to do what is right. That is what I'm apologising for."

"You can be strong, if you finally accept me."

I shook my head. "I'm referring to killing you. Destroying you."

It would be easy, one slip of the hand, a few bubbles of air injected into a vein. This suffering, this torture, this threat – it would be over once and for all. But it was Duncan's life tangled in this web, and I couldn't just throw it away. Not until each and every path was exhausted for solutions.

Duwar didn't reply to me straight away. Instead, he watched me with adoration and abhorrence swirling as one in those lifeless eyes of his. He blinked, and when he opened his eyes again, I knew the man I loved was back in control.

"Then you must kill me, Robin."

I lifted the mirror again and confirmed that Duwar had left me to deal with the repercussions of my angered retort. It was Duncan's face in the reflection, fleeting, but him nevertheless. "You can finish this. Do what is required and end me. *Please.*"

Endless days of these injections, and the same amount of times I heard that plea. *Kill me.* Sometimes it was a demand, a command. Other times Duncan would plead with me, begging like a child wanting a new toy. *Kill me, damn you. Kill me, please. Kill me, save me.* No matter how he said it, no matter the tone or pitch of his voice, it hurt all the same. It never changed.

Neither did my answer.

"I can't."

Because killing him might take Duwar along within him, or it might not. I wouldn't risk losing him for nothing, if Duwar's presence would only find a new way to linger on.

"Duncan is dying anyway," he said, although Duncan's voice no longer his own. The tug and pull between Duncan and the demon becoming frantic and fast. "This body is not made for me. You can either kill him, or I will. But Duncan will die, *unless* you accept me."

"Fuck. You." I seethed until my throat ached, my control finally snapping.

"Coward," Duwar hissed, wide eyed, lips cracking until blood seeped over his teeth. His face screwed up as he continued his internal war for control. "I–it's me. Robin, I'm sorry. I'm sorry. Duwar is scared, it knows it will perish if I–"

Duncan bit down on his tongue until blood seeped out the gaps of his cracked lips.

"Enough," I scolded, speaking to both man and demon.

I held his stare, refusing to look away. Did Duwar watch on, suffering as his vessel was poisoned, weakened, to a pointless and pathetic husk? "Duwar's right. I *am* a coward. But damn it, Duncan, I would be a coward over and over again, if it means getting the chance to save you."

"I don't want to play this game anymore, Robin." When he closed his eyes, Duncan didn't open them again. "I'm so tired. My body is weak, my spirit shattered."

"I know, but I *need* you to fight. Just a little bit longer, that's all. You are doing everything you can, and trust me that I'm also trying to solve this, too." I leaned down and placed a soft kiss to his forehead. His brown hair had grown enough that it spilled around the pillow like serpents. I took my time, brushing it, pretending like life was normal and he was not begging for me to kill him.

"What life is this…" Duncan said slowly, his voice tired, "if I cannot spend it by your side freely?"

A violent shiver raced over my flesh. "I'll find a way to make sure that happens."

Duncan's eyes fluttered open for a brief moment. The deep grooves of tension across his forehead had eased, his dark brows relaxed as the poison worked its magic. "I know you don't believe me, but this power *could* save the world."

Duncan was believing the demon's own lies. They were one and the same, minds and intentions blending.

I ran my hand down the side of his face. "You know, deep down, that those promises are lies meant to manipulate us. Duwar is bad. You are good. Fight it. Remember yourself. Do it for me."

"I'm trying." Duncan fought against sleep but was quickly losing. "But Robin… You need…"

"You," I answered for him. "I need you. Remember, Duwar is not the solution to this problem, but the cause–"

"No," Duncan snapped alert, using the little dregs of energy left. "Listen to me. When I'm gone, you will need… *Erix*."

More words I'd heard, over and over.

I was unable to form a reply. With steady hands, I placed the instrument of torture back in its case. Numb to my core, I stopped at the chair, folded the blanket like I did every morning and made a move to exit the room.

I came to a halt at the door. When I turned back to face Duncan, I did the same action I'd been doing whilst this ordeal had begun. I locked my gaze with his where he continued to watch me. Then I lifted my finger to my eye, then pointed above my heart before gesturing to where Duncan lay.

I love you. Words I couldn't speak aloud because how could I dare utter them after the way I treated him?

Duncan, with weak trembling hands, copied my action. Pointing to his eye, then to his heart and then finally lifting his hand toward me, as much as the chains allowed him to do.

I love you.

I sank my teeth into my lower lip, turned on my heel and left. I didn't turn back again, not until the door was closed, separating me from the room, from my love. My Duncan. That's when the trembling began. It started in my fingers as I locked the door. Then my legs, forcing me to inch down to the floor where I gathered myself into a ball and began to rock back and forth.

If I had tears left to cry, my cheeks would have been wet. But alas, I had cried out rivers, lakes and oceans, leaving me hollow inside.

Unable to face the life before me, or what I'd just left behind, I buried my head into my knees and focused on breathing. It was a challenge, sorting my thoughts into an order I could focus on.

I stopped only when I heard confident footsteps ahead of me. But no one should've been here at this time, let alone in this side of the castle.

Panicked that someone was too close to my secret, I snapped my head up.

Eroan shouldn't have come here. He wasn't due to visit Imeria for another six days, and beyond that, he was banned from venturing this far into my castle. Everyone was. Jesibel never left the gatehouse I'd given her, with the garden she worked tirelessly to grow, in the perpetual silence her trauma had locked her within.

Then who?

Ready to scorn the visitor for ignoring my command, I laid my eyes on the man standing at the end of the hallway ahead of me.

When I'm gone, you will need... Erix.

And there he was, Erix, standing before me. My heart thumped into my throat as I took in the reality that he was mere feet away. His eyes drank me in, bright silver, flaying my flesh until he could see bone. And when he spoke, words sharp as the blade, his tone was as welcoming as soft hands.

"Little bird, I came. I am here."

His cheeks were flushed, his chest rising and falling as if he was breathless. Clearly, Erix had rushed here, panic settling in every flicker of his gaze.

But why?

I'd gone weeks without seeing him, and in the space of a day, this was the second time Erix stood before me. But unlike yesterday, his presence was exactly what I wanted. "*Why*?" I scrambled to stand, keeping my back to Duncan's bedroom door. "You shouldn't be here!"

Erix's eyes fell on the door behind me as if he knew the dark secret I harboured inside. When he levelled his silver gaze back on me, I could've willingly drowned in it.

"You called for me, little bird," Erix said. "So, I came."

Was this some manifestation from Duwar, a punishment for my thoughts? Those where the same words Erix had said in my dream. Unable to face the phantom of him, I buried my face back in my hands and chanted.

"You're not real. You're not real. You're – not – real!"

I fell back to the ground, thumping my fists against my temple, wishing to banish this illusion. I didn't stop until the very tangible, very warm embrace of arms folded around me. Erix knelt, dragging me into him, melding his body with mine. He rested his chin on the top of my head and released a sigh that mirrored the exhaustion I felt. "I'm very real, and I'm here. I have got you, little bird, and I swear no demands from a king will make me turn away. Not this time. Nor ever again."

I drew back enough to look at him through tear-filled eyes. "But you *need* to leave. You shouldn't be here, Erix. It isn't–"

Isn't what? Safe, fair? Neither seemed like the right answer.

"You're wrong, so very wrong." Erix ran a hand down my cheek, his thumb brushing the tears that stained them. "I should have been here for you a long time ago but my own fear of facing the past has kept me heeled like a dog."

"Please, just go." I pushed against his hard chest, but he was as unmoving as a rock in a river.

"I've told you. No." Erix's eyes then flitted to the door behind me again and asked a question that stabbed into my core. "Is Duncan inside that room?"

My silence was answer enough.

Erix gathered me back in his arms, laid his chin on top of my head and folded his wings around us. Then he said something I'd hoped for, but never expected to hear. "I think it's time we talk about what happened in Duwar's realm. Then you can tell me what has happened since we survived it. Deal?"

My blood thrummed through my body, ice clashing inside of me, a storm I could barely hold back. But when I looked into Erix's calming eyes, I knew I couldn't refuse him. "You already told me nothing happened..."

"I lied, to protect you, but I fear it has only had the opposite effect."

Deep down I already knew he'd lied, but hearing it aloud was enough to break me out of my frantic behaviour.

I took a full breath in, clearing the cobwebs of my forced solitary confinement.

"Deal," I said, wondering if Erix's secrets could solve the issue of my own. "I need to know everything. To save him."

"To save Duncan?" Erix asked, but I could tell he already had worked out the answer.

"Yes, but not only him," I replied. "To *save* us all."

CHAPTER 3

"It's almost the same every night," Erix said as he explained that he'd come to Imeria because of a nightmare. Apparently I'd been there, pleading with him to come here. And he did. I didn't have the confidence to ask him what else his dreams entailed, because my heart told me they were connected to those that plagued me. Which didn't exactly make me comfortable, knowing the scene I'd been a part of, bodies entangled, the three of us locked in flesh and desire.

We studied each other, me sitting upon the edge of my bed, him moving before it, wringing his hands just to give them something to do.

"Sit with me, Erix," I said, patting the bed at my side, forcing the dream from my mind. "Your pacing is making me nervous."

So is the thought of you experiencing the same dreams as me. So is the fact that you are here surrounded by all the secrets I've fought hard to keep.

Erix had hardly stopped moving since we'd entered my personal rooms, as though he didn't feel like he belonged. Truthfully, I didn't either. From what Eroan had explained, this chamber was once used by my mother. It was one of many in Imeria, and luckily it hadn't been crushed when the Draeic attacked the castle and caused more than half of it to collapse.

She'd used this chamber on the lower floors in the eastern wing when she was pregnant with my half-siblings – sisters and brothers who King Doran Oakstorm had slaughtered in his desire for vengeance. The connecting room just to my side – a door which was concealed by a large tapestry of mountains, stars, and wild stags – led to the smaller room where Duncan was in his induced state of sleep.

Erix stood before it, scuffing marks into the stone-slabbed floor with his boots. "I'm sorry. This is all just a lot to take in."

Was he apologising for his fidgeting movements, or the fact he'd turned up to Imeria, saying he'd dreamed about me calling for him?

I swallowed down my anxiety and asked the one question simmering in my brain. "How long has it been happening?" Did I really want to know the answer? "The dreams, that is."

"Weeks, maybe months," Erix replied without breath. "In fact, longer. It all blends into one if I'm honest. Sometimes I might not remember what I've dreamed about, but my body aches and reacts as if I do. But the one detail that always stands out is you are there, as is Duncan... both of you requesting my presence over and over."

"You should've told me," I said.

"I could say the same to you." Erix stopped, looked me dead in the eye, the intensity causing me to look down at my lap. My fingers picked at the seam of my trousers, fraying thread. If I had nails left to bite, Altar knows they'd be between my teeth by now. "Robin, you haven't given me, or anyone but Eroan and Jesibel, much of a chance to get close enough to speak to you about even minor matters. And until last night, it has only ever felt like a dream, something my own mind conjures to... punish me. For things I have done in my past, but perhaps also actions I never took."

"This is no punishment," I replied. "At least not in the sense that you are thinking."

Erix's eyes darkened to storm clouds. "It is Duncan, isn't it? He is creating these dreams somehow. Taunting me – taunting *us*."

"Nightmares," I corrected. "And no, I don't think I can blame him either. Not entirely."

It's the monster beneath his flesh that's doing this to us.

"And are they nightmares for you?" Erix asked, a hopeful glint in his eye.

I lifted my gaze, looking toward the tapestry, more so what lingered behind it. "Yes – most of the time."

There was a relief in sharing the burden. Like a weight, not completely lifting from my shoulders, but easing a little. All it would take is to ask him what exactly happened in his dreams, and hope it wasn't a mirror image of those I had.

Limbs entangled, mouths connected, a blanket of desire and love wrapped around us.

"How is it possible?" Erix asked, although I knew he already had worked out the answer.

"You tell me," I retorted. "Or are we going to keep pretending like nothing happened when you saved Duncan from Duwar's realm?"

I studied Erix in the silence that followed, reading the nuances of his expression. The wince in his silver eyes, the deepening of lines across his forehead. How his fists balled at his side, never straying far from the sword belted at his hip.

Before he replied, he finally took a seat.

Erix drew up a chair, opting not sit on the bed with me. It was a wise choice, a cautious one, born from the knowledge of our past, and the fact my present and future was festering in a bed of chains in the room beside us.

Being without Duncan's touch had starved me. I was famished for the comfort a familiar hand could offer. Or was this the remnants of the dream-world lingering? But it wasn't Erix who could offer it to me, and he knew it.

"I fear the moment I tell you, that it will make it all real," Erix said, leaning forwards with his elbows propped on his knees. He looked... exhausted, defeated almost.

I couldn't help but laugh. Not because anything he said was humorous, but because we were finally facing the maelstrom of secrets he'd kept from me. It was a reaction born of relief. "It's real already, Erix. Duncan is… Duncan isn't himself and hasn't been since you saved him." Saved him. Could I even call it that anymore? "Many of us changed after Rinholm, but Duncan… it is different. Darker."

Erix leaned closer, his fingers reaching out for my knee, his touch exactly what I needed in that moment.

"Take your time," he commanded, looking through his lashes at me.

I nodded, gathering myself. "I've tried everything to help him, but I have finally run out of hope." I choked on my emotion as it clogged my throat, control over myself a far-off concept.

"The Gardineum was never for you, was it?" Erix asked, refusing to look away.

I shook my head. "No, it wasn't."

Erix slumped forwards, burying his face in his hands. His breathing came out ragged, so much so that the urge to lay a hand on him so he could feel comfort was a siren call hard to ignore. His hands clawed into fists, the knuckles white with tension. Fleetingly, I reached over and let him feel my touch, to know he wasn't alone. Just as it worked for me, it seemed to have the same effect, because Erix's hand slowly shifted until it lay over mine, keeping me in place for a few seconds.

Then the connection severed, as I knew it would.

"Duwar was waiting for him when we fell through the gate," Erix began, clearing his throat to give room for the self-assured man to tell this story. "The world beyond it was in complete ruin, not a single sign of life. The sky was blood red, the ground leached of colour. It felt like… death, and yet there was something else. A potential for power I could not place my finger on." Erix looked up and met my gaze. "But then there Duwar was, except it was not the demon I expected to see—"

"What do you mean?" I encouraged, needing to know.

"It – it did not look the same as it had when we saw its reflection. Certainly not the same figure we saw in Aldrick's mirrors. Duwar wasn't the horned, fire-and-brimstone form. They looked... normal, almost. A vision I certainly didn't expect."

My breath caught in my throat. I dared not move for fear it would stop the truth from finally being shared. Everything Erix was saying, horrifying as it was, was knowledge I craved since the moment I first knew that Duwar had successfully escaped in Duncan's body.

Erix took a deep breath in, and said, "It was another trick. A lure to get Duncan close, no doubt. And it worked."

It was no different to what Duwar was doing to me now. Using Duncan to lure me in only to ensnare me in a trap.

"What did Duwar do to him, Erix?" I asked, voice trembling. "I know it physically marked him, the scars he had on his chest still don't heal. But surely I'm missing something in all of this?"

Silence hummed between us, Erix barely blinking as if he was trapped in a memory that frightened him to death.

"Please," I persisted. "You need to tell me."

"Duwar was just... talking. Duncan was listening. I – I couldn't hear what they were saying, but Duncan wasn't frightened. He didn't fight back. And then..." Erix shook his head, struggling with the memory.

"What you are going to say may be the key to fixing this. To *saving* Duncan."

"Those marks, the scars that will not heal, that was when Duncan got them. It wasn't because Duwar attacked him, there was no sense of danger between either of them. It... I tried to get to Duncan. I was too slow. If I was just a little quicker, then–" Erix lifted his hand and began slamming his fist into his head.

I felt his pain and suffering as though it twanged down a taut piece of string connecting us to one another.

"Stop it," I cried, leaping from the bed and snatching his arm. It took all my might to stop him from hitting himself. "Stop, Erix. I fucking command it! Do you hear me. Stop this *now*."

The resistance in Erix's arm faltered enough for me to gain control. I stood over him, panting for breath, as I made sure he couldn't hurt himself again. His eyes were fixed on an unimportant place on the floor, his brows furrowed and wings twitching nervously.

"I understand this is hard," I said, laying fingers beneath his chin. I guided his head up until his eyes found mine again. That seemed to calm him. "It's been torture for me. But hearing you speak so freely about Duwar, it makes me feel a little less insane in all of this. And as horrifying as the truth is, it is giving me the comfort I have desired for months."

"All this time and you've been coping with this alone." Erix shook himself, giving up his fight against me, the side of his head bloomed red from the force of his hits. He looked at me through tear-filled eyes, which broke me to the core. The gaze of a haunted man, the very same I saw in my own reflection every time I lifted the mirror beside Duncan's bed. "I can't live with myself knowing I left you…"

"I made you go, Erix. That is my fault, not yours." I wished he not only heard me but felt the sincerity in my tone. "When you are ready, I need you to explain how Duwar was able to trick Duncan enough to get close."

What Erix revealed next was not what I expected to hear from his pale lips.

"It was you," Erix said. "The being I saw Duncan talking with was you. Not the demon-god, but *you*. I think that was why Duncan got close – he was confused because there you were, waiting for him, as if he'd not just fallen into the hellscape that was Duwar's realm."

Another illusion, another trick to make us defenceless.

"Me?" I gasped, wondering how Duncan must've felt when he fell into that realm of corruption and saw me standing there. Did he think I fell in with him? Had he come to save me, only to find himself punished for his selflessness?

"Yes. And I saw you too. That power I mentioned, it was coming from you like you were some beacon. A light, a god. I knew it wasn't real, or was it? I still to this day cannot say which."

Erix fell into silence again.

"Keep going when you are ready." If the fury in my tone, or the command, had the power to stop Erix harming himself, it was the desperation in my eyes that truly rendered him powerless to refuse me.

"Duwar – or you – laid a hand on Duncan's chest. I thought it was a simple gesture, like the greeting of friends... lovers. But clearly the action hurt Duncan. He screamed. Then he fell to the ground and Duwar was gone. I didn't stick around to see what had happened. I picked Duncan up and flew back to the gate before it closed. It wasn't until we were through that I saw the claw marks on his chest."

The wound that hadn't healed in the weeks since it happened. The angry, puckered marks that oozed blood and pus. Neither Elinor's healers in Elmdew, nor any medicine I'd ordered from the apothecary, had been successful in healing the infection that burned there.

"It was some form of transference then," I said, speaking aloud as my mind pieced together the scrambled puzzle pieces. "That was how Duwar was able to enter Duncan."

"So, it's true. Duwar is here... in *him*."

I grimaced at the sharp crack of Erix's final word. "Unfortunately, yes."

I saw the pieces of the puzzle slot perfectly together in Erix's mind.

"I am so sorry, little bird. This is my fault. I should have–"

My legs gave out as I sat back on the bed, hands numb as they rested on my lap. "I've told you. This is no one's fault but my own. I should have never agreed to put my power into the stones. I was convinced it was the only way to prevent this threat from ever affecting our realms again, but instead I only made it a possibility. Now three keys are destroyed, Duncan is possessed and the only way to destroy Duwar is by murdering his host. But I'm just so selfish, I could never do that, Erix. This all could be over if I just killed Duncan, but I can't… I'm too weak…"

"Your self-pity and regret are misplaced, and yet I feel them as if they are mine to harbour," Erix said. "I hate myself for allowing you to deal with this alone. I should've refused you when you sent me away. No matter how you shut me out, I know you well enough to sense that something was wrong. I just never… I never thought it would be this."

Erix's voice cracked as he replied, which made the fissures in my chest widen.

"You'd never be able to refuse me, Erix," I whispered. "We both know that."

He bowed his chin to his chest, his sigh monumental. "Because you are both my greatest weakness, and my greatest strength."

I stood abruptly, putting space between us as guilt racked through me. I couldn't do this, not with Erix – not as Duncan lay, helpless and dying, in the room beside me. It was wrong, and yet it felt almost right. He was comforting me, and I him. And even though my intention was pure, I still suffered with the concept that I was crossing lines that I shouldn't even contemplate.

Perhaps it was a repercussion of Duwar's nightmares, or maybe my own internalised feelings. But having Erix here was both the biggest blessing and an equally terrible allure.

The war inside of me wasn't helping me make sense of the actual battle I had to face. But then it clicked. The draw to Erix had little to do with our past, and everything to do with that fact that I finally had shared the heavy weight of truth that pushed down on me.

This was what I craved, the openness, the ability to share a problem I had previously taken so long to get used to and was forced to forgo.

"I have no right to ask you to stay and help me," I said, forcing the words out and making them sound like I actually meant them. "But I admit that having someone here to share this burden with is… a relief."

"Eroan does not know about this?" Erix asked, surprise creasing his handsome face.

"No, and neither does Jesibel. She's been through enough; I wouldn't put this upon her. I caused this problem, so it's my responsibility to fix it."

"Maybe you enjoy the burden then, but as you said, I am here now to share it." Erix stood too, towering over me to the point that my neck tilted just to keep his gaze. "And I'm not going anywhere."

Shivers passed over my skin so powerfully, I wondered if Erix's gaze at my arms was because he noticed.

"I think it's best you leave," I replied. "It isn't safe for you to be tangled in this web too."

"Is that another command?" Erix asked, all without moving from his seat. "Or will you allow me to make a decision of my own?"

I swallowed down the urge to retract my statement. "Tell no one, Erix. Not Althea, Gyah, Cassial or his Nephilim. This isn't for them to know. I will find a way to solve this issue that doesn't involve you or anyone else. This is my problem alone to face. I opened the gate. I destroyed the keys–"

"You only did what you believed you *had* to do."

I spun around, fury and grief melding to one tumultuous emotion. "I gave Duwar the ability to leave his realm, using Duncan as a vessel. I brought a demon god here, threatening the lives of everyone I love. My actions, my *deceptions*, have spat in the face of everyone who died in the journey to prevent this very thing from happening."

Erix reached for me, clasping my hands in his and refusing to let go.

"Now listen to me carefully, Robin Icethorn." The use of my full name shocked me to stone. "Once again you blame yourself, falling into the ease of self-pity as though it is your one and only option for comfort and support. Enough. You have said this is your burden to bear alone, but it is not."

"How can you say that to me with such conviction, Erix?" I pulled free of his hold, and began to pace. Gathering all the nervous energy burning through me, I put it to use. "I'm a fool. A selfish, desperate child who acts before he thinks, and because of that half of my heart is lying in a bed, chained like a monster, dying, whilst the other half of my heart is trying to justify my mistakes. You only look at me like that because you're too blinded by your care for me to see that I'm no less a monster than Duwar."

"Lies," Erix snapped. "All of it. Lies. You can continue to repeat those things to yourself, and you may believe it, but I do not. I *will* not."

I realised what I admitted before I took my shuddering breath at the end of my speech. There was no ignoring it. My heart, split in two, held in the hands of two men. Perhaps this was Altar's way of punishing me for such transgressions. I could pretend and blame the dreams Duwar punished me with every night, but these crashing waves of feelings began long ago.

That was why I had to refuse Erix. Because if I gave in, I was only failing to Duwar's tests and trickery. The demon brought us together for a reason, and I had to trust it was not a good one.

Erix tried again to reach for me, wings twitching with unspent energy. He caught his lip between his teeth, his silver eyes darkening to forged steel. "I refuse to let you deal with this alone anymore. Fuck your commands. Fuck what *you* want. For once, I am going to do what I want to do, with no one to control me. I'd sooner be locked in the dungeons of this castle, if that means I'm still close enough for you to call on."

It hurt like a dagger to my chest to realise my treatment of Erix was no different to how his birth-father had treated him.

"And what is it you want to do?" I stopped long enough to ask. "Risk yourself for me until fate finally catches up with you?"

"If that is what fate has in store, then so be it." Erix's jaw tensed, the muscles in his cheeks becoming pronounced. "I want to help you. Support you. Be with *you*."

Part of me wanted to fall into his arms and thank him. The other part – the louder, more dominating side of me – wanted to slam my palms into his hard chest and force him out of Imeria myself, for good.

Ice crackled in the air around me, mirroring my lack of control over my emotions. Since the key I harboured in my blood had been destroyed, my power was not what it once was. Before it was endless, now more contained, not weak in the sense of the word, just… limited.

"Why?" I spat.

Erix straightened, contemplating his reply in a moment of silence. As he opened his mouth, I was prepared to hang on his every word. But the shattering of glass in another room stopped him from replying.

I turned sharply, looking toward the direction of the noise. It had come from Duncan's chamber, beyond the hanging tapestry.

Before I could even contemplate what I was doing, I ran. Without thought, Erix was on my heels. I ripped back the tapestry, tearing it from the wall so it slumped across the floor. With a shove, I threw open the door, wood cracking against the stone wall on the other side.

"Duncan," I cried out, seeing his body slumped over the side of the bed as if he was reaching for something. He didn't look at me, his focus entirely diverted. Heavy, tired eyes blinked, and sweat shone on his brow, hair tangled in knots where it hung limp over his face.

"He should be sleeping," I gasped, knowing the administration of Gardineum had happened barely an hour ago. "Why isn't he sleeping!"

It was impossible he was awake – unless…

"Altar, bless us." Erix took a rasped inhale. It was most likely from the shock of seeing how I'd been keeping Duncan, or from the disgust that came from the smell of the room. Clearly, Duncan had soiled himself. It wasn't uncommon, since I couldn't risk removing the iron from his body and allowing him to relieve himself.

I'd need to clean him – bathe him. But for that, he had to be heavily under the influence of the Gardineum and clearly the dosage I was giving was nowhere near enough.

Perhaps it hadn't been for a long time either, and that thought unnerved me more than anything.

I raced to Duncan's side, almost stepping in shattered glass. The mirror, the one I used to check his reflection, was lying broken on the ground. I saw my reflection hundreds of times, wide, sad eyes looking up at me, whilst catching a glimpse of Duncan – and how terrible he looked. But it was him, his reflection instead of the demon beneath his skin.

"He shouldn't be awake, Erix," I said, clearing the floor of glass with my boot. "I've only just given him a dosage of Gardineum. Something is wrong – Duwar is persisting, growing stronger as Duncan becomes weaker."

Erix was stunned to silence, barely moving. I didn't have time to care as I hoisted Duncan's body back over the edge of the bed, assisting with him lying down.

"Talk to me, Duncan," I pleaded, feeling how warm his skin was. He was boiling to the touch, his skin clammy. "What's happened? Do you need something?"

Duncan swept his tired eyes from me to Erix. He wasn't shocked when he saw my ex-guard shadowing us from the doorway. In fact, his reaction was soft, brows lifting from their tense line. Relief, it painted his tortured face.

Duncan sighed, closing his eyes as the lines across his forehead smoothed. "Erix... came... *Good*."

I was dumfounded, utterly shocked as I helped Duncan lie back down. His words settled over my consciousness like embers, hissing and spitting and yet not uncomfortable as I expected they would be.

"I did," Erix replied, tone careful. He took his place on the other side of Duncan's bed, his demeanour taut as if every muscle he had was hard as stone. "Because of you."

Duncan's weak smile tugged the corners of his cracked lips. "You took your... time."

Erix cleared his throat before continuing. "Can I ask why you orchestrated my visit, *Duwar*?"

Duncan winced at the name. "The *power* is resting... you're speaking to me. And to answer your... your question, I brought you here because Robin *needs* you. For that, I need you."

"No." Erix sucked in a sharp breath. "Robin needs you to get better, that is all."

"Wait," I said, snatching a broken shard of glass and lifting it before Duncan's face. Tears welled in my eyes when I saw the reflection of the man I loved so terribly that I'd give my own life for him. "It's really you."

"Yes, darling." Duncan's words were slurred, and yet unmistakably his. "It is me... for now."

I leaned over him, back hunched as adrenaline flooded out of me.

"Erix," Duncan rasped, "you look like you've seen a ghost."

"Not a ghost, Duncan. Just you. I must say you've looked better, friend." Erix scoffed an awkward laugh, but his face was void of any humour or happiness. Seeing Duncan in his state had shaken him deeply, only adding to my guilt.

"I've felt... better too." Duncan extended a weak, shaking hand toward Erix, who took it without question. "I must speak with you, Erix. There isn't time to... waste."

Erix glanced cautiously at me, almost searching for permission. I didn't need to give it, but I nodded anyway as I smoothed down Duncan's greasy hair with a shaking hand.

Slowly, Erix approached. His pace was slow with trepidation, his hand never straying from his sword. Although I knew he'd never use it against Duncan, a feeling I didn't need to be confirmed with words.

"Do I... really look that bad, Erix?"

Erix's face screwed up, lips pouting in contemplation. "You certainly are still the handsome man I first met, Duncan," Erix said as he stepped to the bed's side. I admired his awkward attempt to soften reality, but it barely met its intended mark. "It brings me no comfort to see you like this."

"Try being... in my position, friend." Duncan smiled weakly. "Listen to me." He reached for Erix and wrapped trembling fingers around his wrist. It was so sudden, so full of panic, which reflected in Duncan's unblinking stare. "Robin... needs you. No matter what... whatever Robin says... I ask that you don't leave his side again."

My breath caught in my throat, tears finally falling in rivulets down my cheeks.

Erix spared me a glance. "As much as I agree, I can't force him to do anything. You know this–"

"You would both refuse a man in such a dire state?" Duncan rolled his head and faced me, the inner pain painted in his exhaustion and colourless cheeks. "I made Erix come... for you. Because if I can't protect you from yourself, he can."

"Duncan, you must rest," I began.

"And you must listen," Duncan gasped, struggling to force out the words. "I know Erix will lay his life down for you... and that is all I can ask for."

There was no stopping the sob that broke out of me. I clapped a hand over my mouth a moment too late. Erix noticed but didn't take his eyes off Duncan. The intensity between them was thick. So overbearing I found my knees trembling beneath it.

Erix didn't shy away from the demand. Instead, he knelt at the bedside, clasped Duncan's hand and held it firm. "You need to continue fighting Duwar. Do it for Robin, promise me that and I, in turn, will promise to stay with him."

"I'm so tired... so very tired." Duncan closed his eyes, exhaling a breath through ruined lips. I waited for him to open them again, but he didn't. His breathing evened, his grasp on Erix loosened. And in the wake of the last few minutes, we were left in a gaping void of silence that had the power to undo every fibre of my being.

Time moved strangely. Erix had come round to my side of the bed without me noticing. I could barely think straight, couldn't form a thought long enough before my mind crumbled.

"How about we clean this mess up," Erix suggested softly. "Then you need to rest too."

I looked down, seeing what he pointed at. The glass was everywhere, but I didn't care. None of it mattered, not as Duncan's weak request echoed in my mind.

"I don't know what to do," I admitted. If it wasn't for Erix embracing me, I would've fallen to the ground and stayed there. "I can't – I *don't* know how to fix this."

"Shh," Erix hushed, laying his chin on top of my head, wings folding around me until I was entirely encased. I allowed this moment of connection, because Duncan had been clear in his intention in bringing Erix here. "I am here now and I am not going anywhere. I have new orders to follow now, and I vow to do so until my last breath."

Duncan's orders, that was what he referred to.

Somehow, through the trickery of Duwar's forced dreams, Duncan had woven his own intention within them. He'd brought Erix here, for me. Which opened a new question.

How was Duncan able to use Duwar?

You called, so I came.

I knew, without a doubt, that Duncan achieved this for one

reason. Because he knew that Erix was the only other person who'd give his life protecting me, just as he said.

That's what you did when you loved someone. Even though our love had changed over time, it was still there. Duncan understood that even if I wasn't brave enough to face it.

I looked back to Duncan, recognising the soft smile as he slept. His expression was peaceful, something I'd not seen in a long time. I couldn't help but feel like this was Duncan's way of accepting his fate. He was happily giving up, because he knew I wouldn't be alone. Duncan would die, hopefully taking Duwar with him.

But that was only a theory, not something to throw a life away for just to try.

"I'm so scared," I admitted into Erix's chest. "The path ahead is dark and I – I don't think I'll make it to the end without you, even if my head is telling me to turn you away."

I'd once told Erix I was scared of the dark, but that fear was tenfold now.

"Tell me what your heart is saying?" Erix encouraged. "Speak it aloud, do not let it fester."

I toyed with my answer, either giving him the full truth or just a fraction of it. "My heart is telling me to listen to Duncan's wishes."

In case they are his last.

Erix drew back enough that I could see the utter determination in his gaze. "As I told you when we first met, you only need to call for me and we'll face the darkness together. You're my duty and my pleasure, little bird. But first, you need to rest. Then, and only then, we will begin to formulate a plan."

He released me slowly, but his touch still lingered.

I stood by and watched Erix clean up the shattered glass. Duncan slept soundly, showing no sign that he was conscious. Once Erix had finished, he guided me back into the joining chamber, re-hanging the thick tapestry behind us. I didn't say another word, for fear further conversation would dilute the last thing he said to me.

You're my duty and my pleasure.

It wasn't until he tucked me in bed, pulled the curtains shut to block out the light of dawn, that I was brave enough to make a sound.

"Erix, will you watch over Duncan for me?" I asked. "Would you wake me if – *when* he stirs again?"

I watched him contemplate the question as though I'd asked him to answer life's greatest mysteries. "Only if you promise to sleep."

Not even the thought of what nightmares I'd face could frighten me. Only if Erix stayed close. "I promise I'll try."

Erix didn't hesitate. He left the door to Duncan's room open, giving us a full view of his bed. Then he drew his chair up beside my own bed, respecting the boundary line between us. Even after Duncan's request, I sensed the line between Erix and me, keeping us apart. The respect for my relationship with Duncan shone in Erix – I admired him for it.

Maybe the nightmares would stop haunting me, now Erix was here? I could only hope that was the case. To think straight long enough to find a solution to this issue, I'd need uninterrupted rest.

I opened my mouth to fill the silence, but Erix quickly interjected. "Ah, ah. You promised to rest. No more talking."

My request lingered on the tip of my tongue, unspoken and left alone. I nodded, rolled my back to Erix and closed my eyes. This position gave me the perfect view to Duncan where he lay, his face soft and relaxed, not an ounce of suffering etched into his features.

That was enough for me, for now at least.

Sleep came quicker than it had in a long time. Because for the first time, even with Duncan always close, I didn't feel alone.

CHAPTER 4

"What do you mean a *wedding*?" I spat the last word out as if it was spoiled milk in my mouth.

I couldn't wrap my head around what Eroan had just confirmed. Perhaps I was still half asleep, or maybe it was the confusion of waking as Erix confirmed that Imeria Castle had a visitor. Either way, to say I was confused was an understatement.

I wasn't expecting Eroan for at least another week. And I certainly didn't expect him to bring news about a wedding. I was aware Cassial was arranging some political move with the fey to solidify a new era of relations, but this... not this.

Eroan looked between me and Erix, who stood at the side of my throne. It was one of the items that had been retrieved from the ruined west wing of Imeria Castle. Turned out the rock it was carved from was so strong, not even tons of debris could shatter it.

Shame I wasn't as robust.

"I thought you were already aware of Cassial's proposition," Eroan said, apology lacing his trill voice. "I'm sorry if something has been missed along the way."

I felt as though there was a *but* missing, but Eroan never said it.

"Robin has had much on his mind," Erix added, catching another confused glance from Eroan.

"Then do you care to explain, Erix?" Eroan shot him a

knowing look. I noticed it, like a silent telling-off. Eroan hadn't questioned why Erix was here, nor did I feel obliged to explain. What was more pressing was that Eroan wasn't expected to visit me for another six days, and yet here he stood with a small army of seamstresses behind him.

It was no different to when I first met him, in the city of Aurelia when I ventured into the fey realm. Back when my life wasn't about demon-gods, new worlds and broken hearts.

"Clearly it has been a detail that has got lost along the way, Eroan," I said, commanding his attention back to me. "How would I have known about it, if my own councillor is seeming to not, well, *council* me."

Erix cleared his throat. "Robin, the blame for this is mine. I take responsibility."

My neck clicked as I snapped it around to face Erix. "What do you mean?"

For first time in a long time, I didn't feel so exhausted. However, Erix looked as though he'd hardly slept. Clearly, from the shadows under his eyes, he took his task of watching over Duncan and me very seriously.

"You didn't pass on the invitation?" Eroan replied cautiously, looking between me and Erix. "You told me that you had already informed Robin…"

"I did pass it on." Erix shot me a look. "But I see now that Robin has yet to open it."

My first instinct was: what letter? Then I remembered the note Erix had given me yesterday in Berrow, the one resting in the jacket pocket somewhere strewn in the depressed mess of my room.

"Never mind that," I said, my knuckles pale as I clutched onto the armrests.

I hadn't paid a thought to the letter Erix gave me in Berrow, not with everything that happened upon my arrival back to Imeria. "Someone can break the news to me now."

Erix dropped his eyes to the floor, confirming he already knew the answer to my question. "I'll let Eroan take this one…"

"Your presence has been requested in Durmain, with the leave to be imminent."

Panic flared scolding hot inside of me. "Regardless of the wedding or not, my answer to the previous summons, and any going forwards, is still the same," I snapped, fixing my gaze on Eroan. "I'm not leaving my responsibilities here. Send my apologies to Cassial and those who are celebrating, but I will be staying back to care for… my court."

Eroan looked nervously around his fey companions. "I know your stance on these proposed celebrations in Durmain, but I do think you may want to reconsider this one, Your Majesty. If anything, this is the first time in weeks I've had the excuse to dress someone. If you take this away from me, I will never forgive you."

It was easy to forget that Eroan didn't know about my turmoil. I had to pretend that his excitement was in line with my own emotions, and not jarring like it actually was.

"If you prefer, I could go and retrieve the invitation," Erix interjected, moving slightly from my side. "Then you can make an informed decision."

I shook my head. Invitation or no, I wasn't going to leave Imeria. Erix knew why, and yet one look at him and there was a sense that he thought I should go.

"I get the impression you are dancing around the answer, Erix," I said, voice echoing across the barren, cold chamber.

Erix didn't tell me I was wrong. Instead, he cleared his throat, only adding to the tension building inside of me. "Cassial has been petitioning for what celebration would best draw the fey and humans together, especially in light of the accords that are being drafted. But a… a decision has been made. And it's been decided that the wedding is going to be between… Althea Cedarfall and Gyah Eldrae."

The floor dropped out from beneath me. "Excuse me?"

It was as though a pitcher of ice-cold water had just been dumped over my head.

"Isn't it wonderful," Eroan clapped, practically jumping with glee on the spot.

I couldn't share in the reaction, and he noticed, reigning his in subtly.

"When was this... when did they decide?" I could barely get my words out.

"The decision has only just been confirmed a day or two ago. Cassial's requests for an event that would unite the realms have been going on for the past month, and this was the best suggestion that was offered," Eroan said, taking turn from Erix who was clearly never good at breaking news. "There are no human and fey relationships that can magically be conjured in that time, but it was clear Queen Cedarfall has been smitten with Gyah, so it is just intentions and stars aligning."

"And they just... agreed to this?" I asked.

Of course, I knew they loved each other, Altar, that fact was clear to anyone who shared a room with them. But a wedding... I don't know if it was my surprise that hurt me, or the fact it was proof I'd pushed Althea away so well that I was the last to know about it.

"Yes, Althea and Gyah accepted, in conjunction with Cassial's proposed treaty to unite the fey and humans during a second wedding when the heir to the Elmdew Court, and the young Princess Eugena are of suitable age to be married off to one another. This is a way of getting the heads of the courts in a room, and to follow it up with a party that will be remembered for generations. Althea and Gyah's uniting will kick off what will soon be years of endless peace... peace signed into law."

The wedding and the peace treaty were two separate issues. And the latter I still had a personal problem with.

"But I haven't agreed to sign the treaty yet," I reminded them, suddenly wanting to drink a *lot* of wine.

"I understand," Eroan added. "But you should know that Cedarfall and Oakstorm have. Elmdew is already behind it, considering their heir is still an infant and is spoken for by the council that has been raised until he is of age. You are the last of the courts to agree on the terms. Whether you sign or not, it will be written into law. You must decide to ally with your sibling courts, or be further ostracised..."

My head ached, all this information coming thick and fast. "Is that how you see my decision?"

Eroan looked down to the ground. "I must only remind you of the repercussions of any action, whether I agree with them or not."

"Forgive my hesitancy, but the idea of signing away the future of literal babies isn't something I can just get on board with easily." A draft of the accords had arrived a while ago, outlining very clear, but specific, terms of peace. A new treaty. One that would tie the Elmdew heir to the human princess born to the recently murdered royal family. There had been talks of wedding the children as the grand event, but it seemed Cassial and my ally courts saw sense. Instead, it was Althea and Gyah who would marry. That was the simple part... the joining of two realms in marriage in eighteen years' time. But what wasn't simple was the price paid if either party went against the treaty.

The accords confirmed peace, as long as the fey didn't pose a threat upon the humans. And the same for the humans against the fey, including the Nephilim who'd taken ownership over them. If either realm broke the treaty, it would hand over their land and control to those they've threatened. If the humans acted against us, we would take over complete control until the eighteen years have passed and both realms would unite through the marriage of the two young heirs.

Neither option was ideal in my eyes, even Eroan could agree on that, but it did fend off aggression from both sides. The accords, as Eroan explained, had to be equal.

Perhaps I was so quick to distrust because I couldn't trust myself. Either way, this wasn't something I was happily just going to agree to, knowing I held the biggest threat. By me signing, with Duncan still possessed and with no way to solve his dilemma, I would be doing so knowing the fey realms were vulnerable.

If my refusal meant Icethorn would be separated from the rest of the realms, so be it.

"Whose idea was this?" I asked. "The wedding part."

"From my understanding, it was suggested by Cassial, and Althea Cedarfall agreed without hesitation," Eroan explained. "No better way to encourage peace between fractured parties than free wine and food. The party of the generation to signify the beginning of new times."

I still couldn't get past the fact that my best friends were getting married. Deep down, I was happy for them. And yet the bitter taste of jealousy burned my throat like bile. It was hard to be joyous of love when mine was in tatters.

Erix took a step closer to my throne, his proximity attempting to calm the storm of thoughts inside of me. "Althea would want you there."

I fixed my eyes to him. "I can't go, as you understand."

"Robin, it is high time you leave. Regardless of the little notice, sometimes the best things are the most unexpected. This event has been planned quickly from my understanding, although in line with the proposed date which you previously declined. I've already been preparing for this, just in case you changed your mind."

I wanted to clap my hands over my face and scream, but I had to keep demure. "I will need to think on it," I lied.

Eroan must've sensed it, because he pouted at me, hand on hip. "I believe the invitation was Althea's way of trying to reach you again. As your councillor, I suggest you at least reply. We need the Cedarfall Court for more timber and supplies. Keeping strong relations is important..."

Eroan was right, I knew that. But Althea was someone I'd

distanced myself from for good reasons. "And these celebrations will still begin in three days?"

"Yes, and from my understanding, all is coming together smoothly," Eroan confirmed.

Three days. Three *fucking* days.

"And the Nephilim have agreed to host it, on Durmain land," Erix added.

"Strange place to host a wedding between the fey," I pointed out.

"It is time the humans are not separated from our affairs, but included," Erix said.

"And specifically, the wedding is being held at the border of Wychwood," Eroan added, his army of seamstresses looking around awkwardly. "So, now you know, we really should not waste any more time and prepare an outfit for you. Is Duncan available for measurements–"

"No," I snapped, pushing myself to standing. Erix stepped in closer, prepared to offer me some comfort. Eroan recoiled, a grimace set over his sharp face. "Duncan is resting, Eroan. He's not to be disturbed."

I expected Eroan to press me on the matter, but he didn't. He never did, as if sensing Duncan was a topic out of the confines of what he could inquire on. "So be it."

"Can we have a moment," Erix said. Although it sounded like a request, there was no denying the tone of command lingering when he spoke to Eroan. It was not a "can we" but more a "give us".

"Of course," Eroan said with a bow, likely tasting the tension in the room as I could. "I can prepare the necessary for Robin, and leave them here for you to try in your own time. If that would be preferred. Whatever your decision, it is best we cover all possibilities."

"Yes, it would," I said, too quickly. I needed Eroan to leave so I could sort through all this new information. "I'd prefer that. Thank you, Eroan and… and I'm sorry for snapping."

He bowed, although he didn't take his eyes off me. I hated keeping these secrets from the man I'd come to trust, but it was imperative no one knew. Not everyone would take to the knowledge that I was harbouring a demon-god as easily as Erix had.

"You'll need to be... tidied up, Robin," Eroan added as he prepared to leave. "If I may speak plainly, you look weathered."

"That's if I attend the wedding," I reminded him.

"For the sake of holding up pretences and a relationship between the Icethorn Court and Cedarfall, I'd suggest – as you hired me for this position to do – that you attend. It would be good for people to see Duncan and you living and thriving. Enjoying the world you fought to secure. Hiding away in the ruins of your family's past is only going to separate you further from the ones you love."

I clutched my chest, unable to hide the discomfort his truth caused me. "And what of Jesibel?"

"Jesibel is occupied here," Eroan said. "She doesn't require you to mind her. She has me, after all. And I have given her the task of growing a rose garden, something that requires time and focus in such frozen grounds. As much as I would love to come to this joyous celebration with you, I propose to stay behind and make sure she is well."

Eroan had prepared for this answer, I understood that. He was ready to give it to me the moment I asked, and he was convincing all the same.

"Again," I forced out, throat swelling with emotion. "Thank you for your words of advice, Eroan. I will need to sit on this new information and digest it."

This was a fight Eroan was going to lose, and he knew it. So, he used one last-ditch effort to sway me. "Althea would want you there. Both of you."

"If that was the case, she would've come and invited me in person."

It was stupid, to feel hurt that I'd found out about the wedding with three days to go. I knew why she hadn't come, and so did Eroan. He didn't take that moment to remind me, he could see from my reaction that I figured it out.

It was because I banned her from visiting. After how I pushed her away, it was a miracle I'd even received an invite.

"Just promise me you'll think about it. I know you well enough now to see that you *think* you've already made your mind up on this." Eroan waved his hands and his flock of fey picked up the trunks and cases of outfits and flooded out of the room. "But you must think about the greater picture. That is all I ask of you, Robin."

"He will," Erix answered for me. "I will make sure of it."

"Then you are my last hope of convincing our dear king, Erix." Eroan narrowed his eyes on him, gaze full of silent confusion at his presence. "If Robin won't listen to me, I hope he does you. See that he makes the right decision for Icethorn."

With that, Eroan left us in the wake of ruin his news had caused. Mind reeling, I got up from the throne and left the room without a word. Erix stayed close, always shadowing me. I didn't stop until I got back to my personal rooms and searched the piles of clothes for the invitation stuffed into my jacket pocket. Once I found it, I proceeded to read it three times, just to make sense of it.

Everything Eroan had said was true, as I knew it would be. But seeing it in black and white made it real. It was a wedding invitation for two of the closest people in my life. The celebration was to be held in Durmain, just on the border between realms. A celebration for *all* to enjoy – human and fey.

"From my understanding, the invitation has been extended to every household in Wychwood and Durmain," Erix explained, studying me carefully as I read the invite over and over. "There is not a soul still living who hasn't been invited to experience this... spectacle."

"Glad you see it for what I do," I replied. "It seems like Cassial is really wanting to make this a fanfare event."

Erix didn't tell me I was wrong, simply twisted his reply to something kinder. "Cassial only wants to ensure the peace is upheld, as we all do. With what we both know, I understand it is hard to imagine such a time. But do you really want to prevent all of the people outside these walls enjoying peace, just because Duncan has none within them?

"*Peace* will not last long unless I find a way of destroying Duwar *and* saving Duncan."

Erix gritted his teeth, the micro muscles in his jaw flexing. "Which we will do, together, as promised."

I locked eyes with him, breath itching in my throat as his silver-hued eyes drew me in, forging me in place. "What do you think, Erix? You know what secrets I hide; do you think it wise I leave and play a part in this charade? Who is going to stay back and care for Duncan, administer his Gardineum, stop him from hurting himself or others?"

Erix straightened, his shoulders rolling back and wings shivering wide. "Regardless of the illusion you're trying to uphold, people *are* talking. Questions are being whispered in the shadows about the king and his consort who has not been seen. The longer you hide away, the sooner the light will come looking for you."

"Wise words," I said, hating the bite in my voice. "And yet still it doesn't answer the issue at hand."

"People are excited about the prospect of a celebration, little bird. They deserve it, as do you. I helped ensure everyone in Berrow received the invitation, as per the request from Althea herself. They want as many people as possible – fey and human – to witness it. Althea and Gyah's wedding is the celebration the realms need to begin moving on with their lives. And this treaty will allow all to do so without the fear of another war hanging over them."

Tears pricked in the corners of my eyes, but I refused to let them loose. "And yet you know I still can't go because of the man I can't just bring with me."

"No," Erix replied softly, pacing toward me and taking the invitation from my hands. "*You* can go, it's Duncan who cannot."

"I won't leave him. I can't. He needs caring for at all times. I have to clean him, feed him… make sure he is still living whilst that parasite is still inside of him."

"Then allow me do it for you," Erix offered, voice soft as the brush of his fingers against my hand. "I can look after him whilst you are away. It's three days. That's all."

I narrowed my eyes on him, searching for any sign that his offer was nefarious. "Why would you offer that?"

He held my gaze. "You care about him, so I do too. Duncan is the most important thing in your life, and you… I'll do anything to protect what you cherish. And I do mean anything."

His words broke me, bit by bit, but I had to stay strong.

I opened my mouth to refuse him, but as Erix always seemed to know what I was going to say, he stopped me with a finger over my mouth. "Rafaela will be in Lockinge, you know."

That stopped me from saying another word. Rafaela, the Nephilim who'd tricked her own people into destroying the keys they were sworn to protect. The last time I'd seen her was in the meeting in Elmdew, before she told us that she'd await punishment for her betrayals. Since then, I'd tried to contact her, sending letters to Lockinge – but I'd heard nothing in return.

"You've been trying to reach her, have you not?"

"How do you know that?" I asked, voice barely a whisper.

"Because I know everything that happens in and out of Berrow, it's my duty. Correspondence such as letters written by my king *is* my business, making certain none are counterfeit."

Panic raced up my spine, sending my skin to gooseflesh. "You read them?"

"No, I would never do that." Erix blanched at my accusation. "But I'd recognise your handwriting anywhere. That, and the fact that every week, I get more and more to send to Lockinge. One begins to wonder what Rafaela could offer you, that I couldn't. Now, I know."

"I need answers if I want to save Duncan," I admitted, but not the full truth. "She might have them."

"No doubt you don't need me to remind you this, but be careful what you write. Words on a page are far more incriminating than whispers."

I scoffed, feeling the heat raise in my cheeks. "You don't think I'm that stupid, do you?"

"Far from it. But I still worry."

What could I say to that? My letters to Rafaela, although desperate, didn't mention Duncan or his state. They did, however, ask for knowledge or books on Duwar. The Nephilim knew more about the demon-god than the fey or humans did. No matter how many books I searched, there were no mentions. No answers. If anyone had them, it was Rafaela.

And I put faith in her faith, that she would be open to help me with my search for information.

"So you already know she never replied to me," I said. "Not a single letter back, no matter how many I sent."

"I know," Erix replied. "And I also understand why you had been trying to contact her." His eyes drifted toward the door that was no longer hidden behind the tapestry. That swash of material lay in a puddle before it. "If you think she can help Duncan, this is your chance to go and get those answers in person."

Something sparked inside of me, small but mighty. Hope, was it? I hadn't felt it for so long, it was hard to recognise it. But Erix was right, there was a chance. Although what he wasn't right about was exactly what I needed from Rafaela. It wasn't entirely about Duncan and his affliction.

My request for knowledge led to another secret of mine – one Erix hadn't worked out yet. One I would never share with him.

"Rafaela told me once of Nephilim who turned to Duwar," I said, taking a break from chewing the inside of my cheek. "She said that they were bound in labradorite as punishment."

Erix's eyes widened. "Sounds like a last resort."

I bowed my head, not wanting to look at his eyes. If I did, he would see the hint of something I was keeping from him. "It has to be better than death."

Whose imprisonment I wouldn't say.

Either way, I'd lose Duncan. This lead was the only option I had to help him – help *me*. I could continue poisoning Duncan, keep him locked beneath iron to suppress the fey-magic in his blood, but that wasn't affecting the demonic presence inside of him. Maybe, if I could understand the process of binding someone in labradorite, it would lead to truly saving this world.

"All the more reason that you need to go to Lockinge then," Erix said what I already knew deep down. "And I think you should know that Althea has tried to visit you to invite you herself..."

My stomach twisted in knots at the revelation. "She did?"

"Yes, but I stopped her, because that was what I thought you wanted. Althea hasn't given up trying to contact you, just like you haven't with Rafaela."

I wished I didn't believe it, but I knew Althea well enough not to doubt it. The one time she had showed up at Imeria, unannounced, I'd banished her in a fit of panic of what she'd find.

I turned away from Erix, defeated. "I'd prefer Althea hated me for my treatment of her, than tangling her up in this web of shit. This shouldn't be her issue to solve when she has an entire court, and soon to be a wife, to be concerned about. Duncan is my issue, he is *my* responsibility."

"Ours, little bird. Ours. In fact, the world's issue if you cannot solve it," Erix corrected, laying a hand on my folded arm. "I am here now, with you. And not going anywhere, just as Duncan asked of me."

"Then how do you expect me to leave, and you to stay if that is directly going against Duncan's wishes?"

Erix was too quick to hide his hesitation. "We will figure it out. Duncan will be fine with me. Anything you need me to do, I will. No questions. If it means you get the chance to try and help him, I–"

"I can't go, because I can't leave you either," I interrupted, hardly putting thought into the admission as it flooded out of me. "There you go. Happy now my admission is out in the open?"

"Not at all." Erix hesitated, letting my words settle over him like ash.

My heat thundered in my chest with such vigour I was sure Erix heard it. He stepped in close, reaching for my hand and holding it. "We will find another way then."

"There is no other way."

Erix shook his head, refusing my statement. "Do you trust me?"

"I do," I said after a moment, unable to look at him, frightened at the emotion I'd find. "Because Duncan does."

"Then that is good enough for me." Erix folded the invitation and handed it back to me. "I will inform Eroan that we will be leaving for Lockinge. In the meantime, I will prepare measures to see that Duncan is well cared for–"

"Hold on, I haven't agreed!"

"You do not need to, little bird. I am deciding for you. Hand over some of that mental burden before you're crushed beneath it. That is what I am here for, allow me to do my job."

"Didn't you hear the part about me not wanting to leave you either?"

Erix nodded. "I did. We are going together."

"Duncan–"

"*Will* be in safe hands."

I opened my mouth, gasping for breath. "We can't tell anyone, you know that."

"What did you just say about trusting me?" Erix asked, closing the space between us with another step. "I think you have forgotten that I have taken over my father's creations. The gryvern do as I command. If I want them to practise silence, they will do so."

His gryvern, the soldiers he'd offered to me to help protect Icethorn whilst we rebuilt. "Is that wise?"

"I believe so," Erix replied. "They are loyal to you, because *I* am loyal to you. You and Duncan. Hear that, little bird. And heed it."

A shiver passed over my skin at the use of my nickname. I'd once hated it, now it was all I longed to hear. "If we do this, we cannot tell Rafaela about Duncan. She will kill him if it means destroying Duwar... I must inquire carefully."

"I swear to you that I won't let anything happen to him." Erix's sudden seriousness knocked the wind from my lungs. "Or you, for that matter."

I believed him.

Erix was as convincing as he always had been. Once and always my pillar, offering me the support, the very support I'd craved since Duncan and Duwar merged.

I almost felt guilty for keeping my *real* plan from Erix. There was nothing he could say or do that would make me divulge the truth. When the time came for it, I hoped he'd forgive me. Even though I know, if the tables were turned, I'd never be able to forgive him.

But if it meant saving Duncan *and* the world, then I knew what I had to do. And the answers Rafaela had would only confirm it.

CHAPTER 5

Imeria had always been a quiet place, but when Erix departed – preparing the necessaries for our journey to Durmain – the silence felt like a void. All encompassing, devouring. The wide jaws of a beast, which I walked straight into. A graveyard, which was fitting for those who'd died here when half the castle fell, or when my mother and the family I never met were slaughtered.

And yet, with all the ghosts around me, I *still* felt alone.

I drew up a wooden chair at Duncan's bedside. It was the morning after Eroan dropped the news about Althea and Gyah's wedding. Even after another night's sleep with Erix on his chair beside me, I hardly felt well-rested, but I was better than I had been, at the very least.

Light streamed in through the stained-glass window. Dust danced in the beams, twisting like ropes of gold attempting to entangle any poor soul who found themselves walking through it. One ray shone over the side of Duncan's face, highlighting just how awful he looked. Deep lines, paled blotches of red, dried skin which looked sore and agitated.

He'd be waking naturally after the last dose of Gardineum wore off. It was like clockwork, this routine we'd found ourselves in. Since yesterday, when he woke up even though Gardineum was pumped through his veins, it hadn't happened again.

And just as I expected, it didn't take long for him to stir. When his eyes slowly creaked open, they found me before noticing anything else.

"Good morning, Robin," he croaked, verdant eyes wincing against the harsh light. "Is it that time already?"

I no longer had the mirror to use to see if it was Duncan or Duwar speaking. Not that I needed it. After what I was about to say, this conversation was for me and Duwar alone. The demon would show itself. I had my suspicions who I was speaking with, but my following words would be a draw in case Duwar was still hiding.

"I've been thinking about *your* offer," I said, keeping my voice clear and confident, even though my hand shook on my lap. "A lot, actually."

Duncan blinked, and when his eyes opened again it was as if blood spread across his green iris. "Have you finally come to your senses, Robin Icethorn?"

My nails pinched into my palms at the drawn-out hiss of the demon's voice. I refused to give it the satisfaction of winning, at least not yet. I required answers first, and I didn't have long until Erix returned.

Duwar couldn't know what I planned.

Duncan's body, controlled by the demon, rose from the mattress. He strained against the iron bindings, smiling as though it was some ultimate pleasure. His tongue traced his lower lip, disturbing the already chapped skin.

I flinched back, Duwar's grin faltering. "There is no need to fear me, as I have told you before, I am not the threat you believe me to be."

More words without merit.

"I want to understand, before I contemplate the transference." I knew what it entailed now, after Erix told the story of Duwar using my form to lay a hand on Duncan's chest. Was it truly that simple? "If you would indulge me with a few answers, I would appreciate it."

"Transference," Duwar hissed. The sound of clinking chains made my skin crawl as he struggled to get comfortable. "What is there to contemplate, Robin? This vessel is so close to death;

his will may be strong, but his body is weak; it is not made for the likes of power such as I. We both can agree that his passing would not be beneficial. Your hesitation is the only factor which draws out his suffering, you understand that, do you not?"

I hated myself for agreeing, but Duwar was right. "I do."

Dark eyes narrowed on me, head tilting ever so slightly to the side. "I am beginning to wonder if you even care that Duncan will perish?"

"It would be wise not to worry about my thoughts." I leaned in closer. "And if *you* kill him, you'll be lost forever. You've already made that clear to me, Duwar. Otherwise, you would not be so desperate to arrange for me to serve as your new host."

Duncan's mouth split into a handsome smile. There was nothing dangerous about it, and yet my heart, mind and soul told me to run.

"Robin, you would never let that happen to Duncan." His brows drew down over sombre eyes, giving me a look at the truly worried creature lurking in Duncan's body. "I am merely waiting for you to make the decision. The right one, for Duncan *and* for you. Give yourself to me, and Duncan will be freed from this torment. He made this decision to offer you power, and you have spat in the face of his sacrifice. But I know, as you do, that you shall make the right decision eventually. Or do you need more time to conceptualise my offer, knowing that time is not a commodity that you, or Duncan, has to waste?"

I scoffed, trying to remind myself that I had the power. "You act with the confidence of a creature who forgets he needs my cooperation."

"Your lack of decision is killing him, Robin. You do understand that. I am holding on, as a courtesy for you."

Lies.

"Offering myself up as your new vessel isn't the easiest decision to make," I replied, trying and failing to keep the desperation from my tone. It was written all over my expression. I saw as much in the warped reflection in Duncan's red eyes.

"What is it you must know, to make the decision easier?"

I let Duwar's question hang in the air between us. Erix had been the one to finally divulge what had happened in Duwar's realm. He mentioned seeing me – not monstrous as Duwar's reflection was – but me. He'd touched Duncan, clawed his skin and entered through a wound.

No different to how I'd accepted the Icethorn key.

"Why me?" I asked, my question double-sided.

The answer would prove another one of my theories.

"Because you are power in Duncan's eyes," Duwar replied simply. "He saw the true reflection of what I am, not what the world has made you believe me to be."

My skin itched as Duwar – ever desperate – tried to manipulate me into this lie of theirs. "You are wrong."

"Then you tell me what you think is the correct explanation."

I swallowed hard, longing to claw Duwar out of Duncan with my bare hands. "I think you glamoured yourself to trick Duncan into your web. You showed him an illusion of me to lure him in. Forever hiding the truth of your darkness. Desperation made you pick the only fly that was unfortunate enough to get tangled in your web. Now you have finished with that feast, you are looking for the next."

"Perspective is interesting, is it not?" Duncan turned his head, eyes never leaving me. "You are told that something is evil, and you believe it so willingly."

Ice itched across my skin, begging for release. "You're killing Duncan, that is proof enough for me."

"No, we have already come to the conclusion that *you* are the one killing him. I have told you how you can save him, but still you hesitate. Make the decision now, and he will be saved."

I leaned in close, showing I didn't fear the demon-god, proving that it should fear me. "Why should I believe you will not do the same to me, if I accept your offer?"

"Because you are *fey*."

I leaned back, brushing the comment off with a hand. "That isn't enough of an explanation."

"Your body can heal at a rate that is incomparable to a human's. I never had a hand in creating the humans, and if I had, they would have certainly been stronger than whatever *this* is."

The deranged laugh that burst out of me caught Duwar by surprise. "The fey belong to Altar. The humans to the Creator. We all know the stories."

"And yet you never heard of Duwar," Duwar said, Duncan and the demon's voices tanged as one. The unnatural sound grated on my soul. "There is much you do not understand, possibilities that you would never have even believed. I cannot blame you for your impertinence, but I do pity you."

"Pity me?" I echoed. "It would seem you're confused. You're the powerless one here. All those years locked away, and you find freedom only to face death. Duncan is mortal, which means you will suffer the same as he does."

It clicked into place – the one detail I'd contemplated since this hell began. Duwar lifted Duncan's lips into a knowing smile, as if they read my mind.

"You thought Duncan was fey, didn't you?" I asked, chest aching from the beat of my heart. "You saw his power and took your chance for escape, inside him."

"As you previously pointed out, I was desperate." Duwar looked down at the body tied in iron to the bed, pity flashing in his burning eyes. "Does it pain you to look and see what your prolonging is causing."

"Duncan would want me to let you die."

"But what do *you* want, Robin Icethorn?"

I opened my mouth but closed it again. The answer was simple. I might've said it, but my actions thus far already proved my intentions. I wanted Duncan alive and well. This was my fault. I was the only one who deserved to suffer for helping open the gate.

Peace. I wanted peace.

"Choosing this body, instead of that gryvern who shadows you, was a mistake I will regret. One you will also regret if you do not help me vacate him," Duwar said, the pleading in its tone more pronounced than it had been before. "You think I am evil, but I am not. I am whatever you want me to be, whatever you use me for. A sword can be used for murder, or decoration. I am the sword, now you must decide my use."

"No, you are a *demon*."

Duwar used Duncan's body like a puppeteer and shrugged. "I tried to show you, and still you turn your back to me."

I closed my eyes, watching the scene play out as Duncan had used Duwar to spread life over the ruins of Imeria castle. It had happened when we returned to Imeria, but that wasn't all. There was another part of my return which I had not thought of since, because I made a promise to someone to forget it... forget *them*.

Duwar's display was yet more tricks – more illusions to lure me into the same web that Duncan had found himself bound in.

"Enough of your tricks," I snapped. "You message is clear. You need me in order to survive, and so the choice is in my hands."

"Exactly. I need you, and you need to accept me willingly, if you want Duncan to live."

Willingly. Duwar was speaking on consent as if he gave Duncan that choice. Or did he? Erix had said that what he saw was not contention or aggression. But even if Duncan accepted Duwar into his body, it was only because he thought he was conversing with me.

One thing I knew for a fact: Duncan was dying. Duwar was killing him. My hesitation was killing him. We both would lead to his demise, unless I acted soon. I would lose Duncan forever, and as much as I pretended to be strong, I knew – and so did Duwar – that I'd never let that happen. Which was exactly why I had to speak to Rafaela and understand the binding of a person in labradorite before I gave Duwar my answer.

"It's time you get some more rest, Duwar." I moved for the chest of drawers, fingers brushing over the box that contained the syringe and Gardineum.

"Is this conversation over already?" Duwar asked. "When we last conversed, you bound this body in chains and kept me locked away, but there was still love in your touch."

"I do love–"

"But today you are cold, closed off."

Because I'm arguing with the demon possessing the man I love.

I looked up, aware of the demon's scrutiny. From his winning grin, it already believed it had the answer. "I do not owe you anything but this, Duwar."

Duwar ignored the syringe closing in as he pressed me further. "It is your guard. Erix. You have realised that you can let Duncan die because you have someone else to fall back on–"

"That isn't true," I snapped. I wished nothing more than to claw the demon out of Duncan with my bare hands, to exorcise the presence and free him without giving myself up. "You were the one who brought Erix here."

"No." Duncan's head tilted like an inquiring mutt. "That was *all* Duncan. Once again using my potential to show you the world in which you could live, if only you accepted me. Your love for them both has no bounds, Duncan understands that. He accepts that, somewhere deep down."

"Shut up."

Duwar ignored my command. "You know, I could give you them both. I promised you everything, and everything is what you will get, if you just give yourself to me… the transference works on a willing participant. When – *if* – you give yourself to me, my power will be yours."

"Your lies have no sway over me, Defiler."

I lowered the loaded syringe toward Duncan's body.

"Wait," Duwar snapped, eyes drowning in panic, knowing his last moments of consciousness were fleeting. "Before you do that, ask yourself why Altar created keys knowing that, if used again, it would one day open my realm and set me free? Why did my potential put two gods to war?"

My silence was enough of a response for Duwar to continue.

"Because they knew what I could give them, and they ensured a way that if the time came, I was reachable. You called my realm a prison, but it was merely a waiting spot, a place to bide my time until I was required again. But we do not always get what we want, do we, Robin?"

I shook my head, pushing myself to standing. The conversation was over. I didn't want to hear any more, only because my mind ached with what he just said.

If Duwar was the demon, and he was imprisoned for reasons we will never truly know. Why *would* Altar make keys? Keys are to be used...

"I can sense you finally opening your mind to what I have to say," Duwar continued, taking pleasure in spreading his lies. "Keys were made because even Altar desired a failsafe. He knew that he would need me one day. Just as he tore me out of the ground, using my power to create his children, the fey – Altar knew a time would come when that power would be required. Likely to beg for my forgiveness for his treatment. Maybe to require my assistance in punishing the god the human's call the Creator – the *true* trickster."

I steeled my expression, refusing to give weight to what Duwar shared. "One of these days you'll understand that I'm not so easily convinced."

"Duncan was convinced. He understood the potential."

"I am *not* Duncan," I said.

"No, that you are not. But you are running out of time."

I hated hearing Duwar speak on Duncan as if he believed him to be anything more than the demon he was. "I've heard enough–"

"Let me die then, sacrifice Duncan as a result of your hesitance. I suppose it is a fair price, to save the world from the monster you have all been told I am. But will you truly risk letting him perish, if you have even the slightest belief that I am telling the truth?"

"I don't believe you." I could barely contain the anger in my voice. "I witnessed what you did with Aldrick. I saw, first-hand, the creatures that follow you like hounds. Every time I look in a fucking mirror I see a demon. My perception of you and what you will do to this world is made in the image of your actions thus far."

"As you have just said, your perception of me. You see what you think you know." Duncan tensed his arms, pulling at the restraints. For someone so weak, I was certain I felt the spark of lightning in the air. If it wasn't for the iron, Duwar could conjure a storm in the room.

"Actions speak louder than your plea."

"And what are my actions? What have I done, Robin? Offer humans access to power that Aldrick kept from them? Was my suggestion of balance so terrible?"

"You desire nothing but ruin!"

"I *long* to give the world of my crafting a second chance. I never asked to be used by Altar, I never wanted this consciousness and life. But that was not for me to decide."

"Liar," I hissed.

Duncan's forehead furrowed in deep grooves, worry sent into every crease. "I only wanted a world of peace, Robin. A place in which our creations would live together, equal in power. But no. It was not enough. Ego and jealousy got in the way, deceit between so-called brothers. I am as much a victim as every soul lost in the fight of power and control since my imprisonment."

"I've heard enough," I lied, because this was the first time Duwar had divulged so much information, knowledge that could be used against him if he just continued to spew it.

Hands shaking, I guided the needle toward Duncan's neck, searching for a vein whilst Duwar continued to look at me through my love's eyes. "Ask the right questions, Robin, and you will find yourself with the right answers."

The needle pricked through skin, the liquid Gardineum slowly entering the vein I found. All the while, the demon-god never looked away from me.

"Rest well, Duwar."

The demon winced, the creased lines across Duncan's forehead smoothing as the drug worked its magic. "Time is running out, Robin. For you and for Duncan."

"I know that," I said, tears suddenly streaming down my cheeks. Just one look at Duncan and I could see the deterioration. There was no ignoring that I had to go to Lockinge now. I needed to speak to Rafaela so I could get the answers I required if I was to accept Duwar's offer of transference.

I still could hear it, as clear as it had been spoken the night Duncan awoke possessed by Duwar.

"I will offer you a deal. Provide me access to your body, and I shall give you the world you wish for. The one where you get to have everything you desire."

As the drug emptied into Duncan's blood stream, Duwar faded into silence, his presence departing as the Gardineum overcame his vessel. I half expected Duncan to regain control, but he was too weak to even try. I brushed his hair from his forehead and planted a kiss upon his damp skin. He may not have been conscious, but I hoped that somewhere deep down, he sensed me.

I had to say my goodbyes. I promised to return soon and that he was going to be in safe hands. I was just about to close the door on his room and fall into the routine of breaking down, when a small voice chirped on the bed.

"Darling?"

I paused, daring to look up, scared at what I'd find. Green eyes. Duncan's eyes. They squinted at me, shadowed by dark circles. He could barely lift his neck up to see me, but gods did he try. His gaze flickered behind me. "Why are you alone? Where is... Erix?"

There was no ignoring the genuine concern in his broken voice.

"He'll be back soon." It had barely been any time since he left me, and I craved his return. "Duncan, you need to rest."

"I know." Duncan physically relaxed, as if the drug wasn't enough to do that for him. Clearly, perhaps for differing reasons, he felt the same as I did inside at the knowledge that Erix would be back at Imeria soon.

A shaking hand reached out and grasped mine. I took it, glad for the touch I craved so desperately. "Just promise me one thing, Robin. Please."

"Anything," I leaned in close, needing to close the space between us. "Ask me anything, and I will do it."

Duncan released a heavy breath. "Just promise me you will not send Erix away. Never again. Keep him close... I trust him to care for you as I would..."

Duncan was fading again, his eyes growing heavy, his mouth slack as a rasped breath fought its way out.

I swallowed the urge to scream. "I promise, Duncan."

The most beautiful but weak smile crested over his face. "Good, my darling. That's good."

In those rare moments when he had control over his body, it only reminded me of what I risked losing. It was easier to cope in the silence, easier to pretend Duncan wasn't possessed.

"I love you, Duncan," I said, entire body trembling. "You know that, don't you?"

He nodded, the movement soft and subtle. "I do."

"Which is why I need to leave you, only for a short while."

"You must do what is required. But before you go," Duncan forced out, his words growing sluggish. "Will you... pray... over me?"

Duncan had lost his faith years ago, when he joined the Hunters. But it seemed, when possessed by a demon, he clung to it. Used it as a shield and a weapon against the monster inside of him. Would it harm Duwar to hear the Creator's prayer? It brought me comfort to think it would, and if it helped ease Duncan, that was all that mattered.

I clutched at my chest, wishing to ease the pressure beneath my ribs. "Of course, I will."

Returning to his bedside, I reached for his pillows to fluff them up and give Duncan's weakening body a lick of comfort. It wasn't much, and it didn't make the guilt any easier to combat, but I hoped it showed Duncan that I still loved him, more than words could explain.

"Oh Father, thy being of endless love and resilience," I began, leaning over Duncan as I righted the final pillow. "We pray that–"

I drew back, hissing, to see blood well on the tip of my finger. My eyes snapped to where my hand had been beneath the pillow, but found Duncan's eyes were wide and he was spluttering out excuses, green eyes fixed on my bleeding finger.

"Duncan, what is this?" I asked, voice trembling.

"I am saving… you from making… a decision– " Duncan stumbled over his words, unable to open his eyes as the Gardineum finally took over. "Please, do not take this choice from me."

Ignoring him, and the throbbing spreading down my hand, I lifted Duncan's head off his pillow. What I found turned my blood to ice. Light caught on the shard of glass, the edge coated in my blood. Instantly, I knew it was part of the mirror that had smashed. I drew it out, holding it up as my finger throbbed.

"Glass, Duncan?" I asked, lifting the large shard of glass between us.

Duncan closed his eyes against his will as the drug took hold. His breathing had smoothed out, telling me sleep had claimed him before he could answer me.

"Duncan," I said again, looking down at the horror on my face. "Duncan, wake up! Look at me… tell me why you have broken glass beneath your pillow…"

The only noise he made was the slight rasp of a snore.

I starred at my reflection with a look of pure disbelief. There was only one reason I could understand why Duncan kept the glass there. With its sharp edges, he'd be able to use it to bring an end to his suffering. Was that why he wanted Erix to be with me? So I wouldn't have been alone when I found him, bleeding out, in his bed?

Dread crept up my throat, wrapping unseen hands and squeezing.

Time really was running out. Duwar seemed desperate, and maybe this was why? Duwar knew what Duncan was planning, the next chance he had control over his body.

He was going to take his life, so that I didn't have to make that decision.

Sickness overcame me, every muscle in my body trembling with shock.

I don't know how I managed to leave the room, but I did so, still clutching the shard of glass. I stopped halfway down the corridor, needing to lean against the wall for support. The cold stone seeped into my body, offering me some clear-minded comfort.

I cried until there was nothing left in me. I reached the nearest window, threw it open and threw the shard of glass as far as I could manage.

It was then I saw the three winged bodies flying toward the castle.

Erix had returned to Imeria, with the company he promised. Two familiar gryvern I'd met days prior.

Sensing something had happened during his absence, and before I could talk, Erix made me wash and change whilst he placed the trunks of clothes and items into the carriage which arrived soon after him. My urgency was hard to ignore, but with the presence of our *guests*, I had to keep myself calm.

Duncan was going to take his life. The truth of that made me act upon instinct, as if my body was not my own, moving by the accord of the final scraps of strength I had.

When Erix finally addressed me with the plan, I could barely hear him through the rushing of blood in my ears.

"Maren and Gregory have agreed to watch over Duncan whilst we are away," Erix explained again, as the two gryvern guards stood vigil before me. If I expected them to react with hate, fear and vengeance at the knowledge of Duwar, they didn't. Whatever Erix told them about Duncan, they weren't fazed. I dared not ask for fear I'd give details away, ruining the illusion Erix had spun. "When you are ready, you tell them everything you need about his routine."

That gave me focus, enough to unload all the information that would ensure he was safe, alive and well, upon my return.

I took my time giving them the guidance on how to care for him. They would keep him fed and watered, ensure he was washed and changed whilst also keeping on top of his Gardineum injections – which Erix referred to as his medicine for his mental decline. One of them had to stay guard with him at all times, a detail that Erix didn't question. There was no mention of Duwar or demon-gods, for fear that the more who knew about them, the stronger the god would become, but deep down I knew they sensed the wrongness. I could see it in their eyes, a hesitation to the silent topic that no one brought up.

Belief was power after all.

When I finally told them about the shard of glass – and what I believed Duncan's intentions were – Erix trembled at my side. Secrets on top of secrets wasn't what I needed right now. If Duncan was serious about ending his life, I needed the gryvern guards to stay vigilant.

Erix was right – my secrets were crushing me. If felt… freeing to share at least one with the three before me. Although, one look at Erix when I told them what I found under Duncan's pillow, and I saw the colour drain from his face, replaced with the pallor of soul-eating worry.

"Not a minute can be spared without eyes on him," Erix commanded when I was finished, his lips paled from tension, his gaze focused on an unimportant point on the wall. "Am I clear?"

"Yes," the gryvern agreed in unison.

"Duncan Rackley will be kept in the best hands," Erix confirmed, more to himself than the rest of us. "No harm will befall him, that I can assure you."

I forced a smile. "Then we leave for Durmain before I change my mind."

No one argued with that.

In the end, it wasn't as hard to leave Imeria as I thought it would be. Knowing Duncan was left bound inside the castle walls, knowing what would happen if I failed on this mission for answers.

Whilst Eroan believed I left for a wedding, the truth was different.

The sooner we reached Lockinge, the sooner I could locate Rafaela, the better. Then I would come back and end this.

I *had* to end this. Once and for all.

CHAPTER 6

The day outside the castle ruins was clear, the skies blue. Although the harsh bite of winter winds coursed around us, there wasn't a cloud in sight. Which turned out to be exactly what Erix was hoping for. Eroan had arranged for a convoy to follow, but with our time constraints and my desperation of answers from Rafaela, I had proposed a faster means of travel to reach Lockinge.

"Do you really think this is necessary?" Erix asked as we watched our carriage disappear in the distance. "It will shave off a day, if that, from our journey. But I can assure you that you'd be far more comfortable sitting on a velveteen seat than carried by me."

I turned my attention from the convoy as it faded off up the road, back to Erix. "It's important we waste no time. Eroan confirmed that Cassial is holding council in Lockinge before the wedding. If we want to make it with excess time to find and speak with Rafaela, this is our only option."

Erix flexed his leathery wings; the sharp claw points at their tips caught the light. "Only if you are sure."

I understood that Erix's hesitation came from knowing that our dance of minimal physical contact was about to be left behind us, if he had to carry me all the way to our destination. "I'm very sure, I promise."

Erix nodded hesitantly. "Eroan has confirmed that your belongings will be taken directly to Grove, where you will be staying after the wedding. Eroan has also sent your measurements by hawk directly to Lockinge Castle, so you'll have something to wear in the city during our brief stay."

The mention of the human town I'd grown up in made my stomach tighten in knots.

"Rather organised," I retorted.

"It was at the request of Cassial himself. He is arranging all the outfits needed for the wedding, something about matching an aesthetic."

"Cassial really thinks of everything, doesn't he?" I forced out.

"He has to. Since Cassial has headed the reorganisation of the humans after Aldrick's downfall, he has proven himself to be meticulous. It is in his nature to be well prepared, and thank Altar he is. It is no small feat to lead an entire realm, but so far Cassial has produced nothing but success."

I couldn't argue with that.

There was well prepared, and there was also a person who was obsessed with control. Perhaps it was my lack of trust again, but I felt as though it was the latter when it came to the Nephilim. I'd only met Cassial the once when the Nephilim first revealed themselves, and he certainly wasn't as welcoming as Rafaela and Gabrial had been.

Erix had not experienced the *pleasure* of conversing with the Creator's Shield, as Cassial was previously known as, but soon he would, and then he could make his own decision about him as a person.

"Are you ready then?" Erix asked, arms open for me. "Best go before the weather turns."

I took in his body – garbed in black leathers, armoured shoulder pads and arm braces that looked like scales. A sword was at his hip, extra knives and daggers strapped around his chest. He looked ready for war, not travel.

"Are you sure you can manage?" I asked again. "Lockinge is a long way away."

"Just shy of two days by horse, but I think I can reach the city by sundown if we make haste."

I nodded, knowing the haste was my own doing. Daveed, the human teleporter we met in Aurelia, had stayed there after Aldrick died. To request his assistance would mean more waiting, wasting precious time I didn't have.

Erix read my obvious hesitation, arms crossing over his chest, which made the muscles beneath bunch. "Are you worried about me, little bird?"

"Should I not be?" I asked. It made sense, after all, I was worried about everything else.

Erix's smile was fleeting. He looked down to the sleet-coated ground, his breath coming out of his mouth in a cloud of mist. "I am far more resilient in this... form. A positive side effect of becoming a monster."

"You're no monster, Erix."

Was that where he believed my hesitation came from? After everything – even knowing what I left behind, strapped to a bed, in the ruins of my castle.

"Trust me," I added. "I'm well versed with such things nowadays."

To prove a point, I stepped in, unfolded his arms with my hands until I could melt in his chest. His body bowed around me, and he released a tempered breath. A spark of guilt twitched in my gut but faded when I quickly reminded myself of the promise I made to Duncan. He'd used Duwar to arrange our closeness, that was what I told myself. Although to anyone watching, they'd think the king was embracing his royal guard.

Erix began to tie leather straps around me, attaching buckles to clasps at his chest. I marvelled at the design, and he noticed. "This way I don't need to hold you the entire time," Erix explained when he caught me looking nervously at the straps. "My focus and energy can just be used getting us to Lockinge as fast as possible if I'm not worrying about dropping you."

"Is this your design?" I asked, wiggling in the secure bindings.

"Just something I had an idea about," Erix said, gaze wondering to something over my shoulder. "Although it's the first time I have had the chance to trial them."

"It brings me peace to know I am the one you're testing it on," I mocked, nerves bubbling out of me in a sharp laugh. "Not."

His light chuckle vibrated through my chest.

"There isn't anyone else I've gotten close enough to try it with," Erix replied, but before I could blush at his statement, he continued, "Now you're safe."

Erix released a long exhalation, which sung of untouched words. Then he stretched his wings behind him, blanketing us in a cool shadow. One hesitant arm at a time, he scooped me from the floor. "If, at any time, you get worried, just wrap your legs around my hips and your arms behind my neck."

"I'll be fine," I said, my skin shivering at the command. But to pretend this closeness wasn't undoing me, I would do as he asked. Only *if* the moment required it.

I pressed my face into his chest, inhaling the familiar scent of cinnamon which always clung to him.

"Ready?" he asked.

"Just don't let me go," I replied.

Then, with a gargantuan flap of his wings, the ground fell away. Above the roaring winds, I caught his soft reply. "Never, little bird. Never."

We flew for hours, and not once did Erix relax his hold on me, even with the leather harness holding me steady. His grip was ironclad. Every now and then he'd stop for a brief rest, but I believed this was for me more than him. We ate cured meats, cheese and bread, dark fresh spring water, relieved ourselves and were airborne before a conversation could truly start.

And there was no talking as we speared through the sky. Only the symphony of roaring winds and his thundering heartbeat kept me company. Up here, surrounded by the endless blue, it was easy to pretend – pretend that life could be something I would one day enjoy.

Although I knew this would never be a possibility for me, I would do anything in my power to secure a world in which Erix, Duncan and everyone else I cared about could live in peace. They deserved it, each and every one of them. But for that, I needed Rafaela and the answers she hopefully held.

I was close to sleeping when Erix's wings caught the wind like sails of a ship, stopping mid-air. I drew my face away from his chest, conscious I'd likely been snoring, mouth pressed awkwardly into his leathers. Blinking away my tiredness, I looked down to see what had stopped Erix.

At least he'd refrained from commenting on my snoring again – something he teased me about incessantly.

I looked down at the smudge of land beneath us. A patchwork of fields and hillsides split by rivers and roads. The sky was darkening to late afternoon, which made it hard to make out minor details. I narrowed my eyes on a line of moving… fire? No, not fire. Wagons drawn by horses left what looked like an old castle. Lanterns were held by those guiding the wagons on horseback. There were so many of them – far more than I could begin to count as Erix diverted our flight.

We landed half a mile away from the road. The moment we touched down, I could tell from Erix's pacing that something had unnerved him.

"Something is bothering you." I could read Erix well, but even a stranger could see that he was contemplating something that unnerved him.

Erix studied the dark as if a true monster would slip from it. He pointed at a dark stone structure in the distance. "Do you remember what that place was used for?"

I shook my head, squinting to make out the shapes. "Should I?"

"Yes." His wide eyes flashed with fury. "Because we are just outside of Finstock."

The blood in my veins – cold as my power, though weaker than it once had been – filled my body and bones.

I hadn't recognised Finstock from the air. I'd last seen it from the back of an iron cage, Duncan leading his Hunters before keeping us locked behind the fortress of grey stone. It belonged to Aldrick's followers – until the Cedarfall army cleared them out.

"I thought it'd been emptied," I said. "Cassial's update on progress with the Hunters confirmed as much."

That update came *weeks* back. Then why had there been a convoy of carriages leaving in the dead of night?

"It was *supposed* to be vacant." Erix looked beyond the clearing of forest he'd landed amongst, toward the moving line of flame and cart. "But it would seem someone else has found use for the fort in the meantime."

Throughout the day we'd seen fey and humans travelling toward the boundary of Wychwood in preparation for the wedding. It wasn't an uncommon sight, but clearly this was different.

"Stay here," Erix said, the slight points of his nails burying into the tree's bark. "I will come back to you shortly."

"No," I said, reaching for his hand before he could pull away. "That isn't happening. We go forward together, or not at all."

Erix turned to me, silver eyes drinking me in from head to boot. "If those people are… If the Hunters are regrouping…" Erix inhaled deeply, pausing to control himself. "I can't risk you being seen by them."

"The Hunters would be foolish to regroup when the Nephilim and the fey are searching for them," I added for him. "Do you really think they'd be stupid enough to reclaim Finstock since it was taken from them?"

"I do," Erix replied, chilling me to the core.

"Then I'm coming with you. Have you forgotten that you are also fey, Erix? You are as much under threat as I am. Plus, I have this." Ice crackled around my fingers. The sensation was stunted, odd. But the magic was there – weaker than before, but still useable.

Erix's eyes widened, his mouth parting in clear surprise. "It brings me comfort to know that you haven't lost all your power."

It was a well-kept secret, but then again, I hadn't really had the chance to show Erix what I was capable of. "When the key was destroyed, it took a lot of it. But the magic I had in my veins before I accepted the Icethorn key is still here. Not as powerful, no grand feats to display, but it is enough."

Erix relaxed as if he understood that I was not the powerless little bird he thought I was. "Good, we may need it."

"Hopefully not."

I expected Erix to refuse me again, but instead, he reached for a blade at his waist and handed it to me. This wasn't the first time he'd handed me a dagger, although the last one had been lost months ago. "Magic or not, I would feel better knowing you have steel with you too. I'm sure it's nothing, but we can't leave without checking."

I gritted my teeth, almost excited about the chance of facing Hunters again. "For their sake, let's hope that your suspicions are wrong."

The muscles in Erix's jaw feathered. He looked skyward, noticing the sudden gathering of clouds. When he glanced back to me, it was with a look of pride in his eyes.

I shrugged as I continued to release my power into the sky, bringing winter out of Icethorn and into Durmain. "A little cover will help us get into Finstock unnoticed. I think I can manage that…"

"You truly are brilliant, Robin."

"Back to first names, are we?" I asked, wishing I didn't but being unable to stop the words from leaving my lips. Lips that Erix hadn't stopped studying.

"My apologies," Erix bowed. "Little bird, you are a marvel. Better?"

It was.

I bit down on my lips at his praise. There were so many memories in Finstock. It was where Duncan and I had properly connected. It was where Erix had hunted me down, following Doran Oakstorm's commands. In the little time since, so much had changed. *Too* much.

I stepped into Erix, who wrapped his arms around me from behind this time. He didn't tie the harness back, knowing our flight was only going to be short. Facing outwards so that I had a view of Finstock, instead of burying my face in his chest like before. My stomach flipped as he got us back into the sky. With one hand on the dagger he'd gifted me, the other swirling the gathering clouds like dough in a bowl, we flew into the heart of the fortress, landing on the upper wall.

What we discovered upon arrival was Finstock was, in fact, empty. At least of humans. Although my mind pieced together something we'd seen earlier, and it seemed that the line of wagons we'd noticed had left Finstock. Fresh track marks outside the gate suggested as much.

"They've all gone," I said, looking into the empty courtyard. I searched for signs that they had been Hunters. "The timing is almost too perfect."

"Hmm," Erix grumbled, gesturing us to walk further into the heart of the fort. "Only one way to confirm that theory."

There were no banners with the outline of a hand painted upon material, or old iron cages left behind. In fact, there was nothing incriminating about Finstock, besides the memories that haunted the dark stone walls. Only the old hints of a battle – charred stone, broken windows and a scarred smudge of black against the ground where the Cedarfall army had burned the bodies of the dead.

"If we leave now, we could follow the wagons," I suggested. "We'll get our answers by seeing who exactly left here."

Erix studied the dark fortress, winds caressing the short brown curls he'd grown in the past weeks. For a moment, I caught the glint of someone else. Tarron Oakstorm – his half-brother. It was in rare moments that I got the reminder as to his heritage.

"There're a few more corners of this place I would like to check before we leave." His hand slipped into mine and he was guiding me toward the darkened archway leading into the fortress. "If we follow the wagons, we waste more time. Let's check inside, and if we are confident those were not Hunters we saw, then we leave and head for Lockinge. We can still make it... perhaps a little later than planned but still with enough time to sleep before tomorrow."

Erix was right. This was his way of reminding me that we didn't have time to waste chasing after 'what ifs'.

As predicted, Finstock was empty. It was like the people who'd been here knew we were coming. I knew that was my paranoia, but I couldn't shake the unsettling feeling inside these walls.

Without firelight, it was hard to see inside the many dark rooms. Erix went first, his gryvern eyes more used to seeing in the shadows. Once he was content that the rooms were empty, we moved swiftly on.

We came to a stop in a chamber I'd never forget. It was the fortress's old chapel, the place Duncan had taken me to so I could watch the followers of Duwar sacrifice themselves in front of a crowd. Except, the room seemed different than before.

"What are those?" I asked, following Erix as he inspected piles upon piles of wooden crates. They didn't have a symbol on them to suggest what they held. But there were so many of them, proving that whatever was kept in the room had been there in abundance.

"Looks like whoever was here had been using Finstock as storage of some kind."

"Maybe innocent humans, reclaiming the place after the Hunters were evicted. It's possible. It isn't exactly like land is something to be spared in Durmain."

"Maybe," Erix echoed, although he didn't seem to believe me, or himself. We checked almost every box, but we came up empty and without answers as to what had been here.

I kept looking toward the raised dais, noticing the old stain of blood worn into the steps like rust. If I closed my eyes, I could hear the daggers split necks and the bodies of fresh dead thump to the ground.

A terrifying thought speared into my mind. Duncan and the shard of glass beneath his pillow. What if Duwar was using him to converse with the Hunters – something Aldrick would've done.

I bit down on my lower lip until I tasted blood, trying to stifle the thought. What was better? Duncan wanting to use the glass to kill himself, or Duncan conspiring with Hunters to further Aldrick's plans?

Plans Duwar clearly shared.

I walked to the edge of the room, aware of every noise the stone walls echoed back to me. I was so focused on the dais that I didn't see the glass until I stepped onto it. Erix snapped around, sword unsheathed in a blink.

I raised my hands in surrender. "It's just me, Erix. Stand down."

He sagged in relief, although he kept his sword out.

Lifting my foot, I looked down at the shards of glass beneath my boot. Not glass from a window, but reflective like that of a mirror. In fact, swept into the corner and covered in dust, was a scattering of more broken shards.

Dread sank in my stomach like a stone. I knelt down, just like I had in Duncan's room in Imeria, and picked up a shard of mirror. I held it up for Erix to see. He stepped in close, so much so that I felt his breath on my face. Then he took the shard from my hands, his fingers brushing mine for a moment.

"Tell me this is a coincidence," I begged. "Finding a mirror in a place where Duwar was once worshiped. That is all..."

He turned the shard over, his reflection caught the worry across his brow. "I am not sure."

I swept my gaze over the room of empty crates. Had they all contained mirrors? Or was that just my paranoia talking again. We'd not know without solid proof, and in reality, those crates could've held anything. Perhaps Cassial had used Finstock as storage for the supplies for Althea and Gyah's wedding. Anything was possible.

And yet that stone of dread sank deeper and deeper until it was rooted into my gut like a seed with iron-clad roots.

"We should leave for Lockinge now," Erix said, without taking his attention off the shard of mirror. "Cassial and his Nephilim have been keeping an eye on old Hunter settlements. If anything, they may know what was happening here."

"I'd prefer to look into this ourselves," I said.

"It is not our issue to resolve, not anymore." Erix drank me in from across the room, silver eyes glittering with worry. "Durmain is under the protection, and guidance, of the Nephilim. This is for them to sort. If we were in Wychwood, trust I would make sure we got our answers. But it is best we do not interfere here. Not until the accords have been signed."

I swallowed the lump which formed in my dried throat. "I'm sure it is nothing to worry about," I lied, because if I thought too hard about the mirrors, and my concerns about Duncan, I might've crumbled into a pile.

I needed Rafaela, and for that we had to reach Lockinge. The longer I took, the more this possibility could affect both realms.

We both knew the importance mirrors had to Duwar. Except my memory of last being in this room was clear as day. There had never been mirrors here. Why now? Yes, it was how Aldrick communicated with the demon-god during his banishment, but Duwar was here, lurking in our realm. Surely, he wouldn't need mirrors to communicate with our world now he was in it.

"You're right," Erix said finally, offering me a smile. "Finstock holds far too many bad memories. It is easy to treat it with suspicion, after everything that happened here."

"Exactly."

It was on the tip of my tongue, to again ask Erix to follow the wagons and find out what they carried. But if we were wrong, and they were simply humans travelling to a wedding that was meant to bring together the human and fey, investigating them would only cause the rift between our kinds to linger further apart.

Against my better judgement, we left Finstock and flew in the direction of the human capital. That didn't stop me from searching the darkening landscape for a line of wagons again. Eventually, we saw them, but it seemed they'd separated from their long-lined convoy. I didn't know if that should've relaxed me or made me worry more.

As night slipped over Durmain, swallowing the view beyond in obsidian, my worries shifted back to Duncan. In a matter of hours, he'd wake from the Gardineum-induced coma.

How would he react when he discovered I was no longer there? Perhaps he already knew.

Seeing the broken mirror in Finstock focused my goals and reminded me of what I needed to do in Lockinge. So, when the city came into view, glowing against the dark from thousands of homes lit from inside, I felt a surge of relief.

Relief that didn't last long.

CHAPTER 7

I would never admit it out loud, but it was unsettling seeing how much Lockinge had changed since I'd last been here. Compared to the slow progression in Icethorn – with towns and villages once abandoned now rebuilding as part of a community – Lockinge looked like a city I'd never visited before. It was as if the explosions – atrocities I had caused when we blew up all of the Asp's hideouts – had never happened here. Any sign of ruin had been covered up with golden-trimmed banners with the symbol for the Creator stitched into the material.

Everywhere I could see, there was more evidence of who ruled here now.

The Nephilim, guided by the unseen hand of the Creator.

We landed in the heart of the Cage – the outer slums of the city. It wasn't by choice that we stopped here. The moment we flew close to Lockinge city, the Nephilim were aware. A horde of the angelic warriors accosted us mid-air, armed and poised to protect *their* city.

The welcome wasn't what I expected. Not at the end of a golden blade, with the distrusting glare of a winged warrior before us. Even if the blade was only lifted for a moment before they realised who I was, the unsettling feeling in my gut hadn't wavered.

"King Icethorn," a nondescript Nephilim said in welcome, bowing slightly to show respect, lowering his weapon. "We were expecting your arrival earlier than this."

"Do you greet all guests with drawn weapons?" I asked, nervous at how quick they'd come out, and how quick they were put away. "Or is it special treatment for me?"

"My apologies." The winged warrior swapped his weapon for an outstretched hand. "My name is Zarrel, and Cassial tasked me to be on guard waiting for you."

I took his hand, not wanting to continue this greeting on the wrong foot. "Thank you for your patience, Zarrel."

Erix scoffed from my side, wings bristling. In comparison to the angelic beings that stood before us, he looked much like the monster they'd last known him to be. The monster I had told him he wasn't. But my perspective was certainly different to the angel before me.

"As you can imagine," Zarrel said, shooting a nervous glance in Erix's direction, "the humans dwelling in this city were not long ago terrorised by gryvern. When we received reports of one flying into our skies, it made us... nervous."

"I can confirm that Erix is no threat," I said, unable to hide the irritation in my tone.

Zarrel looked again to Erix. If I wanted to believe their slip up was a result of not knowing Erix had been the one to fly me here, the glint in his azure eyes suggested otherwise.

"What matters is you are here now, and all is well," Zarrel said. "I've been given strict instructions to bring you to the castle where you can rest. As the letter from Eroan suggested to expect your arrival earlier today, any meetings planned have been postponed until tomorrow. Our Saviour Cassial was displeased to hear of your... late arrival, as he was excited to finally host you."

There was no ignoring the bit of disdain in the man's tone. How could I blame him?

I'd helped orchestrate the destruction of the very things they'd vowed to protect.

The keys to Duwar's realm, and thus the only way of keeping him locked away.

"Saviour?" I repeated, not caring for anything else he'd just said. "Interesting. I last remember Cassial being known by another title."

I side-eyed Erix, who looked like he was ready for a brawl. When his lips parted, it was to confirm my statement. "The Creator's Shield, was it not?"

Zarrel flexed impressive wings, downy feathers falling to the ground like snow. "Much has changed in the months past, as I am sure you are well aware. As you can see around you, Cassial has headed a major improvement to Lockinge and those dwelling around it. Dealing with the... damage left behind from your last visit to Lockinge," the Nephilim replied. "If memory serves me correctly."

Was this why they greeted us with weapons drawn? Because I'd been the heart of why so many buildings in the Cage burned to a crisp, and not that Erix had flown us here?

"It has been a long day of traveling," I mentioned, drawing the attention away from the past. "I hope you can forgive our late arrival, the reasons for which I will bring up in my meeting with Cassial. In the meantime, a little rest will be just what we need. Please inform *your* Saviour, that we have arrived in one piece and look forward to an audience with him tomorrow."

"No need, by now Cassial is already aware that you have arrived. There isn't a single detail overlooked in this city." Zarrel paused long enough to offer me the most blinding smile, one that almost reached his eyes, but not quite. "Let us get you into the castle with haste, unless your gryvern would prefer another means of travel to the destination?"

"His *name* is Erix," I snapped, unable to control myself. The fury came thick and fast, half aided by my exhaustion but also at the idea of anyone disregarding him as nothing more than a mindless monster.

Erix laid a hand on my arm. "It's okay, Robin, I am sure Zarrel meant no harm."

"I *certainly* didn't." Zarrel quickly bowed, without even attempting to hide his subtle grin. "Please, King Icethorn, Erix – follow me."

Large white wings beat down, sending the Nephilim skyward. Erix made a move to embrace me, so close that when I spoke, my words were for him alone. "Well, he was pleasant. And by pleasant, I mean prick...ly."

"I'm not going to tell you that you're wrong, little bird. But perhaps it is best we keep pretences up for the duration of our stay. Pissing off our hosts wouldn't be beneficial to our already taut relationship." Erix focused ahead, worry set into his brow. "And to be fair to Zarrel, we are late."

"So? Pissing off their guests wouldn't be a smart way to start this either," I reminded him.

He didn't reply, but I knew Erix agreed.

Erix wrapped his arms around me and the ground fell away as he got us airborne. A cloud of Nephilim hung above us, outlined by the full moon. At the head was Zarrel, eyes fixed to me, an attention I didn't want nor enjoy. He waited for us to follow, his smile still etched into what was an undeniably handsome face. There was something calculating about his stare: a dislike that I understood but didn't have to accept.

The final stretch to Lockinge Castle was brief.

I took a deep breath in through my nose, expecting to smell the stench of shit and ale that infected the slums of the city. Instead, the air was fresh. Better than it had been before. More proof that the Nephilim were succeeding in their new challenge at improving the humans' lives.

I recognised the places where our fires had burned the Asp's hideouts. It had been as a means to draw Aldrick's followers away from the castle long enough for us to break in and save the fey he kept as prisoners. Except, where shells of burned buildings should've been, were now the scaffolding of new buildings. Not homes, but places of worship, each and every one of them. With their spired roofs, it looked as though the Nephilim had hand-picked Abbott Nathanial's church and placed them throughout the city.

So much had changed, in such little time. Even the castle looked different the closer we got. The whiter the stone walls appeared, almost brand new. It was clear that the Nephilim had tried to scrub away the sins of the city since they'd taken control of it. And yet, I couldn't help but wonder what they'd done with the Below – the prison beneath the castle. Had they filled the prison with Hunters – a place hundreds of fey had once been held for Aldrick to harvest for blood like cattle? Or would they keep it empty, just in case they one day required it again?

Deep down, I felt as though I already knew the answer.

No matter how many times I requested, Zarrel – the white-winged Nephilim who'd not-so-kindly welcomed us into Lockinge – refused my requests for an audience with Rafaela.

Waiting until morning to speak to Cassial was easy to accept considering I had not come here for him. But knowing Rafaela was close, I could barely contain myself.

I'd not come all this way only to be denied the one thing I came for: answers.

"I will put forward the request that you'd like an audience with the traitor – with Rafaela," he corrected, although I knew his hesitation was to give me a clear message. "But I cannot guarantee Cassial will accept. But rest assured, King Icethorn, I will do my very best."

Somehow, I didn't think his 'very best' meant much.

I felt every muscle in my body tense as I stood in the middle of the chamber I was given. Erix was, as always, a shadow at my back, studying Zarrel with a wary eye. Our shared emotion for the Nephilim tainted the very air around us. No doubt Zarrel noticed, but likely didn't care. He'd made it very clear the feeling was mutual.

"I made the summons request clear in my letter," Erix said through gritted teeth. "As you have previously confirmed, you already received it."

"We did. But in that same letter you also made it clear that you were to arrive hours prior to this," Zarrel reminded. "It's late. The city is asleep, and so should you both be."

We couldn't argue with that, and the more I did, the more questions Zarrel would ask. I came for answers, not to create unwanted questions from people I didn't know.

Zarrel gestured to the room, the wave of his hand more a dismissal than anything else. "You both have travelled miles and deserve to recuperate your energy. Breakfast will be hosted in the old throne room tomorrow morning. There you will meet with the other heads of the fey courts before a day of council meetings."

"And Rafaela?" I pushed for a final time.

The curl of Zarrel's lip sickened me. His disgust for Rafaela only increased my disgust for him. "I will arrange for you to petition that request directly with Cassial after the morning's activities. I'm not the one who can grant you the acceptance you seek, I'm afraid."

"Does Rafaela not have the ability to answer for herself?" I said, my growing unease now a maelstrom of panic.

Rafaela had told us that she may face punishment for what part she had played in destroying the three keys, but I was beginning to wonder exactly what that punishment entailed.

Zarrel's pause made my skin burn hot. "Goodnight, King Icethorn. Erix. You'll find everything required for your brief stay already in your respective rooms. If you need anything else, there will be guards stationed close by at all times."

And with that, Zarrel turned on his heel and left. I watched, dumfounded, as the door closed behind him. Neither of us spoke, not as we watched the door, dumfounded by the response regarding Rafaela we received.

"Actually, prickly doesn't seem right," I said. "Prick feels more fitting for him."

"I was just thinking the same thing." Erix broke his line of sight from the door, settling it back on me. His silver eyes roamed over my face, noticing details I couldn't see without a mirror. "Although I hate to admit this, you do look tired, Robin. Maybe it is best that we sleep until tomorrow. And by we, I mean you."

I blinked, squeezing my eyes closed as an attempt to will the headache from my skull. "Do you know what they have done to Rafaela?"

Erix paused. I opened my eyes, turned to face him and saw the clear worry across his brow. "No, I don't. But I promise we will find out first thing. Tomorrow, okay?"

We were all aware she'd face punishment. But I'd not found out what exactly that punishment had been. And I admit, I hadn't attempted to find out. With everything happening to Duncan, my mind had been occupied. Guilt was so familiar, it was almost comforting to feel in that moment. Of course, I'd tried to reach Rafaela by letter, multiple times. I believed her silence was because she was too busy with the humans. Now I worried the lack of response was for a more sinister reason.

A reason I *had* to find out.

But since the Nephilim weren't going to help me, I knew someone else who could. But for that, Erix needed to leave me alone.

"Then let's hope that Cassial agrees that I can speak to her," I said, plans forming frantically in my mind. "Maybe he will also have answers as to why I never received responses to my letters to Rafaela."

I got the impression they never reached her, that's why.

"Yes. A solid plan." Erix looked from me to the closed door. There was obvious hesitation in his lack of movement. "You know, if you'd prefer, I could stay in here tonight, with you."

For the past few nights, Erix had taken a seat beside my bed and watched me. I knew he also slept, but having someone so close, someone I could call on when I needed it, was a blanket of relief.

My heart screamed for me to accept him, but my mind had other focuses.

"I'll be fine tonight." I shook my head before I gave in to my weakness for him. "Your room is opposite to mine. I know where to find you if I change my mind."

Stay with me. Don't leave me. I need you.

I couldn't present those demands to him. I wouldn't. My desires didn't matter anymore. All that mattered was answers, and I couldn't wait to get them tomorrow.

I needed them *now*.

Erix looked exhausted, likely the reason he didn't refuse me. There was no denying that, from the deep shadows beneath his silver eyes, to the pallor his skin had taken, hours of flying had drained him. Although his body was not completely fey, not entirely gryvern, he still had his limits.

"Promise you will actually sleep, or at least try."

"You spend more time worrying about me, instead of yourself, Erix." I eyed him up and down. His slumped posture, the shadows beneath his eyes and the heavy drag of his feet all confirmed that he was exhausted. He'd just flown across a realm for me, it was a miracle he could still stand.

"I do, and will. Always."

It took restraint I hardly had to not blush. "Anyway, I'll just be stirring all night. I don't want to keep you up."

"I wouldn't mind the stirring. Besides, I'm used to sleeping through your snoring by now," Erix added, voice soft as he fiddled with his hands.

"Lies. I don't snore."

"Are we really going to have this disagreement again?" Erix released a short chuckle which quickly became a yawn.

Erix had first accused me of snoring when I fell asleep behind him as we rode into Cedarfall lands the day I was saved, saved myself, from execution. The memory was so clear it could've happened yesterday, not longer ago.

"Then be glad you can sleep without the burden of those snores tonight. Sleep well, Erix," I said, opening the door for him before I changed my mind.

He took a step closer, worry set into the lines beside his eyes. "Are you sure, little bird?"

If he tested me one more time, I'd crumble and tell him exactly what I wanted. "Yes, I'm sure. Go. You look like death warmed up. Get some sleep. Nothing exciting is going to happen until tomorrow, you heard Zarrel."

We both glanced toward the door opposite the corridor to mine. There was hardly a physical space between us, and yet the cavernous gap was growing.

"Okay." Erix walked away slowly.

Did he expect for me to call out and change my mind? Perhaps he did know me well, because the urge to do it was on the tip of my tongue. Instead, I forced my lips shut and watched my guard enter his room and close the door.

I stood like that for a while. Focused on his door, listening to the sounds of shuffling inside quickly quieten. Then I turned my attention to the corridor. I could see the junction of conjoining hallways at the end, and the winged guard who walked up and down it. I waited, counting the seconds between his pacing. It took seventy-four seconds for him to complete his walk and return.

A lot could happen in seventy-four seconds.

I slunk back into my room, soundlessly closing the door behind me. Scanning the modest room, I saw there was nothing but a trunk of clothes, a four-poster bed, a low table set up with food and water and an even smaller bathing chamber.

I set my mind to the task at hand – finding Rafaela. And for that, I needed some help. Erix wasn't the only one to send letters ahead of our arrival. All of mine had previously been addressed to the woman I required to see, but the last one I'd sent was addressed to someone else.

Crossing the room, I laid my hand upon the glass of the window.

The winter storm inside of me enjoyed the excuse for release. It rushed up through me with ease, spreading ice across the glass and the wall surrounding it. I didn't stop until icicles hung beyond the window, like the jagged teeth of a monster's jaw.

Then, I did the one thing I'd become good at doing.

I waited.

I took a seat on the edge of my bed, noticing for the first time just how tired I was as I felt the plush bedding beneath me. But sleep had to wait. There was more than one reunion I prepared for in Lockinge.

Minutes stretched out until I caught the slight tap beyond my closed door. I stood quickly, crossed the space and opened it to reveal the face of a ghost. It was half covered by a mask, obscuring the knowing grin she, no doubt, had plastered across her mouth.

"Robin Icethorn," the hooded woman sang my name in greeting, voice muffled by the material across her lower face. She lifted painted nails, pinched the mask and tugged it over her face. Not that I needed to see her to know who she was.

I smiled, beckoning the assassin inside. "Hello, Seraphine."

CHAPTER 8

Just as the namesake of the group of assassins suggested, the Asps were as slippery as a snake. And Seraphine being the queen of that nest, she could get past anything – even death itself.

The world believed she'd died – buried beneath Imeria Castle during the Draeic attack. However, I'd discovered the truth when I arrived back to the ruins of Imeria.

Seraphine survived and was very much alive, a secret I'd since kept for her in trade for the secret she was forced to keep for me.

And here she stood, alive and well, no different to when I found her all those weeks ago. I thought she was a ghost haunting the ruins of Imeria castle when I arrived with a delirious Duncan before Duwar had truly taken hold of his body. That was until she explained that she'd escaped before the castle came down. The rest of her fellow Asps were not so lucky.

Duncan knew that Seraphine was alive, but that was it. And I'd promised to keep her secret, because she kept mine.

Something happened that day, between Duncan, Duwar and Seraphine. A tale I could barely think about without my skin crawling. And yet, every time I looked at the ropes of vines and flowers that now adorned the walls of my ruined castle, I always thought of Seraphine: she'd been there to witness Duncan do it, as well as other things...

"You look like shit, Robin." Seraphine watched me from her seat on the plush reading chair. She leaned forwards, legs spread, resting elbows on her knees.

"I feel like shit," I replied, fisting my hands so she didn't see the stumps that were once nails. "How have you been?"

It was the type of question friends asked after a long period of time apart, and yet I still wasn't sure that I could call Seraphine a friend.

"Coping," she answered, plainly. "Which is as much as you could expect, you know, considering..."

"Considering I'm harbouring a world-ending threat?"

She raised her eyes up to me, the rich colour scoring through my skin. "Yes, something like that."

I hadn't told Seraphine by choice. What had happened between Duncan and me, when we returned to Imeria, was something no one could ignore. If Seraphine hadn't revealed herself in the chaos, I might not have been alive to this day to even have this conversation. But I wasn't ready to talk about that yet, and nor was she.

"I admit that I'm surprised you came to Lockinge," Seraphine said, kindly drawing the conversation away from the secrets we both hid. "When I received your letter, I almost couldn't believe it but here you are... standing out like a wilted rose amongst thorns."

"Did you think I was going to bring Duncan with me?"

She bowed her head. "I did. I can't say I'm not relieved that you left him back at home."

"I wouldn't risk lives like that," I rushed out. "The danger is too great."

She nodded, not needing to press me further on what those risks where. She understood. "Then I imagine you are here for a reason, as my summons also suggests. Although Robin, do you need reminding that my services are no longer available for hire? Or did you simply want me to come for a catch-up, two friends chatting about life in the new world?"

I scoffed at that, eyeing up the half-drunk goblet of wine. "What good is the new world, if it's all some big lie?"

Seraphine didn't tell me I was wrong. "Friend." She laid a hand on my knee, offering me some comfort. "You didn't need to come all this way to accept my offer. A letter would've done–"

"That is *not* why I'm here," I snapped, before realising my mistake. The mere suggestion of what Seraphine had offered the last time I saw her, sent a bout of sickness across my gut.

She leaned back, lifting arms in surrender. "I didn't mean to upset you, only remind you if you needed it."

"No reminder required." I shook my head, before burying my face in my hands. "Sorry. It's been a long day. Fuck, it's been a long few weeks. The days all blend into one at this point."

One last squeeze of my knee and then Seraphine withdrew. "I understand. Go on then, you got me all the way here, what is it you want from me?"

"If I said friendly company, would you believe me?"

"No, I wouldn't." She rocked back, took my goblet of wine and finished it in a single gulp. "So, what is it?"

"A snake may shed its skin, but beneath, you *are* still a snake," I said, looking through my lashes at her.

"Ouch." Seraphine's face pinched into a scowl of disgust, confirming she knew exactly what topic I was dancing around.

"You know what I mean," I added.

"Once an Asp, always an Asp. Is that what you're trying to suggest?"

"Not exactly suggest," I replied. "Hope, maybe."

Seraphine sighed, as if she already expected this. "There is only one life I'm willing to take without payment, and you know whose that is."

Duncan's life. That had been her offer after what happened. She would kill Duncan, because I was far too weak to do it. My answer now, as it had been that day, was still the same. No. "I'm not that desperate."

"*Yet*," Seraphine added, as though I missed the word.

I took a deep breath in. "I need help finding someone, not killing them. Do you have it in you to come out of retirement for a task like that?"

She ran a gloved hand over her chin, mocking contemplation. "And the payment? Don't think about offering me another place to live either, Robin. It seems your idea of home has weak foundations."

She wasn't wrong. I gave her and her Asps Imeria as a home, and it had come crumbling down on them. "Is saving the world sufficient compensation for your assistance?"

Dark horror flashed behind her eyes. I don't think she realised she did it, but Seraphine lifted a hand and ran it down the side of her opposing arm. The last time I'd seen her, that very arm had been bandaged after the skin was flayed by Duncan's lightning.

Lightning meant for me. If anything, I owed Seraphine so much more. She'd left Imeria, harbouring my secrets, with the ability to bring the wrath of the human and fey realms down upon me. Which I deserved. I'd led death to Seraphine's new doorstep and killed the men and women she'd called family.

And being the sole survivor of a family was a hard burden to bear. I would know. Perhaps that was why we bonded so quickly. Seraphine and I recognised kinship in one another. Two lonely souls bound by secrets, forever cursed to wonder the world alone, even with people surrounding us.

"And who do you want me to find for you?" Seraphine asked after a moment of silence.

I took her ignoring my previous answer as an acceptance of my request. "Rafaela."

There was no ignoring the furrow of Seraphine's brow. "The Nephilim?"

I nodded. "She's why I made the journey here. I need to speak to her."

"And here I was thinking you came to celebrate your closest friend's wedding."

"I'm not really in the headspace for celebrating," I said, cringing internally at the mention of the wedding, an event I was dreading. Not only for the joy I was to pretend to share, but also seeing friends I'd pushed away.

"But you are in the capital which has been, rather impressively, taken over by the Nephilim. Can't you ask around for Rafaela since you're here, or perhaps take the hint that she hasn't reached back to you because she just doesn't like you?"

"That may be the case," I said, swallowing the bile that burned at the back of my throat. I blinked and saw her golden hammer in the hands of Zarrel, heard the echo of his refusal to let me see Rafaela and the mention of 'approval' from Cassial. "I think something has happened to her, something bad, and considering I helped her destroy the keys, I find myself feeling responsible for whatever state she is in."

"Careful, Robin. You may just bury yourself beneath the burdens of everyone else, before realising your own are killing you from the inside," Seraphine warned.

"Beautifully put," I replied. "Have you taken up poetry since we last saw each other?"

"Actually, *Your Majesty*, I've turned my hands to sketching. Had to give them something to do since I've put down the daggers and poisons."

My leg twitched, bouncing up and down, fingers pinching into the material of my trousers. "Please, Seraphine. I beg you to help me."

"Must be bad if you left your little demon back in Icethorn, travelled all this way, just to see her."

"She would do it for me if the tables were turned." If Seraphine refused me, I would willingly get on my knees and beg her. "I need to–"

Need to what? Know if Rafaela was okay because I was genuinely worried about her? Or was it because I knew, without her assistance, I'd not be able to put an end to this literal hell on earth? Both, perhaps. Either way, I had to get answers, and nobody else I knew had the ability to carve answers out of nothing but will alone.

"How long do I have for this task?" Seraphine stood from the chair, speaking from a professional place. Gone was the relaxed interaction between us. Once again, I was her employer, and she was my Asp.

"As soon as possible." Relief blossomed within me, like a flower beneath sun. "Or at worst, by dawn. But I appreciate that's short notice."

Seraphine didn't look happy with me, and yet I knew she'd made her mind up. "Is that a lack of confidence in my skills that I hear beneath your words?"

I feigned a smile, shaking my head. "Never."

Seraphine tipped her head and turned back for the door. "You'll know when I have your answers. Don't blame me if it's not what you want to hear."

"I won't. Thank you," I said, chasing her heel until we both stood before the closed door. Before she swept out, I reached out and took her wrist in my hand. "Seraphine, just another moment before you go."

She paused, hand clutching the door handle. "If you want to reminisce about what we've lost, I'm not in the mood for it."

"No," I said. "It's nothing like that. I just… I just want to ask what's changed for you, that you'd help me without payment. Not like you to do charity work, after all."

When she looked back at me, I saw fear in her eyes for the first time. Even when she'd stood between me and Duncan, lightning arching toward her, as Duwar finally took control of Duncan's body, she hadn't looked frightened.

But now, she looked as terrified as I felt inside.

"Because I found something to lose," Seraphine answered. "Just when I believed everything was taken from me, my life ruined. Turned out when you don't go looking, life comes looking for you."

My heart ached at her genuine reply. "What's their name?"

She glanced down to her hand. Although I couldn't see the ring beneath her gloves, I saw the outline of the metal as she ran a thumb over it. "Lindwell. Or Lin for short."

Her hand then shifted from the ring into a jacket pocket. From there she retrieved what looked to be a square of cloth, something sun-faded and frayed at the edges. Slowly, she unfolded it and handed it to me.

"I told you I got into sketching," Seraphine said as my eyes settled on what was in my hands. "A lot can happen in a matter of months, especially when one finally gives up control to the ravine that is life."

I looked down to a picture, drawn in neat, detailed lines. The faces of three people looked up at me. Seraphine stood beside a man, her features sharper than they looked in person but still recognisable. The man, who must've been her husband, Lindwell, stood behind a young girl. I couldn't tell how old she was, and nor did she look anything like Seraphine. And yet there was a tenderness to the sketch, a love that oozed from the heart-shaped face of the young girl, and the soft smile Seraphine offered down to her.

"Altar, Seraphine–" I choked, finding my body rooted to the floor. "I see you've found more than just a husband."

"Lin came with baggage in the form of a five year-old girl. She lost her mother a few years back from sickness, and it would seem I've found myself slotting into her life as the right shape to fit her missing pieces."

I couldn't take my eyes off the sketch. It was only when Seraphine took it back, folded it neatly and placed it back in her inner pocket – the one just shy of her heart – that I looked up to her. "I'm so happy for you, Seraphine. You've found a family, just when those before were taken away from you."

If I was so happy, then why did tears sting my eyes?

"You certainly look it," Seraphine laughed, nudging my shoulder with her fist. "Consider me convinced."

I cleared my cheek of the single pesky tear with the back of my hand. "I really am."

Seraphine shrugged in dismissal. "Everyone else was enjoying this new world, I thought I'd join in on the fun. Turns out, along the way, I discovered the potential of a future and, if I'm honest, I'm thrilled by it. I've never wanted to be a mother, but meeting Amara and Lin, I feel as though life has given me a second purpose."

A lump formed in my throat at the raw emotion rolling from Seraphine. "So, about that payment you mentioned…"

"Save the world, Robin. Fix these problems, then I will consider any debts between us cleared."

I bit down on my lower lip. It was in that moment the severity of our secret hit me. Seraphine had found love, whilst knowing that I kept the very creature that could take it all away from her. I'd thought nothing was stopping Seraphine from taking matters into her own hands and killing Duncan, just as she offered to do. Except, something *was* stopping her and now I understood.

It was the same thing she'd found returning to Lockinge. It was love.

"I *will* fix this," I said to her, refusing to look anywhere else but her eyes. I needed Seraphine to see my honesty, to know that I had a plan and would do anything to see it through. "For Lin. For young Amara. I will do anything to make sure you truly can enjoy the new world that everyone thinks they've achieved now."

Seraphine straightened her posture, drinking me in with a look that sang of pity. "And Rafaela is the key to solving this issue? Pardon the pun."

I winced at the mention of keys, knowing that was what got us into this mess. "Yes, Rafaela should have the knowledge to help me. At least I hope she does."

"And if not?"

There it was… the question I knew this conversation would lead back to.

"Then the next time I call upon you, it will be for that offer you put forward."

"I hope Rafaela has those answers you seek, if that is the case." The muscles in the sides of Seraphine's cheeks tensed. "Robin."

"Yes, friend."

She stepped back as if the title physically struck her. "I finally like this life, even after everything that has happened before it, I really wish to hold onto this one."

I'd never seen such emotion in her. Not even when she'd told me the only reason she stayed in Imeria was because she was personally digging out each member of the Asps from the rubble to ensure they got a proper burial.

She'd bargained a new home for them. A chance at a new life. And although the Draeic came for me, Seraphine blamed herself. And yet it was now, as she looked at me, one hand on the door, the other over the concealed sketch in her pocket, she looked ready to shatter.

"I promise," I said, meaning it.

"Hmm. I can't help but wonder at the cost you will pay, though," Seraphine said, drinking me in with all-knowing eyes.

I had no answer prepared for this, nor the time given to hide the truth. So, for the first time, I said it aloud for someone to hear.

"Me," I said.

There was nothing else I needed to say. Seraphine took my answer for what it was, gritted her teeth and sharpened her stare. "We all pay unfair prices for the safety of those we love."

"We do," I agreed.

Seraphine gave me one last hard look, turned the door handle and opened it. If I expected her to push me for more answers, she didn't. It wouldn't take a genius to understand what I'd meant.

"Tomorrow morning."

"Please."

Seraphine laid a hand on my shoulder and squeezed. "I will send word when I have located Rafaela. Before I go, is that all I'm required for?"

"Not all," I added, noticing her surprise. "I want you to enjoy life. Take it by the reins and rule it. You, Lin and Amara. Enjoy them… make the sacrifices you've previously paid for this second chance worth it. Make sure you enjoy it, for me."

A single tear escaped her eye, matching my own. This was as much a goodbye as it was a reunion. Then, without another word, Seraphine slipped from the room. I held my breath, but by the time I looked down the corridor, she was gone, and the guard was back to patrolling.

I stood like that for a while, speechless and empty. As if saving the world wasn't enough of a motivation for my actions, but seeing the potential of a future, knowing what this meant to Seraphine – who'd lost so much – made my focus only intensify.

My eyes settled on the closed door opposite my room. Erix would be inside, sleeping, doing the very thing I should. But I knew that would be impossible.

I slipped across the corridor before I changed my mind.

Pushing every other thought from my mind, I scanned the dark room and found the outline of a bed in the distance. No matter how carefully I tried to close the door, the click of the latch still woke him.

"It's only me," I called softly as Erix stirred awake. "Sorry to scare you."

"Robin?" Erix replied through a croaky voice. "What's wrong?"

I stood at the entrance to his room, wondering if I left now, would he fall asleep and forget this.

When I couldn't force out a reply, Erix leaned up on his elbows, fixing those bright eyes on me. "Talk to me, little bird. Let me help you."

The use of my nickname broke me. "I – I can't sleep."

I hadn't tried yet, but I knew that it would've been impossible.

I sounded like a broken child, which wasn't entirely wrong. Erix's pondering silence made me fill the quiet with more words – words I knew I'd regret one day.

"I'm afraid of the dark, more so than ever before," I forced out, before the sob in my throat choked me.

In the wake of speaking with Seraphine, the weight of what I had to do, and why, was suffocating me just like she'd warned.

There was a shuffling as Erix manoeuvred his long body, shifting wings out the way. They'd been draped over him like blankets, covering his almost-naked body. My cheeks warmed at the glimpse of undershorts. Erix looked so vulnerable, matching how I felt inside and out.

"Do you need me to come to your room, little bird?" Erix asked, the question having far too much weight to it. "Or you can stay here… with me."

It felt like a betrayal, doing this, with Duncan all alone in Imeria, guarded like a monster, chained to a bed I once hoped we could share together. Why did I deserve comfort, when he had none? And yet my feet moved, my legs drawing me over to Erix's bedside. I stood by the edge of the bed, exhaling tension-filled breaths until a hand reached for me and pulled me back.

"This is wrong of me," I whispered, thinking about Duncan and how pained he would be to know I was standing in this room. "Tell me to go back to my room."

"As long as you sleep, little bird. That is all I worry about, there is nothing wrong with that."

The bed creaked as Erix made space for me to join him. "I'll keep you safe in the dark. Now, tomorrow and every day going forwards. Just as I promised Duncan I would."

If I had tears left to shed, my cheeks would've been sodden. "There will come a time when I must face it alone, what will I do then without you being there to comfort me?"

I craved his response. Although I'd heard it before, I needed it repeated to me as my motivation to carry on. Selfishly, I needed to hear it. And I was nothing but the king of being selfish.

"You will have Duncan, and that will bring me peace."

It was both what I longed to hear, and wasn't. "Why do you do this, Erix?"

"Because it is my duty. You, Robin Icethorn, are *my* duty." *What about Duncan?* I dared not say the question aloud, not that I needed to. Because Erix sensed it and added a final line to his answer. "And I promised Duncan to look after you. I do this for him, as much as I do it for you."

That was all I needed to hear. It snapped me out of my stupor, enough for me to turn on my heel and leave his room.

Erix didn't call out for me, nor did he chase after me. He let me leave, didn't attempt to stop me closing the door and solidifying the boundary line between us, the one *I* had almost crossed.

CHAPTER 9

Erix was, as he always had been, polite. I woke to the tap of his knuckles against the door before it creaked open, waking me from my light sleep. My initial thought was he was going to mention the previous night, but instead he acted as if it had never happened. He didn't give it the power of meaning something as he greeted me, asking how I slept, to which I'd lied when I said 'well'.

"Zarrel has come to collect us for breakfast, so I thought I would wake you," Erix announced, his too broad posture squeezed between the frame. "But I see you need some time."

"Shit," I mumbled, clearing sleep from my eyes. I'd slept, at most, a few hours and was suffering greatly for it. "Just give me... a minute."

Erix nodded, already backing out the door. "I will wait for you outside and keep him occupied." He looked everywhere but at me for too long. "Shout for me if you need anything."

With that, Erix went as quickly as he came, bowing at me almost too formally, as he swept out of my chamber.

My muscles were stiff as I changed into an outfit one of Lockinge's seamsters made for me, as per Eroan's measurements. I felt bad refusing it when I was informed they'd worked night and day to have it ready for me.

The black shirt was buttonless and clung to the narrow shape of my torso. The collar was pointed on either side of my neckline like the tips of Icethorn's tallest mountains. Gold thread had been woven into patterns across my chest, similar to the design on the decorative cloak that I clasped to my overly-padded shoulders.

It had been a long time since I had dressed in anything so fine. Eroan had given up making me lavish clothes when I stopped leaving Imeria. Or at least given up showing me them. My hope, for my duration here, was that no one noticed that I looked as much as felt like an imposter in fine silks and velvet. My reflection in the grand mirror – for all intents and purposes – was that of a king. Even a modest box waited for me, with a replica of the ice-tiered crown I left back at home.

I heard voices beyond the door to my rooms which made me pick up my pace. Before I left, I made sure the silver circlet across my brow was even, ensured my boots were laced tight and the lower parts of my trousers tucked neatly inside. I'd present as a put-together man, with exhausted eyes and a body affected by weeks of worry. Which meant I'd have to put on a rather convincing show when I faced the people waiting for me.

Erix stood vigil at the door, silently stewing beside Zarrel. Neither man spoke to the other when I interrupted them. The tension was so fragile a feather could've sliced through it. The white-winged Nephilim straightened his posture at my arrival, the gold and white armour made him look wider and taller than he'd appeared last night. But compared to Erix, he looked like a boy playing dress up.

"Good morning, *Your Majesty*," Zarrel said, although the last two words sounded more like a bite. "I trust your bed was comfortable enough for you last night. Because if not, please do let me know, and I can arrange suitable modifications for you."

I swallowed hard. There was no point pretending the bed was fine, we all knew I hadn't slept in it for long.

"It will do just fine," I said, offering him a smile. "I do not plan to stick around for long."

"That would be a shame," Zarrel added with a sly glint to his eyes.

I swallowed my distaste for the man, focusing on the important matter at hand. "Have you come to give me some good news about Rafaela, or express your interest in my sleeping arrangements?"

Zarrel's smile flattened, lips drawing into a straight line. He ignored my initial comment. "Nothing of note regarding Rafaela yet, but the day is still young and much can change."

Erix refused to add comment, his pale lips proof of tension. It took effort not to lose myself in the way Erix looked, with the symbol of my court decorating his metal breastplate, the swash of dark grey cloak split in two places to allow his leather wings to fold into his back.

"I was just explaining to your guard here, that if we'd known you'd prefer to share a room, the accommodation would've been provided as such," Zarrel said, slightly bowing his head. It wasn't a sign of respect, but more a way of showing off the golden hammer – Rafaela's hammer – strapped between his wings. "However, if all is well, may I suggest we get moving,"

Blood leached from my face.

"And as *I* explained," Erix began, fists balled at his sides. "The movements and needs of the Icethorn King are not his concern."

"I slept in my own room, Zarrel," I added, feeling the need to explain myself for no apparent reason.

"You are our guests," Zarrel explained, sweeping his gaze between us. "Your comfort is of the utmost importance to us. It was only that your personal guards informed me that you were seen walking into Erix's room last night. I meant no offence with my questioning."

"Then you should train them better because they *clearly* missed my return only moments later. Which, if I admit, worries me. Anyone could come and go without you knowing, clearly," I said, knowing full well that Seraphine had got into my chambers, and no one had noticed.

Zarrel's posture stiffened enough for me to notice. "Then I will make arrangements for tonight, Your Majesty."

"Thank you," I said, forcing a smirk, aware that if this conversation didn't end soon, Erix may give in to the gryvern side of himself, and pluck the feathers from Zarrel's wings with his sharpened teeth.

Zarrel turned on his heel, sweeping a hand for us to move. "Please, if you are both ready, would you kindly follow me?"

I shot Erix a glance, eyes widening in silent warning. *Don't act out*. Then I followed Zarrel, his long strides making me skip a step to catch up.

"Back to my initial question, Zarrel. Is there a reason as to why no news about Rafaela is ready to be given to me?" I asked

"Yes, in fact there is."

My scowl deepened. "And?"

"*And* Cassial would like to discuss the matter with you himself. But first, a banquet has been put on this morning to welcome the four fey courts under our roof. I will take you there to eat and refuel. Cassial will meet you there shortly after."

"I'd like to speak with him sooner, as a matter of urgency."

Zarrel stopped so suddenly I almost barrelled into the back of him. "Pardon me, King Icethorn, but as you can imagine, Saviour Cassial is very busy arranging the final amendments to the peace treaty's paperwork. The ceremony begins tomorrow, and before that there are necessary meetings to be held, signing of papers and the drafting of a highly important accordance which will – if you have not already worked out – truly bring the fey and human realms together, uniting them once and for all."

The king within me rose to the surface, filling my voice with command. "Then I will speak with Cassial immediately on said plans."

"Unfortunately, Cassial is occupied at this time," Zarrel cut in, short and certainly not sweet. "As mentioned, the moment he is free, you may speak with him on any matter you now feel is important."

I dared not look to Erix, but I sensed his bubbling disdain like a shield at my back.

"I – we – don't have the time to waste."

Zarrel's wings flared, itching to spread and show dominance like he was a pheasant. "Unless you feel your personal matters outweigh the good of two realms, please show some patience. Cassial understands you wish to speak with him, but you will have to wait."

I replied through gritted teeth. "I *wish* to speak with Rafaela, but that is clearly proving to be more difficult. I'm beginning to wonder why."

"Do we ask about the happenings in your court?"

A shiver raced down my spine at his question. "Excuse me?"

Zarrel's smile irked me in the deepest parts of my soul. "Forgive me, but I'm simply asking if we, at any point, have shown interest in what happens inside of Icethorn's borders? Do we question you on your people or where they are, what they are doing?"

"You don't need to explain yourself to him," Erix glowered, more monster than man.

His response clearly amused Zarrel, who let out a belly laugh. "Oh, dear. Perhaps we do need to show more interest in the way the fey courts are run. Clearly, as evidence and history show, you all have barely coped residing beside one another. Betrayals, the unjust murders of monarchs and such. Thank the *Creator* we are here to help right wrongs and fix all the damage caused in our absence. I must say, Robin, I expected more from you. Instead, I'm presented by someone who allows their guards to speak for them."

Ice crackled in the air around my balled hands. Zarrel noticed but didn't care.

"Be careful," I warned. "Very careful."

"Of what, Robin Icethorn?" His eyes tracked me up and down. "You?"

"Yes."

Zarrel swivelled on his heel and made a move to leave. The urge to reach for his hand and stop him was a siren call. "Please, do explain."

I took a deep breath, all hopes of staying demure fading fast. "Is there an issue here, between us, I mean?"

It was an obvious question with an equally obvious answer, but this was the chance for Zarrel to address it. He looked me up and down, amused by something he saw. Erix hung back, listening and waiting, but doing as I had silently commanded.

"Why would there be, Your Majesty?" Zarrel finally replied.

Up until this moment I felt as though I was being scorned like a demanding child every time Zarrel spoke to me. "Listen, I understand we have our differences. No doubt you have opinions of me that you have formed due to my... previous decisions and actions. But the past is the past, and we are currently in a future of peace secured by those very mistakes you may believe I made. I think, for the sake of the next few days, you air your grievances with me, or we leave them in this corridor and forget them."

Zarrel took a moment to let my words sink in. Then, slowly but undoubtedly, he began to let his guard down. "You're right, Robin. I have held on to some dislike regarding the events in Rinholm, and perhaps I have let them cloud my judgement of you." He fixed his bright eyes on me, locking me in place. "I apologise."

"Again, I accept your apology," I replied. "Perhaps we don't make a habit of having to continue offering sentiments. And for that, offer the same. For any wrongdoings you hold me accountable for, I am sorry." I didn't need to say what those were, but we both knew that my involvement in destroying Altar's keys went against the very purpose for which the Nephilim were even alive.

I flexed my hands, calling off the seeping frozen magic I'd not noticed had loosed itself.

"Then it is settled," Zarrel added, sparing us both a final glance. "Please, let us move forwards."

Figuratively, and literally I thought.

I nodded, falling into step. "I've built up an appetite after all that excitement."

"Excellent. The food we have prepared for this morning is truly outstanding. Lots of dishes and recipes inspired by our home of Irobel. Tastes you would not even begin to imagine." Zarrel nodded, agreeing to the silent end to the confrontation.

I did as he asked, only noticing the lack of presence at my back when I reached the end of the corridor. Erix was stood stock still, breathing laboured and eyes wide with fury. The last time I'd seen him like that, he'd proceeded to smash his fists into his half-brother – Tarron Oakstorm's – skull until it was a concave mess.

"Erix," I called back, snapping him out of his trance. "Let's not keep our hosts waiting any more than we already have."

Every step Erix took toward me was careful and calculated. It took him effort to calm himself, but he tried. When he reached my side, his gaze still fixed in Zarrel's direction, I laid a hand on his arm.

"I have got you," I said, hoping to draw him back to me with my voice.

Slowly, his gaze swept to mine. I watched the tension lessen in his face the moment his silver eyes fell on mine. "I don't – like – him."

"The feeling is mutual," I replied, not taking my hand off him as we followed Zarrel. "But can you blame him, after what I did?"

What I'm still doing.

"I always thought the Creator's teachings put forwards forgiveness as one of the highest beliefs."

"It would seem Lockinge is not under the Creator's guidance at this time," I whispered, careful to keep my voice low enough for only Erix to hear. "The Nephilim rule in his place. Or Cassial's ego-boosted position as Saviour, whatever that means."

Yet more questions I had for Rafaela when I finally got an audience with her.

Before, the idea gave me some reprieve from my worry. Knowing people like Rafaela – kind-hearted and just – were looking after the humans would've been a positive thing.

I was beginning to believe otherwise.

CHAPTER 10

My heart was in my throat by the time we were escorted in front of two large double doors. I recognised them from when I was last taken here, iron cuff around my throat, my body under the control of Aldrick.

Beyond the great doors, I heard faint sounds from within. Not the stomping and chaotic calls of hundreds of Hunters, excited to watch as Aldrick turned the mundane into powered beings using fey blood. No. This was the soft chatter of familiar voices – people I'd once traversed the world to see, whom I suddenly dreaded to stand before.

There was no time to prepare myself before Zarrel threw the doors wide and exposed us to the handful of people beyond.

Althea Cedarfall was sitting on the lap of her fiancée and most esteemed guard, Gyah Eldrae. Her poppy-red hair sat piled atop her head, held in place by the rich bronze crown that signified her as the queen and last remaining member of the Cedarfall line. I dared not close my eyes for fear I'd see her family, swinging like pendulums in the wind with nooses around their necks.

Gyah's golden eyes narrowed on me, and she patted Althea's lap, who quickly stood and allowed Gyah to do the same. Both were dressed in the fire-red and amber tones of the autumn court, with gold dusting painted over their eyes and the insignia of the burning tree emblazoned on their persons. Althea had it woven in with ruby beads across her corset, whilst the symbol was stitched above Gyah's heart into the structured jacket she wore.

"I hope I haven't kept you all waiting," I said, forcing out the humour to stifle the awkward interaction. Every eye settled on me, flaying my flesh to the bone.

My only option was to drop all worries and anxieties at the door and play pretend, so I did just that.

I was walking into a room of friends and allies, yes. But with every step, my soul told me I was a sheep entering a den of wolves, moments from being torn apart for answers to my actions these past months.

Zarrel, likely delighting in the obvious tautness, shut the doors behind us, sealing me in to face them all. Thank Altar for Erix, who kept close enough that I sensed his heat behind me.

Slowly, Althea drew her gaze from me to Erix, and back again. If anything, his proximity to me got closer.

"Robin Icethorn, it has been far too long since I last laid eyes on you." Sitting poised in a chair opposite them was Elinor Oakstorm, smile lifting to the heavens as her eyes settled on me. "The anticipation of your arrival has been practically *killing* us."

A nervous laugh slipped out of me as Althea and Gyah scrutinised me from the other side of the room. It was like looking at the closest people in my life turned strangers. Because that was the fact. I'd pushed them away to protect them, and here I was, about to face the repercussions of those actions.

The truth was not always the freeing concept people believed. It could also be damning. My secrets not only kept these people from danger, but also from getting close enough for Duwar to start manipulating them into his offer. After all, they were all fey and that was exactly what Duwar wanted in the first place.

Erix finally stepped back and let me walk headfirst into the viper's nest. It took Althea a moment, but she gathered her skirts and copied me, until we stood in the heart of the great room, smothered by the grandeur of it.

"Hello," I said, awkwardly.

She took me in, eyes sweeping me from head to toe. "You look thin."

"Better than shit," I replied. "I've been getting that a lot."

Gyah watched on, always her most diligent protector. I caught her bowing her head to Erix; clearly the issue didn't extend to him.

A soft, jewelled hand lay upon my upper arm. Through the cloth of my shirt, I felt Althea's firm touch like a comforting embrace. "It *is* good to see you, Robin. I am... glad you came."

"Me too," I lied.

Althea narrowed her eyes on me, sensing it. "I was beginning to think that the most important – second most important – person in my life was going to miss my big day."

It struck like a knife as she referred to me being on such a high pedestal.

"I wouldn't miss it for the world." It took every measure of self-control not to expose my inner demons. Althea always had a way of seeing through my shields, which she no doubt was doing. Distracting her, I took her hand in mine and held it up. "Fuck me, Gyah. What mountain did you carve out to make this ring?"

Althea's genuine smile knocked me sideways. Her happiness, her joy... it was everything my lies were trying to protect.

"It's rather modest actually," Gyah said, stepping in close. She wrapped one arm around Althea's shoulder, and the other around mine. With a tug of iron, she pulled us in close until our foreheads were practically touching. "It is good to see you, Robin. Saves me having to drag you here by the short-and-curlies."

I blinked back sudden tears.

"Does your favourite crone get a hug too?" Elinor Oakstorm practically floated over, her azure and buttercup dress clinging to her frame like silken liquid.

Althea and Gyah practically pushed me into Elinor's arms. In truth, I would've rather ignored the offer. Feeling her arms around me was shattering to the little control I had. Elinor was like a mother to me – even in the short time we'd known each other, she had made a mother-shaped impression on my soul. Her story – all her trauma and pain – was so intrinsically linked with my life, I felt somewhat connected to her.

"I have missed you," she whispered into my ear. "Coming here was the best choice you could have made."

"Right back to you," I replied, trying for sarcasm to shield the raw emotions I felt.

"Erix," Elinor called, greeting him next with the same open arms. "I'm glad to see you too. I must ask, since I've got you, have you been having any thoughts about my recent summons?"

Erix stiffened as I laid my eyes on him. "No, Your Grace. I haven't."

Whatever her *summons* entailed clearly made Erix feel a sense of discomfort. One look at him and he practically winced with the emotion. He'd not mentioned receiving word from Elinor Oakstorm, but then again, I wasn't privy to his personal movements.

"Elinor will do." She drank him in, searching every corner of my guard for secrets hidden. "And since you are here, perhaps you can stop hiding from me and we can actually have that talk."

"Are you trying to poach my Lord of Berrow?" I asked Elinor.

She shook her head, eyes closed as she smiled from ear to ear. "Even if I wanted to, Robin, I do not think Erix could possibly be taken from you. Not even dragged by a queen."

"Watch out, Robin," Gyah said. "Once Elinor gets an idea in her head, she is rather persistent."

I waited for Erix to tell me Gyah was wrong. He didn't.

Elinor hooked her arm in mine, giving me a big squeeze.

Her power oozed from her in waves, brushing over my skin, searching for illnesses and ailments to heal. She couldn't help herself, and I admitted the feeling was comforting.

"Court politics," Elinor said. "Boring matters which I was hoping Erix could help with. But alas, let us not bore each other with minor details when we have a fabulous few days ahead of us."

I was glad of the distraction, although I filed away the unspoken topic for a later time.

"How *are* you getting on, back in Oakstorm that is?" I asked, aware the last time I'd seen her, Elinor was struggling with control over her late husband's council. His poison had sunk so deep into the summer court's soil, it would take a burning ray to cleanse the ground.

Luckily, there was no one more perfect for the job than Elinor Oakstorm.

"I have leashed the men who refused to bow," Elinor said, so plainly anyone else would've taken her words for a joke. I knew she was being serious. "And those with a lick of sense, and who've come to heel upon their own decisions, are currently enjoying the fruits of what I can offer…"

"*But*," I added, eyebrow lifting.

"But there is one who continues to petition against me. Doran's brother, spineless little worm that he is. He's gone from petitioning against my rule, to planting seeds that without a direct heir to the Oakstorm line left, he wishes to be named as such so *his* line takes over when I am… indisposed. Which I am sure he is just desperate to happen."

I glanced back to Erix who was doing everything in his power not to look away from his clasped hands. "And you think Erix can help with that?" I asked.

"I'm hoping so. He is Doran's child, after all. But that all depends if he is willing."

"I never thought about it like that," I mumbled, although it made so much sense now it had been said aloud.

Althea leaned in to me, finally saying what was clearly bothering her. "Perhaps you would've known the news, but for that you'd actually have had to accept our invites at the last conclave."

Gyah nudged Althea, whose green-amber eyes were fixed to me. "Or any of our invites."

"I've been… occupied," I said, trying to sound as confident as I could.

"You say it like you're being held hostage. Robin, we have all been occupied." Althea never minced her words, and I loved her for it. "The four courts have never been closer. And with everything lost, all the prices paid" – regardless of her head held high, there was a cloud of grief behind Althea's eyes – "we deserve to enjoy what we have all worked to achieve."

"Which is exactly why I'm here," I said, needing a distraction. As if the universe knew it, a member of the castle's serving staff entered the room carrying a tray of sparkling wine. "May I propose a toast," I suggested. "To the happy couple."

"A fantastic idea," Elinor said, arms sweeping outwards as if she could embrace the entire world. "Nothing goes with buttery scrambled eggs like sparkling wine."

Althea and Gyah made a move to take a glass. Erix took the moment to step in close, lay a hand on my lower back and whisper into my ear. "Are you all right?"

I swallowed hard, a headache brewing behind my eyes. "Coping. Are you though? I didn't realise Elinor was in correspondence with you."

"You have had enough going on, I didn't want to burden you with more problems."

"So, there *is* a problem?" I pushed on.

Erix patted my shoulder, dismissing my question. "How about we talk about that later? For now, if you need an excuse to leave, you just ask–"

"Erix, do you make a habit of drinking whilst on duty?" Althea called over, a spare glass of wine in her hand, offered up to him. "Or will Duncan be joining us this morning?"

Duncan. Just hearing his name made my knees weak.

I'd planned for this very question, so the excuse came out of me with ease. After all, I had so much practice lying. "Duncan was unable to make it. Erix has joined me instead. Duncan felt it was better one of us stayed behind, to keep order in the court over the next few days. Jesibel is still taking time to get over what happened, and Duncan suggested a familiar face was better suited to staying and keeping an eye on her."

As I knew it would, the conversation shifted quickly from missing Duncan to Jesibel.

"That is a shame," Althea said, voice monotone, proving she wasn't buying my excuse. "How is Jesibel?"

I shrugged, discomfort itching at my skin. "She still hasn't uttered a word since we saved her, and if I am honest, I don't think she will again."

"Time is the only thing that can heal her," Elinor added, because she'd previously tended to Jesibel and had little luck. She could fix scars and marks on a person's physical state, but those that wounded a person's psyche were far out of reach, even for a blessed healer like Elinor.

"Good news is we have hope that both Duncan and Jesibel will be attending the ceremony alongside the Icethorn people, making sure they behave themselves no doubt," Erix added, saving me from my reasoning.

It seemed he too was well-practiced with a lie.

"Duncan certainly is taking his new status seriously," Althea added, side-eyeing Gyah. "We are surprised you both haven't seized the day and planned your own wedding yet. Although, you cannot rush perfection, can you? It is not every day you have an angel arrange the festivities."

The concept of a marriage wasn't as pleasing as I think they expected it to be for me.

Gyah planted a kiss on Althea's cheek, leaving the skin crimson beneath. "And I told you, I would have been happy with a *smaller* affair."

"As long as you are waiting down the end of the aisle, I don't care if it's big or small," Althea said, screwing her nose up before turning her attention back to Erix. "At least you made it, Robin, I'm glad for that. And you, Erix. It's been a while since I've been graced with either of your presences, and I've missed it."

"I would not forgive myself if I missed it," Erix replied with a wink.

"You could at least try and convince me better than that," Althea said, handing him the glass. "Well, it's no bother. It seems almost half of both realms will be witness to the wedding. Cassial wanted the humans to see how close our relations can be. And with the betrothing of the Elmdew heir and human princess in another eighteen years, it will be like our peoples were never separated."

"I still think that bit is odd," Elinor mentioned, chewing on a thought like a sour grape. "Both children are not even a year old. To think their lives are put out for them before they can walk is a strange concept. I am sure we can secure peace without signing away the lives of two children."

"Let us worry about that when the time comes to it," Althea added, raising her glass. "What matters is we are embarking on an era of peace."

"Unless either party breaks it," Gyah reminded. "Then we forfeit our lands, as per the covenant in the agreement."

"It's semantics," Elinor said. "The wording simply ensures that neither of us move on one another. The humans and the fey must have clear boundaries. And I have already told you, I have worked closely with Cassial on the wording of the clause. I can assure you, it's fail-safe."

"Enough talk of politics, please," Althea said with a twisted look of disgust. "It will put me off my eggs. Robin, since you suggested the toast, you do the honours."

I reached for the tray, offering the server a smile as thanks. Laying eyes on their face caught me by surprise, so much that it took effort to steel my reaction from the crowd.

Seraphine was here.

No one else had noticed. Like I had when I first saw her, no one expected the face of the dead to ever show up again, so they weren't looking for her. Especially not in a place like this.

Once an Asp, always an Asp.

I reached for the glass, but Seraphine picked it up and handed it to me, slipping something else into my hand with it.

"Thank you," I muttered.

"You're welcome," Seraphine replied in a forced accent. She really enjoyed playing this part.

I felt the rough brush of parchment paper. A quick glance and I figured what it could be.

A note. A message. An *answer.*

"About that toast," Althea encouraged as she pressed so close to Gyah they were practically stitched together. "The floor is yours, Robin."

I lifted my glass, hyper aware of everyone watching me, listening. "To the new world. May it forever flourish."

"To the new world," Althea echoed.

Everyone but Erix echoed the sentiment.

Gyah cocked her drink back and downed it. Althea followed suit. Elinor drank slower, small delicate sips. I was glad for mine, because it gave me a chance to manoeuvre my hand and unravel the note.

Rafaela is being held in the Below.

Rafaela. The Below. Finally, I got my answers to both my queries. Where Rafaela was, and what Cassial was using the prison beneath this very room for. Neither revelation made me feel relief – in fact, my body reacted as though lightning carved through me.

By the time I looked up, Seraphine was gone. Her job complete, just as she promised. How she found out Rafaela's location was beyond me, another mystery of how the Asps worked. But what I cared about now was why would Rafaela be inside the dungeons where the fey had once been kept as prisoners.

"If you're not going to finish that," Gyah said, pointing to my full glass. "I wouldn't mind it. Pre-wedding nerves and all."

I handed it over, screwing the note up before she noticed. "You, Gyah Eldrae, nervous?"

"I'm a changed woman," Gyah said, taking the glass and downing that as quickly as the first one. "Put a sword in my hand and an army at my back, and I thrive. But a wedding, that's an entirely different battle."

I tried to offer her a genuine smile, but my mind was whirling – a vortex of unease.

"Have any of you spoken with Rafaela during communications with Lockinge?" I found myself asking, unable to take my mind off the message and what it could mean.

From the silence and shifting eyes, I knew the answer.

"Should we have?" Althea asked.

I wanted to scream the truth of my concerns but held my tongue. Keeping calm, I added more kindling to the fire, hoping to inspire a spark in each of them. "It's just I have tried to contact her, multiple times, and haven't had any luck." I looked Althea dead in her eyes, hoping she could understand my simmering worry. "I've been concerned about her. We all knew she was to be punished for her involvement in the destruction of the keys. But we never knew what that would entail."

"I know that look," Althea said, clicking onto the thread I was weaving. "What are you suggesting, Robin?"

I felt sick just admitting it, but the note in my hand was practically burning against my palm. I could lie about Duncan, but *not* about Rafaela. There wasn't the need to tell them what I needed Rafaela for, only that she was a friend, and I was worried. "I think–"

The doors opened without warning, revealing a familiar imposing man with ivory-white wings thrice the width of him. The rays of daylight bounced across his blue-black hair, down the impressive set of armour shaped to his body.

"Do not concern yourselves with the whereabouts of sister Rafaela," Cassial said, voice full of unbridled command. "She is well cared for in the hands of the Creator, and there is no better place for her to be."

CHAPTER 11

Cassial entered the room, dripping in glory and power. His shield – the namesake of his position in the Nephilim, was held aloft in one hand. *Creator's Shield, protector of His word.* I could hear Cassial say it, just as he had on the ship from Lockinge to Icethorn all those months ago.

He wore an armour set of pure gold and white – not a speck of damage to suggest he'd ever seen battle wearing it.

It was Rafaela who gave everything, not him. And she was now in the prison beneath my feet. Yet I couldn't admit I knew that with Cassial here.

Volcanic fury rose in me, fierce and frenzied until I was trembling on the spot. Before I released it, spilling into the room in an undulating wave, Erix slipped his hand into mine and squeezed.

Everything unravelled beneath his touch.

Cassial's midnight hair was swept off his face, shiny and slicked back with a thick salve. Everything about him was neat and tidy. Even his thick, dark beard was brushed and full, the edges sharp from recent shaving. Cassial's ivory-white wings shivered, some downy feathers falling to the floor beneath him like snow.

"Robin Icethorn," Cassial announced, the brightest grin plastered across his handsome face.

I stiffened beneath his inquisitive gaze. Unlike Erix's silver eyes, Cassial's were closer to white, giving his gaze an almost endless and all-seeing expression.

"Cassial," I said in greeting, although my posture was anything but welcoming. I found my fists balled, my back straighter than it had ever been before. As if sensing my discomfort, Erix squeezed my hand until I felt his heartbeat in his palm, his leathery wings shadowing the room behind us.

"A little birdy has told me you have been *dying* to speak with me." Cassial's white-toothed smile came across as genuine, but it was no different to a dog licking your hand before biting it. "I am so glad you made it. I was beginning to think I would have to make the journey to see you myself."

"No need for that," I replied. "Although am I to read between the lines of what you are saying about Rafaela? Because if I am, it sounds like she is no longer with us, in this realm."

She is well cared for in the hands of the Creator, and there is no better place for her to be.

It sounded an awful lot like she was dead to me. Even though the note in my pocket suggested otherwise.

"Rafaela is certainly still within *this* realm," Cassial explained, laughing to the watching crowd. When no one returned it, he faltered, snapping his bright stare back on me. I was rooted to the spot.

"Where?" Was all I could manage.

"Not in Durmain," Cassial said, "which I am sure is not the news you have been hoping for, considering your persistent requests for an audience with her."

Not even a minute into his presence, and already Cassial was lying.

"So, Rafaela will not be attending the wedding?" Althea asked, voice sweet but even I could sense the distrust in her tone. "That's a shame. I rather liked Rafaela."

"I'm afraid not, Queen Cedarfall." Cassial bowed his head to show respect, but not enough that his eyes ever left her. "Rafaela has returned *home*. The Isles of Irobel are the best place for her to reconnect with her faith and prove herself worthy in the Creator's eyes once again. With many of the Nephilim here, we required someone of merit to care for our lands until the day these realms are secure, and we can leave them to return home too."

"Liar," I mumbled under my breath. If he heard it, Cassial showed no reaction.

In that moment I longed to tell everyone the truth. Rafaela wasn't in Irobel, in fact she was beneath the very room we stood in. But I bit down on my tongue until I tasted blood, refusing to speak a word.

Yet.

If he was lying, it was for a reason. I knew that all too well.

"Is she not already worthy? After all, she did play a hand in saving the world from ruin," Gyah said, hand never straying from Althea's back. "Or am I missing something?"

My breath hitched in my throat, catching so suddenly I almost choked. I suddenly wanted that glass of sparkling wine. "Gyah makes a good point," I added.

Cassial took his time to drink us all in, his height far taller than anyone who stood before him, to the point he had to look down his sharp nose.

"Rafaela's sole purpose in life was to *protect* Altar's keys and ensure they never were used to open Duwar's gate. Instead, she turned her back on our task and had plans of her own – plans that, I am sure no one here needs reminding, backfired rather grandly." Cassial settled his eyes back on me. I felt every inch of skin flay wide where his gaze touched. "On that matter, how is Duncan Rackley fairing, Robin? Zarrel informed me that he won't be joining us in Lockinge, or for the wedding."

I faked confidence, pushing down every ounce of panic to the pit of my stomach, replacing it with my well-practiced demure nature. "He's doing well."

"I'm very pleased to hear it. It is not every day you face a demon-god and survive." He laughed for a second time, and still no one reciprocated it.

Zarrel shifted where he stood just shy of Cassial's back, carrying Rafaela's hammer as if it belonged to him. If I got close enough to touch it, the truth would come spilling out. Everyone in this room would know my secrets, and the threat I continued to harbour – the threat to the peace everyone longed to enjoy.

"Now," Cassial said, clapping his large hands together. "There is much to do in the next day. Althea, Gyah – plans have been agreed that tonight we will hold a feast and ball to celebrate your union. It will be before this ball that the treaty between the fey and human heirs will be signed and bound. Then, once those minor formalities are completed, we will arrange a convoy of travel for you all to be taken back across Durmain toward the location the wedding will be held. This procession, if you will, gives those who cannot make the wedding a chance to share in the excitement of it. I hope you do not mind, but I have personally seen to all these plans myself, saving you the worry and hassle."

Althea's genuine grin told me she was, in fact, pleased for his help, unaware that I could shatter her trust in him in a matter of seconds.

"You have already been *so* helpful, Cassial," Althea said graciously. "All this assistance, I do hope you find time to enjoy yourself in the days to come."

"Believe me, as soon as the legalities are finalised tonight, I will 'let my hair down' during yours and Lady Eldrae's big day."

"*Gyah*," Gyah corrected, wincing at the use of her new title. "I may be marrying into royalty, but I would prefer my name to be used over my title."

Cassial tipped his head in agreement. "Of course, Gyah. Forgive me for my transgressions, where I am from, royalty is but a concept. I trust that everything else is to your liking. Now, I regret that I do have a few matters to attend to for the rest of the morning. If you need anything, Zarrel will be close enough for you to call upon him."

"Elmdew is it?" Elinor added, looking into her glass as she swivelled the liquid around. "Is that what is keeping you busy?"

He paused, a brow raised above his confused glare. "No, why do you ask?"

Elinor gestured around her, pointing out something I'd yet to notice. "Well, to start, I was expecting to see the representatives for young prince Jordin Elmdew. As of yet, no one has shown their face."

Cassial relaxed his shoulders so suddenly, I hadn't noticed they were tense in the first place. "Ah, yes. Jordin's representative has been occupied, from my understanding. I'm sure she would have preferred to share wine with you over breakfast, but as you can imagine, the care of a young child is of most importance."

Elinor rocked back as if struck, and I was the only one to notice it before she steeled her expression, painting it with a smile. "Yes, I do know that well."

"If that would be all," Cassial said, gesturing for Zarrel to step forwards. "I will see you all shortly."

The idea of Zarrel watching over us was not a pleasant thought. As if he sensed my discomfort, he settled his eyes on me, sinking his attention through every layer of my skin until my bones itched.

"Before you leave," Zarrel added, bringing Cassial to a quick stop. "Robin Icethorn has been persistent in his need to speak with you."

"There will be no need," I replied, considering I had the answers to my question in my pocket. "If Rafaela is not in Lockinge, my request is no longer required."

"If you wish to speak on the matter further, you are welcome to join me."

For the third time, Erix squeezed my hand, keeping me in place.

"With all this food, and being reunited with old friends, I would rather like to stay back for a while," I said, to Erix's relief.

Cassial looked to me for a few beats, then swept his gaze over the room. "If your desires change, please speak with Zarrel again and he can arrange the summons. My door is always open to you, Robin Icethorn."

With that, he left. Zarrel may have followed, but as the doors closed, I knew he would be standing guard outside. Which was a problem, because I had somewhere else I needed to be.

"Erix," I said, turning my back to my friends, hand flexing at my side the second he released it. "Cassial is lying. Rafaela is still here, in Lockinge."

His eyes widened a fraction. Unlike many others might have done, Erix didn't tell me I was wrong. "Tell me what you need me to do, and I will help."

Althea walked up behind us, stopping the conversation. "Cassial has been so attentive."

I snapped around to her, just in time to see the spark of distrust as she narrowed her amber-hued eyes on me.

Althea rested a hand on her hip and leaned into it. "Oh, come on, Robin. Do you think a fancy breakfast, talk of precessions and the promise of a ball, was enough to blind my sense of judgement?" Althea said. "Go on, you two, spit it out. What are you whispering about?"

I held my tongue, wondering if giving Althea a half-lie would suffice, or if it would lead to more questions. Concealing the truth with my genuine concern for Rafaela was iron-clad, so I decided to not keep this from her. At least it would lighten the load of lies, making it easier to sift through them.

"Cassial lied to us about Rafaela's whereabouts," I said with a low voice, aware that anyone could be listening. Of course, Gyah and Eleanor heard – Gyah being the only one who didn't seem entirely surprised.

"Bold accusation," Althea said.

"Bold, yes. But she isn't in Irobel."

"And you are sure?" Althea asked. "Or is this just a hunch? You have never been very good at trusting people."

"I trusted you," I said, hurt by the very true accusation.

"Because I'm special." Althea clearly didn't believe me from the nudge of her shoulder into mine, as if we were two friends joking around.

"Robin *is* sure about this," Erix added for me. "Listen to him."

Althea drew her eyes to Erix, reading into his protective stance and close proximity. She didn't need to say it aloud, but I could see in her expression alone that she was wondering what was happening between us.

In truth, I was wondering the very same thing. My hand still throbbed with the way he held it, but that feeling wasn't entirely uncomfortable.

"Do you remember Aldrick's encampment beneath the castle?" I asked.

Althea winced. "How could I ever forget."

"Well." I was breathless, and yet I hadn't moved a muscle. "Rafaela is currently occupying the Below as we speak. Altar knows for how long she's been down there."

Althea stepped in close, her entire demeanour hardening. "And you are confident of this?"

I nodded. I may have let them into this secret, but I wasn't about to break my promise to Seraphine. "I am *very* confident."

I held my breath, waiting for the inevitable question. *How do you know?* They didn't ask.

"I really did *not* want to have to go back there," Althea said, but I could see she would if required.

"Nor do you need to either," I replied. "I'll go. I'm familiar with the Below. It would be easier for one of us to slip in and out, than a group."

And from one glance to Elinor, the horror on her face, I'd never want her stepping foot near that place again.

"I won't agree to this." Erix's deep voice rumbled across my skin. "Robin, think."

"I am, Erix" I snapped, fixing desperate eyes on him. "In fact, it is all I can do right now. Think and think until I feel like my skull is going to shatter apart. I'm sick to death of thinking, it's time I do something."

His lips parted, but another refusal didn't come out. Erix bowed his head, took a step back and retreated.

"What I don't understand, is why Cassial would lie," Althea said. "He has been incredible thus far. I just don't see why he would need to pretend Rafaela is in Irobel."

"Only one way to find out," I replied, practically buzzing with the need to go immediately and find out our answers.

"Sounds like another prison break," Gyah added with a smile. "It's certainly one way to spice up the pre-wedding nerves."

"As I said, I'm going alone. But there is something you can help with."

Elinor had kept silent, gaze lost to a spot on the floor as her own thoughts consumed her. I worried Cassial's comments about babies had stayed with her, taunting Elinor for all she'd lost.

"Go on," Althea encouraged, hand reaching to her belt on instinct. Usually she kept a blade there, but now it was only a beaded belt.

"I need a *little* distraction," I said. "Something that will keep Zarrel busy whilst I slip in and out."

"I don't like this," Elinor finally spoke up. When she looked up at me, it was not with fear in her eyes, but something else. "Robin, I don't want you to ever go back there."

Elinor had spent years in the dark belly of Lockinge Castle. What she'd experienced during her imprisonment had left scars so deep that no time could heal them.

"I'll be fine, Elinor," I said, offering her a smile I hoped she believed. "I promise."

"Then listen to Erix, and let him go with you. Please," Elinor practically begged.

"If we are both seen missing, it will lead to questions no king should need to answer. I have to do this alone. Not only to keep the Nephilim from getting suspicious but because... if anything happened to her, whatever this punishment has been, it was my doing."

"Hold on," Gyah added. "I'm not one to care about paperwork and treaties, but would this jeopardise what has been agreed, let alone the relationship we have cultivated with the humans?"

"Nothing has been signed yet," I said. "Anyway, this is Nephilim affairs, and has nothing to do with the humans. What problem is it going to cause if Rafaela is in Irobel... right?"

Cassial couldn't punish us for being caught out in a lie, not when he needed us to put ink to paper and sign the treaty he'd worked tirelessly to draft.

"And if he has lied about Rafaela and you find her, what then?" Erix asked the question that was likely on everyone's lips.

"That will be a discussion we can all have with Cassial, but first I need to see what is happening in the Below."

Althea's nervous mask lifted back into a light smile. "If anyone can get away with it, it would be Robin."

I didn't know if that was supposed to fill me with confidence or dread.

"Now, about that distraction," I added. "I need something to keep Zarrel occupied enough that he won't follow me."

"All right," Althea replied, fingers scratching her narrow chin. I felt her eyes search every inch of me, trying to discover what I was hiding from her. "Any suggestions?"

I hadn't thought that far ahead. After finding out where Rafaela was being kept, there hadn't exactly been a lot of time to think.

I was glad when Gyah spoke up. "Erix, want to test out which one of us is more durable, Gryvern or Eldrae?"

"You have *got* to be kidding me," Althea said, rolling her eyes at the suggestion. "Sparring just before our wedding? It's a recipe for disaster."

"As is breaking Rafaela out of prison," Gyah reminded her. "But alas, Robin is fixated on the idea. Don't worry, my love," Gyah wrapped a hand around Althea's shoulder, planting a kiss upon her cheek. "I intend to beat our favourite *berserker* and come out without a single bruise."

"Is that so?" Erix said, cocking his head from side to side, elongated fingers flexing to claws at his side. "Do Eldrae not bruise? Now I think that is a theory I would like to test."

Gyah chuckled. "I suppose we will find out."

Althea's eyes gestured toward the dais at the back of the room. There was a door there, the one I'd been brought through during my last visit, and the same I'd escaped through with Duncan, Kayne, Elinor and Seraphine when Doran and his Gryvern attacked the castle.

Althea wrapped fingers around my forearm, stopping me in my tracks. "Please try to stay out of trouble, Robin."

"Depends if trouble finds me," I replied.

She released me, although not with hesitation. "Make sure Rafaela is okay. If she is, best to leave her where she is, until a proper plan can be formed."

"And if she is not?" I asked, dread squeezing my lungs at the possibility.

"Save her," Althea glowered, then turned away.

If Seraphine was right, and I found Rafaela, I had no intention of leaving her. Treaty or wedding, Rafaela's life was more important in the grand scheme of things.

I gritted my teeth, body buzzing with unspent energy. Everything was leading up to this, and I could almost not wait.

"Hey," I called over to Erix and Gyah. "Go easy, okay?"

"I shall, little bird," Erix replied.

"I wasn't talking to you," I added, eyes flickering to Gyah whose skin was melting into shadows as her shift began.

"Thanks for the vote of confidence," Erix added with a wink just before his wings flared and the serpentine, obsidian-scaled wyvern uncoiled where Gyah's fey form had stood.

Seeing her, for a brief moment, took me by surprise. Perhaps it was my previous trauma, but she looked more like the Draeic than I'd ever noticed before. Just smaller, more compact – but equally as deadly as she settled golden eyes on her opponent.

If anything, this distraction was less about being seen leaving, and more about making sure I wasn't followed.

When the air ruptured with the roar of two monsters, and bodies clashed, I took my chance and ran.

CHAPTER 12

There was one way in and out of the Below, and that was through its only door. I'd visited the prison beneath Lockinge Castle twice before and had vowed to never return. Once was as a prisoner, and the last time was to free those fey held captive – fey the world outside the Below had forgotten existed. Never did I expect that I'd have to step foot in it again. But I trusted Seraphine implicitly. If she believed Rafaela was being kept here, then she was.

I didn't know what I was thinking as I made my way through familiar connecting corridors and grand, linking foyers. If Rafaela was being kept beneath the castle, it would be for a reason. I hardly imagined she'd be without guards. So, when I came into sight of the Below's entrance, I expected to find Nephilim standing vigil.

The entrance was unguarded.

In fact, it was left slightly ajar, as if the universe knew I was coming. Perhaps this was Seraphine's doing? She'd know I was impulsive and would go to the Below the moment I could. Had there been Nephilim here that she'd dealt with? Surely that was the case.

Checking the coast was clear behind me, I opened the nondescript wooden door and slipped inside. The walkway beyond was set on a decline and completely shrouded in shadow. I used my hands, trialling them against the rough stone walls, making sure I didn't walk face first into them.

I continued until a speck of light glowed far ahead of me, signalling the end of the dark corridor. It would soon open up to a cavernous hole, with narrow steps carved into the face of the rocky cave that was the prison.

My body buzzed with the need to reach Rafaela, my mind whispering terrible outcomes, taunting me.

My heavy breathing echoed around me, playing back to me as if I was groaning in resistance. But I wasn't. In fact, I was making as little sound as possible. I held my breath, and the sound continued. I supposed this place, these very stone walls, held the memories of those who suffered here. Or maybe it was simply my mind, tricking me into remembering the atrocities Aldrick used the Below for.

I stepped into the light, ready to get my first view down upon the pit, when I smelled blood.

Fresh blood. One inhalation and the copper taste clung to the back of my throat. Clapping a hand over my mouth, I stepped onto the podium at the top of the stone steps and peered down into the Below.

What I saw almost brought me to my knees.

The groaning that I'd thought was my own doing didn't belong to me. It came from another person, the very one I'd been trying to contact for weeks.

Rafaela.

But *she* wasn't alone.

"Rafaela," I bellowed, panic flaring inside of me alongside magic.

My shout stopped whatever the second person was doing to her. I saw white wings, dark hair and muscle, but as the second person turned up to look at what caused the ruckus, I finally figured out who was with her.

Cassial – all wing splendour and golden armour – spun to look up at me with eyes full of wild fury. In his hand he held a bloodied saw, the vicious metal teeth coated in downy feathers, blood and… flesh. *Her* flesh.

Rafaela knelt on the floor before him, both wrists bound by chain and attached to a bolt in the wall ahead of her. Even from a distance, I worked out what was happening.

Her back, naked and exposed, was no longer shielded by her dove-grey wings. Protruding from both shoulder blades were mutilated stumps of sinew and bone, dripping fresh gore down her skin until it puddled beneath her. Rafaela's head hung low, her body quaking.

Cassial was severing her wings, but from the old scars beneath blood-soaked skin, I knew this wasn't the first time.

I didn't have time to think. There wasn't room for thoughts amongst the roaring maelstrom in my mind.

Only action.

Magic exploded inside of my veins like a dying star, bright, brilliant and desperate.

I had to stop Cassial from continuing this horror. *Now*. There was no time to waste.

There were so many stairs for me to run down to reach her. Instead, my power loosed from its cage. Not as powerful as it had been when fuelled by one of Altar's keys. But I still had enough.

For Rafaela, it would have to do.

I vaulted over the podium's wall, my body dropping through the air like a stone in freefall. Fingers flexing, power seeping outwards, the moisture-heavy air solidified beneath me. A sheet of ice spread like a frozen wave, catching my boots until I slipped down it. My stomach muscles tensed, my thighs burned, but I held myself steady as I shot through the air, guided by the ice floor I continued to conjure from the thick air.

I came to a rolling stop on the ground floor, mere inches from where Cassial stood. His large, imposing body blocked my view of Rafaela, but I'd seen enough. The damage was forever imprinted in my mind.

The blood, the saw, the scars new and old.

Gone were the reasons I came to Lockinge. All I cared about was stopping Cassial from hurting Rafaela. Fuck the wedding and his treaty – all of it.

"This is not the place for your meddling, Robin Icethorn," Cassial sneered, voice booming around the stone pit. He held the bloodied saw before him – something that should only be used for cutting dried wood, not flesh and bone – like a shield.

Or perhaps a weapon.

However, with the magic flooding through me, I hardly felt threatened by it. Which was a shame for him. Because if he had his shield with him, perhaps he had a chance against me.

"The last man… to hold a weapon over me… didn't live for long." I could barely get my words out, as if my body decided words mattered little in a moment like this. In the dark and furious parts of my brain, I saw the Hunter who held an axe above my neck, prepared to bring it down and sever my head from my shoulders.

"It would not be wise to threaten me." Cassial's eyes widened. "In my own city, after we have graciously accepted you as our guest of honour."

Spit and bile brewed in my mouth. I gathered it into a ball and spat it on the dusted floor before Cassial's blood-splattered boots.

"*Your* city?" I seethed. "It seems like this concept of being the Saviour has gone to your head."

Cassial's wings flared wide, the span of them so impressive I was coated in shadow. He flapped them, growling as he prepared to get skyward, the saw dripping Rafaela's blood onto the ground between us.

I wasn't going to let him get away with this.

Before Cassial's feet left the ground, they crystalised in mounds of ice, diamond-hard. He growled a song of frustration, wings pounding harder, forcing blood-tainted winds over me. I held firm, squinting against the force. My magic took those winds and wrapped them around us both. Like unseen fingers, I forced my power of storm and snow into Cassial's throat, until I was aware of every ounce of air in his lungs, his body, his fucking blood–

"You lied," I spat.

Weeks of pent-up emotion was on the brink of exploding out on him. Frost split the air, spreading across the natural sweat across his wings until I turned even his own bodily fluids against him. Ice crept over each feather, making them heavier, until he could no longer move them.

Cassial's eyes bulged, his fear singing straight to my twisted soul. As much as I could've killed him, there was a part of me that knew it would have led to more trouble. So I withdrew enough magic for him to reply, needing his answers. Depending on what came out of his mouth, he would live past the next few minutes or die at my hand.

"This is none... of your business," Cassial gasped, ice cracking over his jaw. "The matters we deal with are between the Nephilim and the Nephilim alone."

I expected Cassial to submit to me, but he didn't. Even with his body heavy with ice, his wings powerless and legs immobile, he never stopped fighting.

"If anyone is the Saviour, it is her," I shouted, pointing toward the all-too-still body of Rafaela. "And yet you *mutilate* her for what reasons?"

"Rafaela belongs to us." Cassial smashed one leg free of my icy bindings. "She is ours to do with as we wish. Her crimes–"

"*Fuck* her crimes." Every ounce of emotion rushed out of me, no longer controlled. "It means nothing, all of it means nothing."

Something snapped in Cassial, as though he read through my reaction and paused. I felt his resistance fade away so quickly, I almost sagged against the sudden draining of my energy. I was no longer a bottomless well of power – I was moments from reaching the end.

Something warm trickled out of my nose. If my hands weren't focused on controlling the ice and wind, I would've found blood slipping over my lips.

Cassial noticed and smiled. "Are you sure, Robin Icethorn? Because of Rafaela's actions, look at you. No longer the powerful King of the Icethorn Court. You have limits, a bottom to a once endless well of power. All because she coerced you into destroying Altar's keys." His gaze tracked over me, from my bloody nose to the slight quiver of my legs. "How long are you going to keep this little party trick up? Until it kills you, or until your meddling in Nephilim affairs ruins any hope for peace between us?"

As if I could ever contemplate peace with you.

I released the reins of my power, reserving the last scraps of it, just in case the moment required it. Cassial kicked free of the ice at his feet and shins, shaking his wings so the capsules of ice on each feather cracked and fell like sleet around him.

He raised the serrated saw, lips drawn back in a snarl, gaze completely lost to his need for vengeance. "I should have known you would come looking for her. As if those little letters you relentlessly sent were not proof of your guilt-born obsession with Rafaela. It would have been wiser for you to take my word that she was in Irobel and leave it at that. But no—"

"I will not turn a blind eye to your mistreatment of Rafaela. Not now, not tomorrow or the days that follow. If you raise a feather against her, do so knowing you will face my wrath."

Cassial stopped, the saw paused inches from my face. I refused to flinch, I wouldn't give him the satisfaction.

"It is too late for such *idle* threats," he seethed.

"Threats aren't something I toy with, Cassial," I said. "Only promises."

He laughed at me, blood splattering over his pristine outfit, reminding me of the almost-too-silent woman chained just behind him. "The treaty is all but signed. The wedding is proceeding." His pale gaze narrowed on me. "You will not ruin any of this, the damage you've caused is enough."

I lifted a steady finger, dropped it on the tip of the saw and guided it out of my face.

"Harm me, and you can say goodbye to the treaty you've worked so hard to finalise. Althea, Elinor, Gyah – everyone back in the hall knows where I am." It was my turn to smile, knowing that I'd gotten Cassial into a corner.

I stepped in closer to the saw, testing him. Cassial knew, just as I had worked out in the wanting glint in his eyes, that if he harmed me, it would start a war. We had found ourselves at a stand-off neither one of us wanted.

"What will it be then, Robin? Will we take the path that threatens the peace we have cultivated in the months since Rafaela's betrayal?" Cassial straightened. "Or the one which leads to contentions neither party will survive?"

"You keep talking about this treaty as if I would ever sign it knowing what you are capable of," I said, reminding him of the fact. "Not to mention Althea. Do you really think she will go ahead with a wedding if she knows what you have done with Rafaela? She will burn this fucking castle down. Cassial, Durmain would burn."

"And threaten the relations between our kinds?" Cassial slowly lowered the saw. "Althea is a woman of measure and thought. There is no future in which she would act against the Nephilim over *one* person. Not like you, however. How selfish you truly are, Robin Icethorn."

"If helping my friend is selfish, then I wear that crown with pride."

Cassial's eyes narrowed on me, the disdain in them palpable. "You know *exactly* what I mean. You dare intervene in the Creator's will, over and over. First destroying the keys, and now you wish to put a thorn in our own beliefs and processes. Do you truly believe you are above *His* word?"

I looked around the pit, unable to stop the sharp-tongued sarcasm from coming out of me. "I don't see the Creator anywhere here. If this... despicable action was something he wanted, he'd be here. Instead, you're the one standing before me."

"I am His–"

"Shield," I spat. "Protector of *His* word. Not avenger or punisher!"

I risked a glance to Rafaela, who was slumped over, balled on the floor with the bleeding stumps pumping fresh blood out onto the stone floor. "Leave, Cassial. Do not make matters any worse than they already need to be."

"What's done is done." Cassial looked as though he was seconds from taking matters into his own hands, again. I had to stop him. "There is no moving past this, we both know that."

A plan formulated in my mind, one I could use to manipulate Cassial into giving me what I wanted. And now, I didn't only need Rafaela for Duncan's sake, but her own.

"Actually, there is something," I said. "If you are willing to listen."

I saw the moment of hope that passed behind Cassial's eyes. If there was one thing clear, besides his vile tendencies, it was that he wanted his well-thought-out plans to proceed. "A proposal?"

"You could say that. I will keep your *dirty* fucking secret," I spat. "No one else needs to know about what you are doing here. But for that, I will need to go back and tell my friends that I have found Rafaela, and she is well, considering each and every one of them know I am here."

Cassial blanched, panic seeping across his expression. "You told them?"

"That you previously lied, yes. I did. But I suppose it was only an accusation until proven, so what news I take back to them will certainly affect how the fragile hours to follow will proceed."

"And you would happily lie to your friends on my behalf?" Cassial asked, head cocked slightly to the side, the very same gesture Duncan used. The rawness of it caught my breath.

"Yes, I would lie to them if it meant protecting them."

It pained me to say it, but it was the truth. In fact, lying to them about Rafaela was no different to what other mistruths had left my mouth.

I needed Cassial to think rationally, and for that I wouldn't tell anyone. If I told anyone else about what I'd found, it would bring an end to the wedding and start a conflict between the fey and Nephilim, thus dividing the world further than it already had been.

My goal was to *save* the world from Duwar. Starting a civil war was counterproductive. And for my plan, I needed Rafaela.

"Not so selfish as you thought, am I?" I asked, the hateful bite in my tone only getting worse.

"Your *word* means little to me." Cassial glowered, large hands balled into fists, wings still out and ready to use against me. "We invite you into our home, host your celebrations, work to unify the world your kind failed many years ago. And here you come, looking in places that do not belong to you. Why would you think I would believe you now?"

I held his stare, ensuring he not only heard my honest emotion but saw it reflected in my dark eyes. "My word is all I have. But I promise, on my life, on Icethorn–"

Cassial smirked. "I will need a vow with more weight, Robin Icethorn."

I swallowed hard. It didn't take a scholar to understand what he was suggesting. "Then I swear it, on Duncan's life, that no one will know of Rafaela. I will play along, but only if you give her to me. See that the only person to touch her is a healer. Going forwards, Rafaela will belong to me. If you believe punishment is justified, let it be the Creator who hands it out. Not you, or anyone else for that matter."

Cassial winced, clearly pained by my reminder that he was no god. Cassial, no matter his angelic proportions, was mortal enough to be affected by an ego. And if I was to win this battle, I had to use that against him.

"Rafaela is Nephilim, we have our ways–"

"I'd suggest you agree to my proposal if you wish peace to last longer than lunchtime today."

Cassial huffed out his nose like a bull readying to charge. If he did, I would stand still and take it. "Would you ruin the relations between the fey and humans over one person?"

"Who said anything about going against the humans, Cassial?" I tilted my head, drunk on the power. "It will be the Nephilim and their *ways* we will fight back against, and you know no one will benefit from that."

Silence thrummed between us, thick as a blanket of iron weighing down.

"If I agree to this exchange, it will only be on the understanding that you sign the treaty. I will give you until tonight," Cassial said, breaking the tension. "Before the ball, you will visit me and sign your name. Give me your support, help confirm a connection between the fey and human realms, and I will take that as proof of your promise that I can trust your word. Do not come to me, and I will understand the defiance for what it is."

My lip curled over my teeth. "I will sign the moment Rafaela is confirmed to be headed for Icethorn lands."

He lowered his head enough that it looked as though he was looking at me through his lashes. "Sign the treaty, Robin, and I will allow you to be the one to take her. Bring her to the Icethorn Court and you can deal with her treachery. She will be your thorn instead of mine." He looked back, pity and hate creased across darkening eyes as he regarded the bleeding Nephilim. "Rafaela has no place amongst us anymore, her betrayal proved as much."

"I accept," I said quickly, body trembling with the need to help her, to get him far away so I could make sure she was not going to die of these wounds.

In his way of agreeing, Cassial dropped the saw. It clattered against the ground, the sound making me wince. "That was the right decision."

"I hope so," I muttered, already making a move for Rafaela until Cassial stepped in the way, imposing with his broad frame.

"You are right, Robin. I am the Creator's shield – the remaining guardian of the Nephilim. But I am also His chosen Saviour. It is my duty alone to save this world, to bring forth the time in which our Lord desired. And I will do anything to protect His legacy. *Anything*."

I gritted my teeth, biting on the insides of my cheeks to stop myself from saying something that would make matters worse. Cassial took my silence as acceptance. I flinched as he reached into his pocket. He withdrew a small key and threw it at me without warning, like a bone to a dog. That was how he saw me.

Cassial smiled down at me like a cat who got the cream, then flapped his wings until he was airborne. He flew out of the Below, landing atop the dais I'd thrown myself from. I held myself firm, forcing the last dregs of strength and control into my legs, until I was confident Cassial had left.

Then I settled my eyes on the damage before me, and all that control left me.

"I'm here," I said, voice breaking, fighting the urge to vomit as I knelt beside Rafaela's raised hands, unsure what to do with them. "Rafaela, it's Robin. Can you hear me? I've got you. No one is ever going to hurt you again."

Her breathing was shallow, proving she still lived. Rafaela was the strongest person I'd ever known. She'd returned to Cassial, knowing punishment awaited her. And I understood that the lack of a locked gate down here, the vacant place where guards should stand, only suggested Rafaela had stayed here out of her own choice.

It broke me, brick by brick, until I was no different to the destroyed half of my castle back home. Because no matter how cruel this treatment, Rafaela believed she deserved it.

CHAPTER 13

I propped my arm beneath Rafaela's neck and lower back as I held her afloat in the pool of azure water in the Below. Her eyes were closed, the water murky as it cleaned new and old blood away from her wounds. I'd covered her body in a white sheet, securing her modesty.

Everything down here was so silent. In the quiet I could remember the time I had washed in this pool. I was alongside many other prisoners, no room to be conscious about my body or situation. Jesibel had been here, shadowing me during my stay in the prison, breaking the noses of those who had threatened me.

The past was a painful thing. It was easy to forget the possibility of a future when I was haunted by so much hurt and loss. And yet, looking down at Rafaela's peaceful face, her eyes closed and lips slightly parted, I reminded myself why I was here.

Because Rafaela could secure the future. She was the key to it, and the lock to secure it.

Once I was satisfied the waters had washed her down, the high salt levels working against any infection in her new wounds, I drew her out onto the rocky shore and laid her down on a bed of blankets and spare sheets I'd found.

There were enough belongings from the Below's previous tenants that I found healing salve that should help numb the area at least.

Time moved slowly down here. If I didn't leave soon, Erix would come looking and my proposal to Cassial would be ruined. I couldn't have him finding out the horrors that happened here without breaking the weak promise I'd made. Yes, I would tell them I found her and make excuses for Cassial's lies, but the moment they knew about her state, it would ruin the securing of peace.

It was the best I could do.

But leaving Rafaela now was impossible. I waited, partly to see if she would live through this, but more because I selfishly needed my answers.

When a groan escaped her lips, the lines formed over her forehead and her eyes fluttered open, I finally let out a breath that I didn't know I'd been holding.

"Steady," I whispered, brushing a soft hand down the side of her screwed up face. "Take your time."

There was no screaming as she came to, no reaction of terror and pain. Just as she had during rest, there was a peace to Rafaela as her obscure eyes settled on mine.

"You should not be here, Robin Icethorn," Rafaela said, her voice rasped from pain and suffering, yet still as assured as I last remembered it to be.

"Neither should you, Rafaela."

Weak hands reached up and pushed at my chest. "Go... you must leave."

I shook my head, refusing to acknowledge her words. "I should have never let you go back to *them*. What Cassial is doing – how they are treating you is–"

"Justified." She closed her eyes, brow furrowing deeper. "I betrayed my kin." Her voice was broken and tired, something I related to. "But most of all, I went against my Maker's desire. I deserve my punishment, and I accept it gladly. Given the chance, I would do it again."

Her sudden smile shocked me to the core. It was twisted and violent, but most of all, it sang of pride.

"Why does it sound like you are trying to convince yourself more than me?" I slumped backwards, picking at the skin around my nails just to give my hands something to do. "This is wrong, Rafaela. No god who vows to protect his people would want them to experience treatment like this."

I'd worked out soon after Cassial departed that Rafaela's wings hadn't just been cut off. In fact, the remains left around her curled body were minimal. Old scars were scored across her back like the criss-crossed marks of a game board. This was Cassial attempting to remove her wings as they grew back, which meant I had no idea just how many times it had happened before I found her.

Two, three... ten... more? How much pain had Rafaela experienced, just because she went against the Nephilim and destroyed the keys she was meant to protect?

Something Duwar had said to me replayed in my mind.

"Altar desired a failsafe. He knew that he'd need me one day."

"Why did the Nephilim want to protect the keys?" I asked, banishing Duwar's taunt from my mind. "When destroying them long ago would've saved the world from Duwar ever being a possibility of destruction?"

Rafaela winced as she shifted on her side. I peered over her back and saw that the sheet was already stained red. Her wounds would need healing again, and soon. "I think you know the answer to that question, Robin."

I swallowed the lump in my dried throat. "Because they wanted the keys alive, in case they needed to use them one day?"

"Not 'in case', but more like 'when' they wanted to use them. But that is no longer an option." Rafaela held my gaze, her pride refusing to crack. "I did what I had to do, and now the world is forever safe from evil, even evil you cannot see so plainly."

Duwar had said that Altar made the keys as a failsafe, a way of using Duwar if and when the fey god required it. But then why did the Creator also want this? What had happened between the gods that turned them each against one another, plotting and planning?

"You believe your purpose is complete," I said. "But you are wrong."

Rafaela didn't stop smiling. "The Creator gave me life, and I took it and did what I felt was right. My purpose has been fulfilled."

"What do you mean when you say the Creator gave life to you?"

Rafaela leaned back, eyes lingering upwards to the far-off top of the cave. "The Creator chose me from all of his fallen because I died in His name – for Him. And I was made into His warrior. I proved myself worthy, showed the Creator that I was selfless. He took my mortal soul and made me stronger, imbuing me with his power. That is how the Creator made His Nephilim – the favoured children. And yet, in the eyes of my fellow kin, I have gone against him. My wings, my power, must be stripped until I can prove myself again. Only then will He free me, when my sins are cleansed. And I have no interest in fitting that mould anymore – I have nothing left to prove. I am done, Robin. With everything."

"I don't believe that," I said. "I can't and I won't."

"It is true."

"No," I snapped, furious at such an evil act against his most loyal warrior. "Because if that was true, your wings wouldn't grow back. Your flesh would not heal. Rafaela, you are no mortal. You are a Nephilim. Remove your wings, take away your hammer, and you are still who and what you are."

"You will never understand," Rafaela rolled over, not without gasping in pain. "Please, now. Let me rest. Enjoy the world I helped secure. Live life, take it and cherish it. Whatever awaits me, I welcome it gladly."

It took effort not to unleash the sickness that stormed through my stomach.

"I can't leave you."

Rafaela's back was exposed to me now, the wound not as angry as it had been. She was healing, slowly, but faster than the mortal she believed herself to be again. More proof that the Creator had not turned His back on her.

"I need you, Rafaela," I persisted. "The world still needs you."

"The world is perfectly fine without me." Her voice broke as if she too couldn't quite believe it. "Please, Robin. I am tired. I must pray in peace and beg for His forgiveness loud enough that Cassial is convinced he does not need to visit."

It was on the tip of my tongue to tell her that it was no longer required. Rafaela was leaving Lockinge, with me. And yet something told me not to tell her, to ruin this clarity she believed she had here.

Rafaela was almost... comfortable.

"What... what if I can help you get it. That forgiveness."

"This is not your responsibility–"

"Yes," I interrupted before she could say another word. "Yes, it is."

Perhaps it was the urgency in my tone, or the desperation, that had Rafaela looking back to me. I buried my face in my hands until she reached up and peeled my fingers away.

"Something plagues you," she said, reading me with those all-seeing dusky eyes. "I sense a darkness in you, a plague of worry that you should not host."

"You're right," I said, bringing my voice to a whisper. "It brings me no joy to admit this, believe me."

"Admit what?" Fear flashed behind her eyes. "Tell me... Robin."

I leaned in, preparing to say the very thing I'd come all this way for. But being here, kneeling beside her, I didn't imagine this would be the situation we'd find ourselves in.

"Duwar... is here," I mouthed, fearful that the admission would echo out of the Below and fill Lockinge Castle until everyone heard.

Rafaela laughed, her sickly tinged skin creasing. "The gate has been closed forever, three of the keys destroyed. Duwar is no longer a threat to this world."

I laid a hand on her arm, begging her to believe me with my stare alone. "Duwar *is* here, Rafaela. I swear it."

Perhaps it was the hot, vicious tears running down my face which convinced Rafaela, or something else, but her laughter faltered, her sore lips straining into a pinched line.

"Where?" She looked around me, snarling as though she wasn't pained and suffering. Rafaela looked like the warrior she was, with or without her wings.

"It is..." I choked, bile burning the back of my throat. I pinched my eyes closed, seeing Duncan's body in the dark of my mind, tied down to a bed, weak and close to death. "It's *inside* of Duncan. Possessing him, controlling him."

I watched as the pieces of a puzzle slotted together in Rafaela's mind. How Duncan had disappeared into Duwar's realm, only to be saved by Erix. The clawed mark across his chest, the agony and suffering he experienced in the days he was unconscious back in Rinholm.

"Are you certain?" Rafaela asked, voice soft but deadly.

I nodded, because I feared if I spoke again, I would crumble to nothing but dust

Rafaela took her time to sit up, wincing as she did so. "Duwar possesses a mortal's body, because it could not leave its realm entirely – not without the use of the final key."

I nodded again, numb to the core.

"Then Duwar is weak," Rafaela growled. "If it is in a mortal body, then Duwar is subject to mortal wounds. You must kill it – before they find out."

She had just confirmed my previous theory, whilst also confirming how I could not do that.

"This is Duncan we are talking about, not some nameless mortal. I cannot just kill him," I said through gritted teeth. "That isn't the advice that I have come to you for. Nor will you slaughter a human, or anyone else offering. Not if there is another way to solve this issue."

"There is no other way."

I bristled. "You vowed to protect humankind."

"If Duwar is here, in our world, all vows are null and void. They will bring ruin to everything."

I scrambled with my words, rushed and desperate to get them out. "You once told me of people in Irobel who conversed with Duwar and were bound in labradorite. An eternal prison."

Rafaela's eyes widened, working out the very plan I'd formed in my mind. "You wish to bind Duncan in labradorite?"

No, not Duncan. "Yes. And I need your assistance with doing it. That is why I am here, Rafaela."

Rafaela took my request in, working out the possibilities silently in her mind. "It is out of the question."

"Help me, please. If you truly believe you deserve this punishment, then prove the Creator wrong. Fix these wrongs, with me, and you will be branded in His glory again. Please, Rafaela. Help me bind Duwar."

Rafaela laid a hand on mine, her trembling fingers clasping mine tight. "What you are asking of me is no different to death. If you do not want to kill Duncan yourself, then why choose this option?"

The final secret I harboured showed some resistance to come out. I had to prepare myself, force the words out before I never had the confidence to share them.

"Because Duncan will not be the body being locked in labradorite."

I knew Rafaela already worked out the next answer, but she asked me plainly for it anyway. "Then who will?"

I held her stare, blinking away the tears as a wave of confidence and strength crested over me. "Me. I will take Duwar into my body, and you will lock me away, forever so no one can ever claim access to such a dark power. If that doesn't work, you kill me. But not him, not Duncan."

I expected Rafaela to refuse me, but she didn't. Instead, her grip on my hand tightened, proving more that she was still strong, even in this state. "I will help you, Robin."

"Thank you." I sagged forwards, pressing my forehead to hers. "Thank you, thank you."

"Do not thank me yet," Rafaela said, grief evident across the pinch of her face. "The road we face is painful, hard. It will require more sacrifice than you could ever imagine."

"I will do it. Any of it. You're not the only one with penance to pay."

Rafaela laid a hand on the back of mine. "Why give yourself up so easily?"

"Because I cannot bear to live in a world without him. Duncan is my life."

"What do you think he would say, if asked the same question, if given the same choices?"

My heart skipped a beat. We both knew that Duncan would choose the same fate. "Enough people have sacrificed themselves in my name. You have faced unjust punishment for your involvement in destroying the keys, it is time I also pay."

"From what I can see, Robin." Rafaela dusted her fingers down the side of my face, clearing tears. "You have suffered greatly already. But I will help you, if you are certain this is the path you wish to take–"

"It is the only path I know of, and we don't have time to locate another."

Rafaela bowed her head. "Then this is what we are going to do. To achieve what you desire, we must go to Irobel. Immediately."

Irobel – home of the Nephilim.

I held my breath and listened to Rafaela's plan, finding comfort in her assistance. Even if her words solidified the end of my story, and how soon that end would come. I would pay it, tenfold.

For Seraphine and her found family. For Althea and Gyah, Elinor and the life that was taken from her for so long. For Duncan, because he had suffered so much, and deserved a chance at a life that Abbott Nathaniel would've wanted for him.

For Erix, the man who would be pacing the floor at my absence, the man who would give anything for me.

And for every life that wished to truly enjoy this new world. I would give myself up a million times over, just to solidify it for them all.

"After the wedding, Cassial will send you to Icethorn with me," I said, hearing the foolproof plan repeat over in my mind. "It has been agreed between us, a way to keep you safe from his… twisted ways."

Rafaela picked at her nails, eyes wide and wild with unspoken thoughts. "Then you have a handful of days to make your peace and say your goodbyes."

I smiled, glad for the closure that would follow. Life had been so unkind, but I'd found so many wonderful people along the way. And Rafaela was right. I had a few days to ensure those I loved knew I loved them, and that the memories I could leave for them would help them understand what I was preparing to do, and why.

"Rafaela… I don't trust Cassial."

"Because you are a good judge of character. You shouldn't trust him. Any of them." Rafaela finished with a snarl.

"He's been calling himself the Saviour, acting both in favour for peace and against it."

Rafaela spat on the ground. "Cassial is *no* Saviour. The promised Saviour has yet to show themselves."

"Promised?" I shook my head, originally believing the title was just given to boost Cassial's ego. "So, the title isn't something Cassial's ego dredged up?"

Rafaela shook her head. "No, not amongst the Nephilim."

"Who are they?"

Rafaela leaned in close, dropping her voice to a husky whisper. "The dawn of the day when Gabrial was chosen as His script, she prophesied a person made from both realms, who would bring an era of peace for the Nephilim. Cassial believes that he is that Saviour, but he is wrong."

"Then who…" I said, feeling my heart beating in my throat.

Rafaela rested a hand on my shoulder, her grip faltering but still strong. "I see a man, born from two realms, who wishes to save them both. Perhaps it is you, Robin. Maybe not. I suppose time will only tell."

CHAPTER 14

Whilst I took the quill and prepared to sign the treaty, Cassial taunted me with his sly scrutiny, and he enjoyed every bastard minute of it. He watched me like a predator watching prey, whereas I couldn't take my eyes off the horror behind him.

Standing proud behind his throne was a glass case, refracting the sunlight in beams of multicoloured splendour. But there was nothing beautiful about what stretched out behind the glass.

Wings. Two familiar limbs held by straps. I had to fight back the urge to scream or release my magic upon him again. Because I knew who those wings once belonged to.

The woman imprisoned beneath my feet. But for her sake, I had to be the demure king upholding the illusion of amity.

So, this was why Cassial changed the location of the treaty's signing last minute. Because he wanted me to see them.

No one else noticed, perhaps thinking it was some glorified decoration brought over from Irobel. But if I looked close enough, I could see the stains of blood soaking into a few feathers.

For a pious man, Cassial held dark thoughts in his eyes. His silence scorched across my body as he watched me sign my name upon the parchment – securing the future for everyone I cared about. A world in which the fey and the humans would live in harmony. I was no mind reader, but one look at him, and I knew just what he wished to do with me. I took pride knowing he would never get the chance once the ink dried.

As the sworn protectors of humans, if Cassial made any move against me, it would forfeit the peace. He was a twisted bastard, but I had to trust he wasn't that stupid.

Once my ink soaked into the page, I stepped back, forcing a smile so no one else around me knew there was anything to worry about. "Is that everything you need of me?" I asked.

Cassial didn't reply with words but bowed his head instead.

I was the last person to sign the treaty. Althea and Elinor had gone up before me, scrawling their names upon a document that would ensure the two realms would become one. A place without borders. A representative from the Elmdew Court, a woman wearing a circlet of silver attached with the ivory horns of a stag. In her hands she held a baby, swaddled in blankets and cooing softly, I knew it had to be the young prince Jordin.

I took my place, stealing myself against any remaining hesitations.

I knew what I had to do to ensure that all this mattered – and with Rafaela's help, I would. First, I had to make it through tonight's ball, and tomorrow's wedding. Then I would return to Icethorn with Rafaela, prepare to journey with Duncan to Irobel, and complete the ritual Rafaela had confirmed might just work.

But before then, as Rafaela had said, I had some peace to make and goodbyes to offer.

"Today, we have made history," Cassial drawled, looking at everyone but me. "We have ensured those who come after us will get to enjoy a world in which our personal sacrifices mean something. Eighteen years to this day, we will return to Lockinge and host the crowning of the human Princess Eugena with the Spring Court heir, Jordin Elmdew, thus bringing our peoples together in more than just spirit. Until then, we begin our celebrations tomorrow with the wedding between Althea and Gyah–" Cassial physically winced at that, as if the idea of the marriage displeased him, but he dared not admit it aloud. It seemed I wasn't the only one to notice. One look at Althea and I saw her eyes narrow. However, she was good at plastering a fake smile upon her face, whereas I was shit at it.

"If that is all," Althea said, the dismissal overspilling in her voice. Even though I hadn't told her what state I found Rafaela in, she certainly wasn't pleased with the 'confusion' about her not being in Lockinge. "I would like to return to my rooms and prepare for tonight."

Cassial bowed, waving a hand in polite dismissal. "That *is* all. Unless anything further is required of me, please enjoy yourselves. I regret I will not be able to join you tonight, but please, raise a goblet on my behalf."

Murmurs rose throughout our crowd.

"Is there somewhere more pressing you need to be?" I asked, unable to hold my tongue.

Cassial slowly swept his eyes back to me. Bless his heart, he really did try and hide the abhorrence he held for me. "Yes, Robin Icethorn. In fact, there is. I'm required at the south border, to ensure our plans have been followed for the celebrations tomorrow. But do not concern yourselves with that, please. Zarrel will stay behind and see to any needs you have. For now, I wish you the best. My one request is that you are careful with the drinks tonight. No fun will be had tomorrow with sore heads."

"Let them have a little fun, Cassial." Zarrel nodded with a knowing smile, clutching Rafaela's hammer in his hands as if it had always belonged to him.

"You are right, Zarrel. Drink us dry if that is what you would all wish."

We were all prepared to depart when the doors to the great hall crashed open, and a Nephilim soldier speared inside. The suddenness had us all holding our breath, although Cassial actually seemed undeterred by it all.

"Your Brilliance," the Nephilim bowed, breathless and faced flushed. "We have news from–"

"*Thank you,* Damious." Cassial's raised hand was one way of cutting the Nephilim off. "But our guests do not need to be concerned with any minor issues."

"Actually, we are rather adept at dealing with issues," Gyah said, hand laid upon the hilt of her sword. "You're welcome to share this, if you choose to."

It was another dig, at Cassial's prior mistruth.

"My betrothed is right," Althea started, sensing the tension in the air. "If there is an issue at play, we absolutely should be included in the conversation."

Cassial stood from his chair, which was better described as a throne. It was impressive how obvious he displayed his comfort whilst sat in it. I'd think that a warrior of the Creator would at least pretend he wasn't interested in control. All that was missing was a crown, and Cassial was no different to a king. "Princess Cedarfall, these are *human* matters."

"And the treaty we have just signed ensures that we are united, does it not?" Althea pushed on.

"It does, but that starts in eighteen years, as mentioned." Cassial's dismissal was cold as ice. "Now please, if you wouldn't mind, I have matters to deal with, and you have a party to get ready for."

Althea and I shared a glance, mirroring that which Erix and Gyah had. Elinor too. But none of us asked questions. Elinor was the one to shepherd us all out of the room, like a mother goose guiding her hatchlings out of danger.

"I, for one, would like to know exactly what has ruffled his feathers," Althea said as the grand doors closed. "Secrecy is certainly not a way to set the tone before the ink has had a chance to dry on the papers."

"In his defence," I said, attempting to dilute the distrust between my allies. "We have kept secrets, as has he."

"I don't like it," Althea persisted. "Minor or not, I want to know what is going on."

I took pleasure knowing that my friend didn't like Cassial.

I knew she had good taste. But for the sake of pretences, I had to keep up my attempt to distil this tension. The first being that my investigation into the Below proved that Rafaela was not, in fact, there. I'd lied and told them she was in her rooms, healthy and whole, certainly not severed of wings.

It was necessary to further *my* plans.

"I'm sure it is nothing to worry about," I replied, offering her a subtle, discarding shrug. "As Cassial said, these are human matters. They've been dealing with them for a while, and we don't divulge matters that occur across our borders. We can at least trust he has it under control."

Althea shot me a look that told me she didn't believe me. "Did you see that Nephilim that came rushing in? He looked rather flustered about something."

Erix was so still beside me, I almost forgot he was even there. It wasn't until he spoke that I remembered his ever-presence. "Hunters. That's what they are discussing."

We all looked to him, shocked at his admission. Before we could ask how he knew, Erix gestured to his pointed ears. "My hearing has improved. Thanks to... you know–" He gestured a hand down his body as if pinning the blame on his new form. "This."

I wondered how many unwanted conversations Erix had heard before now. Like last night, did he know who visited my room? When I entered his, and he woke from sleep, was that all an act?

My own lies were poisoning my judgement, and there was nothing I could do to stop it.

"What else do you know?" Gyah stiffened, wrapping a protective arm around Althea's waist. "We're going to need more than that."

"Cassial has left already. Zarrel is on his way to check on us," Erix's eyes flickered toward the corridor. "I say we go before he discovers we are all stood around discussing matters that, as Robin put, are not of our concern, shall we? We can pick this back up later."

"Should we be worried?" Elinor asked, rich voice dripping with concern. "Because I am."

Erix shook his head. The way his eyes diverted to me, how when he replied his voice shivered slightly, I knew he was lying. "No. Just that a band of them have been found near Lockinge. It's in hand from what I could hear." A creak sounded beyond the door. "Now, scatter."

And scatter we did. I'd no choice but to follow Erix, because he threaded his hand with mine and guided me through Lockinge Castle toward our chambers. The suddenness of the touch, when we had been dancing around it, took any ability to do anything but follow away from me.

Only when we came to a stop, and he dropped it again, did I find I could speak. The lingering warmth of his touch didn't falter.

"You just lied to them," I said once I knew our companions were out of earshot. "Didn't you?"

I knew Erix had the moment the words came out his mouth. How his gaze had strayed, and his left hand flexed on and off at his side. Telling signs, considering I knew him well.

"I did," Erix replied, coldly.

"So, we *should* be worried?"

Erix swallowed hard, the audible thump of the lump in his throat making the hair on my arms stand. We'd come to an abrupt stop, in a narrow hallway lined with empty portraits. Sconces burned with fire, lighting the way, making the golden hue of flames lick and dance across the many banners displaying the Creator's symbol.

"I heard a mention of a convoy. Hunters were seen in a small village not far from here."

"So, it wasn't a lie?"

Erix looked to the shadows, inspecting them for secrets. "The Hunter part, no. But the Nephilim didn't seem awfully surprised. If anything, I heard that the party had been expected."

My first instinct was that something terrible had happened. A pillaging of the village. I had the impression that Cassial's mention of being needed at the border had little to do with the wedding, and everything to do with Hunters. Why else did he not seem surprised when Damious came in? It was certainly like news he expected to hear.

"What did they – these Hunters do?"

In the dark of my mind, I saw a flash of destruction. It was brave, for the Hunters to continue their goals, knowing everything they'd lost – or believed they'd lost.

If only they knew the truth. If only they found out what I had bound to the bed in Imeria.

Erix shook his head, searching the shadows around us for threats. "I don't know. I heard Damious mention something about the wagons being empty. The Hunters are giving something out to the locals, saying it's in the name of the capital. Cassial went into a fury and departed before anything else was said."

I shook my head, unable to make sense of it. "So whatever is happening, Cassial will resolve it."

"Will he?"

I could only hope. "He has no other choice."

"Robin." The seriousness in Erix's tone had me snapping my eyes back up to his. My breath hitched in my throat at the bright glow of his silver irises, next to the red-tinged whites of his eyes. Whatever was bothering him called to the monster inside of him. "If I even get a whiff of a threat, then I am getting you far away from here, wedding or not. Your safety is all that matters to me." His hands gripped my upper arms and held me firm. "I promised Duncan, and I take that vow seriously. Do I make myself clear?"

The severity of his words made my knees tremble. "Loud and clear," I answered, finding words hard to grapple. "But dealing with Hunters is nothing new. The Hand's poison will take more than a few months to purge–"

"It's not the Hunters I worry about. It's *you*. And something is screaming at me, an intuition that is telling me something isn't right here. So, the second I feel like those worries are proven right, we are leaving."

"But that's not it, is it?" His grasp on my arms lessened, but the intensity in his eyes never faltered. "Something else is worrying you. I can tell."

Erix paused, taking in my accusation. That was the thing about him. Erix could read me, just as I could read him. So, when he shook his head and dismissed my question, I knew he was lying again.

"I think our focus should be getting through tonight and tomorrow. Then we can make plans to visit Irobel, with Duncan – and save him."

I looked around, panicked for hidden ears to overhear. "Not here."

"We are alone," Erix said, and something about it sparked a heat inside of my gut. "No one will hear me."

Erix was the only person I had been completely honest with when I left Rafaela. He knew everything that happened, all but a small detail spared. Mostly because I trusted him with my biggest secret; this one paled in comparison. But we were a team, as Duncan wanted. I wasn't going to waste the only true ally I could afford.

"Then you know why we can't cause any issues," I reminded him, clutching his hand desperately. "The next few days must go smoothly for us to get a chance to get back to Duncan. Then we can worry about the charter to Irobel."

Erix calmed, if only slightly, but it was enough. "I have already sent word back to Imeria for my gryvern to prepare for Duncan's movement. I would suggest they meet us at the coast, it would cut the journey back to Irobel in half."

A warmth of thanks enveloped me like the embrace of strong arms, knowing I wasn't the only person to deal with this issue. With Erix, I didn't feel as lonely as I had before.

"Thank you, Erix. I mean it."

He laid a soft hand upon my cheek, my breath caught in my throat. "For what?"

I swallowed hard. "Shouldering this burden with me."

"Of course. As I said it's my–"

"Duty and pleasure," I repeated the sentiment he'd said to me a number of times. "I know."

"Exactly, little bird."

I drew a step back, hyper aware of his hand falling uselessly back to his side.

"You know, we could skip the ball tonight, if you prefer," I said, almost hopeful Erix would agree. "I'm not really in the mood to celebrate after what I saw today."

"As much as I agree, I know that would not be wise," Erix replied.

"Can I ask why?"

"Pretences. I wish I could do as you want, but you must be seen by the Nephilim and human nobility. It is all a game, one you must see through to the end." He stepped closer, the flames reflecting across the hollow planes of his handsome face. Erix refused to look anywhere but at me. "But not only that, you also deserve a night to enjoy yourself. This game of pretend will not last much longer, you may as well enjoy it whilst it does."

My brain told me to step away from him, but my heart kept me in place, our proximity so close I felt his breath on my face. "Is that the only reason?"

Erix mocked a smile, although it didn't quite reach his eyes. "Well, between me and you, I need a belly full of strong spirits if I can even hope to get through another interaction with Zarrel. I'm so close to giving in to the gryvern and tearing him into lots of little pieces."

"Wow," I gasped, "you feel that strongly about him? I'm jealous."

I regretted those last words the second they came out of my mouth. Before Erix could press forwards, I turned toward the door to my chamber, wincing when my back was to him. "I'll knock for you when I'm ready to go back down."

Although I couldn't see Erix's expression, I *heard* it. The sigh he exhaled was so impressive, I felt it in my bones. "And I shall be waiting for you, little bird."

CHAPTER 15

I sank beneath the warm water of my bath, hoping the scalding heat would cleanse some of the sinful thoughts plaguing me. But alas, they were so deep there was nothing in this realm that would abolish them.

Dried rose petals floated around me, the blessed scent of mint and camomile seeping in the mist that danced from the water's surface. I sank lower until the lower half of my face was submerged, my head resting on the curved lip of the tub. As the water slipped over my mouth, I conjured an image of Erix. Perhaps it was my tired mind, or something else, but my thoughts were fixed on him. Instantly, heat uncoiled in my groin. I ached against it, grasping the lip of the tub just to stop myself from reaching down and grasping my length.

Guilt melted seamlessly with desire. There wasn't one without the other when he was near.

Erix clouded my mind. There was no amount of water that could cleanse my skin of him, or dispel the scent of cedar and cinnamon from my nose. Since he'd left me, I'd not stopped feeling the brush of his fingers against my cheek. The tension and ease between us.

Weak to him, I slowly uncurled my fingers, slipped my hand beneath the water and grasped my erection. I told myself that if I was quick, the shame wouldn't last. Yet another lie. The moment my wrist began to move, tugging my hardening length, I knew there was no hope for me.

I arched my back, biting down on my lip to stifle the moan. It echoed across the stone room, dancing up the walls and into the shadowed rafters.

No matter how I tried to fill my mind with thoughts of Duncan, it was Erix who occupied it. Occasionally they would change places. Their bodies, the curves of their muscles, the proud structure of their jaws, shifting from one to the other.

It had been days without one of Duwar's dreams, and I could conjure it as if it had been real.

My imagination had never been the best, but it was like Erix was with me physically, encouraging me with silken words and an even softer touch. Deep in the recesses of my mind I knew something was amiss, but my desire had stolen any sense of clear thought.

It took no time for the heat to fill my length, building into a pressure that could not be held back. Breathless, I cocked my head back and cried out into the barren chamber. As the milky substance burst out of me, clouds of my cum dancing in the bath waters, disturbing my reflection – the desire disappeared instantly.

What have I done?

Only after I'd pleasured myself did it feel like reality caught up. And I felt sick. Unable to think clearly. I pinched my eyes closed, blocking out the world. It was only meant to be for a moment. But between the calming scents, the languid embrace of water and the utter exhaustion plaguing my body, I found sleep welcoming me with open arms.

But no natural sleep came on so fast.

Duncan waited for me, and all thoughts of what I'd just done came flooding over me like a cold wave. I lifted my head to find I was not in the bathtub at all but surrounded by the familiar sheets of a bed. Dust clung to the air, filling my nose, and clogging my throat. As I lifted onto my elbows, I took in the old attic room of Abbott Nathanial's church.

The same leaning ceiling, stained-glass window, boxes of scrolls and a forgotten pile of empty bottles of wine scattered across the dark, oiled floor.

"Hello, darling," Duncan said through a yawn.

I tried to sit up, but he reached his arm up so he could draw me back down to lie on his chest. "You aren't going yet, are you?"

"This isn't real." I persisted, leaning forwards, unable to deny that it actually felt *very* real. "If you've come to punish me, then you're wasting your effort, Duwar."

"Punish you for what, Robin?"

The question hung in the dust-heavy air.

I hunched over, aware that if I just got out of the single shared bed, the dreamscape would end.

I almost did, until Duncan spoke again.

"Stay a while. Please, do it for me." It sounded so much like him. My Duncan. How could I refuse him? "I've missed you *so* much, these days apart. The first chance I get to see you, hold you, speak with you, and you wish to run."

As was normal with these dreams, I knew just how real they were. A place in which Duwar could haunt me, taunt me. Although it had been days since the last, I almost welcomed this one. Even if Duwar was presenting himself as Duncan to disarm me, playing pretend was easier than facing the truth.

"I miss *Duncan* so much," I replied, noticing how small my voice sounded in this space.

"Then lie with me." He paused, fingers brushing down my spine, making me bend to his will. "*Please.*"

That single word broke through my shields.

I allowed Duncan to guide me down, until my face was pressed to his bare chest, his heart beating a rhythm through my cheek. Coarse hairs itched my skin, but it wasn't unpleasant. I missed threading fingers through them, teasing my soft touch across the divots and mounds of his muscular build.

If I simply closed my eyes, I could play pretend like my tired mind wanted me to. So, for a moment of peace, I did just that. A soft hand began to stroke the back of my head, offering me comfort.

"When will you return to me? Home isn't the same without you, Robin. It is quiet and empty. When you are gone, I forget what I am fighting for."

"Soon," I mumbled, words skittering across his skin. "I will be back soon."

"Good," Duncan exhaled with what felt like genuine relief. "And has this time apart allowed you to come to your senses about my proposal?"

That question alone told me who was speaking.

"It has," I replied, unable to lie whilst my skin bristled at the reality of the demon I conversed with. "I know what must be done now. I finally understand."

Reprieve practically unfurled from Duncan's flesh, wrapping around me just as his arms did in that moment. "Your decision will save us. Me, Erix, you. We can finally be together. Then, with my power, you can shape the world into the very image of your desires. Anything you want will be in your grasp."

"Except that isn't what Duncan wants," I said, finally accepting that I knew who I truly spoke with. "You speak on what you believe I desire, but you are grasping at crumbling straws."

"Just as you think I do not know your desires, how can you speak on what Duncan wants if you too are not in his mind, his body?" Duwar purred. His faked warmth of Duncan's skin faded, his skin turning ice-cold to the touch. "He understands that to love you, he must accept *all* of you. That even includes everything you had before him."

"Stop speaking to me as if the tongue you use has free will," I snapped, but my body was immobile.

"Robin, you need this. You know you do, more so than ever. Have you not uncovered dangers that lurk in the shadows that you once mistook for light?"

"And what is *this* exactly?" I asked, refusing to peel away and see the face of the god who looked down at me. I knew Duncan was no longer here, he never had been. But I could still pretend.

"A chance at life."

"And you, God of Ruin, can offer that to me?"

Duwar's laugh slithered over me, uncomfortable as the scales of a serpent constricting around my throat. "I am power, Robin, as I have told you over and over. I alone can offer you whatever you desire. If that is a life with Duncan and Erix, so be it. As long as you give yourself to me, the rest will fall into your open hands freely. This moment can be real, as real as the one you almost shared with Erix last night."

I stiffened, breath catching. "Nothing happened between us."

"No, perhaps not. But I see all. Through reflections, even in a body of water," Duwar said, their voice blending back in with Duncan's dulcet tones. It was in that moment I knew the sexual desire that arose in me during waking was not natural. Had I let my guard slip, complicit because I thought the room had no mirrors when, in fact, I was bathing in one made of water? Duwar's control, its power, was written all over my deceit, and yet that didn't dampen the guilt I felt toward Duncan.

"Think carefully," Duwar continued. "Why else did Duncan arrange for you both to be together again? That was his doing alone. Because even Duncan knows, for success, you need him as much as *I* need you. Erix is the strength you need to make the right decision. For Duncan, for Wychwood and Durmain. Do not let my power fall into the hands of those who would abuse it. Not again."

No one will ever get this power again.

"Promises of the very creature who wishes to defile this world. Not of Duncan."

"When will you learn? I *am* Duncan, he is me. An improved version of myself. Until you see the truth I am trying to show you, I suppose you can simmer in your distrust. Whether you believe me or not, I am only trying to help you." The hand upon the back of my head continued to brush back and forth. "It's clear to me now that you still aren't asking the right questions."

"About?" I choked.

Duncan's hand movement paused. "You understand that Altar kept the keys to my imprisoned state for his future gain, but why do the Creator's children vow to protect them? Because they knew, in time, they would need me too."

It was unsaid, but I knew Duwar spoke of the Nephilim.

"For what, the destruction of the world as we know it?" I bristled, longing to pull away but not daring to make the slightest movement. Because something in what Duncan had just said struck true.

Why *did* Altar make keys?

Duwar dove into my mind, took the question I thought and answered it.

"I have pondered why myself, during my time kept away. I can imagine they knew there was something I could offer them, like the power they fought over in the first place. A power only I had access to. Perhaps even a fresh start, if required. I am all but a tool to use. Either accept that, or maybe another will in your place."

"I hear the threat in your words," I accused, no longer wanting to play this game of pretend. I pushed upwards and swung my legs over the bed, ready to leave this dreamscape.

"Was it not you who said that you do not threaten, Robin Icethorn. Only promise?"

I turned back to look at the body on the bed, to find the soft face of Duncan staring up at me with tired, verdant eyes. It looked like him, sounded like him. Even as his fingers brushed my bare skin, it felt as much like Duncan as he always had.

"Trust no one," he said, a glint of what looked like sadness in his eyes.

"Including you?" I asked.

His smile was sheepish, flickering at the corners of his mouth. The small vision of the real Duncan faded as fast as it came. "Everyone has something they want in this world. A motive. The same goes for the game of gods. Altar and the Creator both desired power, enough of it that it started a war between monsters. Altar stole me from my peace, used me and then discarded me. The Creator went to war over me. And yet, they still kept a tether to me, just in case the game changed, and I was required."

"I have no wish to be a pawn for you to use. I'm not like the gods."

"But you could be," Duwar said, pouting subtly. "If you accept me – when you accept this power, you could be greater than any god the realms have seen before."

"I wish I could trust you," I said, eyes burning with the promise of more tears. "But I have seen what you are capable of."

"And you only focus on the pain I have been used to cause, not the beauty of life that I showed you I could achieve–"

A scene flashed in the dark of my mind. Of vines and roots sprouting out of cold, dead earth, wrapping around the ruins of my castle. How they crept over stone, covering the ruin left behind in flowers so vibrant it took my breath away.

"Convenient tricks," I said. "A rose is beautiful, but it still has thorns."

"And yet it is still beautiful, as you said." Duncan pouted, his stomach flexing with far too many muscles to count. "Robin, even Altar knew my capabilities and used me to make his beloved children. The Creator was jealous. Ask yourself, will you be the one to use my power to create a paradise, or will your hesitance allow for other hands to take me?"

Slowly, Duncan leaned back with his arms behind his head and closed his eyes, peaceful.

"There will be no other hands that ever get the chance to touch you," I said.

"Are you sure?"

Although I knew my answer, I still shot Duncan a look, knowing the monster under his skin was watching. "You'll just have to wait a couple more days to find out."

As I rested my feet on the floor, I banished myself from the dream.

I came to, thrusting up out of the bath my sleeping body had fully slipped beneath. Coughing up water, I clutched the side of the tub for support, willing myself to steady my breathing. All the while, I heard the echo of Duwar's reply in my mind, as clear as day.

"I only hope you have the days to spare."

CHAPTER 16

I longed to compliment Erix on how he looked, but the words turned to ash on my tongue. After what I'd done in the bath, followed by the interaction with Duncan, I could hardly breathe around him let alone speak.

Duwar was playing with me like a dog with a bone, chewing and gnawing until I was nothing but a husk. And it was working, quicker than I cared to admit.

Instead of looking ahead at the ballroom – the marble floor glittering like an ocean of white which caught the glow of the countless burning sconces, displays of white and red roses, music swelling up the large stone walls which reverberated the delicate tune – I stared at Erix's profile.

To the man who Duncan brought back into my life, two times over.

Handsome almost seemed like a pointless word to use, as though it didn't hold enough power for how he looked. Ethereal worked better, but how could I possibly say that to him? Truth be told, Erix was trying everything in his ability not to look at me. I sensed his hesitation as if it was my own. He'd let his control slip when he welcomed me outside of my rooms earlier. His mouth had dropped open, his words lost to him, as I stepped out in my outfit. I'd felt his eyes trace me, up and down, multiple times.

Then, as he'd offered his arm for me to take, he muttered a single word that'd followed me all the way through the castle. *"Beautiful."*

How could I follow that up? Not only the use of the word, but the emotion behind it.

Since then, he had done his very best to control himself.

At least one of us had that ability.

Erix was dressed in silver armour, the metal thin to allow for movement. A grey cloak hung over his back, parting to allow room for his wings. His jaw was sharper than the stitched lines of the Icethorn emblem across his cloak, or the edges of his shoulder guards that looked like scales.

If Erix noticed I'd been looking up at him all this time, he didn't reveal it. Instead, his eyes levelled across the room, drinking in the scene of fey, human and Nephilim, dancing together, or drinking from stemmed glasses, or hovering around elaborate tables of food.

"I should go and..."

"Mingle?" Erix answered for me, still trying everything in his power not to look at me. "Yes, perhaps you should."

Even as he said it, the hand he'd laid over mine hadn't moved. It was anchored to me, keeping me in place, keeping me with *him*.

No one approached us where we stood to the side of the room. Erix had the aura of a guard dog on duty, his constant scowl warding anyone off. Not that there was anyone who'd approach anyway. The Nephilim showed no interest, likely all sharing the same disdain for me as Cassial and Zarrel did. Althea and Gyah were sitting alone – well, Althea was draped across Gyah's lap whilst she was fed grapes one at a time. I spotted Elinor Oakstorm being swept around the dedicated dance floor in the centre of the room, the human she was with looking exhausted but thrilled by the prospect of dancing with a fey queen.

"They all look so happy, don't they?" I said, numb to my core. "Not a care in the world."

This was the picture of a peaceful world I'd painted with brushes of lies and deceit.

"It must be nice," Erix replied, his brow pinching. "To go about life without knowing that more sacrifices must be made. That pain waits around every corner. I envy them, but at the same time I know that they deserve this."

It was the pain in Erix's voice that caught me off guard. I looked back to him and found that he was finally looking at me.

"Are we going to pretend that the thing still bothering you is not worth speaking about?" I asked.

Erix screwed his mouth up. "I am that obvious?"

"I just know you, Erix." I narrowed my eyes on him, and for a moment I found myself transported to another place during another time. "Do you remember the first ball we experienced together?"

"Of course I do."

"Is that what's on your mind?"

Erix nodded, his nose scrunching up. "So much has changed since then, hasn't it? The world is completely different. And here we are still standing in the corner, whilst everyone else around us can exist in ignorant bliss. At least this time you are not drunk on fey wine."

"I wasn't drunk," I said. "I was tipsy – there's a difference."

"You were brash and careless. And it was my job to look after you, a task you made hard during every second."

I withdrew my hand, despite Erix's unconscious attempt to keep it on his arm. "Then I command that you have a night off your duties, Erix. If you want to go and enjoy yourself, do it. You don't need to stand with me. It's not like anyone is going to come and bother me anyway. There is no threat of poison this time round either, no assassins lurking as friends, no monsters waiting to snatch me away and destroy me. This is the peace we have fought for, you might as well start to enjoy it, whether it is real or not."

"And what if I am content being with you?" Erix's tone dropped, the seriousness of his words working into my skin. "It isn't fair. *We* can't even pretend that everything is okay."

"We can try–"

"No," Erix snapped, exhausted. "What I'd give for just one night – one night where we do not have to worry about what is coming tomorrow. But what bothers me the most is, if I am feeling like this, I can only imagine how *you* are suffering. No matter what I would give to change it, I will never have the power to fix the world for you."

He turned and fixed his eyes on me, the first time since welcoming me outside of my rooms. The air cracked, a spark of something powerful and breathtaking threading around us.

"I'm fine," I lied, but if anyone would know, it was Erix. "Or at least I will be. *Soon.*"

Erix was silent for a moment, as though taking in my words and deciding how much weight they had to them. "Do you know what I want most in this world?"

I dared not ask, but the question came out anyway. "What?"

He took a deep breath in through his nose, filling his body with the confidence required to answer. "I wish to see you smile again. Not those fake smiles you plaster across your face when you think the time requires it. I mean the real ones, the type which lighten your face from the inside out. It's been so long since the last time I saw one, and every second that passes without one, I feel as though the world is not worth it. What good am I to you, if I cannot make that happen?"

I couldn't stop the words from flowing out of me. "You have no idea just how your presence alone is helping me, do you?"

Silver eyes held onto my gaze, unwavering. "Duncan deserves to be here with you. Not me."

"I want him here too," I said, clutching at my chest from the sudden pain. "But that isn't to say that I wouldn't want you here as well. Erix, I suggest you should stop worrying about what you think I deserve, and just ask me next time."

Erix's breath hitched, his shoulders rolling back. "Then tell me, little bird. What is it you deserve?"

I was faced with the question, in reality, I was too weak to answer it. Instead of coming out right and saying that I wanted them both – or maybe that was just a new desire that Duwar's taunting made me contemplate as a possibility – I manipulated my answer to stay on the right side of the line between us.

"A distraction," I replied. "From my mind, and my responsibilities."

Erix loosed a broken gasp, his eyes widening a fraction. "It has been a long time since you asked that of me. Different circumstances, different outcomes."

My knuckles brushed his, only for a moment.

"I think we both deserve a night off, don't you? A night where we don't think about anything but the moment. Consider it a challenge, we both distract each other, and at least try to enjoy ourselves. Play the parts of king and royal guard, as we have done before. If not for ourselves, at least to keep up pretences for everyone watching. Just as you wanted."

"Pretences," Erix repeated, taking the reason of my words in, allowing his body to react before he added. "Do you remember what you did, the last time we were at a ball?"

"I got *tipsy*," I answered, finding the swell of heat at the memory. "You just reminded me of that."

That wasn't what Erix was suggesting, and I knew it. But for the safety of this strange boundary between us, out of respect for Duncan, I refused to answer with the truth.

"Hmm. Do you plan to repeat history tonight?" Erix asked. "Cassial has likely requested every possible bottle of wine and ale across Durmain. There is enough to last a lifetime in this very room."

I shook my head. "I hope I don't disappoint you with my answer, but I would very much like to just dance."

Erix laughed. "Dance? Robin Icethorn wishes to dance?"

It was a risk, doing this with Erix. Getting close, knowing what was to come. But more than anything, I forgot that he would be left behind when my plan was successful. He deserved a memory that would make him smile – one he could take with him into the future.

"Not the type of distraction you expected me to ask for, was it?"

His cheeks flushed red. Erix dropped his silver eyes to our held hands and answered. "Well, I am sure Duncan would murder me himself if he heard I refused you a dance."

The mention of Duncan almost had me backing out. I longed for him to be here, holding my hand, throwing ourselves into a dance with nothing but joy and excitement for a future holding us together. But he was not here. And if he was, my mind would be split to another. To Erix. I would always think about him.

My mind was a storm, occupied by two men, both of whom I would never get the chance to have again.

"One night of distractions," I said, shaking his hand. "Nothing… untoward. Just friends, enjoying each other's company."

"Just friends," Erix echoed, doing well to hide the disappointment from his expression. "One night, I can do one night. Now, about that dance."

I gave up control, willingly. For Erix, I told myself, as he pulled my arm and guided me into the heart of the room. Everywhere was loud with the noise of chatter, music and enjoyment – but nothing could conceal the sound of Erix's cloak trailing the ground, or my heartbeat which found its way up into my throat.

I wondered if he felt it, the quickening thump as his hand held mine. Because his heart was a canter, tickling the soft of my palm, telling me the story of his innermost feelings.

We came to a stop just as the excitable sway of music shifted into a languid song. I would've cared for those who watched on, if Erix's intensity wasn't so devouring. Beneath his gaze, the way his breath caught as he peered down his nose at me, nothing else seemed to matter.

"Follow my lead, little bird," Erix whispered as he positioned my hands, one on his hip, the other held tight in his.

"Always," I replied, gaze down on our feet.

With the tip of his boot, he moved my feet into a wider stance. I felt silly, being moved around like a puppet by someone else, but I didn't stop him. There was something truly all-consuming about giving up my control. But part of the power came from allowing myself to hand it to Erix.

We began to move to the music, finding the rhythm, our feet carefully stepping around one another, making sure not to trip or step on toes. It took little time for the music to fade into the background, until the only beat I cared about was our breathing. It entwined together like the vines of roses, weaving and knotting, until it would never break apart.

"This certainly never happened the last time we were at a ball together," Erix said as he spun me, the room and crowd becoming a blur. "You were too busy causing me grief, and getting in my face with threats, if memory serves me."

"Consider yourself fortunate to get a second chance with me."

I looked away quickly, blushing, hating myself for enjoying this closeness. There was a guilt that came to giving up everything to Erix. Until I reminded myself that this was for him.

I did this for him – because this wasn't only the second chance but the only chance.

As Rafaela said, I had my goodbyes to make. I considered this act my first.

"When this is all over, what do you want from the new world?" I asked him, aware of the room blurring around us as we spun and wove amongst other dancing couples. "Indulge me with your answer."

It was a question I'd wondered about. Erix had only ever shown interest in helping me, but he had to have a plan for the future. Something *he* desired beyond my orbit.

Erix took a moment to ponder my question. All without his steel-hued eyes leaving me. "To live long enough to see you find true happiness."

A blush crept up my neck, staining my cheeks. "You couldn't have just said something simple, like building a home, or starting a chicken farm..."

"That is secondary," Erix said, his voice so soft it was a miracle I could hear it. "Anyway, when have I ever showed interest in chickens, Robin?"

I shrugged, spinning again as Erix led me around the room. "I don't know. You must have had interests long before I stumbled into your life. Surely, something you could take with you."

"If you asked me what I had wanted before that fateful day I saved you–"

"Saved me?" I squawked. "From how I remember it, I saved myself. Or did I imagine freezing that Hunter's body in half?"

Erix narrowed his eyes at me, smiling naturally at the memory. "Regardless of the intricacies, if you asked me that question, I would have answered that I only ever wanted freedom. I had run from my home, run from the truth of what I was to Doran. But you, in a way, already gave me everything I wanted. Consider me a partially fulfilled man."

It was brief, but Erix's gaze wandered from me toward where Elinor was dancing, the Nephilim she now spun with smiling brightly. Their whoops of enjoyment were a blessed song, far more potent than the one the band of musicians made with instruments of wood.

"Only partially?" I retorted, aware I was treading on uneven ground. "It sounds like there is still more you want, if you aren't entirely satisfied."

"Well, that would depend," Erix withdrew his eyes from Elinor Oakstorm, back to me. "There are others who have plans for me."

All this time, and I hadn't asked Erix what Elinor wanted to speak with him about. "Is home calling for you again?"

Home. The Oakstorm Court.

"It is."

"And do you want to go?"

Erix settled his eyes back on me, and I felt the force like a blow to the soul. "I have explained to Elinor that I will need time to think over her *offer*. Until then, you are my focus." A flash of sadness passed over him, darkening his eyes to grey storm clouds. "What do you want, little bird, when this is all over?"

"Don't divert the conversation. I asked you first."

"And I answered." Erix swung me around, dizzying my mind.

"That isn't good enough."

"Sometimes in life we do not always get what we want. But there is a beauty in giving up on one's deepest desires, if you know it is for a good reason. Is that good enough?"

His answer was as sharp as a two-sided blade. Simultaneously, he answered my initial question, and my response to him refusing me a complete answer, all in one.

It was my turn to answer. "I want Duncan to be well again, but more than that I want him to thrive in life. His upbringing was… tortured. His adulthood has hardly been any better. I wish for him to experience life where nothing but love surrounds him, because that is what he deserves." I choked so suddenly, balking on the tears that ached at the back of my throat. Swallowing them down, I managed to continue. "And I want you to find another purpose in life. Something that will be your duty, and your pleasure, considering those are your favourite two words."

"Opposed to this life I have?" Erix asked, head slightly tilted.

"Opposed to *me*."

My final word had the power to stop our dance.

Erix looked at me with such intensity, my knees almost buckled. "Impossible, little bird."

I looked away, trying to locate Althea and Gyah in the crowd, but when I needed them most, I couldn't find them. Not that I blamed them, this entire night was a pompous affair.

Suffocating on the tension, I pulled my hand from his, searching for an exit from the dance floor. I spotted grand open doors, leading out to a balcony. If I was not so desperate for fresh air, perhaps I would've remembered what happened the last time Erix and I left a ball together. Althea wouldn't be here to stop us from making a mistake this time.

"Come with me for some fresh air," I commanded. "They say the view from Lockinge Castle is one that would rival the city of Aurelia."

"My view here is just fine," Erix said, looking nowhere else but at me.

I couldn't form a reply. Instead, I tugged his hand, and Erix did as I asked. I felt him trail behind me, like a shadow. There were few constants in my life, but regardless of what happened – the trauma and horrors – Erix always found his way back.

The cool night air encased us the moment we stepped outside of the ballroom. I moved straight for the stone railing, gripping it for support, whilst I swept my gaze out across Lockinge. From this vantage, I could see the entire city. It was aglow with light, homes and establishments open late, preparing for the worldwide celebration of tomorrow's wedding. Nephilim patrolled the skies, some airborne whilst others were perched upon buildings.

Whatever had spooked Cassial had put the city under an intense guard.

A shiver crested over me, not unnoticed by Erix. It wasn't from the cold breeze, but the discomfort of this final conversation I knew I had to have with him. Erix knew that too, but still he unclasped his cloak from his shoulders, and swept it over mine.

"I want to thank you," I said without taking my eyes off the view.

"Is this why you brought me out here?" Erix asked. "I sense there is something you want to say to me, something that could not be said on the dance floor."

I swallowed the lump in my throat, knowing my next words had to be careful.

"I don't deserve you, Erix. Your loyalty, your… friendship." I didn't need to look at his face to know that word pained him. "But I'm going to ask something of you, something I have no right to, but I will ask it anyway because my track record of being selfish in my requests is impressive, so why stop now?"

Erix stepped up beside me, wings splaying enough to block out the ballroom behind us. Here, together, we existed only as one. "My greatest strength is my greatest weakness. Little bird, if you asked me to jump over this very balcony, I would."

"For a man with wings, that doesn't hit the same way you may think it would," I replied, my lips turning upwards at their corners.

"The sentiment is what matters," he replied.

"Why though?" I chirped, knowing my self-control was waning like the moon hung as witness above us. "Why be so willing to do such a thing for a person like me."

"Because I love you," Erix said plainly and without pause. "I have and will for a long time. And with that love comes the knowledge that I can never have you. I am content with that. Because knowing that another man shares the same feeling for you only makes me happy. I did not expect that was possible, but I guess my desire to see you cared for outweighs my need to be the one to provide it to you. That is why."

I fixed my eyes on the distant gates of the city, careful not to blink. If I did, the tears would stream, and I was so tired of crying. Unable to stand the silence, I pretended as though I had not heard Erix, and continued with my own request.

"What I need you to do for me will hurt you. But I'm too much of a monster not to ask it of you."

Erix stepped closer, his shadow falling upon me. "I will do anything."

His fingers tickled over the railing, coming to rest beside mine. The warmth he offered, the comfort – from his touch alone, gave me the power to force the final words out.

I turned to him, mere inches between us. He gazed down, as I looked up, our breaths coming out in clouds of mist beyond parted lips.

"What is it, Robin?" He asked, laying a hand on the side of my face, thumb brushing the pesky tear that fell from the corner of my eye.

"Look after Duncan for me," I said without hesitation. "Whatever happens, whatever comes from the fight ahead of us, I want you to always look out for him."

Erix's eyes widened a fraction, as if working out the final secret I'd not shared with him. "That is not a request you ever need to ask of me. You love him, so naturally I care for him. Anyone with the power to make you happy becomes an important asset in life. But..." Erix took a sharp breath in, using the moment to gather control of his wild emotions. "Why would you ask this of me, if *you* will be around to care for him?"

I looked away, unable to hold his stare, and that was answer enough. Before I could completely turn my back on him, a finger found my chin and turned my face back to his.

"Do not hide from me, little bird."

Overcome with the maelstrom that was my emotions, I did the impossible. It was the only thing I could think to do to stop Erix from pressing me for questions. My desperate attempt to run away from a conversation I knew would happen.

I lifted myself up on my toes and pressed my lips to his cheek.

My eyes closed, misjudging my aim until the corner of his mouth brushed the edge of mine. Trembling fingers found their way to the side of Erix's face, holding him there to stop him from drawing away, or moving the kiss to his mouth. But he didn't even attempt to.

His body was frozen, likely from shock, maybe disgust.

Erix's skin was as soft as I remembered. I wished he wasn't so welcoming, because I would've pulled back sooner. However, I was no strong man. And I didn't know just how much I'd needed this until it happened.

A discomfort sparked in my gut, but I battered it down. This kiss wasn't for me or my twisted wants, it was for Erix. My final goodbye, my way of closing a door, my attempt to settle peace: to leave him with a memory of me that would last an age.

The regret and guilt built in the seconds after I drew away. A tidal wave that swept at my body, pushing me back until the stone railing stopped me. Whereas my eyes were open and searching, Erix had his closed. He didn't open them for a while, not until he slowly lifted a finger to his cheek, convincing himself that the moment was real.

But by the time he opened his eyes, I was gone.

I moved on swift feet, sinking my teeth into my lower lip to stop myself from breaking.

I didn't remember getting to my bedchamber and closing the door. Not until I slumped down from it, staring numbly ahead at the empty room.

What I was left with was the feeling of his kiss – no matter how reluctant it was – painted across my mouth. Even as the tears fell over my mouth, the salt tickling across my tongue, I knew there was nothing in the world with the power to make me forget those seconds with him.

Not a few minutes later, I heard the familiar gait of feet beyond my closed door. They paused just outside. In my mind's eye I imagined Erix standing there, knuckles raised, wondering if he should knock or not.

He didn't. Not long after, the door to his room clicked open, and then closed, and I was left to simmer in this guilt. I found the mirror that I had slipped under the bed when I arrived, the one I was frightened to look in and see Duwar. Withdrawing it from the shadows, I held it up to my face and stared at my red-stained eyes, my blushed lips and the etching of pure agonising guilt that told stories upon my face.

I willed Duwar to show himself, for Duncan to follow so I could reveal the truth about kissing Erix's cheek and explain myself. Only my reflection haunted me, for hours of looking until my eyes ached, no demon showed themselves.

I was alone, suffering and yet knowing that my actions were my only option.

CHAPTER 17

It certainly was a perfect day for a wedding. The sky was clear, not a cloud in sight. There was a warmth to the air, as though spring was finally allowing summer to take over. I was almost too warm in the thick jacket that I was dressed in before dawn that morning, courtesy of Cassial's personal seamstress. I felt weighed down by material, glowing like some pompous prick dressed to be paraded before a crowd – which was exactly what today entailed.

In the open-air carriage, thundering across roads toward our destination, I distracted myself with the view, rather than the stoic guard sitting at my side.

Erix, for the most part, had pretended as though the almost-kiss last night had never happened. Duty was duty, and he played the game well. I did my part in playing along, conjuring small talk and discussing the weather like two strangers would. When in reality, I wanted nothing more than to lean into him and seek comfort for my sins, regardless of whether he could offer me that.

"We should be arriving at the hosting grounds in a few hours," Erix said just as our carriage slowed when our convoy began its descent into a small human town, a few miles outside of Lockinge. It was one of many stops planned along the route, allowing humans to witness our procession, building up the excitement for the wedding and making them feel a part of such a monumental day.

I understood why Cassial ordered for this to happen, but my anxiety was making patience an impossibility. By early afternoon, Althea and Gyah would be wed. By evening, I'd return to Imeria.

Thanks to my lack of sleep, I'd visited Rafaela before dawn crept over Durmain's sky. She had seemed in better spirits, her wounds all but healed, but her inner torment was too great. Since then, I already had word from Zarrel that Rafaela would follow us to Imeria – and with her arrival, we'd complete our plan of *truly* saving the world.

This was, all in all, my last few days.

"I understand the need for charade, to bolster relations and dress up a political move in silver thread and expensive materials, but this feels less like a celebration, and more like pageantry," I said, as I got my first view of yet another town with its main street full of humans. They, like Erix and I, wore their *best* outfits. Humans cheered and clapped – waving as the carriages of fey passed through. Ahead of us, Althea and Gyah led the convoy, doing their bit at thanking the crowds with waves of their own.

"It is all to further the greater cause," Erix reminded me. "There is nothing more powerful to bring two peoples together, then the promise of a party. And to Cassial's credit, he has done an iron-clad job at arranging this."

"I understand that," I replied, trying to forge a fake smile as our carriage began the procession. "Although that doesn't mean I have to like it."

"Not a marriage kind of man?" Erix asked out the corner of his mouth.

I scoffed. "Maybe a long time ago. Now, not so much."

Erix took my hand in his and squeezed. The sudden contact made me gasp. "Maybe that will change again. But for now, smile and wave. Allow yourself a day of enjoyment, you can afford it."

A day. It's all I had – and from the way Erix said it, I believed he was beginning to work it out. My comments last night, my request for him to look after Duncan, it all pointed to the fact that I wouldn't be around to do it myself.

In moments, we were engulfed in the cheers of humans. Crowds of them lined the streets, clapping and whistling, faces flushed with excitement and awe. Oh, how fickle the world was. Not three months ago, I was being screamed at for returning to Durmain, now they celebrated my presence.

A burst of light flashed across my eyes, almost blinding me. I winced back, my smile fading as I lifted a hand to my brow. It happened again, sunlight refracting off glass. I thought it was the reflection off a building, until suddenly the entire street lit up with it.

My blood cooled to ice in my veins as reality set in. The noise faded to the back of my mind as I took in the view of humans – hundreds – waving handheld mirrors at us.

"What *is* that?" I asked, more to myself than anyone in particular.

"I do not know," Erix answered, hands over his brow to block the glare. There was no denying his voice was as distressed as I felt.

I leaned over the carriage, sweeping my eyes from east to west, trying to make sense of what I was seeing. It was like shards of sun shone sporadically in the hands of the crowd.

"Excuse me," I said to the Nephilim leading our carriage. "Everyone we are passing is waving something at us. Do you know what is happening?"

The answer came swiftly. "Cassial has arranged a gift to be sent to every human and fey, to commemorate this special day. Memorabilia of sorts."

"Mirrors," Erix breathed, brow furrowed as more flecks of light cascaded over his face. "They are all holding mirrors."

Discomfort bubbled in my gut, sinking roots and refusing to let go.

"Why mirrors?" Accusation poisoned my tone.

Mirrors started this hell with Duwar. They had since taunted me, going so far as representing the very way Duncan prepared to end his life. Nothing about this brought me a sense of celebration or joy.

"After the poison that was Aldrick, he made many people fear a reflection for what they'd would find in it. There is no need for that anymore." The Nephilim pulled on the reins, slowing the carriage even more. "But that is only my understanding. The workings of Cassial are not for me to speculate. However, you can ask him yourself when we are reunited, which will be shortly."

And with that, the conversation was ended. Cut short, swift as the slice of broken glass across a neck.

I was dumfounded, unable to comprehend why he'd make such a decision, knowing the importance mirrors have had. Aldrick used them to converse with Duwar. Since then, I'd hardly been able to stare at my reflection, for fear of what I'd find. Except last night, when I fell asleep beside the mirror, wishing and hoping Duwar or Duncan would reveal themselves.

And here I was, surrounded by hundreds of mirrors.

It only got worse as the journey progressed.

For the final hours of our journey, every town, village and hamlet we passed through, it was clear these same gifts had made their way across the realm. There was hardly a hand spare.

At some point Erix had placed gentle fingers on my thigh and squeezed. The offer of comfort was welcome, but I barely recognised it beneath the thundering beat of my heart – and the desire to vomit all down the outfit Cassial had made for me.

Despite my discomfort, I recognised our destination as soon as we arrived. I almost didn't have the space in my mind to understand why we stopped here. But I didn't miss the message that was laid here.

Grove – my home, the human village I'd grown up in – was to host the wedding.

"Are we not heading further west?" I asked the Nephilim, who audibly huffed at the question. "I was informed the wedding was being hosted at the borderlands between Wychwood and Durmain, not here?"

"Plans have changed at the last hour," they replied. "There was a disturbance with a small band of Hunters yesterday. Do not worry though, they have been dealt with, but due to the disturbance, the wedding was decided to be moved here."

It certainly answered my question, but that still didn't mean it pleased me. Was this why Cassial left earlier? He said that it was not of our concern, but if the Hunters were massing near the Wychwood border, that certainly was *our* issue to share.

"Did you know?" I asked Erix who simmered in silent contemplation at my side. He didn't need to speak for me to know he was suffering with inner thoughts.

Erix was silent for a moment, staring ahead as the convoy slowed, one by one, and the guests from Lockinge departed. I spotted Althea and Gyah ahead, being shepherded off; Elinor Oakstorm followed with her Nephilim guards. From the looks on their faces they were equally confused, whether or not they knew the importance this place had to me.

"No, I did not," Erix finally replied, eyes wide and unblinking. As his lip curled over his teeth, I saw the twin points of fangs that had been left from his transformation into a gryvern. For a moment, he looked more monster than man.

I kept my gaze strained forwards, not wishing to let the memory of my past blind what was to happen next.

Erix leaned forwards, grasping our Nephilim guard by the shoulder. "We would like to be taken directly to Cassial before any proceedings."

There was no use of please. No room for niceties or manners.

"It will have to wait until after the ceremony," the Nephilim replied, shrugging off Erix's hand.

"Now," Erix growled, fervour pitched in his gravel tone.

The Nephilim regarded him, up and down, sizing the berserker up. Before either could make a scene before the adoring crowds of fey and humans watching, I took Erix's hand in mine, diverting his focus back to me.

"Not now, not *here.*"

Erix snapped out of his trance-like state, following the tilt of my head to the hundreds of people watching.

He calmed down, enough to leave the Nephilim and stay by my side.

As we departed the carriage, I had no choice but to drink in my surroundings. I looked around at the adoring crowd, people I recognised from my childhood. They didn't cheer when they saw me, not like those we'd passed during the day of travel. Early afternoon was upon us, and with it the gleam of bright sunlight. A few clouds had built over the sky, foreshadowing the ominous feeling I harboured inside.

A path had been made for us to walk through, leading directly toward an old church which, in previous years, had been used as a school rather than a place of worship. It was the very place I'd had my education, limited though it may have been. And now it looked refreshed, the walls draped in the splendour of the Creator's emblem, angelic warriors standing guard, wings used as barriers to keep the humans separated from us.

Discomfort seeded deep in my gut. If I had the ability to turn away, I would have. But I needed to see Cassial, I needed to speak with him, understand the need for mirrors.

The church was overflowing with humans, sitting around sharing excited whispers at our arrival. There was barely a space to spare, the room crammed full of life. There was also an overwhelming presence of Nephilim. I searched for fey nobility, hoping to find them amongst the crowds. I spotted one fey, his face familiar with sky-blue eyes. For a moment I thought Doran Oakstorm had rose from the dead, until the stranger fixed his eyes on me and I noticed the subtle differences.

A name came to my mind, spoken by Elinor days ago. Ailon Oakstorm, Doran's brother and the thorn in Elinor's side. He kept to the corner, head bowed once again as though he didn't want to be seen. Perhaps his discomfort came from being the only fey here amongst a hoard of humans.

Erix and I entered last, the doors closing behind us. We were submerged in a blanket of dim light. Candles danced with flames across every surface, offering the only source of light. Any and all windows had been covered with banners, as had the walls. Each one displaying the symbol of the Creator in elegant gold stitching.

"Cassial isn't here," I muttered, catching eyes with Althea and Gyah, who stood before a dais. Elinor had been seated in a chair of dark stone, her arms naturally laid out across the arm rests. Zarrel was there – looming over her, the golden hammer in his hands, not strapped to his shoulders.

In fact, one quick glance around and I saw that all the Nephilim had weapons.

Silence fell upon the room as the clang of the great doors settled. The excited murmurings of the crowd settled to whispers as they anticipated the ceremony to begin.

But nothing happened. No announcement, no grand display that would start the wedding. Only silence, thick and heavy.

"What's the meaning of this?" Althea's voice called out, echoing up the stone walls, bringing with it the heat boiling inside of her. She was swallowed in a dress of pure white. Whoever made her outfit had made the layers of material look like pale tongues of flame. Her bodice was tight, her heels higher than anything I'd seen her wear before. Red hair had been gathered in a bun atop her head, the strands of hair pulled taut across her scalp. Not a detail was out of place. She looked stunning, but that was the exact thing that unsettled me.

This wasn't the Althea I knew.

"Patience, Queen Althea Cedarfall," Zarrel replied, candlelight glinting off his weapon of truth. "Our ceremony will begin shortly. There is a final matter that must be secured before we can begin."

I drank in the rest of the room, seeing doors barricaded by the broad bodies of Nephilim, never a gauntleted hand straying from a weapon. My fingers itched, tingling as though preparing themselves for something I could not yet name.

"What *matter* is this you speak of?" Gyah demanded, the trained eyes of a solider noticing the unbalanced nature of the room. Her suit was form-fitting, a cape clasped to her shoulders, dragging out on the floor behind her. She, like the rest of us, had no weapons to note.

Elinor was the same. I searched for the Elmdew representative then, wondering if they too looked as uncomfortable in their worry. But I couldn't find them, not amongst the crowd. I searched the room three times, and still didn't locate them.

Outside the church, the crowd roared with cheers, reminding us that this was a celebratory day, although it felt nothing of the sort.

"Perhaps you would like to take a seat for the time being," Zarrel commanded, gesturing to the spare stone thrones that had been erected on the dais. A fourth waited for me, opposite where Elinor Oakstorm sat. "Cassial will join us soon. I apologise for the delay, this was not how we planned for this."

Cassial was many things, but lacking in detail was not one of them. Everyone up until now had praised his planning, and yet there seemed to be a problem on the single most important day he had arranged.

Something about that didn't sit right with me.

"Answer the question," Gyah snapped, baring teeth toward Zarrel. A few muffled gasps filled the room, spreading in a wave across the humans who watched from the pews.

Fear, sharp and sudden, filled the air.

"Please, calm down," Zarrel said, but spoke directly to the humans, a sickly sweet kindness spoiling his tone.

Gyah, realising how she'd caused this reaction, simmered back with a blush across her cheeks.

"There is a final guest we are missing, someone of great importance," Zarrel explained, white teeth on display thanks to his plastered, ear-to-ear grin. "Soon enough he will come, and we can begin with the proceedings."

"It looks like there are a few guests missing," I called out.

Zarrel's smile faltered as he turned to me. I noticed his fists tighten around the handle of Rafaela's hammer, which made me reach out for my magic.

What I found inside of me was silence. An abyss of never-ending silence.

Before I could understand why, Erix loosed a keening scream. I spun around to find him falling to the ground, clutching his head as though his skull was shattering apart.

"Erix," I gasped, joining him on the ground, hands reaching, mind a storm of panic. I was vaguely aware that Althea attempted to reach us too, but Nephilim stopped her by crossing spears. If she had access to her power, no doubt those spears would be husks of ash in seconds. But the lack of heat and fire proved that she too suffered the same powerless fate as I did.

Erix rocked backwards, his screams singing of the pain he was in. I searched for the cause, but he was all but physically unharmed. No one had got close enough to hurt him, and yet he was still incapable of speaking, of answering me.

"Someone help him," I cried out, scanning the crowds who attempted to scramble out of the pews. "Please. A healer, someone. Help him!"

The lack of response tore me apart from the inside.

"In good time, Robin. For now though, it would seem we have our signal, and we can begin," Zarrel said, his voice cutting above Erix's suffering.

I watched, through furious tear-filled eyes, as Zarrel turned to his fellow Nephilim. He offered them a nod, a signal, and said, "It's time. Brothers, sisters. Prepare yourselves for the arrival of your Saviour."

Humans fought from the pews, looking to the closed door in confusion. Chaos reigned this small room, filling it with Erix's suffering, and the utter horror that spoiled each and every human.

The guards blocking the door refused to move. They let no one out, and no one in.

"Make it stop!" Erix howled like an animal in a trap when the room exploded in light.

Squinting against the glare, I watched as the banners covering the walls were pulled down, revealing floor-to-ceiling glass. Mirrors lined every possible space, reflecting the horror on our faces, and the placid, expectant faces of the Nephilim.

My reflection looked back at me ten times over, wide eyed and red faced. It made the chamber look far larger than it was in reality, turning the crowd of panicked humans into a horde of scared people trying to flee.

Then, as suddenly as it began, Erix's screams stopped. He gasped for breath, his hands grappling at my arms. I didn't notice as Nephilim swept over to Erix and accosted him, dragging him out of my embrace.

"They are dead," Erix bellowed, eyes ringed with dark shadows, pointed teeth flashing over pale lips.

"Who?" I screamed as rough hands dragged me away from Erix, thrusting me to the ground.

"Maren. Gregory. Cassial has–" A metal-plated fist dove into the side of Erix's face, knocking him to the ground. Humans screamed. Bedlam reigned. The rest of Erix's words came out in the form of blood and spit, splattering against the ground. His lip had split, the mouth I'd touched with my own ruined in a single moment.

Growling, I sprang at the Nephilim, all teeth and nail, a berserker in my own right. I grabbed a fistful of feathers, tearing back with my might, making one of them yell in agony.

"Release him!" I cared for nothing else. "Get your fucking hands off him."

I looked to Althea, Gyah, Elinor – anyone to help. But they were frozen in their seats, unmoving. Physically trapped, whereas their expressions revealed their inner struggle. Althea was the only one who attempted to fight free, but she was bound by stone, thick hands of it rising up from the throne before flattening over her wrists.

"Labradorite," Elinor Oakstorm cried out, straining against the power of the throne, veins bulging in her neck. "They're made of labradorite, Robin!"

I saw the truth in that moment. As light cracked out of Elinor's skin, seeping into the stone as though it was a sponge, absorbing her power.

No, not her power. The key. The final key to Duwar's gate.

I took in the scene of this perfectly laid plan. The ruse that had us sign away control of the fey lands in the place of a baby prince, all for the Nephilim to finally grasp full control.

Magic built beneath my skin, itching for a release, but the heavy presence of something was keeping it at bay, refusing the release I desperately desired. "Resist it," Althea commanded, frantic eyes pinned to Elinor. "Don't give it up…"

Elinor's head dropped, chin to chest, and didn't move again.

"No," I bellowed as Nephilim took my body, forcing me onto my knees. "My magic… I can't feel it, Althea."

"And – mine!" Althea screamed back, continuing to resist her stone bindings. "I can't feel it."

A figure swept in front of me, blocking my view of my friends.

"That would be the small deposits of iron which have been threaded throughout your clothes," Zarrel announced, pacing to where I was being held down by his winged followers. He swung the golden hammer as though it weighed no more than a sack of twigs. Then, as he stepped into me, he held it up, laying the flat cool metal against my chest. "Before you can begin to strip, this room has also been bathed in it. Last night, the food and wine also tainted. For the safety of our guests, above anything else." Zarrel gestured to the humans whose fear and confusion rippled off them. "We wouldn't want such devious creatures to threaten anyone else, now that we know the truth."

At the use of the final word, I felt the draw of power beat between where the hammer touched and my flesh. Rafaela had used it against me once before, but the draw was stronger now, frantic in the hands of a man like Zarrel.

"And yet you stand here," I sneered, muscles straining, a throbbing vein protruding across my forehead. "With weapons held in your hands. Who are you keeping them safe from, us or *you*?"

Zarrel tilted his head, popping a hip to display just how little of a threat he found me. "Well, Robin, that would all depend on you, wouldn't it? Would you like to tell us all what you have been keeping all to yourself, lying to us – your allies – all this time?"

I squirmed against the pressure of Rafaela's golden hammer, but its influence was already upon me. There was nothing I could do to stop the truth rising out of me.

"Duwar," I cried as the name was dragged out of me.

I couldn't look to my friends even if I wanted to, my focus was on Zarrel, the hammer, and the truth was leached from me.

"Do you see how freeing the truth can be?" Zarrel asked, but didn't wait for an answer as he pressed on. "Tell me, Robin Icethorn. Where is Duwar?"

I felt the shocked gazes of my friends scoring into me. But my focus was on the golden hammer, and the drawing persuasion as it forced me to speak the truth. I tried to regain control, forcing out the truth in my own way, trying to save myself some of my secrets. "In – Wychwood."

"Resist it, Robin!" Erix cried out, voice muffled by the blood in his mouth. "Don't give—"

I could only imagine his sudden silence was a result of another fist to his jaw.

"But *where* in Wychwood, Robin Icethorn?"

I sank my teeth into my lower lip, splitting skin, trying everything to stop the truth from coming out. Zarrel forced the hammer into my skin, making the sway of its power impossible to ignore.

As the final answer came out, I bellowed it across the church, so loud the sky far above would hear. "Duwar is inside of Duncan Rackley!"

Zarrel withdrew the hammer, satisfied with the answer. "Of course, I already know, courtesy of our dearest sister Rafaela. Although for the sake of our relations, I appreciate your cooperation."

I didn't have a choice: the hammer had taken away my free will.

In an act of divine fate, I heard the muffled cry of a woman. I snapped my head around to watch as Rafaela, garbed in dirtied clothes, her hunched back stained brown with new blood, was brought out of the shadows. She was held in the arms of two Nephilim, golden blades held at her throat and one at her gut.

One eye had swollen shut, the skin black and blue with bruises. Even her mouth suffered the same fate. But even through her obvious agony, she locked her single eye on mine and said, "I am so sorry, Robin. I had no choice."

Guilt, the familiar friend it had become, rose within me. I'd seen her this morning, and yet left her in the hands of someone like Zarrel.

"Believe it or not," Zarrel taunted, "Rafaela is telling the truth, she really did not have a choice. I only needed to use the hammer on her to get the knowledge out of her. Such a *unique* weapon, one I have grown rather fond of using since it was given to me."

From the pain across Rafaela's face, I knew exactly what means Zarrel had used to extract the information.

All around me, my world was crumbling, and I was helpless to stop it. I fixed my eyes on Erix, finding strength in his unwavering glare. My eyes swept to Althea and Gyah who looked at me like I was a stranger. Then to Elinor, whose soft expression of pity nearly tore me apart like the claws of a beast.

I was a fish out of water, tangled in a net of iron, powerless and helpless.

Then my mind went to Duncan, who was no different. In the moments of chaos, I put together a few pieces of the puzzle. Cassial missing, the gryvern guards protecting Duncan now dead.

I strained against the arms of my captor, not caring for the pinch that bruised my skin. "This isn't a game. Duncan is dangerous–"

"Duncan is a *gift*," came a voice from the mirror – *within* the mirror. "In ways that I could not possibly begin to explain with the little time we have."

Every person in the room turned, human and fey, to find Cassial's reflection staring outwards from the mirrors. A familiar room behind him, an empty bed layered with chains, a sideboard beside it with the hint of a syringe waiting, the vial full of golden liquid.

We were looking into Duncan's room. Back in Imeria.

A keening cry rose up in my throat, but couldn't get past the lump of dread there. Behind Cassial lay two bloodied, torn gryvern bodies. Maren and Gregory – dead – just as Erix had told me. He must've sensed their murder through their connection, which caused his reaction. The pain he felt inside had been theirs.

My eyes finally swept away from the corpses to the man kneeling, head bowed, at Cassial's feet.

"Duncan," I exhaled, an agony unlike anything I'd felt before threading up through every inch of my body.

Cassial's meaty fingers tangled in the length of his dark hair, lifting it up until everyone watching could see his face. There was no denying it was him, and yet I couldn't bring myself to care for my friends' reactions, how they would view me now my greatest lie had been revealed.

For the first time, I wanted Duncan to be the very thing I had feared him for.

Dangerous.

"Robin, Robin, Robin." Cassial beamed with pride, his bright eyes glittering with the hunger of a starved man. "What a deceptive little creature you are, harbouring such a threat behind your walls."

"No," I gasped, hoisted to my feet by uncaring hands. "I was protecting–"

"Lying now will not get you out of this one," Cassial interrupted. "The damage is very clearly *done*."

Then why did he look so pleased? Why did Cassial look like a man who'd just won a game I didn't know I was playing?

"My followers," Cassial shouted, and every Nephilim in the room shifted. "Allow the humans to leave, get them away from this danger the fey have brought to our door once again."

Watching from beyond the mirror, the doors were thrown open, allowing humans to escape from the perfect picture of danger that Cassial was painting.

And yet he was the one with dark blood – gryvern blood – splattered across his armour, dead bodies littered on the floor behind him.

Once the last human escaped beyond the church, the doors were closed once again, the Nephilim returning to their places, weapons held ready.

"Poor humans, what a terrible shock you have put them through," Cassial said, beaming, hands still tugging carelessly at Duncan's head. "Between me and you, I had my own plans to free Duwar today, until I discovered that task was already completed for me. Imagine my relief that you, Robin Icethorn, have been harbouring the power required to fix the unbalance of this world. I should thank you, truly. The effort you have saved me is great. For that, granted you act responsibly, you will be rewarded."

Maybe it was the lack of humans watching me, or the knowledge that Duncan in danger, but I found the energy to act.

My body moved without aid of my mind. Drawing on training and skill, I slipped out of the hands quickly, spinning around and snatching a short blade from the sheath at Zarrel's waist.

This was what Erix had trained me for, relying on my body instead of my power.

I swung the short blade like a mad man, attempting to carve a space out between me and the betrayal suffocating me. Erix tried to fight free too, but the more he squirmed, the more Nephilim came to assist with him being held down. It took little effort to splay him on the floor, positioning his body face down. Those Nephilim who didn't pin him to the ground held his wings at an angle, proving that one tug would rip them free.

"Choose your next action wisely," Zarrel warned, so close to me that I felt his hot breath singe the skin on my ear. "Remember the treaty you signed. Think of all the innocent life outside this church, the humans who will be harmed in this crossfire if you make a move against us. Or, are we too late for that, considering what secret you've been keeping from us…"

My grip faltered enough for Zarrel to take the blade from my hand and return it confidently to his belt.

"*Duncan Rackley,*" Cassial said his name, command lacing his baritone voice. "Open the way for us to pass. We have a reunion to attend."

Duncan's verdant eyes were overwhelmed with the power of the parasite within him. He looked at me, through the mirror, as web-like cracks formed across its surface.

"I warned you," Duncan – Duwar said, voice tinged with sadness that I couldn't ignore. "Your hesitation has caused this, darling."

Not a second after he used his nickname against me, glass shattered across the room, turning the mirror into a doorway. One which Cassial dragged Duncan through with ease, passing through time and space like it was nothing.

Heavy boots slammed against the ground, whilst Duncan's knees were dragged over broken blades of glass. Cassial didn't care for the vessel, only what lurked inside. But I didn't understand. Duwar was the Creator's enemy – the opposing power to the Nephilim's master. If anything, they should want to destroy it, once and for all.

"Duwar is a demon," I spat. "Duwar's very presence goes against everything you live for. Every lie you accuse me of has only ever been given whilst I found a way to solve this problem."

"Lies on both accounts," Cassial replied, followed by a deep belly laugh. "Although I admit, the first has been spread by us for generations. Duwar being a demon, crafting that very perspective to further our own plans. I am confident you have many questions. So, sit and listen. I will do you the honour of explaining ourselves."

My mind was frantic, but I knew what Duncan's fate would be in the hands of the Nephilim.

Death. Certain death. The very thing I had fought hard to prevent.

"Cassial. There is nothing to discuss. Don't do this. I beg you," I hissed, spitting at the Nephilim who grasped me, holding me in place. "There are other ways to remove Duwar from this realm, ways that do not include killing him. If you hurt him–"

"Hurt Duncan?" Cassial pressed a hand to his chest, mocking shock. "As if I could harm him any more than you have, Robin. Look at how you have treated him. The torment, the pain – the punishment. And all because you didn't recognise what you held so dear."

"A demon!"

"Wrong. Wrong. *Wrong*," Cassial replied, lifting Duncan's head again from where it lolled to his chest. "You have been *told* that Duwar is bad. A demon-god. You have been told stories woven by us to believe that Duwar is the Defiler – a beast, ruin, a monster. But the truth is so much simpler than that."

Duwar's words filled my mind, just as the same words left Cassial's mouth. "Duwar is power."

I am power.

I couldn't think – couldn't breathe – as a small spark of relief turned to terror.

Hate pinched Cassial's face into a mask of disdain. He narrowed eyes on me, burning pits of endless promises of suffering. And yet, his smile never faltered. It morphed into something darker, but still drew at the corners of his mouth. "I have no plans to kill Duncan today. Whereas his potential was wasted in your hands, in mine he will help change the world. Fix the wrongs left in the wake when Altar betrayed our god."

I grappled with what he said, but one thing clicked in my mind. "You never wanted to protect the keys. You... you wanted to use them."

Cassial looked at me though his dark lashes, this perspective of his face morphing into something utterly demonic. "Yes, Robin. That is exactly what we wished to do."

CHAPTER 18

My heart thundered under every point of contact as Zarrel clasped my wrists behind my back. He moved me toward a throne of labradorite, seating me next to Althea who strained against her own bindings.

The Nephilim pinning Erix down didn't dare move. Every now and then I would get a flash of his eyes – the whites entirely consumed by the black haze of the monster his bloodline had made him. He continued to fight against them, more monster than man now as the berserker had taken over.

Erix would fight fang and claw to get to me, and I didn't ever want him to stop. If anything, he was occupying many of the Nephilim, which left fewer of them to deal with myself.

"Do you forget yourself, Cassial!" Althea sneered, veins bulging in her neck as she strained forwards in her seat. "We have signed the treaty. You break it by harming us. Your actions alone have forfeited the human realm–"

"I forfeit *nothing*," Cassial snapped, his large hand not straying from the back of Duncan's neck. "From where I'm standing, Althea Cedarfall, the fey have lied to the world. You've harboured power in your realm – a power strong enough to wipe out everyone who opposes you. What would the humans outside this door think if they knew the truth? Not to mention those who'd not long witnessed the events in this room, they have seen what your kind have hidden... they know the truth of whose deceit runs deeper."

That was why they filled the church with humans, so they could witness Cassial, their Saviour, discovering my dark secret and pretending to protect them from it.

Duncan began coughing, drawing my attention from our hope of escape to him. Blood spluttered beyond his cracked lips, staining his chin in gore. Cassial grimaced, drawing back at the sight of the blood, as if he wasn't already covered in it.

"Duncan is unwell," Althea said, but I could see from the pinch of her brow that she knew it was more than that. "This is surely a grand misunderstanding. Do not let this misunderstanding be cause for a war no one will benefit from."

"What do you know of war, Althea?" Cassial spoke from his chest, lifting his chin to reveal just how confident he was. "We – the Nephilim, favoured children of the Creator – will do anything to prevent such a thing from happening again. This is the very purpose of us being here today. And now, with the source of *chaos* that is Duwar, you shall be powerless to stop us from righting the wrongs Altar cursed the realms with his greed."

I sat in silence, my thoughts were a maelstrom, putting together the details of everything. The mirrors in the hands of the humans, that had been Cassial's plan. This illusion of a wedding, to bring the heads of the fey courts under one roof. The labradorite, arranged in a perfect circle – the ground amongst it swirling with mist.

"Elinor," I called out, fixing my eyes on the woman across from me. Her head was slumped, her chest rising and falling with heavy breaths. I knew – without a doubt – that the Oakstorm key was successfully within the throne she sat upon. Proof the transference of power had worked was in the way the mist gathered and swirled, spinning in the centre of the four thrones. "Elinor, look at me."

But without the existence of the other three, there was no hope to open the gate and lock Duwar back in it. However, it was clear that was far from what Cassial wanted.

"Elinor, look at me!" I demanded.

She didn't have the strength left in her to even lift her head.

"Do not waste your breath, Robin. Elinor Oakstorm has served her purpose, let her rest."

"You've tricked us," I said, spearing my accusation like an archer, aiming straight for Cassial. "You brought us here to attempt to open Duwar's gate. That was your plan all along."

"It was, and I have," Cassial admitted with a smile full of pride. "One remaining key was better than all four. I hoped that opening a sliver of Duwar's gate, paired with the mirrors to refract the image of the power – the belief from a world united, all watching, would provide the remaining strength needed to free Duwar. If anything, I could go through, as Duncan and Erix had, and claim the power waiting on the other side. But can you imagine how much time I've wasted, if only I knew that you, Robin Icethorn, have been keeping the power all to yourself. Of course, I had my suspicions. With the incessant amount of letters you sent to Rafaela, I wondered why you had so much interest in our customs. I just didn't think for a moment that it was because you were keeping Duwar to yourself all this time." His lip curled as he regarded me, before spitting his final words out. "Selfish little king."

"So much for protectors of the keys," Gyah hissed. Her eyes were fixed on Cassial, as if he was the only person in the world. It was in the reflection of them that I saw her desire to tear flesh with her teeth. "That is why you punished Rafaela, because she knew what you planned, and she went against you!"

Cassial's eyes darkened at the mention of Rafaela. "Exactly. But in the end, her betrayal matters not. We have what we need, her efforts and the suffering she has experienced mean little. I've won in the end." He snapped his gaze to Rafaela who stood stock still in the grasp of Nephilim. "Isn't that right, *sister*?"

"It is not over yet," Rafaela replied, chin jutting out.

"Is it not?" Cassial replied, sweeping a large hand out to us. "Our purpose was not to protect the keys, you knew that."

Rafaela gathered something behind screwed lips, then spat out toward where Cassial stood. He didn't even flinch.

"Why?" Althea asked, voice calm as a steady flame. "Why the deception?"

"You have been told what we wanted you to know, and you believed it because you were desperate for aid and blinded by Aldrick's movements. The truth was we had come to your realm not to protect the keys, but to *collect* them. That was until one of our own betrayed us. But in the end, Rafaela will be forgiven, because without her involvement, I would never have known the impossible was possible." He bowed his head at her, and she turned away in dismissal. "I should thank you, sister."

"Do not be mistaken, Cassial." Rafaela scowled, lips tensing a second before she spat on the ground. "I would destroy them all over again, if given the chance."

"Shame that," Cassial replied. "Truly a waste of such brilliant talents."

"What do you want, Cassial?" It was the only question I could ask. He had Duncan in his grasp, he had planted the seed to the humans that we had deceived them, that we were the threat.

In answer, Cassial yanked Duncan's head back up, forcing us to all look at his face again. Bile burned at the back of my throat at the state of him. I had done this. My attempts to protect the world had weakened Duncan. He was in no fit state to fight, and perhaps the demon within him had no desire to, either.

Then again, Cassial had confirmed that Duwar wasn't a demon. Just power, a source of great power that the gods fought over.

I wasn't sure what I could believe anymore.

"It is not my wishes and wants that matter, but those of my Creator. This fight began long before any of us were born or made, back during a time where monsters warred, when Altar tricked the Creator, offering a power that was promised to be shared, to his own children."

"All this for a bit of power," Gyah sneered. "Desperate."

"Perhaps." Cassial pondered his next words, deciding that the answer was not required. When he spoke again, it was to Duncan. He brought his lips so close to Duncan's ear, a feral rage exploded within me. Before I could shout, the cold kiss of a dagger pressed against my throat. "We will show the rest of the world what the fey have done here – attempting to free Duwar again and successfully achieving it in you. This scene will be refracted across every mirror in every realm."

"No," Duncan fought out his refusal, surprising me.

Cassial leaned down, lips brushing his ear. "Do it, or find your lover's neck split wide."

Zarrel, as if proving Cassial's threat, dug the edge of the dagger in just a little more until skin parted, and a bead of blood ran down the blade. There was no pain to greet me, not with the tidal wave of fury encompassing every inch of my body and soul.

"Please." Duncan's plea was as broken as his body. It pained me, the ache across my heart intensifying. "Do not hurt him."

Even in his weak state, he still fought for me. I didn't deserve it, not after what I had done to him.

"Do as I ask," Cassial said, "and he will live. I promise–"

"Cassial lies!" Rafaela broke free, using the little strength she had to knock a Nephilim to the ground. "The Nephilim will harness Duwar's power and eradicate every fey from this world." The shout rang out across the church, echoing up the walls of glass and stone. "It is why *we* wished to destroy them. To prevent ruin unlike anything Aldrick could have wanted. It was the *Fallen* who–"

Her scream died in her throat. I didn't need to turn behind me to know why. I could see in the reflection as Rafaela dropped to the ground, hands clasped before her. Blood trickled down her face, courtesy of the fist that had just silenced her by connecting to her jaw.

"Fallen?" Cassial laughed at the word. "We are the *Faithful*, Rafaela. The Creator's favoured who only wish to give Him what was always desired. I am his Saviour, I will bring forth the world the Creator wanted for us, using the very power Altar refused to share."

Rafaela pushed up on trembling arms. "You lost your way many years ago, Cassial. You are no Saviour; you are *no* Faithful."

"Gag her!" Cassial shouted, pointing at Rafaela. "I had hoped Rafaela would repent and see the light, but I can see that her poisonous disbelief runs deep."

Outside the church, a chorus of shouts rose where the crowds were confused about what was happening inside the church. Had the humans who escaped told them of Duwar? Would they turn against us, or run from us like we were the monsters Cassial wanted them to think we were?

"Show the world, *Duwar*. I know you're listening." Cassial tugged hard at Duncan's head again, snapping it back. "Let them see the truth of what happens here."

I cried out, spittle flying beyond my lips. "Stop it!"

Erix roared and fought. Gyah and Althea attempted to break free. Only Elinor was left, silent, head bowed, as the stone drank the power from her blood.

Zarrel clamped a hand on my shoulder, forcing me back into the seat. The blade no longer mattered as Duncan finally opened his eyes, swirling dark with power. My emotions became an afterthought as every mirror in the room shifted and revealed a new scene, unnatural and yet real all the same.

Human and fey looked on, the shock and horror plastered across their faces. If I could see them through the mirrors, I knew that they too watched on from their places across Durmain.

"Citizens of Durmain," Cassial's voice boomed, vibrating the glass at his back. "See for yourselves the lies which the fey have spread. We offered them peace, and they responded with wishes for complete power over us. Duwar was never destroyed, but kept by the selfish king, Robin Icethorn, as a weapon to use against you. Feast your eyes upon their power, see how the fey wished to harness it and become your overlords, using our kindness against us."

In that moment I knew just how the scene looked to those watching. Four fey sat on thrones, Cassial in the centre of swirling mist, clutching Duncan by the neck, whose eyes flamed boiling red with power.

And it was working. Combined with the opened crack in Duwar's gate, the presence of Duwar and with it, the growing belief in the demon-god, ungodly magic was fuelled. Enough that the slither of power left in Duwar's realm broke free, the wrong side of the gate.

This *had* to end.

A seed of knowing grew inside, showing me the one and only path for this to end. Duncan Rackley had to die, to forever remove Duwar from this game of control and power.

What came next was my chance – a gift from Erix.

It was in the reflection of the outside world that I saw them coming. A cloud of grey leather and wings, spearing across the sky in a formation. Gryvern. There'd been a time that seeing the creatures amassed sparked horror in me. They were the weapon of my family's murder, the tool used by Doran Oakstorm. But now, as they filled the skies, their blood-curdling screams beyond the church walls, I welcomed it.

Erix controlled them now. He'd given up fighting against his guards. Instead, he was laughing. Deep rumbling chuckles that built in his chest, ricocheting across the room.

"You wanted monsters," Erix sneered, blood and spit leaking over of his ruined lips. "I'll give you them."

The muffled cheers outside the church melted to screams as the gryvern flocked over their skies. I felt Zarrel relax his hold of the blade, enough to allow me to cock my head back and crack my skull into his nose.

Nephilim or not, his bones shattered, blood spraying. I ducked under the blind sweep of his arms, turned and – for good measure – smashed my fist into his face again.

If the nose hadn't broke the first time, it certainly had the second.

Deep down, it felt good to punch him. *Very* good. I gave him two more swift jabs until he choked on his broken teeth.

The golden hammer dropped to the ground before Zarrel could use it. Face smeared in blood, he tried to kneel and pick it up, but I slammed my boot down on his hand, crushing fingers and then swept my knee up and cracked it into his jaw.

In hindsight, I knew the world would watch on as I attacked one of their famed guardians, but I didn't care.

To save the world, I *had* to act before I contemplated killing Duncan. If I gave myself room to think about it, I would hesitate. Deep down, dread kindled. But I had no choice…

Unless I finally accepted Duwar, just as it offered.

In a heartbeat, the room exploded in chaos. Gryvern tore at the doors to the church, flinging them off as like they were made of paper. The Nephilim inside the church had no option but to fight back, leaving Althea and Gyah with enough of a chance to free themselves.

But they were not the only ones.

Erix cut across the church, wings beating, clashing shoulder-first into Cassial's middle. I was aware that Duncan was flung to the ground from the crack his skull made against the slabbed floor. The mirrors returned to their normal reflections, no longer sharing the scene with the thousands outside this church.

I scrambled to move toward him, but someone heavy crashed into me.

Back on the ground, I was spun up to face the body atop me. I lifted my arms up to protect my face, catching a glimpse of the demonic glower Zarrel shared as he peered down at me.

"You'll be the first of the fey to die," Zarrel jeered, hoisting the dagger up in one hand, his shattered teeth black with blood. "I'll gladly watch the life leave your eyes; you really were an irritating little–"

Zarrel never got the chance to finish his sentence.

There was a blur of gold to his side, followed by the meaty thwack of metal against flesh. I'd seen a head cave in once before – when Erix had smashed Tarron Oakstorm's skull with his bare fists.

I watched the golden hammer arch upon him, driven by a vengeful Rafaela with eyes burning with rage, it dented Zarrel's head from the side. His eyes bulged, then popped. Blood and brain matter rained down on me. Chips of bone and a mass of hair stuck to my skin. I wanted to scream, but if I opened my mouth, it would've filled with the death of the Nephilim.

"Get... up," Rafaela croaked, tears streaming down from furious eyes. "Fight, before we lose our only chance of stopping this."

I took her hand, dragged out from beneath the weight of Zarrel's limp body. I clawed at the gore over my eyes, flicking it down my iron-spoiled clothes. Vision cleared, I searched the chaos for Duncan, only to find his body splayed out across the floor. Nephilim circled, weapons drawn, wings splayed, but it was not to hurt Duncan.

No. Althea and Gyah guarded him – even knowing what lingered within – and they still put their bodies before him, stolen weapons raised, bodies as powerless as mine thanks to the iron in their clothes.

"You welcomed punishment because you knew what you did was right," I said, mind spanning between the labradorite thrones and Duncan. "They do not deserve you."

"Not now, Robin." Rafaela made a move, but I drew her back.

"You knew Cassial always wanted this?"

She locked eyes with me, and her pain was so evident I felt it like a bolt to the gut. "I did, and I had hoped we could solve this before this outcome was ever a possibility. But after you left me this morning, Zarrel turned on me. He used the hammer on me and drew out the truth of why you needed me."

So many emotions rose up, threatening to choke me. All the same, Zarrel's body was beneath me, brain matter leaking onto the old stone floor. I stepped over him, wishing the agony he suffered was great – he deserved it tenfold.

"I know you have questions, and if we survive this you will get answers to them all," Rafaela said, just before she pushed me back and swung the hammer at another charging Nephilim. This one used a shield to block the blow, but the sound of connecting metal boomed over me like a wave.

"I'm sorry, Robin. But Duncan must die."

I gritted my teeth, knowing she was right but still clinging to my final hope. "Let me accept Duwar, then you do what is needed. You end this."

A fierce sadness passed behind her eyes, and then she nodded. "Get to Duncan – complete the transference and I will... finish this."

Finish you.

The plan had always been so simple. This was how it was to end. But without being in Irobel, Rafaela couldn't bind me in labradorite. Death was the only option. It was Duncan, or me. I knew what I preferred. But for that I had a room of warring angels and demons to get through.

My body buzzed with a rush of pure adrenaline. I quicky tore the dagger from Zarrel's stiff, dead fingers and ran for Duncan. The Nephilim were so focused on Althea and Gyah as they fought side by side, they didn't notice me come in from behind them.

I drove the blade into the middle of one of their backs. From the way their legs gave out instantly, I knew I'd severed an important nerve. The next Nephilim had some warning that I was to attack. Before I could thrust the dagger forwards, their wings spun, shielding them. Amongst the mound of feathers, the force ripped the blade out of my hand. Before they could turn their full might on me, Gyah pounced. She wrapped her thighs around the Nephilim's neck, grabbed his head and twisted harshly to the side.

There was a sickly snap of bone. Nephilim fell to the ground, their body softening Gyah's fall. She sprang up, turned fast and threw herself at the next. She spared me a glance, snarling teeth. Despite her Eldrae form being suppressed by the iron, she fought as though she had embodied the beast within her.

She nodded at me, then moved on, ready to tear at the next feathered warrior who stood in her way.

Althea fought with the grace of burning fire. Swift and sure, she danced with four Nephilim, holding them at bay, blade swinging without hesitation.

"I trust you have a plan," Althea shouted, ducking beneath the thrust of a spear, before driving her stolen sword up and through the sternum of her opponent. "That's why you chose to keep this from us?"

"I did – I *do*," I said, regretting the secrets. Hating that these would be the last words I ever shared with Althea.

My lips moved, preparing to offer the apology, but Althea silenced me before I could speak.

"Then I trust you, Robin. Fix this before we no longer have the choice."

I gritted my teeth and nodded. There was so much I wanted to say, but barely time to breathe let alone speak.

I left Althea without saying goodbye. Duncan was my focus. It took surprisingly little effort to reach him – considering he was currently Cassial's focus. But Cassial fought against Erix who, lost to his innate fury, fought even harder.

"Duncan." I knelt beside him, careful to turn him onto his back, fearful of what I would find. "I'm here, I've got you."

Blood soaked the side of his head, likely from where the fall had hurt him. I ran my hand down his clammy skin, feeling just how hot he was. My relief to find him breathing was short lived. I took his limp hand, and placed it to my chest, speaking to the demon instead of the man who harboured him.

"I accept your offer, Duwar. I allow you into me, to be used as your vessel."

I held my breath, not sure what to expect. A few long seconds passed, but nothing happened. If I didn't hold Duncan's hand to my chest, it would've fallen helplessly back to his lap.

"I accept," I tried again, mentally opening myself up. "Duwar, my body is yours. Take it, use it…"

Slowly, Duncan found the last scraps of energy and lifted his face to meet mine. He opened his eyes, enough for me to see the brilliant green of his iris. I saw pain; I found suffering and dread.

But I did *not* find Duwar in their reflection.

"You're too late," Duncan groaned, shaking hand reaching for my face, tears streaking down his dirtied face. "Duwar has been…"

"No," I spluttered. "I accept. I accept the transference. I'm willingly giving myself to Duwar. Please. I *beg* you. You can't die, I will not let you do this for me. Let me pay this price, let me fix this."

"Duwar has been… taken." Duncan's eyes shifted over my shoulder, peering at something behind him. His brow creased, his eyes closing and refusing to open again. I turned to see what he had, to find Cassial afloat in the pews of the church, wings beating down foul wind upon us.

His eyes glowed with fire. Light spewed outwards from his hands, but there was nothing angelic about him. Power – pure, undiluted chaos – filled Cassial's veins, making him more god than man.

It wasn't Duncan's fall that severed the refracting vision spread across the mirrors. Perhaps it had never even been Duncan to open it. That was just part of Cassial's glamour – making us and the world think we were the monsters.

The truth was far more horrifying.

Cassial had been in control all this time. He played the part of the victim, showing the world a well-painted scene of the fey attacking them, Duncan's body a puppet for a demon god. Duwar was inside of Cassial.

"He told me you were…" Duncan flattered, eyes rolling back into his head. "Cassial tricked me in Imeria."

Duncan confirmed the transference had happened before they even stepped through the mirror.

That was why Cassial looked like he had won. Because, in his opinion, he had. And from his smile, the waves of undiluted power pressing out from the fine hair-line cracks across his skin, he knew.

Duncan's death would be meaningless. My chance of taking his place and paying the great sacrifice no longer a possibility.

I looked around for Rafaela in hopes that she had worked it out quick enough to act. If Cassial died, Duwar would perish. That was what we had to do.

Gyah was screaming bloody murder as four gryvern lifted her from the room. More gryvern rushed for Elinor, clawed fingers tearing at the stone bindings. I saw it then, the concentration on Erix's face as he attempted to orchestrate an escape, using his monstrous siblings as our means.

I had to do it.

Begrudgingly, I made a move to leave Duncan. There was a blade not far off to my side, one I could use to kill Cassial and end this.

As if reading my mind, Cassial snapped his head around to me. A resounding crack exploded through the room. Beneath my splayed hand, the floor was crumbling, dust and stone shards rising upwards, guided by an evil power.

"No longer will this world be threatened by the power of Altar and his children," Cassial shouted, shadow and light swirling in his upturned hands.

All around him, the church walls shattered, the ceiling splitting into chunks of stone. I looked toward the blade, then to Cassial, just as he turned his hands upside down.

The stones began to fall. Large chunks of wall and ceiling crumbling upon everything. This was what Erix tried to get us away from. He'd recognised Duwar using Cassial as a new vessel, the danger of that truth.

A chunk of wall fell upon the blade ahead of me, burying it.

Althea shrieked at my side. I risked a glance, cowering over Duncan's unconscious body, to see her running toward Elinor Oakstorm. But she was too late. A chunk of the church's ceiling fell atop Elinor, crushing the fey queen and the labradorite throne she had been bound to. Dust billowed outwards in a wave, swallowing everything it touched.

Death came for Elinor swiftly. I was only thankful that she was already unconscious. Hopefully her suffering never registered in those final last moments.

Elinor Oakstorm's death was only the start of an avalanche that was to come.

I reached a hand toward Althea, who stood as still as the stone raining down around her. My throat closed on itself as I attempted to call her name. The Nephilim who chased after her exploded beneath chunks of the building, as did Erix's gryvern who attempted to reach for her.

But I was helpless to watch as Althea disappeared beneath debris, her eyes closing softly just before the stone devoured her from view.

"No!" I screamed, throat bleeding with the force. "Althea. *Althea*!"

In a matter of seconds, two of the most important people in my life had perished.

I turned to Cassial, murderous intent in my eyes. But before I could so much as act, he positioned the swirling mass of power toward me and unleashed it.

The church continued to crumble without prejudice to who it killed.

There was a peace to come at the end. A silent lullaby that blocked the world out. Where I expected pain, I found nothing but a sense of relief.

I screwed my eyes closed, rested my body over Duncan's like a shield and laid my head on his chest. Any moment I'd feel Duwar's power flay my skin from my bones, but what came was the press of a warm shadow.

Just as I placed myself over Duncan, Erix landed atop me, coating Duncan and I with the shield of his wings.

The last thing I heard as the church came down on us was the soft voice of regret from the man atop me. "I have got you, little bird. Both of you. I will never let go."

Then there was silence.

CHAPTER 19

A figure stepped through the curtain of mist and shadow. Death, the physical embodiment, come to welcome me into their realm, to crown me with my failures.

I released a breath, soft clouds of shadow parting like snakes around me.

It was said that when you died, your loved ones would greet you on the other side. Even in my state I felt a swell of relief at the knowledge. But it was not my mother or father who parted the mists. Nor was it any other friends that I had lost along the way.

"Jesibel?" I said as her form revealed itself, corporeal in a place where I had no body to feel.

The thought that Cassial had killed her too ruined me.

She ran toward me and threw her arms around my middle, before my knees gave way. It was only then that I realised I had a body in this place. Looking down I saw my arms materialise, enough for me to return the hug.

"I'm so sorry," I sobbed into her embrace. "I know I have failed."

All my hesitations, all my lack of actions had ended up leading to the path of ruin I tried to steer away from.

Jesibel drew back, looking me up and down. She ran her hands over my body to check that I was, in fact, real.

Her mouth opened, but no sound came out.

In life, Jesibel had power over dreams. But this was just a trick again, surely. Something to punish me.

Shaking her head, Jesibel waved her soil-caked hands, and a parchment and quill conjured out of nothingness. Frantically, she began to scribble, until words were visible.

You are not dead, Robin.

I read it twice before the words faded, replaced by new ones.

This is a dream.

"Really?" I gasped, daring to hope.

She smiled through tears, not bothering to clean them from her cheeks as she began to scribble again.

The world thinks you have perished. All of you. The courts have fallen. Alive.

I could barely grasp onto my reality, to understand what the last memory I had was. I remembered darkness and death. Elinor crushed beneath stone... Cassial the vessel for Duwar and...

"Althea," I gasped aloud.

Jesibel scribbled down something quick on the paper and held it up. What was waiting was a single word, one that cut deep.

Alive–

It wasn't the violent ache in my shoulders that woke me. Nor was it the bite of metal cutting into my wrists, rubbing the skin raw. What finally had the power to draw me out of the dream was the shock of freezing water cascading over my face.

I gasped, jolting forwards as much as my bindings allowed. High levels of salt in the water made the numerous gashes and wounds across my body sting.

The cry that broke out of my torn throat sounded like the dying chirp of a small creature. "Jesibel–"

I was silenced by a hand pressed firmly over my lips.

"Good morning, Your Majesty." The water cascading over my face blurred my vision from the person before me. Their voice I would recognise in both life and death.

"If I was you," it continued. "I'd keep your screaming to a minimum. Otherwise, you'll find the Nephilim will be here in seconds, and we need a few of them to spare."

I blinked away the water, my mind swirling with impossibilities. As the figure before me came into focus, it was like looking into the face of a ghost. I couldn't shake Jesibel and my dream, the words she wrote on parchment were burned into the backs of my eyes.

"Seraphine?" I gargled her name against the press of her palm.

Her sharp brows rose, eyes bright with scheming. "The one and only. Now, do you agree to stop your shouting, okay?"

I couldn't manage to even nod, not as the true agony my body was subject to came into full focus. As did the room. All at once, without order, the details came rushing in.

I was in a room made of wood – a room that was swaying from side to side. It was lightless, not lit by candle or flame. Only the small circular window allowed for a beam of daylight to cut through. The view beyond was of the endless blue sea, waves occasionally lapping over the glass and bathing my room in darkness.

We were on a ship. That detail was as clear as the fact I wasn't dead, just like Jesibel had believed when she first entered my dream. Turned out I hadn't been crushed by a falling church or buried beneath rubble.

However, being alive wasn't all it was cut out to be.

The first haunting thought was of all the people I'd last seen before the church came falling down on us. Erix. Duncan. Althea, Gyah, Rafaela. The names threaded through my chaotic mind all at once.

Jesibel had confirmed Althea was alive, but Seraphine had woken me before I got the chance to ask after the rest.

My second instinct was to move, but I couldn't. Because my wrists were held above my head – fingers numb from the limited blood flow. My ankles weighed heavy by iron chains.

Panic seized my lungs. I inhaled, only to be assaulted by salt, blood, sick and the overbearing odour of sun-bleached wood.

Seraphine must have noticed I was panicking, because the palm over my mouth soon became a claw that grasped my jaw and held my face in one place.

"Look at me," Seraphine demanded..

I couldn't make sense as to why she was here – Altar, I couldn't make sense as to why *I* was here. I should be dead...

Duncan. Erix. Gyah. Rafaela.

My heart jolted in my throat, choking me.

Duncan. Erix.

"Robin. Focus on *me*," Seraphine hissed, ever the snake she was. "Now isn't the time to panic. Focus. I need you to calm down, and so do your allies, if you want to make it off this fucking ship alive."

All I heard within her words was 'allies' and 'alive'. It was enough to cool the fire in my gut.

Slowly, she removed her hand, keeping it poised just in case she needed to cover my mouth again.

I didn't shout, but kept my voice as quiet as hers had been

"What's – going – on?" I forced out between hulking breaths.

Anxiety had taken full hold, using me as its puppet.

"I was hoping you could tell me," Seraphine replied, her thumb sweeping away a tear I hadn't realised I'd released. "Almost every soul in both realms saw what happened during the wedding, and those who didn't watch through the reflection of mirrors have surely been told by those that did. The fey have been accused of harbouring Duwar, preparing to use the power to take over the human realm. Then the vision in the mirrors stopped. Next thing we knew was the church had come down and Cassial pronounced you all *dead*. That was two days ago."

Two days. Two fucking days had passed.

I shook my head, fury bubbling in every bone and vein. "It was a trick. The Nephilim lied. They..." I couldn't get my words out, nor did I need to. "Cassial planned for this."

Saying it aloud didn't make it feel any more real.

"I'm not as easily led as the rest of the people in this forsaken world. I see the game the Nephilim have played, and unfortunately for you, it is to the detriment of our people."

I held Seraphine's gaze, locking on and refusing to look away. "He *killed* us."

"That's what Lord-All-Mighty Cassial the Winged Saviour blah blah *blah*" – Seraphine spat that last part – "wants the realms to believe. But the truth is much worse, Robin. He ordered those who survived the church's destruction to be taken to the Isles of Irobel. What they will do with you there, I don't know. But it can't be good. Thank Altar I've come to save your arse. *Again*."

Seraphine stepped back, her hand rubbing across her jaw as she began to pace. That's when I got a proper look down at myself. I was topless, the iron-infused trousers I wore barely hanging on. I couldn't begin to count the number of marks on my body. Blood and dust, grime and sweat, all blended into one across my pale skin. There was a puddle of dried sick on the floor at my feet, a splash of it smudged down my chest and stomach.

Beneath me, sawdust had been sprinkled across the floor to soak up any unwanted fluids, but it just made the stagnant puddles coagulate and hold the stench. Seraphine paced over it, unbothered.

"Cassial used us," I spat, my throat demanding water, anxiety giving way to anger. "He... he got us together hoping to open Duwar's portal. But–"

"*But* he found out you had Duwar all this time and modified his plans last minute. Regardless of the truth, the world believes the fey had nefarious plots all along and the scene that was shown to everyone with those fucking mirrors has only solidified the lie. Altar doesn't even know difference between the truth and a lie now."

I knew she was right. "If enough people believe in Cassial's lie, it becomes a truth in its own right."

"One that is currently being used to prepare a strike on Wychwood and eradicate the fey from existence. Why, I hear you ask? Because the fey have the power to fight back, and that will forever be a problem for people who seek control." Seraphine stopped her pacing and faced me again. "And what I bet my life on is you're going to help me fix this. For Wychwood, and for us."

In other words: *this is your fault, Robin, fix the shit you caused.*

I hung my chin to my chest, aching body and soul. "This *is* my fault. My hesitation, my wasted time... all led to this. If I was strong enough to kill Duncan, this wouldn't have–"

"Shut the *fuck* up, Robin. We don't have time for self-pity. Only action. Whether you killed Duncan whilst he still had Duwar within him or not doesn't mean you have failed. It just means you have humanity, and that isn't a weakness."

She was right, but I wasn't wrong either. Otherwise, she would've told me as much. Regardless of my plans for Duwar, my hopes to destroy the demon-god, or whatever Duwar was, for good, my hesitation to kill Duncan only ended up with the power falling in the wrong hands, just as Duwar had warned.

I gritted my teeth, swallowing a cry of discomfort as the ship swayed against the waves, making the bindings around my ankles and wrists ache. "Do you have a plan?"

"Barely."

I narrowed my eyes. "I can practically see the cogs turning behind your eyes, Seraphine."

She winked, actually winked. "Once an Asp, always an Asp, aye?"

I nodded, wanting free of these bindings so I could unleash my rage upon Cassial.

"Well, to start, we will be getting you out of here," Seraphine said. "But for that, I need a key. I don't need this weak version of you either. I need Robin Icethorn, the king. The powerful, ice-wielding fey who I'd heard so much about. So, are you capable of becoming that version of yourself again? Or are you going to continue shedding tears and wasting time?"

The answer was simple, and the only one I could offer. "Get me out of these, and I will show you."

"Good," she said, scrutinising me for any underlying concerns. "Your guard will return shortly to top up the dose of Gardineum in your system. When he comes in, I will allow you to play the weak version of you, just to give me enough time to do what I need to. I'm not going to ask if you can do that, because you will. The fate of those you love depends on it."

"They are here?" I gasped, needing to hear her answer. "All of them survived?"

Pain creased her face. No, not pain. Grief. She quickly looked down to her feet and replied. "Just be ready."

I jolted forwards, as much as the chains allowed. "Seraphine, who... who hasn't made it?"

She refused to look at me. "Help me with this next part, and I will tell you."

"If someone has died," I shouted, not caring who heard, "I deserve to know."

Elinor Oakstorm had been crushed beneath the church. Perhaps she referred to her? Somehow, I felt like she didn't: something else was amiss.

Grief hung at the edges of my mind, but I refused it's power, which allowed for panic to sink its talons deep into me. I suffocated against the ache of it. There was a part of me which relied on the feeling, as if it was the only emotion I deserved.

Someone else had died, back in the church, as it fell upon us. Althea, it couldn't be her – Jesibel had said she was alive. Gyah. Duncan. Erix. Rafaela. There were possibilities as to who it could be. I didn't dare think about it. It would ruin me before I had the chance to act. But, in a way, I'd known something was wrong the moment I'd woken up. Like an empty part of me, a hollow ache, as if the universe had carved someone out of my own soul.

"Just be ready, okay?" Seraphine didn't wait for my answer as she walked to the corner of the room. A barrel waited, the lid taken off. From the puddle seeping from its base, I guessed it contained water. Was that how she'd made it onto the enemy's ship?

One look at Seraphine and I knew my questions had to wait; there was no time for answers. She climbed into the large barrel. Before she lowered the lip atop her, she gave me a final command. "When I contest the Nephilim, I need you to clamp your mouth closed and stop breathing."

"Stop breathing?"

She lifted a hand, revealing a small glass vial pinched between her fingers.

"Poison," Seraphine said. "Inhale it, and you will die, and that wouldn't be good, would it? I didn't have enough time to get more antidote, so we will need to make do."

Seraphine guided the vial to her mouth and placed it between her molars. Then she sank into the barrel and closed herself inside. All the while, my mind reeled with the fear of who had died. Who had Cassial taken from me? Or was it my own actions that led to it?

There was no knowing how long it would take for my guard to return. Minutes, maybe hours. But every second that passed left me without answers. Perhaps that was why Seraphine refused me them, because she knew me well enough. She knew how I'd act.

So, I began to scream.

I took all the physical pain, all the metal agony and balled it into a chaotic storm. And I made sure every soul on the ship heard. It wasn't exactly a word that came out of my throat, but a string of furiously fuelled sounds.

Soon enough heavy footsteps sounded beyond the door, followed by the jingle of keys. It swung open after a beat, and a Nephilim entered. He was tall and narrow, with wings speckled black and white. I expected him to wear the tell-tale armour of the Nephilim, but it seemed my fit of screams came unexpectedly, because he was dressed in more casual attire. The closer he drew, the more I smelled the alcohol on his breath.

He shut the door behind him, but didn't lock it.

"Shut up," the guard demanded, hurrying toward me.

When I didn't stop screaming, he drew back a hand and slapped it across my face. The pain was fresh and sharp. My teeth bit into my cheeks, splitting skin. Blood filled my cheeks until I gathered it up and spat it into his face.

Unbothered, I watched as the guard withdrew a familiar vial and needle. It was the same I'd used on Duncan, weakening him, punishing him, for the thing that lingered within his body. Gardineum, the golden liquid, swirled in the glass vial, the dosage far larger than anything I'd given Duncan before.

The guard didn't just want to shut me up, he wanted to see how close to death I could get.

Focused on filling the vial, he didn't notice Seraphine slip out from her hiding place. To be honest, I didn't either. Not as I faced the very people that lied, tricked and used us to start a war they'd been planning for an age.

No. This was no war.

It was an extermination.

"Let us see if this shuts you up until we reach our destination," the Nephilim growled as he moved the needle closer to my neck. "Steady now, you don't want me slipping up where I inject."

I snapped my teeth, fought against my bindings, all to give Seraphine more time. When the tip of the needle cut into my skin, she pounced.

Seraphine latched onto the Nephilim's back. His eyes widened in shock, and I smiled, watching my reflection in his dark gaze. The clamp of her thighs prevented his wings from spreading, but it was the handful of grime-sodden sawdust that she stuffed into his open mouth that shut him up.

I didn't think. Only acted. I thrust myself forwards as much as I could, cracking my forehead into his nose. The force made him gasp, allowing the sawdust in his mouth to fill his lungs.

The Nephilim began to choke. The sound was the most beautiful thing I'd heard in my life. He was forced to inhale through his nose, which turned out to be exactly what Seraphine wanted.

Then, with the elegance of an assassin queen, Seraphine spun around, took the needle and stabbed it into the Nephilim's eye. The pop of wet flesh pleased my core. She forced the needle as deep as it could go, but it wasn't long enough to kill him.

Just like a serpent coiling its prey, Seraphine spun around his body to face him. She clenched her teeth. I heard the crack of what sounded to be glass, the vial breaking beneath the force.

Her lips parted and Seraphine spat a coagulation of liquid onto his face.

I stopped breathing, just as she commanded. I turned my face away as a fume of gas and liquid clouded over the Nephilim's face, drawing into his nose and spoiling his one good eye.

As the poison sank into him, Seraphine dropped like a cat, withdrew another vial from her pocket and emptied the dried contents into her mouth. I could only hope it was the antidote she mentioned... the only one she had.

Thank Altar, the Nephilim was the only one to die in this room. He dropped to his knees, skin peeling freely, blood running down his ruined face. Wherever his hands clawed, more peeled away. A few enjoyable seconds later, and his body thumped against the sawdust-, vomit- and grime-covered floor.

I was breathless from adrenaline, reeling off the death this monster deserved. Seraphine looked down at him, waiting for proof that the poison had worked. When a purple-toned liquid began to spill out of his nose and ears, pooling beneath his melted face, she sprang into action.

"Neat trick," I said, bile scorching my throat.

"Turns the brain to mush," Seraphine said, already reaching for something tied to the Nephilim's belt. Her hand withdrew, holding the set of keys. "Risky way of doing it, but I really didn't have long to decide which poison I was bringing with me. I had to pack light."

"You... you could have... died," I stammered, noticing her casual lack of care that she almost ingested the same poison that made the Nephilim's brain leak out of his orifices.

"Not today, Robin." She thumbed through the keys, trying a couple in each of my locks. "You wouldn't know this, but an Asp is trained to use their last words as a means to guide someone else toward their final goal. Not a breath is wasted, not a word is worthless. If I was going to die, you would've known it. Remember that the next time you face a threat like Cassial, all right?"

How could I remember anything when I'd just woken up a captive on a Nephilim ship, with one Nephilim's brain matter pooling beneath his down-turned face?

"And now that's taken care of, we won't have long before the others come looking for their missing companion." There was a click as she finally found the right key. As the lock fell, she began undoing the rest that kept me in place, one by one.

It took a few more minutes until I was freed. I slumped to the floor, catching myself on numb hands, the wet kiss of brain matter staining my palms.

"Get out of those clothes and get yourself in his," Seraphine snapped. "Do it quickly!"

I did as she asked. My skin shivered with disgust as we undressed the dead Nephilim. There was no time for modesty as I took my trousers off. All I cared about was the almost instant relief that came with the return of my magic, ridding myself of the iron deposits.

My skin began to tingle as the cuts and grazes knitted together. It would take time to completely heal, but the return of some strength was a blessing. I would need it for what waited outside my cell door.

"What now?" I asked the assassin.

"Survive long enough to save the world," Seraphine replied. I'd never seen her so panicked. Likely because she had some idea of how many Nephilim were on this ship with us. She knew what we were up against, and from her expression, she had little confidence that we were going to get through this.

"How many are there?" I asked.

"Thirty winged pricks, give or take." Seraphine looked to the door, expecting them to come barrelling in any second. When she looked at me, her brow furrowed and eyes darkened. "I *need* you to be up to this."

I clicked my neck, aware the ache was slowly fading. "I am."

"Good." Seraphine pocketed the keys.

"The Nephilim are powerful creatures. The Creator's own monsters. If we have a hope, we should free the others first." I blinked and saw fire in the back of my mind. A ship engulfed in flames, feathered wings singed to black stumps. "We need Althea."

For the second time, Seraphine looked away from me. My heart sank to the pits of my stomach. "She is unable to help you now, Robin."

When Seraphine looked back at me, I saw the answer before she said it. "Cassial has Althea back in Durmain."

I heard her but didn't understand her. Unable to see the sadness in Seraphine's eyes, I pinched mine closed and faced the darkness. In it, my mind replayed the moment the church came down on us, how Althea disappeared beneath chunks of falling stone.

Seraphine had just confirmed what information Jesibel had given me.

"No." A rush of frozen winds uncoiled within me. "No. No. No."

Hands grasped my shoulders. "There is a reason I didn't tell you until now."

If Seraphine wasn't holding my arms down, I would've been slamming my fists into my skull, hoping to banish the truth out of my mind with my fists, one punch at a time.

"But she *is* alive?" I spat, remembering what Jesibel had said.

Seraphine paused. "For now—"

"No," I said, fury building.

Seraphine's gaze faltered to the side, unable to look in my eyes as she spoke. "Althea's fate is worse than death."

"Why does Cassial have her?"

A political prisoner, a bargaining chip to use against us. Insurance in case his plans failed him.

Knowing that Althea was alive was one thing, but the knowledge of her with Cassial didn't quell the storm inside of me. In fact, it made it stronger, more violent and ferocious.

Seraphine clapped a hand over my thunderous heart.

"Take your pain and turn it against them. For the sake of everyone else, for the sake of Wychwood," Seraphine said, looking deep into my eyes. "We need you, Robin."

Seraphine didn't need me. She needed my *power*. And when I opened my eyes, the tears crystalising to blades of ice on my cheeks, it was ready for release. I had no words. Nothing to say. If I opened my mouth, the winter inside of me would've consumed the entire ship.

Which, from her knowing grin, was exactly what Seraphine wanted.

I turned to the door, knowing Seraphine followed like a shadow. It wasn't until I stepped out on steady feet, my heart pounding a beat in my bones, that I let the power free.

All of it.

Not an ounce was spared as I welcomed the ice-cold hate in my heart, gathered it up and encased the entire *fucking* ship in it.

CHAPTER 20

I was a weapon. A thoughtless, emotionless void of a creature.
I was winter and pain. I might not have held the Icethorn key
beneath my bones anymore, my magic could no longer freeze
the ocean or turn the sky to ice.

But what I had was enough – *I* was enough.

And I held nothing back.

It didn't take much to locate the Nephilim. I followed
the raucous sound of laughter, the clinking of tankards and
the drunk singing. Seraphine stayed close, her presence
my shadow. It was only when we were outside of a door,
the room beyond full of off-duty Nephilim, that she finally
stopped me.

"Don't waste your energy on these Nephilim," she
warned. "Because you have an entire guard on deck to deal
with next. Be cautious with your attack, stay sensitive to
your reserves."

Hearing her worries aloud only further proved that I wasn't
the powerful wielder of storm and snow that I once was. And
yet her concerns were something I'd already contemplated. "I
have a plan."

Seraphine didn't ask me what it was, but if she had, the
answer would've been simple.

Revenge. Suffering.

To cause these people the same agony that warred inside of
me.

My victims were unaware that death waited outside the door. I was in the lower decks of the ship; and before me was a room occupied by the Nephilim which must've been some sort of mess hall. I got a glimpse of the celebration through the circular window in the door. There was a table full of food, tankards full of ale, but more importantly, seats overspilling with winged warriors.

Alcohol tainted the air – lathering my tongue with each inhale.

They celebrated whilst Althea was captured, and Elinor was dead. They drank as though they'd won already.

Oh, how wrong they were.

I grasped the handle of the door. Ice crept over the brass knob, passing up and over the wooden frame until not only the door, but the entire portion of wall was encased in my power. For good measure, I called upon the moisture inside of the lock and froze it solid. Mist hissed into the room, quickly catching *my* prisoners' attention. They looked up through frosted glass to see my outline.

That is when their shouts began.

Like living butterflies pinned to cork boards, the Nephilim began to squirm.

Their joyous shouts turned to screams of anger and terror as my winter devoured the room. A carpet of ice swept over the floor, encasing the legs of chairs. Those who were unlucky enough to be standing found themselves frozen up to their waist. The Nephilim in chairs were worse off as flesh and material forged to wood. One of them screamed as they attempted to stand, tearing away the backs of their legs in the process.

I relaxed my power, keeping it to the surface whilst allowing it some rest. Before their shrieks got the attention of the Nephilim above deck, I needed Seraphine to do something.

"Go and free the rest of us who can fight," I commanded. It was an almost out-of-body experience, to hear the numb emotion in my voice. I imagined what I looked like to Seraphine – someone lost to grief. I wanted to ask who was on that list, which one of my loved ones hung from chains on this very ship – but I feared the answer I would get.

Most of all, I feared that Seraphine would miss out a name from my list.

Knowing Althea was alive was enough, but recognising Elinor Oakstorm – the person that I looked most to as my second chance at having a mother – was dead *ruined* me.

"I'd prefer to stay with you," Seraphine said as dust rained down through the panelled ceiling above her. Thunderous footsteps sounded as the Nephilim made their way to us. "It is safer to fight them off before we–"

"Leave," I replied, managing only one word.

Seraphine regarded me again, looked to the corridor at her back, then back to me. "Are you sure, Robin?"

I swallowed the lump in my throat. My body was trembling with unspent desire to cause destruction. I feared if Seraphine stayed close, and the true storm inside of me released, she'd suffer the same fate as the Nephilim.

The part of me I was about to give in to was a place of no control.

"The Nephilim's strength comes in battle when they're airborne," I said, a devious smile pulling at my lips. "What better way to cull the flock, than clipping the little birds' wings?"

Little bird. Just saying it aloud made me think of Erix. If Elinor died from being crushed by falling stone, how did Erix fare after shielding Duncan and I from the debris?

If I contemplated the outcome too long, I would break apart.

"Survive this first move on the game board, Robin." Seraphine clutched my arm, drawing me back out of my thoughts. "And good luck."

My brow furrowed. "I'll be fine."

Because no physical pain could compare to the turmoil inside of me.

Seraphine left me, sweeping back into the shadows of the corridor, slithering away to locate my allies. I had just enough time to move myself into a better position to greet the Nephilim.

Focusing my intent, I walked carefully to the end of the corridor, nestling myself in the crook beneath the stairs. Just in time, because the door above deck flung open and Nephilim came racing down into the belly of the ship. I counted five of them, and inside of my prison of ice there were almost twenty. That left a handful still unaccounted for, as per Seraphine's information.

I'd worry about them next.

The Nephilim, wings folded and weapons drawn, turned toward the room of screaming comrades. I slipped from the darkness, following behind them, revealing myself only when they were cornered between the frozen door and me.

In each of them, I saw Cassial. No matter their physical differences, they were all the same. Angelic warriors meant to disarm us, make the world trust them with their ringlet curls, bright eyes, feathered wings and the promise of a new world.

It was all a lie. All of it.

And Elinor Oakstorm was dead because of them.

My power didn't need encouragement to leave me. Before the first Nephilim could turn around and find me behind them, I released it.

Roaring winds ripped down the corridor, blasting the five warriors in their backs. One was forced into the frozen door, the others smashing into the walls around it. I smiled as one of my enemies yelled out for help as half his face was left stuck to the frozen door, dripping blood quickly crystalising.

I wanted them all to scream.

I searched for moisture, anything I could find. In the air, on their bodies, even liquid inside of them – and whatever my power touched, I turned to solid ice.

Screams died on lips, turning to puffs of mist as my magic reached deep inside of their bodies and overcame them. I forced my way into every possible orifice, filling mouths, ears and eyes. Then, as their skin turned to fragile ice, their veins hardening, I weighed their hearts down with ice, cracking them with my power, just as my own had splintered in my chest.

I grabbed the neck of one of the Nephilim, fragile, glass-like skin beneath my grasp. They looked up at me with haunting fear clinging to wide eyes, face a mess of blood and ruin. One jolt, one harsh squeeze was all it would take for me to kill them. It took effort not to give into that dark desire… not yet at least.

"Answer my question and you will live to see another day," I spat.

The Nephilim broke into snivels and whimpers, aware that their friends and allies lay around us in chunks of smattered flesh. "Any – anything."

"Is Althea Cedarfall alive?" I knew the answer but required confirmation from the beast's mouth. Jesibel, as much as I hoped she'd walked into my dream, it was still up for debate. But this Nephilim beneath my grasp could confirm my hopes and fears with a single word.

My fingers dug deeper, as if clawing the answer out.

"Yes," they panted. "Althea Cedarfall is – is with the – Saviour." Their expression changed from fear to hate, lip curling, teeth bared. "And he will destroy–"

Magic burst from beneath my hand, encasing the Nephilim's head in my power. All it took was one harsh tug, and their neck tore free, the head tumbling off their shoulders from the lack of support. Their spine had become fragile beneath my magic, breaking like a twig to stone as it tumbled onto the death-ridden floor.

"That's for *Althea*." I forced out my words, knowing that the five warriors didn't hear them because they were already dead.

I turned my back on the corpses, flexing my hand at my side. I left the weakening Nephilim beyond the door to slowly perish in the low temperatures inside the room, with nothing but the view of death outside of their little window. My focus was elsewhere, my power all-consuming, still begging for more torment.

I wouldn't remember walking to the deck of the ship. My legs moved of their own accord, my mind lost to thoughts of my friend – her poppy-red hair, sarcastic quips, beautiful smile and eyes once full of life.

Such wonderful details now in the hands of someone with the power to ruin them.

Cassial killed Elinor like she was nothing; what was to say Althea's end would not be the same?

As I stepped out into the bright glare of light, I lifted a hand to my brow. In the shadow my hand made, I made out the remaining winged warriors. Some stood on deck, others flew in the sky as our ship continued its path through the unsettled sea.

All it took was one of them noticing me, covered in the blood of their allies, and they all sprang to action. They called out something, rallying each other for a battle they believed would be easy to win. But what they didn't account for was my lack of care. I had none of it. There was nothing left inside of me.

I stood still, giving myself to the remaining dregs of my power, trusting it would protect me by instinct.

The first two Nephilim nosedived down, golden blades drawn, reflecting light across my face in attempts to blind me. I closed my eyes, the spray of waves cresting over the ship's rail and soaking me from my side. As the next wave came, I grasped the salt-spray, froze the water to bullets and cast them skyward.

With my eyes closed, I didn't see the damage I unleashed as frozen magic sprayed outwards in an arch. But I *heard* it. Wings tore beneath pelting ice, flesh ripping apart. Then there was the tell-tale thump of two bodies landing on either side of me, cracking wood beneath the force.

I opened my eyes in time to watch the edge of a sword swing toward my neck. I welcomed it, wondering if the blade would hurt as much as the crushing weight of stone. Did Elinor feel pain when she died, or was it instant? Would Althea's demise be swift, or prolonged to cause those who loved her equal amounts of agony?

No matter the answer, I would make these Nephilim feel her suffering tenfold. My misery alone would kill them.

Sidestepping the blade, I swept my hand, fingers dragging through the thickening air. Spikes of ice and blood rose upwards, piercing through the Nephilim's side. In through their stomach, then up at an angle, the sharp points revealed themselves through the soft flesh of the Nephilim's neck.

I lost count of the number of Nephilim I killed. But I knew it wasn't enough. Just as I quickly gave up the final dregs of energy, my magic was spent. As the final three Nephilim charged toward me, I couldn't so much as conjure a blast of ice-cold winds.

I bent down, collected the golden blade from the pierced and slumped corpse of the Nephilim. Wielding it high, I faced the onslaught and smiled with blood coating my teeth.

"Come on," I screamed, like some feral beast, spittle flying past numb lips. "Come get me!"

If this was my end, I would go knowing my loved ones would meet me in the afterlife. But before that, I had a few more people to take with me.

My lessons with Erix came back, my muscle memory overtaking my numb body. I countered the first swing of a blade, knocking it back then sweeping mine outwards. It nicked across armour, the song of metal against metal screeching. I ducked, feet slipping over frozen blood, just in time to miss another jab. That was the thing about the Nephilim: their imposing bodies and proud wings made fighting side by side impossible. They could only attack one at a time, but they did so with honed training.

Heavy, continuous sweeps of their blades kept me on my knees. They were playing with me. Keeping me down, weakening my arms. I had to hold the blade with both hands, the muscles in my shoulders screaming against their force.

A desperate cry ripped out of my throat, all the while I refused to look away. On and on they attacked, smashing the full force of their strength down atop my blade. Each hit reverberated up my arm, making my bones ache. But those attacks suddenly stopped as another sound responded to my cry.

A roar. Deep from the gut of the ship, so powerful it shook the very foundations of the wooden frame.

My mind pieced together exactly what that sound promised, and it was my turn to grin up at the Nephilim, sensing the tides of victory shifting.

Gyah Eldrae was coming.

I knew that was who Seraphine had freed first. Just as she used my reaction to Elinor's death as a weapon, she must've told Gyah about Althea. Whatever the answer, it would not be Gyah who helped finish our enemies.

It would be the monster beneath her skin.

Before the three Nephilim could react, the floor beneath them splintered, and the body of a black-scaled, winged beast thrust skywards. In the jaws of an Eldrae, a Nephilim was dragged upwards. I heard the crunch of bone, the tearing of flesh and snapping of wings. Blood rained from a clear sky as Gyah flew up and up, her serpentine body twisting, talons racking the bodies apart as she devoured the remaining Nephilim one by one.

They attempted to fly away, but no matter how they tried, Gyah was faster.

Intestines fell down, smattering the deck of the ship like sun-bleached ropes. Feathers fell slowly, like snow, covering the death and destruction.

My neck ached as I sat slumped on the deck, looking up as Gyah moved with vicious but organised momentum.

It seemed to last an age before Gyah landed back on the deck of the ship. Her tail flicked back and forth, her gargantuan neck moving side to side, searching for more revenge. Her roars of ferocity became a whimpering sound from within her blood-stained maw. Then she settled two golden eyes on me, bowed her snout and released a world-shattering roar before my face.

As her foul breath washed over me, I dared not move. I faced the Eldrae, recognising her agony as it echoed within me. My adrenaline left me like the racing tide. Gyah's Eldrae form melted away, black smoke catching in the winds, leaving behind a slumped figure. She was on all fours, back heaving as she panted. Braids whipped in the winds. I almost didn't hear what she was repeating, until I crawled to her and gathered her in my arms.

"Althea. My Althea." She cocked her head back. "My wife!"

If I wasn't broken by the revelation before, I was utterly shattered now. In pieces. Gyah slumped into my arms, each of our bodies holding the other up. I didn't dare cry as I consoled her. My grief would wait. In this moment, I needed to be her crutch.

"They killed her, Robin!" Gyah screeched to the skies as if she had the power to rip it apart. "They killed my Althea!"

I reached for her, clasping firm hands to her trembling arms.

"Althea is alive, Gyah." The truth rushed out of me; I only hoped it was strong enough to cut through her grief and make her believe me. "Jesibel... she dream-walked and confirmed. I – the Nephilim confirmed it too. Althea *is* alive..."

Gyah paused momentarily, looking for someone behind me. "The Asp, she told me that Althea was dead."

Discomfort twisted in my gut. I knew the reason behind Seraphine's lie, it was a way to turn Gyah into a weapon, and it had worked.

Althea was in the hands of the enemy. I could only imagine the feeling of losing Duncan and my body would want to implode. Then I thought of Erix, losing him, and the feeling intensified.

"She is not dead, I promise." I had nothing but the words of Jesibel to believe, and the confirmation of the Nephilim I'd interrogated. That had to account for something. "We will save her."

Gyah fixed golden eyes on me, boring through my soul. "Captured and held by Cassial is no better than death. It… it is worse."

"I know," I said, laying my chin on Gyah's head as she rocked back and forth in my arms. "I'm so *fucking* sorry."

My betrayal, my lies and my deceit, all of it had led to this.

"Althea!" Gyah bellowed, only capable of speaking one word. Then her voice dove to the deepest pits of tone and she growled another name. "Cassial."

Gyah roared it to the skies, demanding in every syllable of the name, as if she commanded the gods to return her love to her.

No one answered.

"He will suffer for what he has done." I refused to let her go. I wouldn't – not now, not ever. I swept my gaze over the ruin around us, the splintered, blood-soaked wood, torn bodies and ice. All of it, and it just wasn't enough. Whether or not I had the power in me to destroy them all, I would find a way.

Neither of us heard the footsteps until a large shadow passed over us. I looked up into the faces of two men. Bright verdant eyes beside a gaze of polished silver.

For a second, the ability to breathe failed me.

Erix had Duncan held at his side, an arm wrapped around his shoulders. Both men hobbled out of the ship's belly, squinting against the light, skin coated in dust and wounds. And I wanted nothing more than to turn to them and allow them to console me.

"Oh, my darling," Duncan said, sorrow painted across his handsome face. He drew away from Erix, his gaze falling on him for a beat longer than normal. Then he slipped to the ground and wrapped his arms around me. As his arms encased me, I didn't let go of Gyah.

The three of us held one another. Comfort came in the form of our connection, but something was missing – someone was missing. I looked up to Erix who watched on. I could see in the lines of his face that he shared the grief but also something else. Relief. It was relief in finding me alive.

So, I extended my hand to him and gave him a command. "Come."

And Erix did. He knelt before us, wings shifting to give room. Then he put an arm around Duncan, another around me and lowered his forehead to mine. Erix tensed against the storm of emotion. I could see he was equally as broken over the news about Althea. And still he had it in him to offer me the strength with calm, collected words. "I am here, little bird."

I closed my eyes as Gyah's sobs quietened and Duncan's breathing matched pace with mine.

"You always are," I replied, aware of the comfort he offered me but also feeling as though I didn't deserve it.

Erix's exhalation washed over me. "And I always will be."

When I heard more footsteps, I lifted my face out of our bundle of bodies to see two more people step out of the stairway. Seraphine came first, hands clasped before her.

"That is everyone accounted for," Seraphine said, sorrow drawing at her thin brow. "No one else is on board, only the dead."

I swallowed the bile down, looking around the small band. Someone was missing – a person who had been with us in the church. It wasn't until the second shadow behind Seraphine parted, and stood in the light, that I saw them.

Rafaela.

Relief rose its head, before shattering like glass to stone as Gyah released a vicious snarl.

Gyah uncoiled from us, standing tall as she cleared the tears from her cheeks with a blood-coated hand. Her gaze settled on Rafaela, and the sound she emitted was a promise from the Eldrae lurking beneath her skin. "*You* did this."

Seraphine positioned her body in front of Rafaela, who stopped her with the sweep of a hand.

"You are right, Gyah," Rafaela said, refusing to break eye contact with her. "In part, this *is* my doing. And there will never be enough words to share just how sorry I am for the price paid for my deceptions, but I assure you, I *am* on your side. I have *always* been on your side. Everything I have done is to work against the Fallen."

Rafaela hobbled a step forwards, wincing as the dirty material drew across the twin wounds on her back, where wings once were. She gazed over us, drinking in the weakness and grief.

"I think it is time you tell us everything," I said, wanting nothing more than to stay in the arms of Duncan and Erix, but knowing that we didn't have the luxury of time to waste. "And I mean everything, Rafaela."

She bowed her head, unable to hold my gaze. "I intend to. But first we must ensure the ship stays on course for its destination."

"What we need to do is turn back," Gyah growled, the whites of her eyes now stained red.

"Not yet–"

"Cassial has Althea," Gyah screamed, voice twisted with the creature inside of her. "I will not wait another moment before I skin the fucking flesh off his bones."

"All in good time, Gyah," Rafaela said, hands raised before her. "Althea is safe for as long as Cassial believes we have all made it to Irobel and faced the imprisonment he ensured for us. If he catches wind that we are alive, Althea will go from comfortable captive to a tool used to torture us. So, we must gather ourselves beforehand. We are in no state to go against an army of the Fallen. Cassial will face the judgement he deserves, just not yet."

"I won't wait…" Gyah bent over, clutching her chest as a wave of physical pain overcame her. Erix released me and moved for her, offering his body as a pillar to lean on. No one spoke until Gyah had the energy to finish her sentence. "I must save her."

Rafaela took a careful step forwards, a soft hand lying upon Gyah's back. "I promise, Gyah, you will. But only when we are ready. Cassial is currently the host of Duwar, stand in his way, and he will ruin you before you get the chance to act. It is imperative that we first recoup, gather our numbers and return when we have the strength to go against him."

"We are alone in this fight," I reminded her. "The humans hate us. The fey are scattered, and the Nephilim were never on our side—"

Rafaela snapped her eyes to me, the seriousness in them had the power to silence me. "Not all of the Nephilim believed in Cassial's plans. The Fallen have ruled long enough. I didn't believe in him, nor did Gabrial. But there are plenty more who have gone against the Creator, just as I once told you. And it is those souls who will help us."

"Who?" I spat.

"The Faithful," Rafaela answered. "My sisters and brothers, a slumbering army that we will rally together. But for that, we *must* reach Irobel. Either we turn back now weak and broken, or return with a power that even Cassial will struggle against."

Fallen. Faithful. Titles that were new to me and made little sense.

"Why should we trust you?" Erix asked the question we were all likely thinking. "Continuing to Irobel is what Cassial wanted. The land of the Nephilim – home to *our* enemy."

"There is much I need to explain," Rafaela said. "A web of lies and betrayal that must be untangled if we are to hope to put a stop to Cassial's regime. But for that, you must understand the truth. Starting with *Duwar*."

"The demon-god," I said, looking at Duncan, who had been uncomfortably quiet this entire time. Although his eyes had never left me, his hand never straying far from me. It shocked me when it was Duncan who replied on Rafaela's behalf.

"Duwar is not a god, nor is it a demon," Duncan rasped, voice monotone, so weak the winds almost caught it from his lips and snatched it away. I had heard him, we all had, as clear as day.

His forest eyes fixed to mine, a deep-rooting regret lingering behind them.

"Duncan is right," Rafaela said.

Discomfort bubbled up through me. "Are you saying this to make me feel a type of way about refusing to believe it?"

"No, darling," Duncan started, but broke into a barrage of coughs.

Rafaela continued for him. "You are not to blame for your disbelief, Robin. We have manipulated your perspective of Duwar to think it was evil, to see it for what we wanted you to see it. That is only something *I* can take responsibility for."

I faced Duncan, drinking in his face, his body – aware just how weak he looked because of my treatment of him. "Is this true? I don't understand."

He lifted a shaking hand and traced his fingers down the side of my face. There was so much he wanted to say, weeks' worth of unspoken words. "Yes. Duwar is corrupted, but to no fault of their own. Years of solitude in that realm broke it, twisted it… but at the root… Duwar is power."

"*I am power*," I said, drawing on the words that had played over in my mind since Duwar had said them using Duncan's mouth.

Duncan blinked, and I found myself missing those eyes with fever. "Duwar is a source to be drawn upon. A power that Altar and the Creator warred over, tricked for, played a game to harness and control."

I shook my head, dragging up the reasons why Duncan was wrong. "But I saw Duwar. Their reflection. Duwar is a demon, and it used you to–"

"Duwar did not use me in the sense you think," Duncan

said, dropping his hand from my face. I found myself leaning into thin air, wishing he would touch me again. It was all I craved – but then I looked to Erix and reminded myself of the line I'd crossed in Lockinge.

Rafaela saved me from my thoughts, by finishing Duncan's revelation for him. "But Cassial *will* use Duwar, the source of chaos and power, to bring an end to the fey. He has the power behind him. And Althea will not be the only one to die if we act before we are ready."

"If Cassial wanted Althea dead, she would be." I knew it, deep down, as if someone whispered the truth into my ear. "He needs her..."

Gyah's lips curled over teeth. "Exactly why we must turn back for Wychwood now."

"We will, I promise." Rafaela's eyes turned north, out toward the endless sea. "But Robin is right. Cassial will need a fey once his body is not compatible for the power source. She is safer with him, as much as I know it is hard to believe that, it is true. No harm will come to Althea as long as Cassial wishes to utilise Duwar."

Duncan nodded to himself as if agreeing. "What is it you... suggest, Rafaela?"

"First, I must return home. There is something I must see through to give us a chance in this battle."

"Hand us over to the Nephilim waiting there?" Erix asked, a growl edging his words.

Rafaela shook her head, braids catching in the harsh winds, whipping them like snakes around her tired face. "The only Nephilim left on Irobel are those imprisoned in labradorite, which is exactly the reason why you all were being sent there. The same ritual Robin wished for information on..."

"All this because the gods warred for power," I spoke my thoughts aloud.

"Power that belonged to neither... of them," Duncan said, still struggling in his weakened state.

"You are both correct. This is a war of the gods' puppets," Rafaela said. "One that has been in play for too many years to imagine. A being, like Duwar, is very much determined by perspective. One's monster is another's Saviour. Look at Cassial; his actions determine he is the worst of us all, and yet people still follow him."

"Blindly," I added, pushing to standing as my thoughts raced with all the half-truths Rafaela had shared previously with me. "You told me that the Nephilim bound in labradorite were there because they believed in Duwar, they wanted to use the demon – the power source. Was that more lies?"

"Lies, yes. But lies to protect you," Rafaela said. "All said in good faith."

That was something I could relate to.

"Look how that turned out," Gyah growled. "With Althea captured, Elinor Oakstorm dead, the world in the hands of *your* people."

"The Fallen are *not* my people. They are Nephilim who forgot their way a long time ago." A storm passed behind Rafaela's eyes, and for a moment I saw the power in her again. A focus. A fiery determination that dwindled the light of any belief. When she spoke again, it was with a clear voice of authority, the same that I had last heard when we fought beside each other. "But the Faithful, we will help you, just as Gabrial prophesied. And I swear that I will help right these wrongs. Be it on my life, Cassial will fall."

"On your life," Gyah spat, vicious tears streaking down her face. "I will hold you to that."

"I know, Gyah Eldrae." Rafaela faced each and every one of us. "Now, shall we take this conversation to more comfortable lodgings? Irobel is a day at most away. Before we reach the boundary of the isles, it is best you understand the truth. All of it. Starting with the previous Game of Monsters and how we will prevent it from occurring again–"

"Not yet," I interrupted, eyes fixed to my boots.

My distress must have been obvious, because both Duncan and Erix called for me at the same exact moment.

"Darling."

"Little bird."

I felt as though I was seconds from combusting.

I lifted my gaze, aware that everyone was looking at me. In the face of chaos and disorder, I found myself most comfortable when taking control. So that is what I did.

"Gyah," I said, facing my friend, reading the agony in her face like the lines of a recently written obituary. "There is currently a room below *full* of Nephilim who may be dead, or may still be hanging onto life. If the cold hasn't killed them, do you feel up to extracting some information from them about the state of Durmain and Wychwood? Maybe insight into Cassial's immediate plans, knowledge into where he is keeping Althea and for what purpose?"

It was wrong of me to ask Gyah to do anything, but she was not the type to simmer in anxiety and do nothing. She found comfort in action, and the promise of more vengeance. From the spark of light in her eyes, I knew I was right.

"I will not be long," Gyah said as focus took over her mind. "If you hear screams, ignore them. They won't belong to me."

I pitied the Nephilim who may have survived my magic. They wouldn't be so lucky after facing Gyah.

"Rafaela," I said, her name lodging in my throat. "You can help clear the ship of the dead. Feed their flesh to the ocean dwellers for all I care." I found it hard to hold her eyes, knowing that the lies she'd revealed still had more lies beneath them.

Rafaela gritted her teeth. I waited for her refusal, but it never came.

"I will help her," Seraphine added quickly, which translated to *'I don't trust Rafaela, so I will keep a close eye on her'*.

Not to my surprise, Rafaela agreed.

I looked to Duncan, my heart lodged in my throat. He was alive, freed of Duwar, but the price had been great on him. But after losing Elinor, the raw pain of it, I couldn't bear to imagine if it was Duncan who'd died.

Or Erix.

I turned to Erix, drinking in his straight posture, his ever-present concern for me evident in the way he winced as if I was glass moments from breaking. And I knew, more than ever before, that I couldn't live without either of them.

"We need to talk," I said to them both.

There was guilt I had to bare before we could continue.

"Go and be with Duncan." Erix bowed out, stepping back as if he hadn't noticed that the 'we' included him too. "I will make sure Gyah is okay with her endeavours."

I opened my mouth to explain myself further, but Duncan beat me to it.

"Erix," Duncan said, voice as weak as he looked. "Robin means for you to join us."

At that, Erix fixed his eyes on Duncan. The muscles in his jaw feathered. Although, I'd be a fool not to notice the softness to Erix's edges as he took in the man at my side.

"The three of us? Talking?" Erix laughed awkwardly. "What could possibly matter enough when the world is crumbling around us?"

"He does," Duncan said, nodding at me. "Robin matters, which you agree and cannot dispute. So, we shall talk."

I swallowed my reservations and panic.

Finding even the open air suffocating, I fought the sudden urge to walk away. But I'd never get far, not with the ties from both these men always anchoring me. "Yes, Erix. It's time we have the conversation whilst we have the time."

Erix didn't ask me what I meant. He knew. We all did.

Perhaps it was Althea's capture that triggered this confidence in me. It reminded me what I had to lose. And like Gyah, I'd devour the flesh of any being who took either Duncan or Erix from me.

Before our group departed, it was Gyah who added the final sentiment. "And when we are all back together, I would like to know how you are alive." She pointed to Seraphine, whose lips curled into a smile.

"Once an Asp, always an Asp, Gyah Eldrae," Seraphine replied. "And by Altar, do I have a story for you."

Seraphine looked from me to Duncan and back to Gyah. If there was one conversation I dreaded having, it was what happened when Duncan and I returned to Imeria. But it was time for pointless secrets to no longer stay buried.

But first, there was one secret that was eating me alive. And that involved me, Erix, the balcony and a kiss.

CHAPTER 21

We found a cabin which must've belonged to the captain, from the grandeur of it. This was no bunk for those without a station, from the large oak bed to the well-crafted furniture and plush curtains and rugs – this belonged to a person of importance.

Had belonged, I corrected.

The bed took up the back wall, large enough for the Nephilim to sleep in, accommodating their wings. A case of gold weapons hung on the wall: swords, spears, daggers and a strange ball-shaped weapon attached to a chain and a handle. Erix was looking at it, pretending to keep busy, whilst the awkward silence hung heavy around us.

"How are you feeling?" I asked Duncan, although the evidence was clear before me.

He didn't look *well* at all.

It was hard to look at him for long, to see the shadows beneath his eyes, the sickly pallor of his skin. Duncan looked like he'd been to hell and back, which in a sense, he had. Sometimes by my own hand. When he moved, I caught a glimpse of the multiple angry wounds at the side of his neck. Marks I'd made with the continuous injections of Gardineum.

If those were the wounds I could see, I hated to think of the scars left that my eyes could not reach.

"Free," Duncan answered, back hunched as he sat on the edge of the bed. Even the slightest movement made him wince. "I would say I'm relieved, but the cost of my freedom is far too great. I was hoping, for good or bad, that I would perish and take Duwar with me – but you had other ideas, darling."

Duncan had just confirmed, in a manner of speaking, that the glass I found beneath his pillow was meant for harming himself.

I sat beside him, feeling the bed shift beneath my weight. "I'm so sorry for–"

"*Don't.*" Duncan placed a hand on my knee and squeezed. It took him considerable effort just to do that. "Don't apologise to me, Robin. Everything you did was because you loved me, I know that. I have no ill will toward you. I'm just relieved we even get to have this conversation in the first place."

I hung my head, chin to chest. "But what else can I say? After what I've done to you, I should grovel at your feet for forgiveness."

Not only for the pain I caused, but for the pain I was about to give him.

"Darling, please," Duncan exhaled. "As much as I like the idea of you being on your knees for me, perhaps we can wait until I'm feeling better. I fear that I can barely sit up properly."

I turned to face him, just in time to catch his wink. Even in his state, Duncan could find his mischievous side. Altar, I'd missed that. Missed *him*. In a sense, I had mourned Duncan long ago, feeling as though a moment like this would never happen.

Now I was faced with the conversation I dreaded.

I cleared my throat, finding it dry and in dire need of water. "There is something I need to tell you, Duncan."

At that, Erix turned on his heel across the cabin and faced us. "It wasn't Robin's fault," Erix snapped. "If anyone should be laying their sins on the table, it is me."

Duncan looked between us, his bloodshot eyes slow to follow. When he blinked, his eyes would stay closed for a second longer than normal. I took his hand from my knee, threaded my fingers between his and melted beneath the true warmth of his touch.

"No," I said to Erix, then faced Duncan. "No, I won't let him do that."

"Do what?" Duncan asked, eyes widening a fraction.

"Erix is doing the gallant thing and trying to take the blame for something that happened between us. But it was entirely my doing. *My* fault. I will not have anyone in this room thinking otherwise."

"Robin," Erix said, voice stern, attempting to stop me. "This is not blame you need to burden right now."

"Both of you, just stop." Duncan laid weak fingers on my knee and squeezed, his words shocking me to silence. "If this is about the kiss-on-the-cheek incident, you really have nothing to worry about."

"You know?" I asked, tears stinging my eyes.

"I do. However, it's something I expected to happen; after all, I brought you together for a reason."

I shook my head, doing everything not to look him in the eyes. "But I kissed him, Duncan. I kissed Erix, cheek or not. Regardless of whether you know or not, you deserve to hear the truth from me, and the apology that you are owed." The tears began to fall, cresting over my cheeks, clearing a path through the grime coating my skin. "Whilst you were suffering in Icethorn by my hand and decisions, I was in Lockinge trying to find a solution. And… I *betrayed* you."

I bowed my head, but my chin was caught by two firm, calloused fingers.

Duncan lifted it back up, so our eyes met. "Is that all? Is that the only burden that weighs on your morality?"

Is that all? Three words, one question, and I found myself almost admitting that it could not have been. More could have happened. I searched for comfort in Erix, almost selfishly laying myself next to him in bed. Not to mention Duwar's dreams. My betrayal to Duncan went far beyond that kiss.

I dared not speak, so instead I just nodded my head.

"Why are you crying, Robin?" Duncan swept the tears from my cheeks. "I don't understand why you are reacting in such a way?"

"Because I love you, and I did the unspeakable. I broke your trust..."

I caught Erix in the corner of my vision. His knuckles were between his teeth, his brow furrowed so deep the lines across his forehead were cavernous.

Duncan pondered my reply, drinking me in, refusing to look away. "I don't doubt that you love me, darling. But I do doubt that you really believe you broke my trust." He took a deep breath in, the sound harsh as it rattled in his chest. "Let me tell you both this, plain and clear, you have broken no trust, nor have you done anything I did not prepare for."

"I... missed you–" I choked. "I swear. Everything I was doing, everything I planned for, was to help you."

"I know, darling." Duncan trailed his trembling fingers and placed them over my cheek. He was so cold to the touch, the tips of his fingers like ice. "However, since we are in the conversation of truths, I want to ask you something. I beg that you answer it honestly."

I knew what was coming before the words left Duncan's paled lips. "I'll do my best."

Duncan's eyes lifted to Erix and rested there. "Do you love *him*?"

Him. Erix. My Erix.

I pinched my eyes closed, blocking out the view of the room. It was as if Erix held his breath for my answer, whereas Duncan's breathing was even, his heart beating calmly in the tips of his fingers.

I thought of Elinor and how quickly someone could be taken away. My mind went to Gyah and how she was needing to exist knowing the love of her life was in the hands of our enemy.

If Erix had died... it would have destroyed me.

The answer was simple.

"Yes," I said, the only word I required to share. "Yes, I do."

It took bravery for me to open my eyes and see the reaction, but I did it. Because if it caused Duncan pain, I deserved to see it. I couldn't hide anymore. Not from reality – not from what I wanted.

Erix stood stockstill, silent, his hand now at his side. Silver eyes were fixed to me, so bright I blamed the light coming in from the porthole, only to find that it was tears in his eyes that made them glow.

"I should go," Erix said suddenly, body springing into flight, ready to run away from the ruins my admission had likely caused. "We are exhausted, and our worlds have been turned upside down. Robin – you don't know what you are saying…"

I longed to tell him to stay, but it was Duncan who spoke for me, *again*. In fact, he gestured to the bed at my side and gave Erix a command. "Sit, Erix. Don't run from this. Life is far too precious to waste, especially in the face of a chance like this. Especially when I know how you really wish to respond to Robin's admissions. Walk out that door and you will regret it, I know you will."

I held my breath as Erix pondered Duncan's request. It felt like hours went by before he made his decision and walked *away* from the door. He paced the room, closing the space between us, then sat at my side.

I was sandwiched between the two most important men in my life.

"I need you both to listen to me very carefully," Duncan began, leaning forwards so he could see Erix. There was nothing sad in his verdant eyes, no nuance of an expression to suggest that he was surprised or hurt by what I'd said. "I haven't flirted with death, been given a second chance at life, only to waste it."

"You barely look like you have been given that chance yet, Duncan," Erix said, eyeing him from across me, drinking in the same weak state. "This conversation can wait until after you are healed."

"It will happen now," Duncan said, but I sensed there was more to it. Something Duncan was not telling us.

Losing Elinor had been the trigger for me to stop hiding the feelings inside. The guilt, the angst, the turmoil. What did it all matter if, one day, I didn't have the chance to ever say it.

"I was the one who brought you both together," Duncan said. "Me. And I did it because I love Robin so much, that even in the face of my potential demise, I knew I couldn't leave him alone in this world. And Erix." He spoke directly to the man at my right. "I trust no one else, in this realm or the next, to care for Robin like I do, besides *you*. I recognise that you care for him, with the same intensity that I do. In fact, I have known as much since you saved me from Imeria. I'd be a fool not to see it, and a double fool to not use that to my advantage."

"It was my duty to look out for Robin," Erix said, hands fiddling on his lap. *It was my pleasure.* "As his guard, I only did what I had to do."

Duncan released a small laugh. "Don't lie to me, Erix, or yourself. You deserve better than that. In this room, we only speak from a place of honesty. Unless you wish to tell me that I'm wrong, and you don't hold a flame for Robin? Look him in the eyes and tell him that you don't care for him in equal measure to me."

I already knew the answer, because Erix told me during the night of the ball.

I was about to turn away, but something in the intensity of Erix's gaze had me pausing. Then the words left his mouth, I felt my entire body crumble.

"I love him with every fibre of my being," Erix admitted. "If it came to it, I would lay my life down for him happily, if it meant he got to survive another day."

My hand moved without thought. It was a need – a desperate and selfish desire that had no concerns. With my left fingers entwined with Duncan, I put my right hand upon Erix's balled fist.

Like a flower blooming beneath spring sun, his fist uncurled, and my hand melted into his.

"This isn't fair," I said, speaking to both of them. "You deserve someone who can give you their entire heart. Not half of it. Both of you."

"Darling," Duncan said softly. "A heart is not something you can split. Mortals are not bound by such constraints. You admit you love me, and you love Erix. To me, the path forwards is clear. But it is a path that we can only take together, not only hand in hand, but side by side."

Erix's eyes widened. "The dreams. The visions that plagued me every night. Those were because of you, weren't they?"

Duncan nodded, his thumb brushing circles on mine. "Courtesy of Duwar. The Gardineum may have kept me asleep, the iron may have dulled my magic, but nothing could truly dampen the power source that is Duwar. I couldn't use it often without my body paying the price – but in moments when I knew it was desperate, I tried to bring you together. And now we are here, alive, with the potential of a tomorrow ahead of us, I think it is time we discuss it."

My cheeks bloomed with heat, knowing that the dreams I'd had, had potentially been shared with Erix.

"What are you suggesting, Duncan?" Erix asked, voice calm although his face was pinched, revealing his internal struggle.

"Boundaries. But the way forwards is not for me to come up with alone. It is not only Robin's desires that matter, but ours also. We must all be on the same page. Up until now I simply laid out the possibility of a path, but without the consent of all parties, what is possible will be meaningless. We can walk out this door knowing we tried, that's what matters."

I fixed my eyes on an unimportant place upon the floor. This conversation, although breathtaking, was almost ill-placed. After everything that had happened, I couldn't help but feel as if this could've waited. But Duncan spearheaded it, and it had to be for a reason.

One I was far too frightened to accept yet.

"I have so much I want to say, but I don't know where to start," I said.

"Then say it all, Robin. I need to hear the words come from you." There was a pleading edge to Erix's tone. "Tell us what you want."

"I don't know," I said, finding lying easier.

"Yes, you do," Duncan replied. "I'm not telling you how to react, nor am I asking you to provide me with an answer right now if you are not ready to give it." Duncan paused, taking a hulking breath in, as though what he had to say next required it. "But I am suggesting an option for us all. One where the three of us can be... one."

Erix stood abruptly. His fingers pinched the bridge of his nose, his eyes screwed shut. I jolted up to reach for him, but it was too late. My right hand felt empty without him, as if a physical piece of me had suddenly been taken away.

"I fear I have pushed this too quickly," Duncan said, leaning back, eyes blinking closed.

"I should go and help... they might need me." Erix reached the door in four large strides.

"Erix," I called after him.

Duncan pulled me back. "Let him go. Choice is important, he deserves to make his own when he is ready. As do you."

I tugged free of Duncan's hand, only to regret it when he grunted in pain. I was literally stuck between them both, unsure if I should go after Erix, or help Duncan as he suffered.

"Erix, please," I begged, just as he took a step outside the door.

"Little bird, I am not walking away from you, or Duncan." He stopped, long enough to look back at me. "I just need some fresh air. Time to think. Today has been... a lot."

How could I refuse that? In what realm did I have the justification to tell Erix how to feel or how to react?

"Will you come back?" I asked, voice cracking with hopefulness. "I don't… I can't lose you too."

In a manner of speaking, I had just told Erix what I wanted. Him. Duncan. Both of them. A tomorrow when we could all be as one. Even if that tomorrow was under threat every second that passed.

It was impossible to keep Althea's capture from my head. It sprung out of the shadows, like an assassin, ready to slay me with the reality that she was gone. Losing her reminded me what was important in life.

Erix bit down on his lower lip, contemplating my request. "That's the problem, little bird. I'm strong enough to know that I could *never* leave you for long." He settled silver-clad eyes on Duncan and added. "Nor you, Duncan."

Then, with that, Erix left us.

The door swung shut behind him, leaving me to simmer in the possibilities. I stood there, rooted to the spot, staring at the door as if Erix would come barrelling through it again.

When he didn't, I released a heavy sigh and faced Duncan again. His posture had slumped further, as if the last dregs of adrenaline had left in the wake of Erix's departure. All thoughts of the conversation faded as I saw the obvious discomfort he was in. In seconds, I was on my knees before him.

"Why are you doing this, Duncan?" I grappled for his hands, noticing how he didn't have the strength left to hold me back. "It is your turn to tell me the truth."

"Because… I never ever want… you to be alone in this life."

"But I would have you," I choked. "You'd forgive me for my transgressions, and be with me?"

Duncan closed his eyes. "I hope so, if I can hold out that long."

Panic surged through me, blinding any hope of saying anything else about the matter of me, Duncan and Erix.

"You need to rest," I said, knowing Duncan needed more than that. He needed a healer – someone to tend to his weakness and fragility.

Duncan winced. "All I have done is rest. I don't want to waste a moment of waking again."

I looked up at him, wishing to imprint myself on his body, just to prove that this was real, and he was here.

"I really thought I was going to lose you," I said, carefully studying the nuance of his expression.

Duncan refused to look at me when he replied. Nor did he tell me I wasn't going to lose him. "Because of the Duwar-possession part, or the Erix part?"

A sharp prang of pain shot through my chest. "Both."

Duncan's smile was weak, but bright. The most beautiful thing the world could offer me.

"I would be a fool to give you up so easily, darling." Duncan used the last possible speck of energy and reached for my face. He drew me up from the floor, pulling my body atop him. He felt so small beneath me, as fragile as glass. Regardless, he wrapped his arms around my back and held me upon him. "That is why I know Erix will come around."

"Why do this for me?" I said, peering across minimal inches between us.

"Because I love you, and Erix loves you. You are the hinge that keeps us together. But I am not only doing it for you. I am doing it for me, and for Erix. I care for him, deeply, and I have seen into his mind to know that he shares in that feeling. Mutual understanding is important in this journey, Erix's, yours and mine. We must make this decision together."

"And will you be by my side, to experience this together, regardless of the answers?" There, I said it. Got the haunting question that lingered in my mind.

Duncan's answer was the same as it had been. "I hope so."

Not a yes, not a no.

"I don't deserve either of you," I admitted my insecurity aloud. "That is how I feel."

"Shh," Duncan said, lips quivering. "Saying that is like suggesting we don't deserve to make that decision ourselves."

I leaned in, resting my forehead on Duncan's. "I missed you, darling," he said.

"I missed you so much," I replied, the words breaking out in a violent sob. "I don't want to ever lose you again. Either of you."

A strange, imposing weight lifted from my shoulders.

I waited for Duncan to tell me that he wasn't going anywhere, but of course he didn't. We both knew his tomorrow was yet to be secured. He was suffering in the wake of Duwar – greatly.

"I could never leave you," Duncan whispered. "Not for long."

He lifted his finger and pointed to his eye, his heart and then to me.

Our signal. Our way of saying I love you without words. Seeing him do it, this side of surviving Duwar's possession, ruined me. So, I did the only thing I could think to do, and I laid my mouth upon his. The moment our lips touched, a small chirp erupted from deep within me. A sound born from the mixture of relief and sadness.

"I love you too," I gasped against his mouth. "So much, Duncan. So, *so* fucking much that it burns inside of me."

His shaking hand traced up my back, fingers knotting in my hair. Duncan tightened his grip, holding me to him as our touch melded into one. The kiss was not frantic or desperate, but slow. It was as if he longed to draw out the moment, just as much as I did.

When I drew back, Duncan didn't open his eyes again. His chest rose and fell, the tension in his face lessening as his exhaustion caught up.

I moved to get off him, but he moaned, proving he was still awake. "Stay with me," he pleaded. "Just a little longer."

I couldn't refuse him. Duncan was as much my weakness as he was my strength. So, I curled on the side of the bed, nestled my body into his. I would need to speak with Rafaela about a healer – someone on Irobel who could help him. Duncan would need time, or a miracle. I hoped both were possibilities.

"Robin," Duncan whispered so quietly it took effort to hear him. "As much as those chains weren't meant to excite me, I think I actually miss them. Maybe when the world goes back to normal, we can give them a try?"

My laugh was honest, born from a place his sarcasm touched. "You're terrible, Duncan!"

"Silver linings," he exhaled, voice sleepy.

"Silver linings," I echoed, finding the spark of happiness fading again. I was almost relieved when Duncan didn't speak. His rasped snore told me he slept. Which left me to ponder the world we'd left behind.

I couldn't find the silver lining in this story. Elinor was dead. Althea was a captive. Duncan was still suffering. Wychwood had been handed over to the Nephilim, just as they plotted, risking the lives of millions. And we were sailing away, leaving it all behind, without a foolproof plan of how to return and fix this colossal issue.

Maybe once the rest of my problems were solved, I could face my own battle between my heart, and the hearts of the two men I held, one in each hand.

CHAPTER 22

Sailing upon the endless blue, it was impossible to keep track of the minutes, let alone the hours. The day beyond the cabin's window had swiftly passed into night, and with it my mind was fixed on Duncan and Erix.

The three of us.

Sleep came and went, if I could call it that. My only constant was lying beside Duncan, who'd not woken since our last encounter.

Unable to sit around, hiding in the cabin, I left Duncan to sleep whilst I obtained the answers waiting on the deck.

I found Rafaela standing at the bow of the ship, staring out across the stretch of ocean, her eyes lost to an unseen spot in the distance. What she saw was beyond me, because all I could see was glittering stars reflected off a blanket of black. The moon hung like a pendulum, acting as our guide as we sailed toward it. My mind drifted to the unseen creatures lurking beneath the hull, tailed serpents or water dragons from the old tales. Regardless of such monsters, it was the person who stood beside Rafaela that made the breath catch in my throat.

Erix was at her side, the wind making his wings dance. I hesitated, looking back to the ship's helm. Seraphine gripped the gargantuan wheel, lean muscles straining as she kept the ship on its path. Lanterns had been lit across the deck, casting enough of what was around us in a glow. She nodded at me, short and sharp. It was the encouragement I needed to push forwards.

Erix, as he always seemed to do, noticed my presence before I announced it. He turned his head slightly, enough for the silver glow of moonlight to dance across the planes of his face.

I couldn't tear my eyes off him, and the feeling was clearly mutual.

Rafaela noticed. When her eyes settled on me, I saw regret and pain. The faint whisper of words Rafaela and Erix had shared stopped, making me feel almost awkward for interrupting.

"Duncan is still sleeping," I said, excusing the lack of his presence. "Sorry I haven't come out sooner. It's the first time I've been able to share a bed with him since before–"

"There is no need to explain yourself, little bird," Erix said, laying a hand on my shoulder and squeezing. "Never, okay?"

I smiled awkwardly at him, knowing that if Erix had stayed in the cabin with us, we would all likely still be in it.

"What have I missed?" I asked.

In answer, Rafaela offered me an update on Gyah. "Your friend has requested to use a vial of Gardineum that the Nephilim had in stores. Gyah is suffering greatly from her separation from Althea – it is easier for her to rest her mind and give it a reprieve from reality."

I couldn't begin to imagine the heartache that poisoned Gyah. If she wanted to sleep, with the aid of the poison, then that was her choice. Not something I had the grounds to make comment on. "Gyah will be going through a lot right now. I know the pain of being parted from the person you love. It eats you up from the inside out."

I caught Erix's eyes, hoping he knew that I spoke about him as much as Duncan.

There was so much left unsaid between me and Erix, that I expected him to acknowledge the interaction he'd not long walked away from. But he stayed silent, until a handful of words left his perfectly bowed lips. "I'll leave you both to get reacquainted."

With that, Erix made a move to sweep past me. I found my arm snaking out and hand gripping his. "I know I'm in no position to make requests of you, Erix. But can I ask of you one thing?"

"Robin." I hated when he used my name. There was once a time I'd rather him use it, but now, with everything that had happened between us, it sounded foreign on his tongue. "I could never refuse you; you know that. Ask me of what you need, and I will see it done."

"Can you sit by Duncan's side?" I found myself asking the question, proving just how desperate I was. "He is not well, and I would prefer that when he wakes, he isn't alone."

Erix leaned in and laid his lips to my cheek. The suddenness of it shocked me to silence, made every hair on my body stand on end. He withdrew enough to be able to whisper in my ear. "It would seem the stars have aligned, because that was exactly where I was going anyway."

"You were?" My voice lifted in pitch, reflecting the hope that dwelled inside of me.

"I was," Erix said. "There is a matter I would like to discuss more with him."

It was on the tip of my tongue to ask what matter he spoke of, but I guessed I already knew the answer.

Erix left me to simmer beneath the tingles his lips left on my cheek. Swiftly departing from the ship's bow, I was left to Rafaela, who continued studying me. Only when Erix had disappeared into the belly of the ship did she speak.

"I would ask how you are faring, but I worry that I already know the answer," Rafaela said.

It didn't matter how I felt, what mattered was fixing all the problems around me. Starting with Duncan. "Duncan needs a healer the moment we reach Irobel."

"I am aware." Rafaela looked away from me, making me think she was hiding something still. "Duncan is the first known mortal to host Duwar in all of time. Having Erix guard him is wise. We will be unsure of the damage he has suffered, lasting or not, so it is best not to take any chances with the small band of people we have left."

My mouth dried, my tongue turning to sand in my throat. "Then you agree that I should be worried about Duncan?"

The signs pointed to his suffering, the clawed marks on his chest as pronounced as they had been when I last saw him.

"I *hope* not." Rafaela leaned forwards, facing across the ocean again. I joined her at the rail, glad for the physical support to prop me up.

Stars glittered across the dark oceans, sea-salt breeze tangling my black hair. "How long do we have left of the journey?"

"If the winds are swift, and the oceans our ally, then I hope we will reach land sometime tomorrow," Rafaela said. "I sense we are close, like a tether is pulling at me, pointing my inner compass toward home."

"You speak on these isles as if they haven't harboured monsters all this time." My accusation caught in the winds, amplifying the disdain in my voice.

"Home is home, whether the memories there are painful or not."

I took a deep breath, feeling it rattle in my aching lungs. "Why didn't you warn me? When I came to the Below, you could've given me a heads up about Cassial's plans and prevented this from happening."

Rafaela released a heavy sigh that carried on the winds and into the dark. "I could not tell you Robin, because if I had, you would have felt like you had no option *but* to kill Duncan yourself."

"And was that my only option all along?"

Rafaela spared me a glance, proving to me she already knew I had the answer. "I did what I had to do."

"Because Zarrel could've got your truth out of me with the hammer?" I asked, already knowing the answer.

"That was always a risk." Rafaela didn't tell me I was wrong. "It was better, this outcome."

A shiver passed down my spine at her comment. "Althea has been captured because of this game you continue to play against your own people. Elinor is dead," I seethed, finding the fury coming out of me without warning or control. "I don't see how this outcome is better than any others. Wychwood is left without its leaders to guide it. We have lost, Rafaela. Surely you can see that?"

"No, we have not lost. Not yet." Rafaela laid a cold hand on mine. It was then I noticed just how tight I held onto the railing. My knuckles were white, the veins protruding out the back of my hand. I eased my hold slightly beneath her touch.

"I will not lie to you and tell you that we are on the road to victory," Rafaela said. "Many more innocent lives will be taken from this realm, and more so will feel the pain of that loss. But this was the outcome that *had* to happen. We – *I* had to return to Irobel if we had any hope of going against Cassial. Duncan had to return to Irobel."

"What do you mean return?" I asked, feeling my heart swell in my gut. "He's never been there–"

The look in Rafaela's eyes stole the breath from my lungs. "What do you know of Duncan's parentage?"

It was one story I was confident about. "They were killed by Aldrick who lied and told Duncan the fey murdered them, just to manipulate and use him."

"Then you see that the Nephilim are not the only creatures capable of lying, Robin Icethorn. You of all people should know that."

"Thanks for that." My grip tightened on the railing, knuckles turning white. "Listen, for the sake of our frayed relationship, Rafaela, I strongly suggest you stop speaking between the lines and get to the point."

She tipped her head in agreement, looking back out of the dark waters. "The prophecy I told you about, the one Gabrial – rest her soul – had many years ago. It is the heart of this conflict, and the key to solving it."

"The prophecy about the Saviour?"

Rafaela winced at the use of the word. "Before Cassial and his Fallen took over Irobel, we – the Faithful – continued with our life's work. Duncan *is* the product of those plans, a child born from angel and man. Someone…"

"Made from both realms," I answered, repeating the words she had shared with me days ago. My blood hummed through my veins, so loud that my ears rang with it. Duncan, made from angel and man. I couldn't begin to understand how this was possible, and yet my mind told me it was. "You said that you thought it was me that prophecy spoke of. Half fey, half human. But you lied."

"I admit there have been so many lies that I have long forgotten which hold truth. But yes, I may have suggested that you were the prophesied Saviour in case Zarrel got the information from you and discovered the truth. Turns out I placed my worries in your mind being invaded, and did not worry about my own."

I clutched my gut, wondering if the sickness was from the rock of the boat, or the upturn of all these truths. "I no longer care about what you have said before now. I need only to know every detail, no matter how small you may think it is to the matter. I need to know what part Duncan has to play in this game."

As if the game hadn't already ruined him.

Rafaela took a deep breath in and held it. She released it only when she was ready to tell me all the secrets she kept. "I was the one who sent Duncan back to Durmain as a child. One of many, who would act as failsafes if we ever required them. For generations we have been cultivating children for the sole purpose of discovering the Saviour. Of course, at the time we did not know what they would save us from. But as time went on, and the prophesied Saviour did not reveal themselves, others upon Irobel began to birth ideas and ideals of their own."

"If Cassial believes he is the Saviour, then that means he is also born from both realms?"

"Made, not born."

Made. There was something in her emphasis of the word that had my brain turning. "Who were Duncan's parents?" I asked, regretting the question as soon as the answer came.

"Cassial was his father." A devouring silence lay over me, threatening to drag me into its depths.

"Cassial?" I breathed.

"Unfortunately, yes. And his mother was a human woman who had devoted herself for generations to help protect our history."

I balled my fists so tight that my fingertips ached from lack of blood flow. When my knees wobbled, I knew my sudden weakness had no corelation to the boat's movement. A sudden and sharp need to turn back and run to Duncan's side, to share this information with him, overcame me. No matter how horrifying this revelation was.

"Duncan deserves to know this."

It had once been his life's mission to discover his parentage until Aldrick's lies made him believe they were long dead.

"And he will, in time. But it was important we got him back to Irobel, to play into the prophecy and ensure Duncan is the one to save the realms."

"Duncan is in no state to stand up on his own, let alone save anyone," I snapped.

Rafaela leaned into my shoulder, her touch exactly what I needed to calm the ice leaking from beneath my hands.

"Which is why he must reach Irobel. Duncan was born, but he must be *made* – do you understand?"

I shook my head, information tangling in my mind "Nothing makes sense anymore."

"It will, in Irobel, I promise."

"What's so special about Irobel?" I asked. "You made us believe all the Nephilim left. Not that we want their help when it is clear they all share the same vision that Cassial and the Creator have. The eradication of the fey, once and for all."

"Not all the Nephilim shared in that vision," Rafaela said. "I don't. Gabrial didn't. And there are thousands of others who also did not wish for the downfall of the fey."

"And yet it is happening," I said, shivering to the bone. "We are too late."

"Not late, simply delayed." Rafaela blinked heavily, her dark skin glowing as sea-salt spray crested over her.

"So where are these thousands of Nephilim who share your beliefs?" I asked, looking out into the endless dark, wondering if our hope of salvation sensed our pending arrival.

Rafaela took a deep breath in and finally released her hand from mine. "There is much I have told you, and much more that I have not. You must first understand that I was chosen as the Creator's hammer. Protector of his word. But with the spreading of his truth, I understood the importance of lies. How they played a part in, hopefully, saving the world from the inevitable repeat of history. The web of them is iron-clad and tangled, but I want to unravel them, so you understand."

"Then do that," I pleaded. "Help me understand."

Duncan. Cassial. Prophecies. Saviours. So many words, and they all made as little sense as the next.

"It began with our arrival to Durmain. We told you that we came to protect you from Duwar – a demon-god. That was the first lie, and not a singular one. Duwar is no god, nor is Duwar a demon. Duwar is simply a source of the world's power."

I am power.

"Duwar told me that," I admitted, "but I didn't believe it."

"Because you were made to believe Duwar was evil. You trusted in a truth you believed, that is not your fault. And with all power, it is not inherently evil or good. It is how power is used which determines that. The same goes for people. Gods. Nothing is simple. Look at the power that is in you, compared to what Doran Oakstorm coveted. You see, it is the wielder of a weapon with bad intentions that is evil, the blame does not fall upon the weapon itself."

"I understand that," I said, "but what I don't understand is why I saw Duwar as the demon... their physical reflection. How can my mind debunk what my own eyes saw?"

"Perspective, Robin Icethorn. You saw what you were made to believe. Just as humans look to Cassial as a hero who saved them from evil fey; it is merely their perspective and not the truth as we know it." Rafaela turned her back to the view of the sea, leaning against the railing with powerful arms folded over her chest. "Duwar has always been the epicentre of a great divide between the two gods. Altar and the Creator – before their kin gave them names – were simply beings using chaos, or Duwar as you know it, as a means to sculpt the world as we knew it. On Irobel, we have texts on texts about it, describing a time we have named the Game of Monsters. It was those texts that Duncan's birth mother looked after – until Cassial decided she was not worthy enough to continue her task and gave her a new one."

There was pain in Rafaela's voice, suggesting that Duncan's mother had met her end long before this day.

"Altar and the Creator warred over... chaos?"

Rafaela nodded. "They fought over who could use Duwar, and who could not."

"A Game of Monsters," I repeated. "Duwar also mentioned this."

But again, I didn't believe it.

"It was given that title by the Nephilim. A time when Altar used Duwar to create his children, the fey, and the Creator believed the harnessing was unjust and unfair. The Creator, no matter how he tried, was unable to make beings to rival the power of the fey. The humans were simpler creatures. It was only by giving of the Creator's own matter – blood and tears – that he was able to make us. But that was to his own detriment. The Nephilim were the result of the Creator's demise. But by the time he discovered this, it was too late and Duwar had already been locked away, the gods weakened due to their conflict."

"You told us that the Nephilim were meant to protect the keys. But you really came to find them before Aldrick, and use them."

"No, I came to destroy them. That was never a lie. Cassial though, he wanted the very same as Aldrick." Rafaela sucked her tongue over her teeth, followed by a sigh. "In truth, we didn't know of the existence of the keys before Aldrick started searching. Likely because even that knowledge was not given to the fey. It wasn't until Aldrick began his expedition to free Duwar and harness the power to change the world in his desired image. Because Aldrick was half-human, Gabrial was able to read his intentions. It was how we discovered the possibilities of these keys and used that to come over to your realm, under the guise that we were to protect you."

"Aldrick, was he one of these Saviours you mentioned?"

Rafaela looked into my eyes, straight through my soul. "Yes. Aldrick was a child born from two realms – but not made. This was our biggest mistake. Although Aldrick was one of our many attempts to start the prophecy Gabrial shared, as you can imagine, he was one that was almost successful. Except he was no Saviour because he was born."

"Not made," I added, still not knowing what that entailed.

"Exactly."

The sickness rose its head again. "And the difference is?"

"To be born from two realms is easy, but to be made is something entirely different. It requires a change, a physical alteration. It has nothing to do with realms and races, but gods. Made from two realms. Mortal and divine."

"So, Duncan is..."

Rafaela shook her head, reading my thoughts. "He is no god. But he is something close, because he has the potential to touch the divine and survive it. Thank the Creator, otherwise he may not have lived through Duwar's possession for this long."

I simmered on all the knowledge unloaded upon me, trying not to drown in it.

"This is why the Nephilim punished you for destroying Altar's keys." It was beginning to make sense, even if I didn't want to believe it.

"It is."

My stomach cramped with the urge to vomit, but I held it at bay. "You and Gabrial both planned to destroy the keys to keep them away from Cassial."

"You see now that her death, although painful to me, saved her from suffering at the hands of her own people. She is with the Creator now, in his kind embrace."

Kind. I laughed at the word. There seemed to be nothing kind about him.

"Robin, I should have faced death by Cassial's hand, but from my understanding, the letters he received from you attempting to reach me planted a seed of interest into your need to discuss our practices. If you had not attempted to reach me, I may have been killed long ago."

Instead, she suffered. Over and over. Just a glance at her wingless back proved as much.

"And the gate, the one Gabrial showed me in her vision. More lies. More deceptions. You were not protecting it."

Rafaela bristled, wrapping her arms around herself to fend off the chill of night.

"Some of us were, others wanted to open it. The gate within Irobel has been the attempt of the Nephilim to *free* Duwar. For years the Fallen have tried. Using old texts, trying to reverse Altar's ultimate deception to the Creator. But over and over they failed. Until Aldrick showed them the way to success."

"And what of these thousands of Nephilim that you mentioned, the ones who didn't believe in this? Why didn't they – *you* – stop those who had been corrupted?"

"We were outnumbered, it is as simple as that. Yes, there were thousands of us, but there were more of the Fallen. Poison spreads faster in willing veins, and Cassial ensured those who worshiped him were malleable subjects."

Another thought came to mind, one which tied me back to something Rafaela had told me before.

"You told me the Nephilim influenced by Duwar were then bound in labradorite as punishment. That was the crux of why I needed you. The plan we made – was that more lies?"

"Yes *and* no." Rafaela hunched forwards, losing a breath full of tension. Russet stains had dried across her tunic, mirroring where the stumps of severed wings lay beneath.

"Our practice of binding a person in labradorite was one of our experiments of freeing Duwar, gone wrong. It will be easier for me to show you when we arrive. But you must understand that the Nephilim we bound in labradorite were *not* those supporting Duwar, but those opposing Cassial's goals to free the source of power. Hundreds... *thousands* of my kin have been locked away for generations under the belief that they would never be free. To kill a Nephilim is to return them to the hands of the Creator – death is far too kind for those who wished to stop the Fallen from succeeding in the Creator's ultimate plan. But the binding, the defiling of a Nephilim in the bones of an opposing god, *that* was punishment. An eternal prison that was believed to be forever. But it is not."

"It isn't?"

Rafaela smiled. She actually smiled so bright that her entire face beamed. "The process, if Cassial was interested in understanding, is reversable. Which is why Duncan's return to Irobel is important if we hope to stop Cassial. Yes, I believe Duncan is the Saviour. But not only of your realms, the Saviour for the Faithful, those locked in stasis for generations, waiting for him to call them out of stone and to freedom."

"So this detail is the crux of Gabrial's prophecy?"

Rafaela nodded, jamming a thumb toward herself. "Duncan is the only one capable of saving *us*."

"Duncan has one foot in the land of the dead," I said, hating myself for speaking the truth aloud. "Unless we find him a healer, he will not survive long enough to help you."

"Duncan must survive," Rafaela said, jaw tightening as she gritted her teeth.

"Must and will are two entirely different things, Rafaela."

Rafaela shot me a sideways look, one that sang of her own desperations. "He is our last hope, just as the prophecy said."

"And how do we stop an angel imbued with the power source of the very world? What can Duncan do about that!" My hands were shaking; my entire body trembling with unspent energy.

Rafaela didn't seem to share my nerves as her smile only brightened. "Cassial is the product of the Creator. Unlike the fey, who were made with the use of Duwar's power, we and the humans were not. So, our incompatibility will only lead to Cassial's death, just as it weakened Duncan. Cassial is many things, but stupid is unfortunately not one of them. He will refrain from using Duwar for as long as he can – until he is provoked. Our issue is not fighting against Cassial, but ensuring he does not use the power to cause destruction that cannot be reversed."

My mind went directly to Althea, slotting her in place in Cassial's plans.

He kept her because he needed her.

"Duwar wanted me. I was told that Altar used them to create the fey – that we are compatible. I could have stopped this if I just accepted – I could've prevented Duncan from this suffering..."

I couldn't bring myself to mention Althea in all of this.

Rafaela nodded. "I understand you believe that your treatment of Duncan was destroying him, but that is simply not true. I do not need my hammer to see the truth of that. Your self-imbued guilt is written across your face. If anything, keeping Duncan in the state you ensured was perhaps the only thing that saved him. We will see."

We will see. Three words that should've relieved me, but they did the very opposite.

"I don't want to wait and see. Duncan is going to die if he is not seen by a healer." I finally said it. Spoke the truth that I knew just by looking at him. "No more talk of prophecies until we locate one in Irobel. I can manipulate the winds, try and get us to our destination faster..."

"There is no one in Irobel to heal Duncan, Robin. Only statue and stone reside in Irobel now, unless Duncan can free them."

We were going round in circles, and still an answer was just out of reach.

I gawked, pain gripping my chest and squeezing. "Then why are we still going?"

"Because there are other ways in which we can help Duncan on Irobel," Rafaela said. "Our practices do not simply include the binding of a person in stone. As I said, that was only discovered during failed attempts to utilise Altar's bones. There are practices we have perfected–"

"Can you save him?" I shouted, eyes bulging. "That is all I care to know. Can *you* save Duncan?"

"I can try, but it will not be my will – no matter how I wish it to be – that saves him."

A frigid cold crept through my veins, ready to strike against the world. "Then who? If there are no healers, who is going to decide if Duncan lives or dies."

"The Creator." Rafaela narrowed her eyes, focusing on the distance. The tension quickly ebbed out the lines of her face, as if her final secret had finally been shared, and she was free from the burdens of her web of lies.

"If you think I will put Duncan's life in the hands of a god whose own children wish to destroy us, you must think I am a fool!" Rage erupted within me, refusing the answer Rafaela had just given.

"I'm sorry, Robin, but there is no other way." Rafaela fixed her eyes on me, boring through my soul and out the other side, sorrow pinching her thick brows together. "I cannot promise you that Duncan will be saved, but I do trust in Gabrial's prophecy and hold hope that we will find salvation in Irobel, and not further pain and suffering. I know that isn't enough for you to hold onto but know that I would not be doing this if I didn't think there was a chance."

There was so much I needed to say, and yet I couldn't get the words out. Instead, I turned on my heel and marched away from Rafaela. If not, the magic that drummed in my bones would've broken free.

I found myself back outside the door to my and Duncan's cabin when I heard voices from within. As soon as the dulcet tones of the two men I loved sounded past the thin wooden door, I found all my emotions from my conversation with Rafaela dissipated.

Leaning my ear against the door, I fought to still my beating heart just enough to hear what was being said.

"I want nothing more than for you to be happy," Erix said, voice soft yet firm. "Before I make my decision on what happens next, I need to hear it from your own tongue that this is what *you* want."

My palm pressed against the door, wishing to push it open, and yet I didn't want to interrupt this.

A broken, weak voice rose up and replied. "Erix, this will only ever work if we each equally desire this. Love comes in many forms. My love for Robin is vast, as I know yours is the same for him. But my love for you... comes from knowing that you hold those very same feelings that I do. Robin, he is our everything and for that you are my everything, and I know the feeling is the same. I see it in your eyes, but most notably Duwar saw it in your soul. Answer me this... please." Duncan must've paused, because for the next few seconds I heard the rasp of his strained breathing.

"Take your time," Erix whispered, his encouragement palpable even through the wood between us.

"Will the first step forwards together be harder than the one it would take to walk away?"

It was my turn to hold my breath, waiting on tenterhooks for Erix's answer. When it came, I found myself smiling.

"No, it would be easier to move forwards. I know that."

"Your hesitation is beautiful, Erix. It shows that you have time to contemplate and come to your own decision. This... this door that has opened for the three of us will only stay open if we are all, equally, on the same page."

"If it closed, I would kick it down," Erix replied, voice dropping to a faint whisper. "That I know."

At that I pushed the door open to find both men looking up toward me. They must've noticed my smile, because both returned it, Duncan's fainter than Erix's due to his exhaustion.

"Little bird," Erix stood from his seat on the edge of Duncan's bed, his hand gathering away from Duncan's which was laid out and stretched across the sheets toward were Erix sat. "I didn't expect you so soon. Are you okay?"

I shook my head, because lying was not how I was going to start this. "No, but I will be, once we reach Irobel, I hope."

Erix looked beyond me to the dark and quiet corridor. "It is late, I should–"

"*We* should rest," I said, gesturing toward the bed. "All of us need it."

Duncan leaned back on the pillow, face pale and eyes closed. His voice was quiet as it rose from the mounds of bedsheets. "I cannot argue with that, darling."

I kicked off my boots and paced toward the bed. Erix watched my every move. "You need to sleep too, Erix."

"Are you sure?" he asked as I climbed onto the bed, pressing myself into Duncan's left side.

I patted the space at my side.

"I am," I replied, guiding Erix with my eyes to the other side of Duncan. "But only if you are?"

His actions answered for him. Erix followed suit, moving to the right side of Duncan and climbing onto the bed. Whereas I lay on my side, facing them both, Erix put two arms behind his head and looked toward the ceiling.

This felt… easy. The three of us, connected in different and yet powerful ways. I could've said something more to Erix, but the peaceful quiet was exactly what I needed. Instead, we shared a final look, a soft smile and a silent promise that tomorrow would be full of answers.

"I don't want to choose," I admitted, voice a small whisper.

"Then don't," Duncan said, fingers tickling my side. "Why choose anything, when you all know what outcome we want."

I spared a glance to Erix, whose lip quirked upwards at the corner. He noticed me looking and rolled onto his side until he faced me.

"Why choose," Erix repeated, toying with the words in his mouth.

No one spoke again. With Duncan between us we slept soundlessly, giving into the sense of peace that I'd not felt in days.

Until a shattering noise broke my reality apart.

CHAPTER 23

A whistle rang out across the ship. I sat bolt upright in the bed, aching from the deep slumber I had fallen into. Light cut in from outside, proving some hours had passed. Dawn was upon us, and with it a new chance.

Erix and Duncan were still sleeping when the whistle cut the skies. Not wanting to disturb them, I rolled out of bed and made a move toward the top deck.

Rafaela stood where I'd left her, at the bow, as if she'd not moved a muscle in hours. The sun hung heavy in the sky above her, plastering uncomfortable rays down upon the wood. The scent of warmed salt and polish filled my nose, but it was not that which bothered me. Rafaela turned to me, tired eyes wild as she pointed at something in the distance, hand raised to her brow, blocking out the glare of the sun as it sank beneath the islands ahead of us.

"Look," she shouted, a singular tear rolling down her cheek before being snatched away by the winds. I did as she asked, facing the distance, just in time to watch a collection of islands appear through the mist. One by one, formations of rock and stone revealed themselves, some large and others smaller.

"Home," Rafaela muttered as more tears fell from her eyes. "I have made it home."

I understood the feeling she was filled with, looking at a place she likely never imagined returning to. But it was not the islands that she pointed at, but something on them. I didn't differentiate

what she was actually referring to until the ship sailed closer.
What looked like portions of stone protruding across the flat
islands and rocky crops were actually statues. Hundreds of them.
No, thousands. The clear outlines of Nephilim, forged in dark
stone, looking out across the ocean as if guarding the shores.

This was our army.

This was Rafaela's home, not the place but a people – all
bound in labradorite and left behind.

What I witnessed was unlike anything I could imagine.
The ship slowly passed into the collection of islands, sailing
between them. One detail I couldn't ignore was just how silent
of a place Irobel was.

Far in the distance I caught a glimpse of a formation of
buildings, white stone buildings of pillars and pitched roofs.
But I didn't get long to drink it in as my name rang out from
across the ship.

"Robin." Erix stood, face drawn in horror. I shivered at the
use of my name. But it was the tone Erix called it with that
made the blood in my veins thrum.

He must've just woken up to find me missing from our bed.
Surely that wasn't enough to spark such fear in his eyes.

Erix fixed his eyes on me, skin pale and wide eyes bloodshot.
And an unspoken truth hit me with the force of a thousand
arrows to the chest.

"Duncan," I gasped, already reading the panic across Erix's
face, the taut posture of his body. I knew Erix well enough that
I could read him and understand he was worried – no, he was
terrified.

Erix broke my line of sight and locked eyes with Rafaela.
She released a small gasp, like a broken chirp of a bird. There
was only one possible reason she could've reacted like that.

Because my horrors where confirmed.

"No," I whispered before the horror exploded in me like a
dying star. Then I screamed, so loud it had the power to wake
every Nephilim bound in labradorite. "No!"

Erix reached me before my body hit the floor.

My hands clawed at his chest, my eyes locked to his. "Tell me he's okay. Tell me, Erix!"

Erix held me close and whispered his reply. "I'm sorry, little bird. I tried to wake him…"

I saw it then, understanding the truth that was held back in Erix's apology. He wouldn't lie to me, but he didn't have the strength to tell me the truth either. All he could do was draw me close, whilst repeating a promise over me. "He won't wake up, Robin. No matter how I tried, Duncan will not open his eyes… His breathing is–"

"We will save him," Rafaela snapped, guided by her hope now we had returned. "But for that we must make haste."

Gyah ran out from the belly of the ship in that moment, eyes heavy with her recent use of Gardineum. "Jesibel, she visited me in my – have I missed something?"

"Duncan is dying," I said, voice trembling with my pleading. It hit Gyah so hard that any remnants of exhaustion left her expression in a second. "I can't… I can't lose him too."

"What do we need to do?" Gyah asked, focus set across her brow.

"Get him to land," Rafaela answered, thrusting a pointed finger in the direction of the islands. "Now!"

I jolted forwards but stopped as a firm hand clamped down on my shoulder. Rafaela held me in place, words scarred with command. "There is a chance Duncan will survive, but I still need your consent. I will not do this against your wishes."

Duncan's survival rested on the will of a god, a god whose children petitioned to destroy all of fey-kind.

I fixed my eyes on Rafaela, unable to ignore that this was my only option. Giving Duncan over to her for whatever judgement he had to face with the Creator. I didn't have to like it to know that this was my only chance to save him.

"If he dies…" I couldn't finish my threat. The words clogged in my throat, like hands tightening around my airways.

Rafaela straightened. "Duncan was *born* for this. Put trust in me, if anything, and I will uncover all the false truths you have been led to believe. He must now be *made* if we have hope in him saving the realms."

Fuck the realms, in that moment I cared only for Duncan. Selfish or not, he was half of me. The *best* half of me.

"I will only do it if you agree," Rafaela echoed, refusing to look anywhere else but into my soul.

She knew I was stuck between a rock and a hard place. Only she presented an option to me, I was actually without them. It was let Duncan die or give him the chance to live.

"Do it," I snarled.

Rafaela's eyes fell on Erix next, and her question surprised me. "What about you, Erix. Do you consent?"

It was a quick moment, but profound. Rafaela understood the invisible ties between the three of us, and respected it enough to ask for his permission, and not only mine.

Erix was quicker to answer. "Save him. I beg you."

Duncan lay in a pool of cobalt water, his eyes closed and arms crossed over his chest. I refused to look away from him, dared not so much as blink for fear I'd lose him. So I fixated on the rise and fall of his chest, the slight rasp his breath made, not the fact that he was being handed over to the Creator for judgement.

Sunlight speared in through the glassless windows, dusting an unbearably warm breeze over my skin. The water rippled against it, spinning with motes of glitter. This was no mundane water – Rafaela had just explained as much.

I was jealous that the water and winds got to touch him, but I couldn't. If it wasn't for Erix holding me to his chest as we watched, I would've climbed the shallow steps into the pool and wrapped my arms around Duncan and refused to ever let go.

The pool was one of a kind. It was set into the mosaic

flooring in the heart of a domed building. White stone walls offered shade from the overbearing heat. All across them, images in faded pale paints took up space, showing angels with wings, weapons of yellow gold, spilling from the hands of an unseen figure. I hadn't focused on many details after Erix had told me of Duncan's condition, but the few I did stuck to me like sap.

The Isles of Irobel were a collection of islands scattered across the ocean. Set beneath a blazing sun, the air curdled with heat, so much so that I was soaked in sweat the moment we disembarked from the ship. What greeted us on Irobel's main island was silence. Strange, pillared buildings stood empty, stone-laid streets untouched. The only presence of life came in the form of the statues, countless bodies frozen in stone, watching on from hillsides in the distance.

Irobel was a graveyard. Rather fitting, considering Duncan's life was in the balance the moment we stepped off the pier, as Rafaela ushered us toward our current destination.

"I will ask you both a *final* time for your consent," Rafaela enquired from where she stood behind Duncan, waist deep in the bright pool. If she wasn't holding Duncan by the back of his neck, his body would've sunk. "There are still risks. He may not be deemed worthy for the necessary alterations…"

He would. Whatever test or trial Duncan had to face, he would succeed.

I gritted my teeth, finding myself waiting for Duncan to wake up and speak for himself. But if he had, we wouldn't be here. There was so much he deserved to know about his story, details he never had the chance to know. And wouldn't if I didn't accept that this was his only chance of survival.

There was no ignoring how weak Duncan was now. He'd not opened his eyes since last night. His breathing was shallow, and the faint beat of his heart barely enough to rival the beat of a butterfly's wings.

He was fading – I could not only see it before my eyes but feel it in my soul.

"Yes," I said.

"Do it," Erix added.

We held Duncan's life in our hands. Rafaela had made clear the dangers of this practice. Although the details were faint, my mind unable to hold onto any facts beside Duncan and how close he was to death.

Erix squeezed my hand, never letting go. "Duncan will be fine. He will come out of this, just as he has with all the trials that have been set out before this moment."

I swallowed the bile in the back of my throat, forcing it deep down. "How can you be sure?"

"Because if I knew I was leaving you behind, I'd fight tooth and nail to get back to you."

I warmed at his response, clinging to the feeling of hope it offered.

"Even if you had to go against a *god*?" My question echoed around the domed room, skipping between pillars and large block walls. Not to mention a god who inspired enough hate in the Nephilim to go against us.

"Even that, little bird."

"The Creator is many things," Rafaela reminded, chin jutted. "But his desires are not for us to decide. The assault on the fey is due to Cassial's warped sentiments, not because the Creator wanted this future. What Cassial and his Fallen desire is not in line with the rest of us."

I looked at her, dead in the eye. "You say the rest of you, but you stand alone."

In the dark of my mind I saw the unseen number of statues littered across the terrain of Irobel. The rest of her 'Faithful' were bound in stone, guarding the islands like sentinel guards.

"I am not alone," Rafaela said, laying a hand on her chest. "Nor are you. If only you know where to look."

I turned to Erix and buried my face in his chest. "I can't lose him, Erix." My knees buckled, the force of the very real chance weighing heavy on me.

"Then have faith," Erix encouraged. "Do not give up on him yet. Duncan is, as you well know, persistent. He has survived a change before, he can do it again." He lowered his lips to my head and whispered.

"I'm scared," I admitted.

"Me too." His hand brushed down the back of my head. "I don't want to lose him either."

Knowing my tether to keep Duncan in his realm was not solitary helped, if only a little.

"This is different," I said, voice shaking. "No outcome is guaranteed."

"But remember, Duncan *is* different," Rafaela reminded me. "He was born for this. Born to be made."

Small brass bells danced in the winds, casting a gentle sound around the room. It swelled around me, pressing in on my skin, until the very notes were etched into my bones.

"This process is not pleasant," Rafaela warned. "I would advise that you both wait outside until it is complete."

"No," I said, swallowing my weakness, trying to grapple the little strength I had left. "I'm not leaving him. Not for a second."

I caught Rafaela looking to Erix for assistance, but his silence was refusal enough. When she understood neither of us would leave, she offered us a final warning. "Do not let go of one another. Stay beyond the pool. If you interrupt the ceremony, it *will* hinder the results... possibly ruin them, in fact."

It was not a request, but a clear warning.

Rafaela didn't wait for our agreement, because there was no room for an answer. It was clear and simple. Don't interrupt, don't stop the ceremony.

"You've done this before?" I asked just as Rafaela reached for Duncan's lips and parted them with her fingers.

"Many times. I have even faced this judgement myself. The Creator has seen my heart and deemed me worthy – which suggests that He does not support Cassial's plans. Remember, it is the wielder who is evil, not the weapon. The same sword, in a different hand, can either protect a person or kill them."

I couldn't argue her point, nor did I have the energy left to do so.

The bells chimed louder, casting an unnatural ripple over the already unnatural waters. I couldn't believe what they were at first, not as Rafaela had hurriedly explained the process on our way here.

"After the Game of Monsters, the Creator hid within the cracked and ruined remains of his lands and wept for his loss of Duwar. It is in those tears of grief that we offer our mortal bodies up for judgement. It was from those tears that his first Nephilim were made, from the bodies of his fallen humans, altered and given the Creator's own strength. And from that day, the practice had continued. If worthy, the transformation will begin. If the Creator does not find an offering worthy, then death befalls them."

"Please, Rafaela. Do everything you can to make sure he survives this," I commanded, toying with the idea of praying to a god I had never believed in, or cared for.

But Duncan once did, under the wings of Abbot Nathanial. Comfort came in small measures at the knowledge of that.

I wondered if Nathanial knew the truth about Duncan. All those orphans he cared for; had they been delivered to him for a purpose? How many more people like Duncan lingered in Durmain, left to play a part in this strange turn of fates. He'd told me an angel once came to him, and I put it down to age and a fragile mind.

Now I knew the truth.

"Duncan, I swear you better survive this," Erix whispered, lip curling as he spoke to the floating body beneath us.

I risked a glance at him again, to find a furrowed brow and determined gaze fixed to the unconscious body in the pool of the Creator's tears.

When Erix spoke again, it was to Duncan directly. "Do you hear me? Survive this for Robin. For me. Fuck, do it for us. We have unfinished business."

Unfinished business.

"It is time I begin," Rafaela said, her gentle fingers still covering Duncan's mouth.

She swept her gaze between Erix and me, and we both agreed with the bow of our heads. That was all she needed to continue. Rafaela began to mumble strange words beneath her breath. What she said had a rhythm to it, as if she spoke in line with the bell's chimes.

Slowly, she parted Duncan's mouth until it was held open. Then, with one hand on his forehead, the other on his chest, Rafaela forced him beneath the waters.

I was expecting it, but that didn't stop the scream from bursting out of me. Erix locked his arms around my waist, holding me back, as Duncan was held beneath the pool.

His eyes flared open, panic singing in the bright, forest green. He'd not woken since last night, but the fright had just dragged him conscious at the wrong time.

Bubbles escaped his lungs, as the waters flooded into them. He tried to clamp his mouth closed, but he couldn't.

The damage was done.

Water splashed over the lip of the pool, cresting over my boots in waves. All the while I continued to shout for Duncan, whose frantic eyes searched for me. In the chaos, Seraphine and Gyah rushed into the sacred room. They saw what was happening, combined with my cries, and Rafaela concentrating on her prayer as she offered Duncan's life as payment to a god.

"Get him out of here!" Rafaela broke her flow enough to shout at us, a wave of power radiating out from her body. It wasn't magic. It was authority: the command of a Nephilim who was chosen by the Creator as his enforcer. "Now!"

Erix hesitated, but Seraphine and Gyah didn't. With their help, and brute strength, we were guided out of the chamber, leaving behind Rafaela to continue holding Duncan beneath the pool, her words echoing between stone walls.

As it turned out, it didn't take long for a person to drown. I noticed, as I was swept away, that Duncan's body had stopped thrashing, that the rush of bubbles leaving his mouth had slowed – proving no air was left within his lungs.

CHAPTER 24

Even beneath the blanket of night, Irobel's heavy, warm air was insufferable. I sat upon a wicker chair, digging my fingers into the knots of twine as I looked out across the island void of life. My eyes fixed on the reflection of the moon across the ocean's calm surface, because looking at anything else made this wait unbearable. No matter where I found my eyes falling, I thought of Duncan. Short storms rolled in quickly but left even quicker. Lightning flashed in the distance, speckled amongst thick clouds, only to pass on. In the moments after the lashing of rain, it gave the air some reprieve. But alas, the comfort didn't last.

Every now and then I'd catch Erix out the corner of my eye, dressed in a loose linen tunic which hung to his chest, tied over one shoulder. I supposed a positive about being in Irobel was that most of the clothing was made for creatures with wings.

Erix barely removed his attention from me. If it wasn't for his encouragement, I wouldn't have drunk the water provided or touched the plate of fresh fruits that had been picked by Seraphine for us to feast on.

Grapes, Seraphine had explained, a strange, small fruit that were sour to chew and coated in a thick skin. Tart orange slices that tasted more savoury than sweet. I could only manage a handful before sickness gripped my stomach.

Without Duncan beside me, I felt so alone. But the reality was I was surrounded by the people I loved.

Gyah was sitting by the door, gaze fixed to the wall, mind lost to her loss. I couldn't imagine how she felt, waiting for news on Duncan's second chance at life, while Althea's life was in the hands of a murderous zealot. Just the thought alone tore me up from the inside.

Seraphine kept herself busy too. A pile of books sat beside her, each 'borrowed' from the library she stumbled upon as she mentally mapped out the island and what was on it.

Once an Asp, always an Asp.

The texts were handwritten, likely biased accounts written by Nephilim over the years. I didn't have it in me to ask what she was researching, or even to care. I did, however, wonder if those texts had been touched by Duncan's birth mother. Were her stories inked onto those pages?

Every detail led back to *him*.

I practically held my breath as I waited for Rafaela to return with an update on Duncan's fate. But as the hours passed, dusk tumbling into the dead of night, I found that the only thing with the power to occupy my mind was *home*.

What state would the realms be in upon our return? Who else would be taken from this world, joining Althea in capture or Elinor in death?

If I had it in me to sleep, perhaps I would dream of Jesibel and find news. But every time I closed my eyes, I saw Duncan drowning in those cobalt waters.

"*The Transfiguration* success rate is rather high," Seraphine spoke, hardly looking up from the tome in her hand. "And can you believe the Nephilim have been taking humans from Durmain for generations? There is even a section in this book that mentions a festering sickness that swept across Irobel, leading to the demise of multiple Nephilim. With their numbers low, they were desperate for newer recruits – focusing on religious leaders in Durmain who continued the spreading of the Creator's belief. So the angels from religious stories show up, say that the Creator has a task for them, trick humans into coming here to be 'changed' and then ta-da, more winged warriors."

I hadn't told them about Duncan's truth – it wasn't fair they knew before him. So, I kept my mouth shut, knowing the twisted truth of the prophecy and what it made people like Rafaela and Cassial do.

No one replied to Seraphine. I tried to force up a sound to at least acknowledge I heard her, but my voice cracked and that made Erix jolt toward me as if something was wrong. Seraphine didn't notice, filling the awkward silence with more findings from her reading.

"I have found some more information about the binding of Nephilim in labradorite as well." She lifted her gaze and settled it upon me for a beat. "They called it the Severing. Severing a Nephilim from the Creator, by binding them in labradorite stone, and believe it or not, it is our dearest Rafaela who discovered it. No mention of a reversal, but if she is confident that it can be done, she would be the one to know."

I stretched my gaze out across the ocean again. There was a small island just off the coast of the one we stayed upon. Its jagged rockface was lined with the statues of bound Nephilim. To the naked eye, no one would believe they were anything but figures carved from stone. The truth was darker. And this was the promise of our army, a chance to save the world from Cassial and his use of Duwar. And yet we were wasting time trying to save Duncan – one soul – instead of an entire realm of people. Was that where my priorities lay? My small world, not the one around me?

No one suggested as much, but it was all I thought about.

It went on like this for a while. The room simmering in silence, only broken when Seraphine found something else to share.

"This tome explains that when Altar stole the power source of the realms, which was soon after named Duwar, it left behind an endless black chasm in the far north of what is now

Wychwood." Seraphine turned the book around so we could see the pages, and on it was a sketch of a familiar map of land. "Look here."

I did, narrowing my eyes on the location. "Is that…"

"The Sleeping Depths," Gyah answered for me. It was the lake we had visited all those months ago, when Althea's brother Orion had died at the hands of a Hunter. "That would explain why nothing that enters the waters of that lake survives."

Because Altar stole the power of the world and used it for his own gain. There had to be a price to pay, and that was what we knew as the Sleeping Depths. I remembered how no light reflected off the waters, and how eerily quiet it was as if the lake repelled anything natural.

"…*with desperate hands, Altar took something which never belonged to him. And with it he used the power of chaos and life, weaving it amongst his creations, giving them access to powers that no mortal deserved to hold.*" Seraphine paused, her fingers lingering on the sentence she was reading. "There is further comment on how the Creator willed his powerless humans to hunt down any powered fey and cast them into the abyss of nothingness, thus removing them from ever being a threat. But it was years later when the fey moved into the realm now known as Wychwood, but at this time there was no border. Do you see."

As she turned the book around again, nail pointing toward the map, a sound of footsteps rose beyond the closed door.

Heart in my throat, I stood before it opened. All thoughts of fey, gods and death-filled lakes left my mind in an instant.

Rafaela stood beneath the arched entrance to the room, puffing slightly from her rushed visit. Her eyes found mine and held them. "Duncan lives."

Something was missing in Rafaela's admission. Like a 'but' or 'for now'. I sensed it, read it in the silence of her abrupt stop.

I couldn't move. I didn't make a sound. I worried it would break this illusion and the real truth would catch up to me.

Erix closed into my side, offering his strong body as a frame for me to lean into. His presence alone gave me the strength to force a few words out.

"Can we... see him?" I asked, knowing I spoke for two people, no longer just one.

"Yes, but only if you are careful. The Transfiguration will still take time to complete. For now, Duncan has spiritually survived the Creator's will; we must now wait for his body to catch up, so to say." Rafaela looked exhausted, but even through it she didn't stop smiling. Hope glimmered in her bright eyes, making them almost shine like they were filled with tears. "I only ask that you allow him to... wake when he is ready."

"What do you mean?" I said, the question changing Rafaela's demeanour in a flash. Suddenly her smile faltered. Rafaela's hands wrung together, eyes downcast to the floor, shoulders hunched. "If he lives, he has been successful, no?"

"It is not as clear cut as that."

It was Seraphine who added more context. "According to this text, the final step of the Transfiguration is some sort of metamorphosis of the physical body. The Creator accepts the soul as worthy, but the body must always complete the change."

I knew what she meant. I'd seen and fought against enough Nephilim to know their bodies, and how different they were. I hadn't contemplated how Duncan would survive this, forever changed.

Would he be the same man I knew, or different in ways that go far beyond his flesh? Either way, it was his soul I loved. Put it in the shell of a beast, and my views of him wouldn't change.

"We would like to see him," I said, already taking the necessary steps toward Rafaela, Erix following like a shadow. "If he is going to wake up – *when* he wakes – I want us to be the people there to greet him."

"Of course," Rafaela bowed, clutching the doorframe for support. "Just be cautious, that is all I ask."

It was on the tip of my tongue to thank her, but until I saw Duncan breathing and the world freed from Cassial and Duwar's threat, I would keep my lips sealed. Superstition weighed heavy on me, but that didn't stop Rafaela from recognising my emotions when she caught my eye.

"You have worked valiantly," Erix said to Rafaela as we passed, his brow softening over tired eyes. "For that there will not be enough thanks that would suffice."

Rafaela bowed, a sombre smile flickering at the corners of her lips. As I got past her, she grasped my arm, fingers pinching into my skin. "Erix, what you find in that room will be a shock to you both."

"As long as he survives, I don't care—"

"No, Robin. I didn't mean a shock for you," Rafaela released me, parting from the door to allow room for me to pass. "I'm referring to Duncan. When he wakes, the world will be different for him. I ask that you are careful with him. Give him time to adjust."

"Time," I choked on the word. "It's not exactly a luxury we have."

When we returned to the ceremony room, Duncan was no longer in the pool of sacred water. The first thing I noticed was that he was missing, and my heart skipped a beat, panic seizing my lungs immediately. If it wasn't for Erix gesturing away from the pool, I might've screamed so loud it would have woken every stone-bound Nephilim on the island.

"It's okay, little bird. Look. Duncan is still with us."

I followed Erix's finger and took in the almost impossible view before me.

Hanging from a gelatinous stem on the ceiling was a pod. It wasn't the outline of a body, but a shapeless formation of wet yet solid material. My mind went to the cocoon of a caterpillar, except this dripped as though the Creator's tears had coagulated into a mass that held its shape, whilst dripping pools of bright blue water onto the stone floor.

I stepped free of Erix's shadow, feet squelching over the thickened liquid. The evening breeze continued to blow against the many brass bells, filling the space with a light tune. But there was another sound to accompany it. The definite thump of a heart.

Duncan's heart.

To prove my sanity, I laid a hand on the outer shell of the pod, and through it I felt Duncan's strong beat echo against my palm.

Thud. Thud. Thud.

It was my Duncan, loud and strong – his beat as proud as I remembered it.

I trailed my hand over the wet pod, wondering if Duncan was conscious within. Could he feel me? Sense me? My fingers came back webbed with slime, but I didn't care.

I leaned in close to the scentless material and whispered. "I'm here, Duncan. And I swear to any god, I won't leave you again."

"Rafaela said to wait for him to wake in his own time," Erix said, closing the door, sealing us in the room together. "I didn't imagine this was what she was referring to."

I could barely understand what she meant, and I was stood looking at it. Like the transformation of a weak creature into a beautiful butterfly, I could only imagine what was happening to Duncan. As much as I wanted to claw my way through the pod to reach him, deep down, I knew better than to do that.

I was toying with a pawn of a god, a player on a game board. The unknown was frightening, yes. But when the unknown was in relation to the man you loved, it was world-shattering.

Erix walked in from behind me. His hand found its way atop mine, resting so we were both connected to Duncan's cocoon. My heart swelled in my chest, so large my ribs ached. Seeing his hand splayed on mine, pressing against the strange shell encasing Duncan, filled my soul with a sense of calm.

"Do you think he knows we're here?" I asked, the words echoing around the chamber.

"I think he will always know when *you* are close," Erix replied. "It is impossible not to."

I dropped my hand, forcing his to come with me. I turned and faced Erix, leaving my back to the cocoon. "He'll be happy you're with me too. Duncan, I mean. Your presence is important to him: I know that, as do you."

Their private conversation replayed in the back of my mind, warming my soul from the inside out.

Erix swallowed, a smile creeping at the corners of his mouth. "I do."

We were so close to one another, Erix had to look down at me where he stood. He lifted a finger and traced it down the curve of my cheek, sending shivers across every inch of my skin. "Duncan has two reasons to get better and see this through to the end. Then he can tell us exactly how much he cares for us himself."

I shivered but the feeling wasn't unpleasant. My thoughts, although frantic and unorganised, seemed to go back to something I hadn't had time to think about in the moment. "There is something I need to admit to you."

I hoped Duncan really could hear me as well.

"Tell me," Erix encouraged softly.

Stealing myself, I refused to look away when I spoke again. "When you went to check on Duncan, I heard you speaking. I didn't mean to eavesdrop, but I did, and I admit it."

"Then you know what we spoke about," Erix said plainly.

"I know," I said, hearing the words repeat in my mind. "Me. I mean us, the three of us."

The kiss of fingers melted into the soft caress of a palm against the side of my face. Erix released a sigh, followed by the most beautiful smile I'd ever seen. "The conversation was brief," he explained. "Duncan reiterated his reasoning behind wanting me with you. He truly believed his end was near, and he seemed content knowing you would not be alone if death came for him. But that wasn't all. I think even Duncan sensed a hope that if he was to survive, his desires going forwards would be the same. The three of us. Me, you and him."

"Together," I added. "Not just for the present, but for the future too."

Erix bowed his head. "Duncan has had time to contemplate this path forwards, but I had to ask him why. Why he feels as though he can share you with another person, when the thought of that has never crossed my mind until now. I knew there was a reason, something he wasn't telling us. And it was because he knew he was dying. I understand now. He loves you so much, he cannot fathom to leave the world knowing you would be alone in it."

Duncan knew that I had Erix, and that if he were to die, it would be with the peaceful knowledge that Erix would still be by myside. And yet, something still didn't make sense to me about that.

"Duncan is a man of his word, Erix."

"As am I," Erix replied, dropping his hand and stepping back.

"Care to further that statement?"

He lifted his silver eyes over my shoulder and laid them on Duncan's shell. "I realised that Duncan never planned to *share* you. That wasn't what he meant."

"Because he thought he was dying?"

Erix shook his head, fixing his gaze back to mine. "No. His offer was not solely born from a place of worry that he was going to be taken from you. It was made from the hope that, if given another chance, he simply wishes for the man he loves to be happy. To be whole. At least, those were his words."

I did want those things. But the same went for Erix. If it was Erix in Duncan's shoes, taking his path, I would have reacted the same. I knew that. The fear I harboured at the idea of losing either of them made me sick to my core.

"Duncan knows me well," I said, finding that it was all I could get out. "As well as his own desires. However, this decision must be made with equal power between not two, but three of us. Tell me, Erix, what is it you want? Because if Duncan survives this, we are once again faced with this tug and pull. I love you, and I love Duncan, but I don't want to be stretched between you."

"Why choose, hey?" Erix took a step closer until my chest pressed into his.

"Surely it isn't as simple as that?"

Erix drank me in, all silver eyes full of love, and lips glistening from the trace of his tongue. "We would not be the first in history to fall in love outside the norms of what society dictates. Sometimes love is not as clear cut as we believe it to be. It is as wild as a ravine, and as embracing as the waters within it. So, I ask you, what do you want, little bird?"

I took a deep breath, filling my body with the incense-heavy air of Irobel. "I want to exist between you both comfortably, like a piece of a puzzle finally finding the place it belongs. But that will only work if you are both matching pairs."

His eyes narrowed, the tension growing thicker between us. "Then it seems our desires are shared. I told you long ago that it is my duty to ensure you are cared for," Erix added, a single brow lifting over inquisitive eyes. Tired, inquisitive eyes that were haunted by everything we'd been through. "That duty is the same for Duncan. And truthfully, I care deeply for him. On a level I never knew possible. My love for Duncan stems from *his* love for you. And I understand now, after my conversation with him, those feelings are mutual."

I longed to touch him, to trace my fingers along his jaw and memorise him for an eternity. "It's as if life finally makes sense, right?"

"My thoughts exactly."

I found my gaze drifting to where Duncan lingered inside the strange pod. "When Duncan wakes from this, I will still need you. I can't explain it in words, not yet. However, I know Duncan is right. I'm only whole when the two halves of my heart are kept together. He holds one half, and you the other."

Erix shuffled on his feet, turning his body to the side until we both looked to where Duncan rested.

Moonlight swept in through the glassless windows, bathing his profile in an iridescent glow. It caught the single tear that slipped out of his eye, which was strange, because Erix looked the happiest I'd seen him in a long time.

"Are you crying because you are sad?" I asked, already knowing the answer.

He shook his head, lips tugging wider. "Robin, I thought I lost you. I grieved for you after… after what Doran made me do. I accepted my actions and the consequences they led to, and it destroyed me. But it was Duncan who encouraged you to speak to me in Berrow all that time ago. It was Duncan who ensured I stuck around. For you. He recognised, even then, that you needed me, even if neither of us had worked that out. I owe him my life for that."

I didn't understand the concept of being with them both, but what I did know was it involved consent. If all parties were not on equal footing, then it would fail before it began.

It was my turn to offer Erix some comfort, for his words sank as deep as a knife inside of me. I lifted my hand up and laid it on his cheek. Erix closed his eyes, his expression soft with relief. He leaned into my touch, quickly covering my hand and holding it in place.

"I never stopped loving you, Erix," I whispered my admission. "Just as I know I'll never stop loving Duncan. My

heart is big enough for the both of you, equally. I see it now...
that it is not about separate halves or sharing. It just simply *is*."

"You have no idea how I have needed to hear that, little
bird," Erix smiled, the emotion glittering in twin silver-flamed
eyes. "No idea."

"Then hear it, and take it in," I said. "Don't ever forget."

"I will not, even though I still recognise I'm not worthy of
such an answer, not after the pain I have caused you, but I do
hear you."

"Who determines if you are not worthy of my love, but
me?" I asked.

The pause stretched between us, a gaping mouth of darkness
ready to swallow us up for judgement.

"Perhaps we can continue this conversation when
Duncan decides to wake up?" Erix said, putting a halt to the
conversation. "I want him to hear my definitive answer. It
would be pointless if he wakes and has changed *his* mind, now
he knows that death is behind him."

"I told you already, Duncan is a man of his word."

Erix lifted his eyes toward the hanging sack that Duncan
dwelled within. "We shall see."

Then he stepped back, leaving my hand to hover strangely in
the air where he'd been. His gaze swept the room, searching for
something. "I think it best that we both get some rest. Duncan
would also kill me if he knew you hadn't slept properly whilst
in my care."

I was aware that there was no bed in the room. But I had no
plans to leave, and Erix didn't need to be told that either. I put
it down to Erix realising that if the tables were turned, and it
was me who'd just faced a death, he'd have to be pried away
to leave my side.

I smiled at the unspoken knowledge.

"Come here," Erix said, taking my hand and leading me
off to the side of the room. We stopped before a thick pillar
of cool marble. Threads of black veins spread amongst the

stone. Erix sat himself against the pillar, spreading his legs out on either side.

He patted the space between them. "Lie down with me."

Altar, that command almost brought me to my knees.

I tried to find an excuse for him to go find a bed and to leave me. But it would've been wasted breath. So I did as he commanded. I nestled myself between Erix's legs, laying my head on his chest. His body was hard with muscle, and yet I melted into him, feeling at home even surrounded by this strange place. There was no need for bedding in such a hot climate. But Erix rested a wing over us, offering me the cool air in his body-made shadow.

I looked up to where Duncan's cocoon hung ahead of us. Even from the distance, I could still hear the strong thump of his heart, and how it played in symphony with the chime of bells.

But there was another beat that sang to me too. Erix's heart echoed through my back, spreading across my chest until I was full of him.

"Erix?" I said, closing my eyes to hide myself away from his reaction.

"Yes, little bird?"

I took a deep breath in, drinking in the scent of him. "Do you remember the dream you had, the one Duncan used Duwar to give you?"

"I could never forget it." Erix lowered his mouth to my scalp and pressed a kiss to it.

"Can you tell me what you experienced?" I asked.

You called for me, so I came.

"It was of us." Erix's wings tightened, holding me close. "The three of us, that is."

I exhaled a breath full of tension. My mind came up with an answer to Erix's concern from moments ago. "So, even back then, Duncan was showing us the possibility of a future."

"I suppose he was."

In the moment, I thought it was Duwar taunting me, using a weakness I didn't know I still had against me.

Erix took a moment to pause, thoughts swirling behind those bright eyes of his. "All we can do is wait for him to make it through, and once he is in his right mind, we will see what he says."

"And if the proposal is the same?" I asked, hope glittering across my words.

I found myself holding my breath for his answer.

"Little bird, I made a promise to never leave you again. I too am a man of my word. I plan to stick to it."

"Good," I said, wishing it was physically possible to press into him more.

"Now sleep," Erix said. "I'll wake you if anything changes with Duncan."

"What about you?" I asked. "Surely you are tired too."

"Exhausted," Erix answered. "But for just a moment, I would like to enjoy this. Us. The chance of a tomorrow."

"There is a chance for more than just a tomorrow, Erix. There could be so much more."

So much more. Me, Erix and Duncan. But first, we had a world to save.

I woke from a dreamless sleep, startled beneath the sky-shattering boom of thunder. My eyes opened to a dark room, but it wasn't because night still ruled the sky outside. A storm had finally rolled over Irobel, casting the once-blue sky in a blanket of dark cloud. But unlike the others, this was one was here to stay.

"Robin – where?" Erix mumbled frantically, sitting up, jolting me forwards.

"It's just a storm," I said, looking back at him. Sleep crusted the corners of my eyes and my mouth had dried. My body was covered in a sticky film of sweat, but it was the best sleep I'd had in a long while. So much so, it took me a moment to work out where we were.

Then I remembered Duncan and turned to his cocoon.

My world shattered at what I found.

The cocoon had broken apart. Half still hung to the ceiling, but the rest lay in dried patches of cracked shell across the floor. Amongst the dried shell and puddles of thick masses of goo, white feathers led like a path toward the window.

And Duncan was nowhere to be seen.

I was up in seconds, standing on trembling knees as I scanned my eyes over the entirety of the room. Erix joined me, sharing in my panic. Lightning cast the room in a stark purple glow. It highlighted the broken shell and missing body.

"I'm sorry," Erix shouted over another clash of thunder. There was barely a second between the lightning and the world-shattering boom. "I fell asleep when I was supposed to keep watch. I should not have... I–"

As another bolt of bright light cast across the sky, my panic faded to nothingness. I laid a hand on Erix's arm, wishing he shared the same revelation as I. "Erix," I said. "This is not a normal storm..."

"What?" His eyes were wide open, fear painted in the bright hues of his irises.

"It's him."

Him. Duncan.

Even more snakes of purple light passed over the sky, proud and strong. I knew in the deepest parts of my soul that they belonged to Duncan. For this was his power. I couldn't explain it, but from the way the panic left Erix's gaze, he figured it out too. As if the same tether inside of me was also bound around him.

Another unspoken need was my desperation to be taken to him. Erix sensed that. In seconds I was swept up, his muscle-hard arms holding me close to him.

Erix beat his leathery wings against the thick air, the floor falling away from us. Then, with the grace of a dove, we speared out of the window, directly into the sky beyond.

Rain lashed down over Irobel, blinding me. Warm winds whipped at my skin. Erix flew up and up, until the building was nothing but a speck beneath us. But that wasn't the only thing I noticed.

The sky was full. Not only of thunder and lightning, rain and wind. But of Nephilim. They were everywhere, wings beating, keeping them afloat. My first instinct was to gather my magic, bringing ice to the surface, ready to turn rain to spears that would rip through flesh.

But the Nephilim paid us no mind.

There was a flock of warriors, hundreds of them. No, *thousands*. Not a single one looked at Erix or me. Their gazes were focused to a spot in the centre of the storm, where another figure hung, white wings beating as purple light sparked and crested around their body.

A body I knew as well as my own, except it was different to the last time I saw it.

"Duncan," I breathed, almost choking on the name. When I repeated his name, it came out as a desperate scream. "Duncan!"

Perhaps he couldn't hear me, or maybe he just chose to ignore me. But that didn't stop me from bellowing for him, over and over, until my throat felt as though it bled.

Erix attempted to fly closer, but the lightning kept us at bay, as did the sky full of Nephilim.

It seemed, with every passing second, more joined the sky.

But from where?

More lightning. More thunder. I watched as the lines of stark light left the white-winged figure. Instead of threading through the clouds, conducting in the warm air and setting the sky on fire, they crashed into the earth, spreading across every island in Irobel – atop statues of stone.

"The Saviour," I breathed, studying this impossibility. "He really is the Saviour who Gabrial prophesised."

324 A GAME OF MONSTERS

As Duncan's lightning struck Irobel, it shattered stone. Not stone, but the statues themselves. And from those statues, more Nephilim flew skyward. An endless stream of bodies. And I watched, from Erix's arms, as the hope of saving the realms suddenly became a possibility.

Duncan had not only survived the Transfiguration – the Creator's judgement and the physical change to his body – he was using his fey-given power to free Rafaela's promised army. And with each strike of burning light, I felt the kindling of hope spark in my chest, growing hotter and hotter until it was impossible not to let it consume me.

Born from two realms. Made, with the blood of the fey threading through his heart.

I smiled, pride beaming from my soul for him. Because Duncan Rackley's survival had just changed the tide of the future's fate.

CHAPTER 25

The sun broke through storm clouds, bathing the chasm before me in rays of pure gold. The beams danced across a silent crowd of flesh and feather – Nephilim filling every possible space. Those who couldn't stand to watch had to fly, wings a multitude of blacks, greys, whites and creams beating against warm air, their eyes pinned to the man who had freed them.

I edged closer to the cliff's edge to get a better look at them. My feet walked over a smooth man-made path in the rockface, until I came to a stop on a threshold that overlooked Irobel. All around me I could see the ocean, interrupted by the smaller sister islands to the heart of the isle. But my attention wasn't spared to anything or anyone else. Only *Duncan*.

Trousers clung to strong thighs, but his chest was exposed to the elements, light reflecting off the hardened lines of muscle. Wind tussled his feathered wings, making the dark hair upon his crown dance like serpents.

Even the crowd of Nephilim who filled the chasm looked up with adoration in their eyes to Duncan, who stood front and centre.

I understood their obvious respect. Not a single soul spoke or made a sound, which was impressive because there had to be thousands of winged warriors looking on at this miracle.

My miracle.

I shared their same emotion. My heart had lodged in my throat for every second we were apart.

Erix stayed at my side. Rafaela and Seraphine had arrived not long ago, on the back of Gyah in her Eldrae form. I noticed the hesitation from the crowd as the obsidian-scaled creature flew into view, but one raised hand from Duncan was all it took to calm them.

He oozed authority and power. Stood tall, his skin exposed to the world, there was not a muscle hidden. Even his back rippled with them – muscles my fingers and mouth had not yet explored. Whatever had happened during the Transfiguration had changed him in *every* aspect. He no longer looked like the weak man I had worn down with my treatment. Duncan stood tall, shoulders rolled back, likely a result of the two imposing pure-white wings that spread from protruding mounds beside his spine.

I was desperate to speak to him. Every time our eyes locked, I felt that need build, alongside the hiss of electricity racing over my skin. My body was a chamber of overboiling lava, seconds from bursting. But I had to keep control, to focus on keeping myself calm, all whilst I watched Duncan address the sea of Nephilim watching him.

Rafaela gripped my arm, knees weak as she was overcome with relief. Her whisper seemed to be a shout as the world around us was so silent, even the winds calmed in the presence of a being like Duncan. "He has come. Gabrial's prophesied. Our Saviour."

Hearing her refer to Duncan as the Saviour warmed my spirit, kindling the hope that couldn't help but rage inside. Simply looking at him, seeing what he'd achieved, even I couldn't dispel the concept of the prophecy.

"So, the fey-hunter survives *again*," Gyah drawled, the moment she shifted back into her form. "Are we sure Duncan is not part cockroach or something?"

"He is something incredible," I said, voice clear cut and swelling with pride.

"When we saw the Nephilim we thought Cassial had come for us," Gyah admitted. "As much as I'm glad to see Duncan alive and kicking, I am disappointed I don't get to tear out Cassial's throat today."

I stood, dumfounded, and fixated on Duncan's back. "Soon," I promised Gyah, knowing it was truly a possibility. "His fate awaits him."

Now more so than ever before.

"Duncan Rackley has faced the judgement, survived and has returned to us with a purpose," Rafaela added, eyes fixed, gaze locked on Duncan. "We are now in a position to go against Cassial in a way that he will least expect."

"I like the sound of that," Gyah replied, closing in. "But my question is when. Now our purpose here is complete, I want to leave Irobel immediately."

"We will," I promised, sharing in the same want as Gyah. "Althea is our priority."

Gyah looked back to Duncan, a grimace pinched across her face. "I hope so."

Seraphine leaned in, hand over her heart – likely pressing down on the folded sketch of those she left behind in Durmain. "I must say Duncan has such an impressive wingspan. I can see the appeal now, Robin."

Her comment conjured a belly-cackle out from me. But before I could reply, Duncan finally spoke up.

"Children of the Creator." His words boomed across the island, as if the clouds of his conjuring magnified his voice.

The hairs rose on my arms, not from his command but the lightning that still thickened the air around us. The storm may have passed, but when Duncan was close, it never strayed far.

"The Creator's Faithful warriors. You have been locked away for sins that never belonged to you. It would seem the years have confused our brothers and sisters; the path we've walked for generations has faded and many have lost their way. You paid the price. Shut away in the continued effort to prevent history from repeating itself – cast into stone simply for doing what was right. No longer shall you be hidden away. No longer will you face the endless imprisonment. The time to right the wrongs of the Fallen is upon us."

A perfectly synchronised cheer rose from the chasm. The sound shook the very sky, with more power than any conjured thunder could. It split the clouds further, bringing forth more rays of golden light.

I could practically taste the admiration they all held for Duncan.

"And who are you, Duncan Rackley, in the eyes of the Creator?" Rafaela shouted, voice rising in pitch as she directed it to Duncan. I was surprised Duncan heard. He slowly turned to face her, his severe brow softening as he laid eyes on Rafaela. There wasn't anger, but the sorrow of someone who understands a price paid.

Rafaela had lost so much, Duncan recognised that.

Duncan offered his hand to her. Everyone watched, not daring to breathe, as he lifted her from the ground and drew her to his side.

When he answered it was personal to Rafaela, and yet he ensured the entire crowd heard him.

"My given name is Duncan Rackley, although you know that was not the one I was born with." The sorrow in his verdant eyes told me that Duncan had already uncovered the secrets of his birth. I wondered what else the human god had whispered into his ear. "I have been given true life by the Creator to give the Faithful a second chance. There has never been a time when your iron-clad faith has been more required. Duwar has been freed – chaos has, once again, been taken by the hands of those undeserving. The Creator knew, in his last moments, that keeping Duwar out of play was the only way for peace. He faced his regrets in those last moments, and yet some of his creations seem to have disregarded his enlightenment for the hunt of power and control. And as we were first designed, from the grief and loss of the Creator, we must ensure that His regrets do not continue into our future. For that, I stand before me, as Duncan, *Herald* of His word. Bringer of change."

Rafaela fell to her knees, hands clasped in prayer. Tears spilled down her face, staining the dusted ground beneath her. "Gabrial promised this day. She saw it, in a potential future, one of knotted paths and shadowed potentials. And now the Creator has proven He understands the damage Duwar will cause – how it tore Him apart from Altar. This is proof to the world of what we must do."

Belief, religion and prophecy blended into one, forced into the vessel that was Duncan. Everything had led to this moment. All the lies and betrayal, the secret plays on a game board that I never knew we were a part of.

Duncan's wings flared wide, further proving Seraphine's earlier statement. His wingspan cast a shadow of his form down over the crowd, gathering a gasp of amazement from the Nephilim watching.

"We follow you, *Herald*." Rafaela was renewed with a sense of authority, as if Duncan's presence reminded her of her possibilities. "Tell us how we are to right the sins of those who betrayed us, and we shall see it through."

Duncan drank in Rafaela's words, power flashing across every inch of him.

"Cassial has lost his way. It's up to us to offer him the right path, show him the way back into the Creator's arms." Duncan ensured his gaze fell on every possible watching soul. All but mine.

What I'd give for him to turn around and look at me, recognise me. I was beginning to think he ignored me for a reason. Perhaps the physical change was not the only thing that had altered during the Transfiguration. It didn't pay to contemplate what else was different.

"If unchallenged, Cassial will fulfil the Fallen's hopes of bringing forth a new world in which only the humans shall thrive. An imbalance. The fey are not the enemies of mortals, but the protectors as Altar intended them to be. It's up to us to prevent any other future from happening. I ask you, forgotten children of our Creator, discarded warriors – will you stand beside me in the name of what is right, to fix the wrongs before us and stop our enemies from threatening the realms again? Will you fight beside me, human and fey, to ensure a world in which we finally can live beside one another in complete and irrevocable harmony?"

A chanting began in response to his questions.

It started with the stomping of feet, then every set of wings began to thump as they were contracted against powerful bodies. Soon the sound filled the island, even sinking deep into my body where I felt it in every vein and vessel.

"Then, it shall be. We leave for the mainland soon." Duncan turned to face Rafaela, dropping his voice so only those on the podium of rock could hear. "See that you are prepared. If we are to get close enough to Cassial to stop him, he must not recognise a difference in our warriors from his own. To succeed we need to infiltrate Cassial's ranks, take him down from the inside. But before that, a contingency plan *must* be made."

"Certainly, Herald," Rafaela said. "The necessary plans will be drafted with your guidance."

Already the world weighed too heavy upon Duncan's shoulders. I sensed it, as did Erix, from the tight draw of his lips.

Duncan, too, stiffened at the title, but only I seemed to notice his discomfort. "We do not have long to act. Once you organise the Nephilim, see that a space is made for the rest of us to discuss these important matters. If we are to succeed, we must leave by dawn tomorrow."

"Anything else?" Rafaela asked, head bowing.

"Yes, actually. In the meantime, I would appreciate a moment alone–"

Duncan lifted his eyes over Rafaela's shoulder and fixed them to me. My breath caught, as though lightning shot between us and struck my chest. His expression was serious for a beat, until his lips curved and parted, forging into a gentle smile that tugged at the scar down the side of his face.

"With *them*," he finished.

I looked to Erix, following Duncan's sweeping gaze. His eyes were wide and watching, locked to Duncan who gave him a subtle wink. If my heart had skipped beats before, it practically leapt in that moment.

"Unfinished business, isn't that right, Erix?" Duncan said, stepping in close, bringing with him the air of power around him.

"It is, indeed, Saviour." Erix nodded to Duncan, whose smile seemed to widen. There was relief in his verdant eyes, a happiness I'd not seen in a long time.

"Duncan will do," he replied. "It's the name I am used to hearing and much prefer. It's not my future that defines me, but my past and present."

"And what are you going to do with the present?" I asked, voice cracking from nerves around him. "Now that... that you have secured it."

Duncan didn't reply at first, but I *sensed* his desire in his silence.

It was in the way he looked at me. It was as if the wings and strength, the power and command all faded away, leaving the man I'd first come to know standing before me. "You, *darling*. Both of you, as I told you, I am a man of my word."

I laid a hand over my chest, as if that had the power to still it. Duncan had heard us from his cocoon, and that filled me with the greatest sense of relief.

Duncan offered a hand to me, and then his other to Erix.

"Althea," Gyah said in reminder, brow creased over storm-filled eyes. "That is where our focus must be. Not Cassial, but Althea."

A thrum of emotion filtered over the crowd. Duncan fixed his gaze to Gyah and then to Seraphine. Although the space was silent, not a word spoken aloud, I saw the slight widening of Seraphine's eyes and got the impression of a message being shared between them.

She nodded, in agreement it would seem, then took Gyah to the side and whispered something to her.

Duncan squeezed my hand, then said two *distracting* words. "Shall we?"

I couldn't form a reply for fear I would break down. Instead, I took his hand and melted into the warmth of him. My palm tickled against the residue of his power – like called to like.

I longed to say something, but I couldn't force the words out.

"I'm sorry I had to leave you both this morning," Duncan said to me, his voice back to his normal self. "As you can imagine, I had some business to take care of."

I swallowed hard, the sound audible even as the roar of Nephilim took flight around us. "I can see that."

"But I'm back, and no longer is my focus split."

"For the record, *Duncan*," Erix said from my side, laying his hand in Duncan's waiting palm. "My wingspan is definitely larger than yours. Not that it's a competition or anything."

"Is that so?" Duncan's brow lifted in jest, turning his attention to me. Altar, his smirk had the power to warm my insides. "What do *you* think, darling?"

Heat unravelled in my groin, hot and sudden.

"Careful with your answer, little bird," Erix warned, mischief simmering in his silver eyes.

I gathered the confidence to address Duncan. And when I managed to get the words out, I spoke with the one emotion that came naturally. With the same sarcasm that always rose as a shield in times when I needed it. "Ask me after I get the chance to investigate for myself."

CHAPTER 26

I stood between the two most important men in my life, finally facing the possibility that I could accept them both equally.

Duncan stood to my left, his white wings folded, his exposed stomach hardened with rejuvenated muscles. A handful of downy feathers had fallen beside his feet, blanketing the stone floor in a carpet of soft white.

Erix waited at my right. I watched the trickling sweat roll down his temple, wanting to reach up and clean it for him. My desire to tell him that his hesitance was not warranted burned on the tip of my tongue.

But how could I say that, when I shared in the feeling?

Part of me wanted nothing more than to beg them both to close the space between us and touch me. I craved it. *Desperately.* But it was as if we each waited for the verbal consent to take this first frightening – but thrilling – step.

"So, Duncan," Erix said, peering to him. "You are a Nephilim now?"

Duncan's wings shivered as if they were sentient and understood Erix. He looked down at this new body, then back to Erix. "I suppose that is part of it. As well as the fact I'm still myself. Human. And I have fey blood pumping through my heart too. Bit of a monster, I guess."

"They say that a cat has nine lives, and here you are already proving you've got at least more than two," Erix added with a light laugh

Duncan's warm chuckle rumbled across the room in response, dusting over my skin. "What can I say, I have a lot to live for."

His eyes fell on me, snatching my breath out of my lungs.

"The prophesied Saviour," I announced, aware of just how odd the words sounded in my mouth. "Besides the wings and your new title, dare I ask what else has changed?"

Duncan refused to take his eyes off me. I fought against the urge to look down, worried at what his answer might be.

"Nothing else of merit. I'm still the same man, just with some added limbs," Duncan said, stepping into me. He swept a hand through his dark wash of hair, brushing the strands away from his eyes. "I've been given another chance at life, and this time I refuse to waste it."

"I – I still can't believe this." The words came tumbling out of me. "It feels like I'm dreaming."

"This is very real, darling." Duncan pinched his eyes closed and laid his forehead against mine.

If I closed my eyes, I could pretend that none of this had changed. That we were two people, existing in Abbott Nathanial's attic, with no concept of time or responsibility.

"I can leave if you prefer," Erix said, filling the silence. "You both deserve some time–"

"Erix, tell us what you really want," Duncan interrupted. "If you wish to leave, then you can. But only do it because you want to, not because you *think* that's what we want."

A light sparked behind Erix's silver-clad eyes. "I want to stay," he said slowly. "With you both."

I locked eyes with my guard, wanting nothing more than to feel his closeness, his touch. "I need you here, Erix."

Duncan nodded in agreement, stretching out a hand for Erix.

"Robin," Duncan began, taking my hand until we were all connected in a thread of flesh and bone. "What do you wish to do with the chance of a new world?"

"With a tomorrow," I corrected, catching Erix's eyes as I repeated his sentiment aloud.

"I like that," Duncan said, eyes dusting down my neck, my torso, lifting back up to meet my eyes. "This tomorrow, what does that look like for you?"

"Life," I answered, looking between them both. "One together. With you both by my side, no expectations, no anxieties to rival us."

"Well, I can only speak for myself when I say this." Duncan brushed fingers down the side of my face, leaving a trail of shivers in their wake. "I will never leave your side, darling."

I looked to Erix, waiting for his response.

He took a deep breath in, straightening his posture beneath my gaze. "How could I turn my back on you, little bird? If you asked for the sun, I would find a way to give it to you... and Duncan."

"I don't want the sun," I said, softly. "I simply want you, Erix."

"Then that is what you shall have," Erix replied, lifting his chin high in feigned confidence.

Duncan lifted a strong hand and laid it on Erix, smile singing of his pride. "I exist better knowing Robin has you in his life, and I have you too. Tomorrow, we have the chance to secure the future we deserve. But today, right now, we simply deserve to exist in it." Duncan drew Erix closer then took precise steps toward me, wedging my body beneath them both.

I looked at them both, making sure they could read the silent desire lingering in my eyes. Then, I slipped my hand in to each of theirs and gave them an order. "Sit with me."

I stepped backwards, aware the bed was close enough to reach. My heart was in my throat by the time the back of my knees hit the bedding. I sat, drawing both men to join me. Duncan to my left, Erix to my right. The bed shifted beneath our conjoined weight, the frame groaning audibly.

I allowed myself a moment of pause. Just a second was all I needed. Eyes closed, I took a breath in, filling my lungs and clearing out the cobwebs of my own hesitation.

It wasn't simply a want to have them both, but a need. Recognising that, taking control of it, was what would see me through.

"Can I be selfish for a moment?" I asked, looking between them, skin itching for their touch.

"Go ahead," Duncan said.

"Please do," Erix added, the corner of his lip quirking with what was only anticipation.

No more hiding. No more worrying. If there was ever a moment to show both Duncan and Erix just how deeply I required them in my life, it was now.

I turned enough to face Duncan, threading my fingers into his hair, nails tickling over his scalp. A pleased sign escaped his parted mouth, just before I silenced him with a kiss. As my lips melded with his, my tongue slipping in and entangling with Duncan's, I ensured my spare hand never left Erix's knee.

The kiss was everything I'd craved in the weeks past. Warmth spread across my groin, making me ache against the feeling. But, out of respect for them both, I had to take my time.

I drew back, bringing my hand from Duncan's scalp to lay it across his cheek. Then it fell further, reaching for the curve of his wings. As soon as I touched them, Duncan's entire body shivered, a small chirp bursting beyond his lips.

"Are they sensitive?" I asked, the word fumbling in my salivating mouth.

"*Very*," Duncan purred, his gaze serious as his tone. "I'll get used to them, as will you."

I smiled up at him, allowing myself to finally release all those emotions I'd pent up since the last time I was able to share such a time with him. "Duncan, from the moment I met you, I knew that there was a part of me that had been missing until then. Even though you captured me, I still recognised your truth, behind the illusion of Duncan, the Hunter. I saw you, the man I then came to love." As if that wasn't enough, I repeated myself, making sure the next five words were the clearest I'd ever said them. "I love you, Duncan Rackley."

His green eyes softened at the edges, his pink wet lips curving into the most beautiful of smiles. "And I love you."

I shifted my attention to Erix. There was no ignoring the way his breathing caught in his throat, as if our sudden eye contact was enough to shock him. Duncan's hand lay on my back, encouraging me to continue my admission.

"Erix," I breathed his name, feeling the weight of it, the emotion behind it.

"Hello, little bird," he said, his nerves endearing and no different to my own.

"Thank you," I sighed, desperate to kiss him but needing to get one last thing off my chest first.

"For what?" He tilted his head, laying his hand atop mine and squeezing.

"For existing. For everything." I took a deep breath in, preparing to unlock the final bolt upon my emotions, and let them out. Vulnerability always made me feel weak, but for the first time, the release of it made me the most powerful man in the world. "Thank you for sweeping into my life and showing me the person I never believed it possible to become. Without you, without the profound effect you've had on me, I don't think I'd have had the strength to dare to love another person. You showed me the parts of myself that were hidden, and for that I can't do anything but thank you."

"Oh, Robin," Erix exhaled my name, as if the moment warranted the seriousness of using it. It was my undoing. "You have always been my anchor, even when my mind was not my own."

"And you fought against it, for me."

"He did," Duncan agreed. "And for that Robin, take the first step and show Erix *how* you feel."

Encouraged by Duncan's words, I leaned into Erix, closed the space and placed my lips to his. The kiss – as it had been with Duncan – was tender. Full of emotion and unspoken words. I delighted in the taste of him, drinking every possible second as if this was a dream. When in truth, nothing had ever felt so real.

Erix was the one to break it. I didn't need to ask why as he reached over me, took Duncan's hand and spoke to him directly. "We both love him."

"More than words could ever begin to explain," Duncan agreed.

"Your actions have made that clear, both of you," I said, looking between them both. "Whether I'm deserving of it or not."

"You are," Erix whispered. "I have decided."

"We can both agree on that," Duncan confirmed. "Words are strong, but actions are ever so powerful. Let's use them to show one another exactly how deep we feel, and how sure we are."

How could I refuse?

I rocked back as both men closed the space and laid their mouths on my neck. One from either side.

I faced skyward, eyes locked to the domed ceiling. Pleasure was a tidal wave. A release. I lost myself to the feeling of their mouths, the graze of teeth and the languid sweep of tongues.

It was one thing to lie with one of them, but having them both was otherworldly. If there was any scrap of feeling that I was not worthy, it faded away as Duncan and Erix devoured me.

I was worthy, because they saw me as that. And if I expected them to accept the same feeling, I had to first take it and confidently welcome it too.

I couldn't get enough. Without words or commands, I begged them each to take turns on my mouth. As Duncan expressed his need for me in the passion of his kiss, Erix would continue roaming his mouth down my neck. At one point, Erix had reached for the button of my tunic and offered me a simple question.

"May I take this off, little bird?" Erix asked.

Duncan withdrew from my mouth just long enough for me to reply.

"Yes," I exhaled. *"Please."*

Erix wasted no time. He began undoing my tunic, tugging the lose material over my shoulders so his mouth could continue its exploration. His tongue lapped up the salt across my skin, whilst leaving a map of marks down my upper arms from his nipping and sucking.

Desperately, I returned my lips to Duncan's mouth, luxuriating in the divinity of him. There was no stopping as I moaned into him. Clearly it was exactly what he wanted to hear, because he growled in return, his fingers deepening against my skin.

In the moments I found the energy to open my eyes, it was to watch the encouraging glances Duncan and Erix gave one another – as if continuously offering their consent and acceptance to what was happening.

By the time my tunic was discarded on the floor, the possibility as to what was coming hit me. I laid a hand on both men's chests and pushed enough to signal I needed a moment.

"Are you all right?" Duncan asked, voice a soft encouragement.

"Perfectly fine," I replied, smiling at him and then at Erix. "In fact, never better."

I stood from the bed, leaving them both to sit and watch me. Perhaps they expected me to change my mind, that my standing was a physical sign that I wanted this to end.

It couldn't have been any different.

I knelt upon my screwed-up tunic, using the material to soften the press of my knees against the stone. Then I gave both men a command of my own. "Sit closer for me."

"Not even a *please*, where have your manners gone?" Erix said in jest, already shuffling up to Duncan's side until their thighs touched. Seeing their closeness, seeing the comfort of their proximity, made the fire inside of me burn wilder.

"Since when has Robin ever had manners in the bedroom?" Duncan added, peering down his nose at me. His stomach muscles flexed with every inhale and exhale. Gone was the fragile body he'd found himself in. Not that the muscles mattered to me… but it was certainly an added bonus.

"Duncan," I said, proving him right, edging command into my tone. "Undress Erix for me."

Without another word, Duncan turned his attention to Erix. "Are you comfortable with that, Erix?"

"I am *very* comfortable with that." He nodded, silver eyes drinking in the angel at his side. "After all, what Robin wants, Robin gets."

"As much as that sentiment burns a fire in my groin, this is actually about what you want, Erix." I fixed my eyes to him, searching his soul for a reason to call a stop to this. "You are not here to fulfil my desires, but to share in them with me."

Erix's expression hardened for a moment. I knew that look – although it had been a long time since he looked at me with eyes glittering like that, I recognised it. He was serious about this, deep to his core.

"I want this," Erix answered, making sure I understood each word and the emotion behind it. "Duncan, get to work. Undress me."

My breath hitched in my throat, threatening to suffocate me. And with that, Duncan laughed, leaned forwards and began unbuttoning Erix's shirt. With deft fingers, it took moments for it to peel away, revealing the impressive form of my personal guard.

"That's much better," I said, rubbing one hand up each of their thighs, drawing their attention back to me. Silver and green eyes devoured me, each as hopefully as the other. "But not completely perfect, at least not yet."

"What would make it perfect for you?" Duncan asked.

"This." One at a time, I undid their trousers. Duncan was first. He leaned back, lifting the weight of his arse as I pulled the material down the swell of his thighs. He was, as I already knew, hard as stone. His cock leaned upwards, the tip perfectly pressed over his bellybutton.

Erix was next. His heavy breathing ruffled across my hair as I remove his trousers, and then his undershorts. My cheeks reddened, heat racing up from my groin and filling my entire body.

There was a power in seeing both men hard for me. Their desire literally revealed inches from my face. I wanted them so desperately that I didn't give pause before I reached with each hand, took them in it and held on as if my life depended on it.

"Slowly," I said, as if reminding myself and them. "I want to savour this."

"In your own time then, darling," Duncan simmered, looking down at his cock in my hand. "All in your own time."

I brought Duncan's length to my mouth and wrapped my lips around its crown. The moment my tongue brushed against the curved tip, I tasted his seed. It was the encouragement I needed as I lost myself to the rhythm. From the sounds Duncan was making, he was enjoying every second. Which was why I was surprised when his fingers threaded my black hair and tugged me off him.

Lips wet with spit, chin dripping with escaping dribbles, I was forced to look up at Duncan whose face was pinched in pleasure.

"Now, Erix's turn," Duncan said, urging me gently toward Erix's cock. "Show him what you have shown me."

My cheeks pricked, filling with saliva and want.

As my mouth lowered to Erix's cock, guided by Duncan's hand on the back of my head, I remembered the last time we'd shared such a moment. The excitement and thrill. How Erix had always been so gentle with me, taking his time, always wondering about how I was feeling.

I made sure he got his answer as I locked eyes with him. Not only did I fill my mouth, but I also took Erix in so deep within my throat that a gag of enjoyment rushed out of me. Clearly, it was exactly what he wanted to hear. His moan echoed in response, mirroring my own.

With Duncan's guiding hand movements on the back of my head, Erix lost himself to my mouth and tongue. As Duncan had, I tasted the sweet pleasure of Erix's seed as it filled my cheeks and lathered my tongue. The more I sucked, the lap of my tongue brushing his balls the deeper I took him in, the more Erix seemed to seep into my mouth.

I made sure my time was equally spent between them both. No matter the building ache in my jaw, I enjoyed every moment. So much that at a point, I'd reached into the band of my trousers and palmed my own hardening length.

Breathless, I pulled back and told them exactly what I required. "I want to feel you both. Share me. Experience me. And *please*, don't make me wait another moment."

It was as if the invitation was all they needed to hear for them to spring into action.

"There are those manners I find so endearing," Duncan said, mouth wet and poised for me.

"How could I ever refuse someone so polite," Erix practically growled when he spoke, a deep guttural longing for what was to come.

It was Duncan who swept me off my knees, lifting me with unimaginable strength, until my hips were wrapped firmly around his waist. His mouth was on mine – tongue desperately sharing in the taste of both men. He spun me around, the room a blur, then laid me on my back. When he pulled back, it was to allow Erix to lean in and begin pulling my trousers down.

They both worked in tandem, never getting in the way of each other, even with their wings shifting and moving with excitable energy.

An angel and a monster – both mine.

I leaned up on my elbows, as they both looked down at me as if I was a feast. One that could be shared and enjoyed. And they did just that.

Both men got on their knees and began devouring me. They took my legs and lifted them, trailing mouths and tongues across my thighs and shins, Duncan even getting down to my feet where he nipped at my toes, playfully sucking on each digit as if they were deserving of his full attention.

Erix took a break from the inside of my thigh, long enough to let the gathering of spit in his mouth fall to his fingers. Sensing I was watching, he locked eyes with mine. I didn't watch his hand move – but *felt* it. He lowered his spit-glistening fingers to my entrance. I arched my back, but a firm hand laid on my lower stomach and forced me down again. Leg up and over Erix's shoulder, he began to brush the wet tips of his fingers over me. The feeling was indescribable. As he kissed the inside of my thigh, Duncan continued his devouring, Erix worked at preparing me for what was to come.

Always the gentleman, forever making sure I was ready and comfortable.

Taking one of them in was a feat unto itself. Knowing that I would experience them both was a fucking miracle.

I didn't dare touch myself, for fear I'd finish before this truly began. Instead I fisted the thin sheets, bunching them up and locking my hand in place. A small moan escaped me as Erix slipped his second finger inside of me and held it.

"I think Robin is ready for you, Duncan" Erix sang, slowly inching toward the tender spot deep inside of me. "I can *feel* he wants it."

"*Needs* it," I corrected, so lost to pleasure I could barely hold my head up to look down my body at them. "Needs it so fucking bad that if you don't fuck me, I will scream this island down."

Duncan lowered my leg, all whilst looking at me. He placed a slender hand on Erix's shoulder and used his body as leverage to stand. "Then we shouldn't keep you wanting. Should we, Erix?"

"No, Duncan. We shouldn't."

"Take him first," Duncan said before leaving Erix's side and climbing onto the bed. "I want to watch."

Duncan knelt beside me, his length so close to my face, teasing me with it.

"Put it in my mouth." I demanded, needing something inside of me to stifle the brewing screams of pleasure. "Now."

Duncan, never one to disappointed, guided his cock onto my outstretched tongue. I took him in, digging my fingers into his thigh. He placed a hand on the back of my head and thrust deep into my throat – slow, long movements that made tears stream from my eyes.

"Good boy," Duncan groaned, wings flaring as pleasure overcame him. Before he could draw back, I grasped a handful of feathers and held him close.

"You wanted to watch him fuck me," I said, withdrawing him enough to speak. I was breathless and overwhelmed, tears of enjoyment and strain glistening in my eyes. "Then watch."

Duncan leaned down, hands grasping my jaw, and pressed a desperate kiss to my mouth. "I'll never take my eyes off either of you."

I opened my mouth to reply, but the pressure of something large worked against my entrance. The shock and delight came out of me in a sky-shattering cry.

Erix drove his shaft into me, all the way to the hilt.

"He really *is* a good boy," Erix agreed to Duncan's earlier statement. "Taking me in like his body remembers me."

"It does," I cried out, back arching before Duncan put a hand on my lower stomach and formed me down. "It never forgot you."

I caught Duncan smiling out the corner of my eye. I was vaguely aware of Erix lifting my legs up and over his shoulders. He shuffled me closer to the edge of the bed, pulling Duncan out of reach for a moment.

The pressure against my entrance intensified as Erix slowly withdrew and then pushed into me. He didn't stop, not until his hips met the soft flesh of my arse, which he held open with either hand.

"Gods," Erix bellowed to the ceiling.

Duncan brushed my hair from my forehead, caressing me with his gentle touch. Erix pressed my leg, breathing heavy against my skin as I tightened myself around him.

"Say my name," I said as he began to move in me. "I want to hear you claim it. Claim us."

Erix's eyes were distant, as if the feeling of me around his cock had transported him to another realm entirely. But not enough that he refused my request. He looked me dead in the eyes and answered me. "Robin."

"That's it," I said, pleading for more as Duncan continued caressing me.

"Robin," Erix said again, his movements picking up in pace, his eyes rolling into the back of his head.

"More," I demanded, not speaking to Erix alone. "I want more!"

Duncan heard me, picking up on what I meant. He said my name next, breathing it against my mouth as he brought his lips down to me. "Robin, my darling. My beautiful, beautiful man."

I gripped the back of Duncan's neck, holding his forehead to mine. Our eyes locked. My breathing came out ragged as Erix fucked me, and Duncan looked down at me as if I was the only important being in the entire world.

"Enjoy this," Duncan asked beneath Erix's groans. "You deserve this. You deserve us both, and equally as we deserve you. Together. The three of us."

"The three of us," I repeated, finding the words fall out of me. "I love you. *Both*. So much that it hurts."

Erix and Duncan replied at the same time, without a beat or second difference. "I love you too."

It went on like this, Duncan devouring my mouth with his, offering me soft words of encouragement as I took Erix inside of me. He told me how well I was doing, his words of affirmation edging me.

Erix came to his end so suddenly, there was almost no warning. I thought he came inside of me, until he quickly withdrew, his warm seed splattering up my belly. Reaching down, I ran trembling fingers through his cum, spreading across my hardened stomach.

Erix looked to Duncan, who had been patiently waiting.

"He is all yours," Erix said to him.

Duncan looked back to me, eyes wild with desire. "Can you take me too? If you say no, we can wait–"

"Fuck me," I interrupted, practically shouted with the overboiling need. "Do it."

Duncan didn't need to be told twice.

It was Duncan's turn to give commands, this time to the breathless man who was still locked to his pleasure. "Erix, lay on the bed beneath Robin for me."

As we moved positions, Duncan lifted me up, his wings spreading to balance his posture. His hard cock rubbed against my arse as he held me afloat. Only when Erix was on his back as Duncan commanded did he lower me back down.

"On your hands and knees," Duncan said to me. "But position yourself over Erix. I want you to face him whilst I fuck you."

I did as Duncan asked, adoring the control he took. Without another wasted second, I crawled atop Erix. He smiled up at me, looking at me as if I was the only source of light in his life. He leaned up, enough to press his mouth to mine. The kiss was exactly what I needed; *he* was exactly what I needed.

Duncan came in behind me, spreading either arse cheek with his hands. Erix helped, needing to give his hands something to do. He clamped his touch at the bottom of my back, pushing down until my spine became the perfect arch for Duncan.

"Robin, tell me if you need to stop at any point." What followed Duncan's reminder of consent was the feeling of pure, blinding gratification.

Indulgence.

Duncan took me from behind, whilst I looked down at Erix. Both men offering me praise – telling me how I was doing such a good job, how impressed they were and how good I felt.

I swear their words alone would make me finish.

Erix took time to kiss me, never taking his eyes off mine. At one point Duncan reached around and took my cock in his hand. Between thrusting into me, he began to work up and down with swift tugs of his wrist.

Whatever doubts I had that there was a chance for a future together had completely faded by the time Duncan finished inside of me. I concluded, as I too reached my end, my splattering cum down over Erix whilst he kissed me feverishly, this was exactly what life was supposed to be for me.

I'd never have fallen in love with two men if I didn't have enough in me to share.

"That was incredible," I said, body thundering with waves of pleasure.

Time was an odd concept in the wake of the sex I had just experienced.

"Incredible almost… seems like too little a… word," Duncan replied, words broken and breathless.

I flopped down beside Erix, rolling off his chest until I was lying at his side. Our bodies were coated in sweat, sodden to the touch. Duncan joined, nestling his naked body into my other side, until I was wedged between them both.

We laughed – the sound so natural and full of genuine emotion. I refused to let either of them go. I knew, if we did, we had a world outside these doors to save to ensure moments like this could happen.

"How long do you think we can hide away from our responsibilities?" I said, rolling my head to look at them both in turn.

"A few more hours, I'd wager," Duncan replied, voice dipping as reality seeped into him.

No matter how I wished to shield him – shield all of us – it wouldn't last.

"I can cope with a few more hours." Erix leaned in and pressed his mouth to my cheek. Duncan followed suit, curling up beside me. Each held me close, either man laying a wing over me, covering my naked body.

"No more talking," I said, wishing to block out the fact that a realm lingered outside this room, and it was one we had to save. "Can we just exist for a little while longer."

"Of course," Duncan said, reaching over and taking Erix's hand. Once they were connected, they rested them on my stomach, so we were all connected.

"I like the sound of that," Erix added, using his spare hand to tickle shapes into my chest.

In the silence that followed, as their breathing evened out and I was left to the company of my haunting thoughts, I finally recognised the possibility of *us* – the three of us. But with the warmth of that truth, it also made me face one harsh and very real possibility. It reminded me of what I had to lose. But that wasn't all. Because having them, *experiencing* them both, was exactly the reminder I needed.

Any future sacrifices I made would be in their honour.

CHAPTER 27

Even with the hours between our shared experience, I could still *feel* Erix and Duncan. With every step, my body echoed with their touches. They were the gift that kept on giving.

After lying in silence, we'd bathed together, taking time to wash skin with gentle hands. It took so long that the water had cooled by the time we finished. And yet even that couldn't remove their touch from my skin, or the sensitive ache between my legs.

I imagined nothing had the power to distract me.

My theory was debunked as we met with Rafaela. The moment we entered an open-air chamber, me at the lead, with Duncan and Erix flanked behind me, I knew something was wrong.

Two empty seats sat waiting, tucked neatly beneath the table. Untouched.

Rafaela stood abruptly, quite clearly aghast. Tension hummed in the empty room, catching in my lungs, making breathing a challenge.

"Where is Gyah?" I asked, tongue thick with the anticipation of an answer. "And Seraphine?"

Rafaela settled her dark eyes on Duncan, as if waiting for guidance. I looked back to see his reaction, and it was one of calm. A serenity that came with knowing. Whereas Erix matched my energy, scanning every possible nook and cranny for Gyah and Seraphine.

"Gyah has already left Irobel," Duncan said, so calm it felt misplaced.

"What the fuck does that mean?" I asked, feeling the anxiety pop in my chest, one bubble at a time. "Why would Gyah leave?"

"Because she has an important part to play." Rafaela winced as she spoke to me without taking her eyes off him.

I feared that if I moved a muscle my body would shatter into a million pieces.

"Answer plainly," Erix said, warning evident in every syllable.

"Shall we sit?" Duncan added quickly, gesturing to the chairs. "And all will be explained."

Duncan knew before we even left our rooms. None of this was a surprise to him.

"Duncan?" I said, head tilting to the side. "Why has Gyah already left?"

"Because Althea is still alive, but we believe this will not be true for long. I could not expect Gyah to sit around and wait for us to be ready, when the next moves on this game board we find ourselves on are the most pivotal to our success."

All it took were those words and my entire world shattered all over again.

I shook my head, as Erix voiced my inner thoughts. "What the fuck do you mean Althea's not got long?"

The silence that followed was so tense, I could only hear my heart thundering in my ears.

"Cassial is goading the fey into starting a war, but there is resistance," Duncan explained, his eyes almost distant as though pulling information from the deepest parts of his soul. "Cassial plans to use Althea as bait because it has not worked; he is growing desperate. And his desperation will result in Althea's life being under threat."

"How do you know?" I gasped.

Duncan tapped his head. "A gift, from the Creator. I can sense other Nephilim, like we are connected and–"

"He is going to kill Althea, to start a war?" I spat, not caring about magic gifts from gods.

"In a manner of speaking, yes."

Suddenly I was glad Gyah had left already. If anything, I wanted to claw my way out of this room and follow her. But my body sagged forwards until the table crashed into my hips. I placed my hands across the wood, unable to stop the creeping freeze that erupted from beneath my fingers. It took seconds for the table to engulf in ice, before cracking down the centre.

"You knew?" I spat, catching Duncan's warped reflection in the mirror that was my ice. "All this time, you knew?"

"No, darling. The information was only revealed to me after the Transfiguration. I gave Seraphine the information she required to make sure Gyah left Irobel quickly. All is well, you do not need to worry."

"Fuck all of that," I shouted. "We all should've been informed about this..."

Instead, I had given into my selfish desires and lain with Erix and Duncan, all whilst Gyah left Irobel to save the woman she loved.

I couldn't wrap my head around what was happening. My eyes met Rafaela with force. "What about you. Did you know this was happening?"

I waited for her to tell me the answer, but I saw it in the gleam of her eyes. "No. I discovered the truth alongside Gyah."

"Then who told her?" I shouted, the table shattering into pieces beneath my hands. "Duncan, you were with us the entire time, you didn't get the chance to speak to Gyah..."

Rafaela took a deep breath in, clutching the hilt of a sword at her waist. "Seraphine informed us that Cassial has grand plans for Althea in a few days' time–"

"As per my request," Duncan reminded.

I gagged on the sudden rush of bile, clapping a hand over my mouth to stifle it. I was hit with both relief and anger – blinding fury that I'd been made to believe my closest friend was dead.

I expected Rafaela and the Nephilim to lie, but not Seraphine – never Seraphine. She would've told me, she would've kept me in the loop as she had from the beginning…

"What plans does Cassial have?" I dared to ask.

"To use Queen Cedarfall to start a war."

I don't know who said it, Duncan or Rafaela, but the truth sank in my chest like a stone of dread.

Hearing it aloud only further proved what my mind had already made up. "And how… how long has Seraphine known this?"

My knuckles whitened as they tightened at my sides, waiting for the answer.

"Long enough to get ahead," Duncan said. "This panic you feel, this anger at being in the dark… you can place it upon my head. It was my doing."

I winced, eyes closing so I could give into the calm darkness behind my eyelids.

Rafaela took a seat first, settling herself down as if the floor shook.

"Cassial wasn't only keeping Althea hostage," Rafaela said, her defiant gaze fixed to me. "He's been biding his time to use her against the fey. You would have turned back for her."

"Of fucking course I would have," I shouted, unable to move a muscle beside my eyes that flared open once again. "And yet we've left her, in Altar knows what state, for how long?" I spun around, winter winds crackling around me, searching shadows for the Asp. "We need to leave. We have to catch up with them."

I was moments from exploding.

Pinching my eyes closed, I saw the Cedarfall family, dead, in the dark of my mind. The image of their bodies swaying like pendulums. After everything Althea had endured, we'd left her in the hands of a man who'd soon see every fey killed.

Duncan placed a hand on my shoulder. The touch lasted a second as repulsion uncoiled in me. Shrugging him off, I took steps back, pressing into Erix who waited.

The emotion that stormed through me was destructive and hungry. It needed release.

"You could've told me," I spat, pushing my finger into Duncan's chest, so hard that nail bent against muscle. "*Should* have told me! I deserved to know if Althea's life was under *imminent* threat."

Duncan looked down at me with an expression of sorrow that irked my soul. "There wasn't the time–"

"Because you were too busy *fucking* me?" I screamed, no longer caring who knew. "Althea means everything to me, Duncan. If I'd known she was going to be used as a pawn to start the war Cassial is so desperate for, we could've saved her."

"But Duncan would have died in the process," Rafaela reminded me. "Coming to Irobel was imperative to our success."

"Success is not guaranteed! We only came here to further test *your* prophecy. Because of your twisted beliefs and manipulations," I barked, spinning on her, brain aching from the constant whipping of my head. "He is your Saviour, freeing those Nephilim bound in stone. But who will be Althea's saviour?"

"Gyah, for I have seen it," Duncan muttered. "I know what she must do, and I have faith it will work."

My eyes settled on Erix, to find him trembling with the same unspent rage I was lost to. His pupils had shrunk, giving his eyes the impression of being pools of silver. "Take me away from here, Erix."

He didn't reply. He looked down at the table, eyes flickering between his splayed hands.

"We only did what had to be done, to save the world," Rafaela began, but I cut her off.

"And yet you didn't think for a moment that Althea *is* someone's world." There was something in her words that sent Cedarfall-conjured fire through my veins.

I couldn't blame Gyah for leaving. I would've done the same. If anything, I only wished I had the chance to leave with her.

"Whether you knew about Althea or not, I have little doubt you would not have divulged the information if it meant keeping Duncan from his fate. Gabrial's promise of the Herald was the only thing ensuring we could stop the Fallen."

Duncan lay a firm but gentle hand upon my shoulder. "There have been no secrets, Robin. The moment I woke, I shared the information I had with Seraphine and explained what I saw in the threads of endless possibilities before us. I asked her to keep it to herself until we were further prepared. Gyah knew the truth of Cassial's plans soon after."

"And yet you didn't tell me!" I snapped, drawing away. "Gyah has gone alone to face god knows what plans Cassial has."

"She is not alone, she has Seraphine," Duncan reminded me, soft fingers reaching for my face.

I leaned into it, delighting in his warmth. It grounded me against the maelstrom of anxieties rupturing through my body. "I should be there."

"Giving Cassial access to another fey royal to control isn't what we need right now. You are safer here, and Althea Cedarfall will be safe as soon as Gyah reaches her. Trust in that." Duncan's voice was so loud it was as if he was shouting, except his furrowed brow and drawn lips showed he felt nothing but regret.

My eyes flared wide as realisation of a missed detail made itself known. "Cassial would not kill Althea so flippantly. He will need her, just as you said. He needs a fey to host the power…"

"A willing fey," Duncan reminded me. "Althea would sooner die than become a pawn for Cassial to use. I *see* how this will end." His fingers dropped to my chin, lifting it up until we were eye to eye. "Do you trust me, darling?"

"Trust is a shield, *not* a weapon, Duncan. We don't have time to waste talking about this," Erix said, hands wringing together before him. I could feel the press of his body behind me, how he trembled with emotion, limbs quaking. I had no doubt that he got close to me in case he lost control and needed an anchor. "Robin is right, we must follow and stop them."

Rafaela looked to Duncan, fixing her eyes on him. I read the nuance of their silence and discovered Erix's answer before either of them said it. They weren't going to let us ruin whatever they had planned.

"Don't you dare," I spat, finger pointing at both of them, my heart aching at the betrayal laid out before me.

"Robin, please," Duncan pleaded. "I know Cassial needs a fey, one of Altar's descendants, to house Duwar and survive the power source. I do not think his plans are to murder her, but to use her. It will be Althea who chooses death over that outcome."

"I hate to say this, but you are right," Erix said, head bowing. "Cassial needs Althea because she is going to be the next vessel. She is safe – as long as we don't intervene, or as long as she doesn't refuse him."

"Gods," I cried, forcing my eyes closed, imagining Cassial in a state of pain and weakness as Duwar ravaged through his body.

"They will not help us anymore than they have," Rafaela said, looking away from Duncan.

"That's right. Their meddling is over."

"What… what has changed?" I asked, bile stinging the back of my throat, tears pricking in my eyes. Not from sadness, but fury.

"Cassial is desperate because he is growing weak. And now we are ready to face him." Duncan rolled his shoulders back, lips drawn in regret. "I wish I told you earlier, but it was imperative to our plans that Gyah went ahead."

"We should be with her," I snapped, feeling a distance growing between us. "That was not your decision to make, Duncan."

Duncan sighed. "I am sorry."

"Are you?"

He straightened, something clicking in his gaze. "Gyah has left to head straight to Wychwood and warn those gathering for battle not to attack. *I* am heading straight to Cassial too. If you really wish to meet up with her, to stop Gyah or help her, you can do so by getting to Wychwood."

"What about you?" I said, desperately needing him, whilst wanting distance at the same time.

"I must go to Cassial, that is what the Creator has asked of me."

Erix tore his hand out of mine and began to pace, the pent-up emotion becoming too much for him to control. I could see from the darkening of his eyes that the berserker was close to the surface. "The fate of Wychwood and all its peoples falls on Althea's shoulders until we can get to her. She will do anything to save them – even if that means complying with Cassial and his needs. If harnessing Duwar for Cassial's gain serves to protect Wychwood, she will do it."

"Well fuck those plans! You've just sent an Eldrae into the midst of this fucked-up war we still know little about. Gyah's presence will not only inform Cassial that we all have survived his attempts to banish us. But any hope that he'll spare Althea will cease the moment our secret is revealed." I could've laughed at how ridiculous this all was. If I didn't laugh, I'd scream or cry.

"Gyah will *not* risk Althea," Rafaela said. "That is why Seraphine is with her."

"*An Asp may shed its skin, but beneath it is still an Asp,*" I muttered the very sentiment Seraphine had shared. I'd placed my trust in someone who had her own motives. But why? What game was Seraphine playing keeping information about Cassial's intentions to use Althea?

"Then we follow after them," Erix said, nodding to himself, mind whirling. "How long ago did they leave?"

"Hours," Rafaela answered. "Gyah has flown back to Durmain. It's quicker travel than a ship. It is important she informs as many nobles and military leaders in Wychwood as she can of Cassial's plans, so they can react in the right way."

"And do we know where Althea is being held?" I asked. "That's where Gyah will go next."

There was no hesitation as Rafaela answered. "Seraphine knew, but the information was not shared. Even that was not something Duncan was privy to. When I asked, Seraphine said we would figure it out."

The web of knots that were Seraphine's motives were becoming more tangled by the moment.

"She is stalling us," I said. "Because she knew we would follow after her."

A thought came to my mind, thick and fast.

Jesibel could find out where Cassial was. If I connected with her through my dreams, Jesibel could walk into Althea's mind and discover more information. I hated to ask Jesibel to do anything; I wanted her to experience nothing but peace. But if she didn't help, there would be no peace left for anyone.

"Seraphine is giving herself more time," I said louder, wanting everyone to hear. "She has a plan, to further yours, I just don't know what it is yet."

"I can find out Althea's location," Erix added quickly before I could offer the same, pressing fingers to his temple. "Communication with the gryvern has been difficult at this distance, but if we leave for Durmain and I can reach one, then I may be able to locate Cassial. But for that, we need to go – now."

I expected Rafaela or Duncan to refuse again. Their silence suggested they expected this response. I kept communing with Jesibel in my back pocket. Sleep would be impossible for me, I knew that. But Durmain was a long way away, I had the time to try.

"Then the rest of us must prepare to leave immediately." I studied the Nephilim carefully, watching to see how they would react. "If we have any hope of stopping Cassial, we do it together. No more secrets." If I had nails left, they would've bitten into the skin of my palm. I fisted my hands so tightly, I felt my heartbeat within them. "Seraphine has a plan; I have to believe she does."

Seraphine had so much to lose. The new world meant a lot to her, more than I could even imagine. She wouldn't commit deceptions and betrayals if it wasn't for a good reason. There was no way she would just stand by and let Gyah go in alone, putting not only her, but everyone else under threat.

I had to believe that.

"If what we believe about the fey army is correct," I said, skin itching at the possibility of war. "Then Cassial is playing with them. They think we are all dead, and Althea is the last member of a court's family surviving. It is in their blood to protect that."

"Cassial's plans are simple and – if we do not act – unavoidable," Duncan said, voice brimming with authority. "He is goading the fey army to attack first, proving to the humans that Cassial's lies were all true. Once the initial attack occurs, he will do the necessary to use Duwar and lay waste. But he will not do that until the power is safely inside of Althea. Cassial is many things, but he will not risk his own life for the sake of his hopes and wishes. Ego is the crux of a weak man's downfall."

And if the world believes we are dead, so would Althea. There was a chance Jesibel already informed Althea of the truth through her dreams, but that was not worth putting all my hope into.

"Cassial is blinded by desires," Rafaela added. "He will be so entirely focused on the army before him that he will not see us coming in from the back. After all, we have one advantage: he will never expect the dead to attack."

"So, he must not become aware that we have survived." Duncan's white wings flexed outward. "Just as Cassial wants the fey to attack first, solidifying them as the enemies, having our Nephilim attack his Fallen will only confuse the humans. I have no doubt that he will use the mirrors handed out across Durmain to continue spreading his misinformation. If we act at the right time, we can use this to our benefit."

"That's why you didn't stop Gyah from leaving, isn't it?" I asked, already knowing the answer.

"Gyah is a messenger. She can slip through the realms and reach the people we need. Whereas if we are seen, then it is over."

I knew, deep down, that was not the only reason. But there was no time to waste arguing.

These next moments were for action only.

I had prevented a war before, only for the promise of it to be back on the playing board. There was no doubt in my mind that Doran and Tarron Oakstorm would be smiling in their graves at the thought.

"Cassial is likely tired of waiting, but he will only make the first move if he feels like there are no other options. What we must do is bring him an option he hasn't thought of yet." Duncan straightened, snow-white wings flaring on either of his sides as sparks of power danced around his clenched fists. "Faithful against the Fallen – but to the humans they will simply see Nephilim against Nephilim. That alone will plant a seed of doubt in their minds as to who is the *real* enemy."

Erix was silent still, focusing on reaching his gryvern. It had been days since the last time he had managed, but if anything had changed since then, it was Erix's determination.

I laid a hand on his, offering him my confidence. "You can do it. I believe in you."

Erix's eyes widened. Although they were focused on me, it seemed as though he stared right through me for a moment. I held my breath, praying to whatever god would listen that Erix would be successful.

"Duncan," Erix broke his silence, the lines of concentration smoothing out across his forehead. "Cassial is at the Wychwood border. Finding him will not be difficult, my gryvern informed me that his host is large. I can inform them about Althea, see if they can assist with–"

"No," I snapped. "If the fey armies feel that Althea's life is under threat, they will attack, feeding into exactly what Cassial wants. We need more time before we act."

"Time is already something we have agreed is lacking," Rafaela reminded me.

I stormed to the wall and drove my fist into the stone. "Fuck."

Over and over, I continued to punch it, stopping when firm hands pulled me back. Torn fists dripped blood onto the floor.

"Stop it, Robin," Duncan hushed into my ear, breath cool and tickling.

"I – I can't save her," I stammered, fumbling over the words as my deepest fears came out, knuckles cut to shreds. "Althea will never let Cassial use her. She would die by her own blade before…"

"Which is why Gyah had to leave," Duncan whispered, leaning in close. "Please, trust me."

"I want to, Duncan, I really do." My words clogged in my dry throat, making the next thing hard to admit aloud. "But I can't help but feel like you are not telling me something."

He rocked back as if physically slapped, then downturned his gaze to the floor between us. When Duncan spoke again, it was with a detached command. "The moment you can get sleep, try and reach for Jesibel. She must warn Gyah that you are coming after her. If you really wish to stop Gyah's next move, give her a good enough reason. It will be her choice to listen to you. Otherwise you will understand why I, or anyone else, has no right to prevent Gyah from saving the one person she loves. Just as I would not want anyone standing before me when it came to you."

I heard Duncan, his last words settling on my soul like the kiss of ash. Duncan's hold on me loosed when he was sure I wouldn't take my fury out on the wall. Stepping free, it took effort not to turn on him with a fist.

"I have to do it," I said to him. "I am sorry."

Duncan didn't resistant when I turned my back on him, facing Erix for some semblance of strength.

Erix gritted his teeth, fighting his own urge to take me into his arms. "Robin is right, we must make haste. If we wish to use Gyah's next moves for our benefit, we must follow. Otherwise Robin will be the only Wychwood royal left–"

"That isn't true," I interrupted, fixing my eyes to his. "I'm not the only royal by blood left, Erix."

He winced, turning his head, refusing this part of him. "We follow your command." Erix placed a hand over his heart. "The gryvern are yours, little bird. Tell me how you need them, and they will act."

There was so much more I needed him to believe. Erix was more than my guard, he was Oakstorm by blood. We would need an Oakstorm to face what was to come. But the conversation had stunted, disregarded by Erix as he turned his back on his heritage.

"As are the Nephilim." Duncan followed suit, placing a hand atop his heart, regret creasing his strong brow. "They've been freed to change the fate of this world. I follow you, darling."

Do you?

"You're the Saviour," I said, the title souring on my tongue. "Isn't the world yours to save?"

"I have put the parts in play as the Creator asked." Duncan shook his head, swashes of dark hair falling over verdant eyes. "And as you pointed out, my purpose was to unify the Faithful and right the wrongs of the Creator. Not to fix the world. I, like you, cannot do that alone."

"Okay," I said more to myself than anyone else. The wheels of my mind were moving, speeding through. "Okay..."

The room suffered in silence. It was so quiet my heartbeat sounded like thunder in my skull.

It was incredible how quickly a plan could come together when one knew there was no time to hesitate. I felt it form inside of my very core, fixing together into a solid iron, with very few chinks in the armour.

"This is what we're going to do," I said, sweeping my eyes across the room. "Cassial wishes to learn from previous mistakes in history and prevent a war again. He wants his domination to be through the path of least resistance, otherwise he would've attacked by now. So, I say we bring it to him. Erix." I fixed my eyes on him. "I need the gryvern to sweep through any human settlements near Cassial's encampment. He will have set himself up in a built-up area. The more humans who die in the crossfire, the more it will benefit his attempt to vilify the fey. We need to evacuate the area. Whether the humans listen to the gryvern or not, they must be moved. Scare them out if asking nicely does not work."

Erix bowed his head to me. "I'll see that it is done."

I looked to Duncan next, finding his full attention fixed to me, pride glittering in his verdant eyes. "What do you need of me, darling?"

Only the truth, but how could I request such a concept that even I had put to the wayside for months?

"Show Cassial the full might of those his campaign punished. Set upon him the full force of the Nephilim at your disposal. You want to go straight to him, then do it. *Kill* him."

Duncan's shoulders rolled back, as though my command offered him some relief. "Better Cassial fights against his own. Keeping the fey out of this mess will only benefit the mess we will have to arrange after Cassial is dealt with."

I agreed. If Cassial was waiting for an excuse to use Duwar against the fey realms, we had to make sure he was distracted enough not to act. At least delay it.

"Our first step is showing both realms the truth. No more betrayal. No lies or further deceptions. If we can show the humans through the veil of Cassial's lies, then we may find they come to our aid. It will take the full might of both realms, the effort of humans and fey, Nephilim and monsters, to ensure the new world we were promised becomes a reality. One no longer threatened."

"And what of Duwar?" Rafaela asked. "That is still a power on the game board that we must ultimately deal with. I hate to say this, but there is a chance that killing the host will not also destroy Duwar. There has never been a recorded possession before Duncan."

A seed of doubt spread roots as soon as Rafaela stopped talking.

"Then we find another way," I said. "We bind him in labradorite, we make sure both Cassial and Duwar are wiped from the face of the realms."

Erix cleared his throat, demanding attention as he said. "Seraphine mentioned something in the texts she was reading. About Duwar and the Sleeping Depths."

He was right, and with his words those roots of doubt ceased their spreading.

Immediately, my mind went back to the story Duncan had shared with me. The story of Altar first calling upon Duwar, drawing the power from the earth, stealing it from its resting place. The Creator believed it was unfair, how Altar stole the power and used it to create the fey. His feelings were justified. Just like the use of power, Altar or the Creator were not inherently good or bad. Duncan passing his judgement had proved that. It was what we did with power that mattered. And Duwar – the demon god, the source of chaos, whatever we wanted to believe it was now – was an issue our gods created, and one we had to solve.

No one deserves to hold power such as Duwar. Not a fey, nor a human.

We couldn't lock it away like the gods had done when they called a truce. But I could return it home. And I had a hunch of where it all began – but to give my plan a chance, I needed to get Cassial away from his army.

"We stop using it, and allow Duwar to be free," I answered. "It is time for Duwar to return to its place of rest. Chaos does not belong in the hands of mortals, or gods. No prisons, no more gates and keys. We give it up – just as Altar should've all those centuries ago."

* * *

"I'm sorry, Robin," Duncan said, tracing his hand down my cheek. "I should've told you everything, but I trusted that a change was coming. I *had* to put faith in Seraphine and Gyah. Selfishly I'm trying to protect you, doing a duty that I haven't been able to do for months."

I looked up at him, aware of the crash of waves that sounded at his back. The sky was clear, the sun unbearably hot. As much as I wanted to hate Duncan for holding the truth about Cassial's plans back, I had to believe it was for a reason.

"Save your apologies for when this is all over," I replied with a smile that didn't reach my eyes.

Duncan noticed and sighed, his gaze falling to our hands held between us. "We *will* see that new dawn. Together." He looked over my shoulder, to Erix who stood watching at a distance. "All of us."

I swallowed, forcing down all the things I longed to say. Except one statement that was far too demanding to hide away. "I don't want to leave you."

"But you must," Duncan replied, wincing at the dark thoughts harbouring behind his verdant gaze. "And it will not be for long. The path ahead is full of trials, but I trust that we will make it to the end. I have to."

"I know," I echoed, looking to Erix who waited at a distance. "I'll be safe with Erix."

"He will be safe with you, darling." Duncan ran a soft hand down my cheek, so enticing I leaned into it and allowed myself a second of his touch. "I know you will both be fine, although that truth doesn't make *this* any easier."

Erix stood just shy of the lapping waves, boots sinking into the sand. His leather wings were stretching, preparing for the flight back to Lockinge. As were the thousands of Nephilim Duncan had freed. They were perched across every speck of land I could see, waiting for Duncan to lead them. Rafaela was amongst them, her wings not yet healed, so she would be carried.

"If all goes to plan, we will not be apart for long." I fought the urge to cry. But I couldn't show weakness, not now when the tide was about to change. "If Erix is right, Cassial will be stationed on the border of Wychwood. If you can create a distraction with your arrival, Cassial will be forced to send his fellow Fallen to meet you. The fewer he has with him, the easier it will be to get in and deal with him."

"There are risks," Duncan reminded me. "Don't forget that this is not something for you to deal with alone. We act together, as one. No more running in blind to save a world. It is a burden you no longer need to bear alone."

"Everything worth something has a risk attached to it," I replied. "Sometimes we can't ignore that."

If Duncan noticed my lack of acknowledgement to his latter statement, he didn't show it. Instead, he leaned down, meeting his lips to mine. I reached up on my tiptoes, delighting in the kiss, no longer feeling hesitation or regret. When I thought of Erix, it wasn't with the worry of how he would feel. Our boundaries were set in stone.

Duncan took my hand and guided me to Erix. "The same goes for you, Erix. Stay safe."

The men clasped each other's forearms, the intensity in their gaze enough to set fire to the air between them. They embraced, my heart leaping at the vision. I wanted to burn it into the dark of my mind and never forget it.

"I expect to see you, alive and well, in a matter of days." Erix refused to look away from Duncan as they finally drew apart. "Do what is required, then rush home to us, okay?"

"Everything I do is to ensure that very possibility," Duncan said. "Home certainly sounds like something worth fighting for. And I've had so many *homes* in my life, and never one as alluring as the one with you both."

My shattered heart cracked just a little more. It was a sentiment we all could relate to. Me with my desire to know who I was. Erix with him running from his birthright and the curses that came with it. And Duncan, handed from Nephilim as a babe, then passed from human to human.

I stepped in close, laying a hand on each of them, connecting us in a chain of flesh. We didn't share final words, or goodbyes. Doing so would only encourage the pain inside of me to triple. And right now, I had to focus.

We had a war to prevent – *again*.

"Are you ready?" Erix said, fixing his silver eyes to me.

A lump formed in my throat. "No." I choked. "Are you?"

"Not really." He took my hand and squeezed. "But what does that matter?"

"Exactly. But I have got you. Duty and pleasure, remember?"

"Duty and pleasure," Erix echoed, smiling down at me. "Always, little bird. Now, let's get to Wychwood and make sure we stop this war before it begins."

CHAPTER 28

It took almost two days to complete our journey. Two agonising days of dark thoughts plagued by the 'what ifs' for a future. And it was on the second night that Jesibel finally entered my dreams.

She parted from whisps of silver shadow, clutching a long stem in her hand crowned with the most luscious rose I'd ever seen. I barely got a word out before she handed it to me, the thorns sharp and yet they didn't prick my thumb as I took it. I asked after Althea, and silently Jesibel nodded with a smile. No words came out as we conversed, at least from her. I asked Jesibel if Althea knew we lived, and she nodded again vigorously. Then I asked if she was well. A brief grimace passed across her face but lasted but a second. It was enough for me to know Althea was still okay, that she was holding on for help to come.

The dream stayed with me in the hours after I woke.

In an attempt to distract myself, I studied the patchwork map of the human realm, reminding myself of what we fought to protect. Erix carried me through the clouds, enough to keep us concealed and yet my fey sight caught hints of what lay beneath us.

I'd expected to see Cassial's army as we reached Lockinge, but the city had been close to empty. A handful of humans stood beyond their homes, hands raised to their brows, as they watched our arrival.

A GAME OF MONSTERS

To them, the flock of our Nephilim had arrived to join Cassial's efforts against the fey. I felt their relief in every scream and cheer, a celebration as aid arrived. Erix held me closer to his chest, lifting high above the line of Nephilim, concealing our obvious unbelonging.

The same went for the flight across Durmain's horizon. Towns, villages, hamlets and farmlands; it was all much the same. Empty. Quiet. As we came closer to Wychwood's border, there was one detail that became prevalent – I saw no signs of people.

Where was everyone? Had the gryvern been successful with their attempts to remove humans, getting them away from the conflict? If that was the case, we would've seen leagues of people moving across the land.

So far, we hadn't.

"It's too quiet," Erix announced as we landed after hours of flying on the second day. "It's like we left here and have come back to find a realm of ghosts."

It will be if we don't save it, I thought.

Erix had voiced the concern that had grown inside of me. The last of our Nephilim army had just flown out of view, leaving us alone for the first time. They would stop only when they reached Cassial, slowly infiltrating his ranks, poisoning his army of Fallen with Faithful, without him realising.

"It is," I agreed, looking out at the ramshackle farmland beyond the window. "And I don't like it, not one bit."

"Me neither, little bird," he said, protectively stepping into me, not trusting even our own shadows. I glanced back at him to find his body slouched, a sickly pallor clinging to his once sun-kissed skin.

"I'll be all right to carry on in a moment," Erix announced, reading the concern in my eyes.

We had to catch up to Gyah and Seraphine, and as long as we kept pace, we'd be only hours behind them. But one look at Erix, that was all it took, and I knew he wouldn't make it.

Exhaustion told stories across every line and shadow across his brilliant face.

"You need to rest," I announced, leaving no room for him to refuse, nor did he try.

I looked around, scanning the area around me for an answer.

On all sides, fields of grazing livestock were left unattended. Chickens ran around without purpose. I'd lived near enough to farms like this that I recognised the keening screeches as requests for food, and the smell. In the distance was a ramshackle building, almost leaning to the left slightly as if the foundations were far too relaxed to hold it.

"Over there," I said, pointing with one hand whilst taking Erix's hand with the other. "We can afford a couple of hours to rest. Maybe we'll find some answers as to why Durmain is so quiet..."

I was relieved to find the farmhouse empty, but it also added to my concerns as to why. There no one here. No one but me and Erix, filling the rooms of someone's home like unwanted guests.

Erix had finished checking the small dwelling set into the farm's heart, confirming it had been recently vacated. I tried to convince myself that whoever had been here had moved on to better things. But drawers were full of clothes, vegetables and meat were left to rot in their respective storages.

It was like the humans who lived here had upped and left with little notice.

Giving myself something to do, I knelt before the hearth, running fingers through cold soot. The stone around it was also cold to the touch, proving it had been some days since it was last lit.

"And your gryvern have shared the same update?" I asked again, stomach cramping from hunger and worry.

Erix nodded, hesitant eyes scanning the empty room as if an assassin would spring from the shadows and murder us. Distrust was evident in every crease in his brow and nibble of his lip. "It would seem that Cassial has *already* ordered the evacuation of any dwelling close to Wychwood. He beat us to it."

"If that was the case, we would've seen those refugees making their way to Lockinge." Yet the roads had been empty, the streets of the human city almost void of life. "Humans don't just disappear in a matter of days, so where did they all go?"

"I don't know," Erix said, clearly displeased with the lack of knowledge. His eyes fluttered closed, his attempts to keep them opening failed over and over.

"No more questions and answers," I said. "Get some more sleep."

"If I can. Perhaps the Nephilim are built for such long journeys, but I feel like my wings are seconds from falling off. Hopefully when I wake my gryvern will have more news on the humans' whereabouts, and you will have conversed with Jesibel on the passing of your messages."

Erix looked like a man struggling. Shadows clung beneath his eyes, even the usual bright hue of silver looked more akin to dark storm clouds.

Unlike Erix, I'd slept some of the flight, finding it easy to focus on his heart's canter and the beat of his wings. I'd woken when we passed over Lockinge, so I was as rested as I needed to be. We briefly stopped just south of the city, in a nondescript building that had once belonged to the Asps. I'd been inside it once, after we escaped Lockinge, only to return to it. In truth, with the combination of being close to the fey realm, and knowing Duncan was on his way to infiltrate Cassial's league, I hardly imagined sleep would be a possibility until this was all over.

"Wake me in an hour," Erix grumbled, head leant against the side of the worn chair.

"You can take more than a few hours," I said. "If all goes to plan, Duncan will be able to reach Cassial just after Gyah reaches him. Then your gryvern will follow."

"It is Gyah I am worried about," Erix echoed my own unsaid thoughts.

"I trust Seraphine will not let any harm come to her," I reminded him, and myself. "And Cassial is going to be so focused on the Wychwood border that Duncan's attack will surprise him threefold and from three different sides. We *must* have faith that the distraction will be enough."

Whatever game Seraphine played, it was full of overlapping lies. I trusted the Asp, or at least, I knew our hopes for a future were aligned. But she'd had a reason not to involve me in her plans. I just hadn't worked out what those were yet.

"Are you trying to convince me, or yourself? Erix asked, a single brow raised.

It was natural for my mouth to draw into a tight line as I shrugged. "Both."

The plan was simple, and really the only option we had. Duncan would take a handful of his followers to Cassial, leaving the rest nearby with Rafaela to await further commands. It was best Cassial didn't discover the full might of the freed Nephilim.

A few of them would go unnoticed.

"No more talking," I said, talking behind Erix and allowing a moment of selfishness. I placed hands on the back of the chair, leaned in and planted my lips to his. "The sooner you sleep, the sooner we reach Wychwood and catch Gyah before she makes any rash decisions."

"Gyah is not one for rash decision making," Erix said. "She is one for sharp teeth and vicious nails."

That was exactly what I was worried about.

Before I could draw back, Erix planted a hand on my face. Erix's eyes opened, as if the lack of my lips had suddenly sparked a bout of energy inside of him. "I'll never get over this."

"Over what?" I asked, ambling toward the kitchen, already aware of the handful of root vegetables that would be okay to eat. I was no cook, but I could whip something up for him.

"You. Me. Duncan." Erix answered, whilst drawing out a pause between each word. Likely, for dramatic effect. He was like that. "The contrast between the world being under threat, and me finally having everything I have ever wanted. It is like I cannot allow myself to be happy, whilst the reality is that all I feel is happiness."

"It's odd, the feeling. But, if anything, it inspires the hope inside of me to burn that bit brighter."

"*Hotter*," Erix added. "I am glad our thoughts align, I worried that time apart would lift a haze from over us and you'd changed your mind."

I shook my head. "Impossible."

Erix may not have watched my lips crest into a smile, but I was confident he heard it in the light chirp of my voice. "If anything, it is giving me a real reason to continue it. I want this over so that the realms are saved. I want this over so that you never need to worry about danger again. And I want this over because the past two days without Duncan have been unbearable."

Erix sighed, slouching into the chair as if it could swallow him whole. "I feel the same. So much has changed, hasn't it?"

"I can hardly remember what came before all of this. If I think about it too much, I'll lose my focus." I let my eyes lose themselves in Erix – from the set of his jaw to the focus in his silver eyes. He was a fantastic distraction, but he was also so much more than that.

Yes, I missed Duncan like a gaping hole in my chest. But Erix was here, and that counted for something powerful. I needed him, and I wasn't ashamed to admit that without him with me, I wouldn't see this through.

"You need to put those worries out of your mind for now," I said, gesturing to the worn reading chair set before the hearth. "I saw some food that would be edible in the kitchens. You'll need as much replenishment as possible, before we need to move on. Rest whilst I will rustle something up."

Erix attempted to wave me off, all whilst snuggling into the chair. "Don't stray too far from me."

I hesitated, fixing my eyes on the burning hearth before me. "Never."

Erix mock-closed his eyes and pretended to snore. Little moments like that made me laugh, further proving how important his presence was for me.

I'd dumped a handful of potatoes, carrots and a chunky, wonky turnip into a large cooking pot, and filled it up with water from a pump outside in the yard. Once everything was prepared, I snuck it back into the same room Erix slept in. Trying everything in my power to keep quiet, I lowered the brass pot atop the hearth, allowing water to boil and vegetables to cook.

By the time he woke, it would be ready.

I felt, in a way, like I was playing house with Erix. Testing out what the world could be like, if we made it through. I sat and watch him for a while, drinking in his relaxed expression, the soft curve of his smile. I wondered what he dreamed of, hoped that whatever it was offered him reprieve from the horrors of the world.

I cringed when the vegetable broth – because soup was far too generous of a word – began to boil. The noise it made caused Erix to stir awake. It had barely been over an hour. My heart told me he needed more, whereas my soul was ready to leave for Wychwood.

"I really do love waking to this view," Erix said as his sleepy eyes fixed on me across the room.

"And yet you *still* should be resting," I said, getting up to remove the pot and stop it overcooking.

Erix yawned, mouth wide as a monstrous sound rumbled from the back of his throat. "Impossible when I have such company."

"You always know what to say, don't you?"

He lifted himself up, fixing his slumped posture. "When you have spent a long time apart from the person you love, you get a lot of time to overthink every little thing you would say if given the chance. I am, if anything, a well-practiced man."

My skin warmed beneath his words, pleasant and needing. "You thought of me that much?"

"I did, back when I thought I had truly lost you, I found that imagining a tomorrow was more painful than remembering the past. It was the past, our memories, that got me through. Now, all I can do is look forwards. I don't want to miss a moment of it."

My hands shook as I carried the pot and rested it on cold stone slabs beyond the fireplace.

"And what do you want, when this is all over?" I asked, already knowing the answer, but desperately needing to hear it from his lips. "Indulge me, if you would. I want to hear your answer again."

Erix sighed. Not a sad sigh, but one full of relief. "Exactly what I have got now. You, little bird. I want you. This. Duncan and the life we will all carve out together. Now that I understand that is a possibility, I can barely retract my claws from it. My answer will never change. Ask me it over and over, and you will always find the same, I promise."

"As you've said, a lot has changed, and can again." I hated to be the bearer of bad news, but I couldn't sit here and play pretend. "Promising only leads to disappointment."

"Lies. And how do I know? Because my feelings did not change before, so they will not going forwards." Erix leaned up as much as his tired body allowed and patted his knee in invitation. "Life – that is what I want. A good one, with those I care deeply about."

Not wanting to disappoint, I joined him, forgetting about the broth as I rested myself across his lap. Erix embraced me, laying a hand on my lower spine, the other wrapped around my waist.

There was no guilt anymore – not when sharing these moments with Erix. Yes, I thought of Duncan, and wished he could've been here with us. But I knew that this is what he'd want.

Duncan had brought us together, and for him, we would stay forged as one until he returned.

"I like the sound of that tomorrow," I admitted. "But at some point, you are going to realise that there are other responsibilities awaiting you."

This was the first time I'd laid a finger on the topic of Erix and what his blood tied him to since Elinor's death.

"Such as?" he asked.

I almost didn't answer, but what was the point of dancing around the facts? "Oakstorm is left without someone to rule it. Only you can take that mantle, Erix. If anything, it is what Elinor wanted."

I felt him physically recoil beneath my touch. "That is not something I am ready to comprehend yet. I have spent most of my life running from the borders of Oakstorm, it is going to take more strength to turn back for it now."

"Sometimes we have to put aside our desires, for the betterment of people who rely on us." I turned to face him, laying both hands on his spread knees for support. "I might be wrong, but you look at Oakstorm as a place you inherited the bad sides of yourself from – sides that I don't think are inherently bad, let me make that clear. And yet you didn't only get those wings from your father, you have his blood, and with that, the right to rule. To change a place for the better, as you have changed me."

Erix exhaled, tugging me closer. "Altar willing, we'll have many tomorrows ahead of us. Maybe during one of them I can think about Oakstorm. But until then, I want to selfishly exist with *you*."

"Well, you know I'll be by your side when the time comes to make hard choices," I whispered. "Just as you have done for me many times over."

"No one wants a monster to rule Oakstorm, Robin."

The use of my name shocked me. "You say that as if monsters have not ruled Oakstorm for generations."

"You know what I mean," he said, voice heavy with emotion. I knew there was much more to say, but Erix was still exhausted. Burdening him with the potential of responsibility, when tomorrow wasn't even secure yet, was wasted effort.

I swivelled, enough to face him. Erix looked at me through the opening of one squinted eye. His smile was soft and genuine. I found myself looking across every inch of his face, drinking him in. His pores, the bow of his lips, the dark lashes that lined his eyes. I'd take in every detail until the image of him, in the dark of my mind, was fully formed.

"You really need to get some more sleep whilst you can," I whispered.

"I know," Erix said, fighting another yawn. "Just not yet. A few more moments of this bliss is better than any dream that will be offered to me."

To help Erix relax, I came to stand behind his chair, and ran my palm across his head, brushing hair in languid strokes. His throaty groan told me it was exactly what he wanted, as did the hardening press of his cock, which pitched in his trousers.

"Better?" I whispered into his ear, lips brushing flesh.

"Mmhm."

I continued to touch him with careful hands, guiding him into an existence where he could rest well.

"Little bird," Erix whispered.

"Do you want me to stop?" I asked, noticing Erix clutch at his groin, the veins on the back of his hands bulging.

Getting Erix hard was certainly *not* the type of rest he needed.

"No. Please, do not stop. Not ever. I just… would you tell me what tomorrow looks like to you? I want to hear what *you* want when this is over. Paint the picture for me."

"I can do that," I said, running my fingers over his scalp, eliciting another moan from him. "But only if you close your eyes."

"Don't tell me what you think I want to hear," he added, before shutting his lids. "I want to hear *your* truth."

He'd asked me this question before, and my answer had been a lie. What do you want from the new world? How could I have answered that, knowing I didn't plan to stay around and enjoy it.

But this was different.

So different.

I took a deep breath, moving my fingers from his scalp to the side of his face. Before I began, I offered him another kiss, something soft. He puckered into me, longing to keep the kiss going, even as I pulled back.

Then I answered, pulling my truth from the inside of my soul. "I want to return home, with you and Duncan beside me. Not to Icethorn, a castle full of empty memories. But to Grove, back in the house I grew up in with my father. I want to spend days locked inside, living in my truth, with the two men who helped me find it. I want to see humans and fey as one, no longer separated by the past. I'm a bad king, Erix. I never wanted it, never asked for it. I tried to play pretend, but that path was never meant for me. And do you know something? I never truly believed in a home.

I spent my youth wondering after my mother, chasing after her ghost, believing I'd find the place I belonged when I finally reached her. Along the way, as I finally got everything I thought I wanted… I found out that I was wrong. Because it wasn't the destination my soul craved, but the people I found along the way. You, Erix. Duncan too. Those were not split pathways to the end of my story, but a single one that broke off but found its way coming back together. Because the crux of what I want for my tomorrow, is allowing myself to accept that I deserve one. And I deserve you. I deserve Duncan. And I believe that you deserve me, just as Duncan does. That is what I want." I paused, gathering my breath for the last part of my truth. "I want the home I believed I was searching for, but realised that I found it, long before I truly understood it."

By the time I'd finished, Erix's breathing had evened out. A smile was painted across cherry-red lips. His grasp of my hip eased enough for me to pull away without resistance. As much as I longed to sleep alongside him, to enjoy his touch and the gentle brush of his breath against my skin, I couldn't.

I leaned in, bringing my lips to the smooth skin of his forehead. "I love you, Erix. So much. I always did. It's my pleasure to chase tomorrows with you. Always."

The final kiss was light. I expected Erix to wake, but he didn't. He was far too exhausted. I sat myself beside the burning hearth, feeling the heat radiate off the warmed pot.

I thought of everyone I met along the way, those lost and found, who helped write this story. Those whose lives facilitated this very moment being possible. And, as I stared into the dancing flames, I silently thanked them. Allies and enemies. Because the path may have been treacherous, but we'd made it this far. And I planned to make it to the very fucking end.

For Duncan. For Erix. And, most importantly, a truth I finally recognised and accepted, I'd do it, for *me*.

CHAPTER 29

Peace never lasted long. One day it would, but for now, it was an impossibility. We could pretend for a few minutes, hours at most. But reality always came knocking. And it came in the form of Erix's gryvern kin.

I felt sick to my core. I clutched at my stomach, unable to stand still, as the news continued to repeat in my head.

"Cassial knows exactly what he is doing," I shouted as we burst out the farm's doors, Erix and a cohort of his gryvern warriors following behind.

They'd arrived hours after Erix had fallen asleep, just as the pot of broth cooled, forgotten. I hadn't had time to ladle it into bowls when I heard them arrive – bringing news from the frontlines.

"It is insurance to him," Erix called after me, still visibly tired, but such details no longer mattered. "He is using innocent lives as a shield against the fey. It isn't just about using the fey to further his campaign, that was never enough. But pitting them against the powerless humans, that is Cassial's way of cementing his future. He will turn the fey into the monsters he needs them to be."

I spun on one of the gryvern, the only one dressed in armour. "Are you confident this information is correct? We cannot afford to move on this unless you are sure."

The gryvern bowed their head toward me. "I wouldn't have brought this information to you unless I was completely sure, Your Majesty. We've checked through every dwelling as requested, attempting to move the humans away from the fight, using fear. But everywhere the gryvern have been is empty. I have personally got close enough to the Nephilim encampment to see the humans we searched for – men, women and children... hundreds if not thousands of them..."

Children. I couldn't fathom it. Blindly led by the Creator's promised warriors, but then used as a shield before them. That was where all these people had gone. I imagined the family this farm belonged to. How they left their home to stand between the Nephilim and the fey, not knowing the death that awaited them.

Cassial had put the people he was supposed to protect on the front line, a band of flesh and bone to separate them from our army lingering beyond Wychwood.

"He's a *monster*. This is what Cassial has done with them all," I snapped, wondering if the owner of this farm was also an unsuspecting victim of Cassial's plans. Did the angels show up at their door, promising them salvation from the fey-monsters, offering the promise of the Creator as their protector?

Deep down, I knew the answer already.

"Have they been given weapons?" I asked, voice trembling. "Tell me they are at least prepared for the fight that Cassial is hoping for?"

"No." The gryvern couldn't look me in the eyes. "They haven't. The humans are a shield, that is all. If the fey attack, the humans will die."

"It would strengthen Cassial's plans to ruin any hope of relations in the future," Erix added, equally as distraught. "We will be the bloody killers, Cassial will continue pressing his agenda of being this Saviour."

I snapped my attention to Erix and the other gryvern who flanked him. The rest, unlike the warrior I conversed with, were like mindless hounds, monstrous forms too far gone in their transformation to find humanity. Yes, Erix had control of them, but that still didn't stop my heart from skipping whenever we caught eyes.

These creatures had killed my mother. The family I never met. They were Doran Oakstorm's pets – twisted creations of his seed.

But just as Cassial was trying to paint the fey as monsters, I understood that such a feeling was all down to perspective. The gryvern were not monsters by choice. Just like Duwar was not a demon-god, but a power determined by how it was used.

"Then we must reach Wychwood now. I need to speak with the fey lines and inform them of this news," I said, body practically erupting with unspent energy. "We *must* withdraw, but they will only do this with the order of a fey leader. I can't be sure they will listen to anyone else but me."

"If they see you, nothing will stop news of your survival reaching Cassial before our plan has been completed," Erix reminded me.

"If Gyah has reached them by now, she would've told them," I said.

There was a niggling thought in my mind. If Gyah had informed Wychwood that the Icethorn king still lived, why had we not seen a convoy sent to search for us?

"And if she hasn't?" Erix voiced the same concern, likely noticing that one detail I had figured out.

"The lives of hundreds of humans are not worth the risk. Althea would say the same." I could almost hear her voice in my ear, telling me that my decision was the right one. "No life, human or fey, is more important than any other. Regardless, our fight is against Cassial. *Not* the humans. Especially not humans who don't hold a weapon or shield. Their faith in Cassial as their Saviour will not stop them from dying."

But I can.

No one told me I was wrong, but that didn't stop me from adding a final sentiment aloud. Perhaps I wasn't even speaking to Erix or his gryvern, convincing them of what I was saying. Maybe those final words were solely meant for me.

"I've stopped a war between the realms before, I will do it again."

"That you have," Erix confirmed, the confidence he held for me made his gaze glow, his posture straighten. "We will reach the front lines and inform them of Cassial's plan. No matter what, our armies must not attack. Doing so will only give Cassial reason to use Duwar against them."

"Duncan, Gyah and Rafaela must be informed too," I reminded him. "If they don't know about this... it would ruin all hopes of retreat for those humans that Cassial is using. We need more time. We need another plan."

With the news brought by the gryvern, my previous plan had crumbled to dust in our wake.

Erix nodded, his brow fixed in a harsh frown. "You heard your king; take this news to Duncan and his Faithful. Make sure all parties know of how Cassial is using the humans and put a hold to any planned attack until further commands are provided."

Our fey would not survive the attack. Nor the humans. And I had no reason to believe that Cassial wouldn't attack, even with the humans still positioned before him. At the chance of ridding the world of the fey, what was the cost of a few human lives? If anything, it would truly solidify us as monsters, setting a dark path for any who survived long enough to experience the type of future Cassial and his Fallen wanted.

"Then we go now," I commanded. "To Wychwood."

I thought of Duncan, who'd soon expect us. How would he react when we didn't follow through with our signal? Without me, the rest of his Nephilim wouldn't be able to reach Cassial. But I couldn't encourage a war until the innocent lives were protected.

What good was the promise of a tomorrow – a new world – if we *all* couldn't experience it?

CHAPTER 30

I was breathless from anxiety the moment we touched ground beyond Wychwood's border. I hadn't expected to find the fey encampment so easily, but I was proven wrong. A sea of tents had been erected within the cover of Wychwood forest. Concealed beneath thick foliage, there was no missing it as we flew over the border into fey land.

All around me fey looked up as if they'd seen a ghost. Erix had barely released his hold on me before I was running.

"Where are your leaders?" I shouted at those I passed, no room for the act of a demure king.

It was one soldier, a tall woman with rich skin and eyes of amber, who pointed to the largest tent set in the middle of the encampment. I barely got out my thanks as I forged ahead.

The further I gained into the camp, the more my mind was stunted at what I saw. I'd seen the fey army once before, but never something of this magnitude. In the far north of the Cedarfall Court, when I'd visited Farrador, I'd had my first glimpse of what a fey army could look like. But what waited here, a scar of flesh and armour stationed before Wychwood's border, was like nothing I'd seen back then.

For the first time in our history, all four courts had come together.

We were a force of destruction and ruin, which was not a good thing.

With a conjured blast of winter winds, the curtained entrance flung open. Between seeing a glimpse of the fey army, and the sheer number of soldiers waiting to advance on Cassial, I was even more eager to share my news and put a stop to any planned attack.

"You must call back our numbers and put a hold to any advancements," I shouted before the curtain settled at my back. "*Immediately.*"

No one replied. Not at first.

I swept my gaze across the tent, across every face. I recognised Lady Kelsey Cedarfall first – Althea's aunt, whose skin turned an icy white at my arrival. She leaned forwards, hands splayed on the large table before her. Around her stood other fey men and women, each looking up toward me, equally pale and wide eyed. Someone gasped, drawing my attention – Eroan, clutching at his chest as though his heart was seconds from bursting out.

"Robin Icethorn. You're alive." Eroan's eyes widened at the sight of me, blinking rapidly as if the illusion of my presence would dissipate.

I held my chin high, aware that the rustling at my back was Erix catching up. "I am."

Eroan was the first to bow, a heartbreaking sob bursting beyond his pale lips. He practically folded in half, mumbling his thanks to Altar that I wasn't dead. Lady Kelsey followed next, just as shocked.

Eroan proudly wore the Icethorn emblem as a pin on his jacket. Lady Kelsey was dressed in the fire reds and rich golds of the Cedarfall court she represented. There were more. A young woman who wore the emblem of the Elmdew court. My eyes went to the familiar man again, trying to discern why I felt as though I knew him. He was older than the rest, with thinning white hair, and bulbous sky-blue eyes enlarged behind round spectacles. His bloated fingers rose to rest upon the symbol over his heart. The symbol of the court he represented: Oakstorm.

I'd last seen him lurking in the back of the church before

Cassial's ambush. And now here he was, poisoning the very space I'd walked into.

"I cannot believe it," Eroan gasped, hardly looking at me as if the vision before him was too painful to imagine. Questions painted his lips, drawing them in a line of tension. "How is this possible? Erix too–"

"I will explain when we have the time," I replied, "but for now I need you to listen very closely."

Eroan bowed again, gasping out another sob. "Time is not something we have, Robin. We were hours away from setting off our campaign to save Queen Cedarfall from enemy hands–"

"No," I snapped, reaching him in strides, taking his frail arms in my hands and lifting him. "That cannot happen!"

Eroan bowed again as if my words scolded him.

"We have time for bowing and shock later," I added, scanning the tent. "For now, you *must* send word to the front lines. Draw back, retreat. It's important we do not engage with the Nephilim. A war must not proceed under any circumstances."

"The war has already begun Robin Icethorn," said the Oakstorm man.

He stepped around the table, hobbling slightly on a bad foot. It was then I noticed the details of the table, how the oaken top was carved into a familiar map of the realms. Wooden figures had been carved into the shapes of soldiers, some placed on the familiar borderline between the realms, whilst others looked to gather east, far away from this encampment. The only detail missing was the hidden Isles of Irobel.

"Under whose order?" I snapped, seething at the patronising tone he spoke to me with. "Surely not yours, Ailon Oakstorm?"

He blanched at the use of his name, then smiled sickly toward me.

"You are now the second ghost to walk into this tent, King Icethorn," Ailon said, coughing into a stained hanky. He looked behind me, settling his dominating stare upon Erix, and resting it there. "Are we to expect any more to follow?"

I could read the distrust in his face. It was so distracting I almost missed what he'd said. But Erix didn't.

A growl built in the pits of Erix's throat. "Care to expand on that, *uncle*?"

"Lord Ailon Oakstorm will suffice, *boy*." He sneered in Erix's direction, disgustingly turning up the corner of his lip. "Let us not begin to use such titles when you have never bothered with them before. It would not seem appropriate, considering what has happened since we last saw one another."

I quickly realised that Ailon was not here as a representee of his court, but a replacement to Queen Elinor Oakstorm. And he was loving every minute of flashing his authority before me, just like his brother once had.

Before he was killed.

"Ailon." I had no energy for manners. "I trust Gyah Eldrae has arrived too, good. I need to speak with her. Someone fetch her—"

"Unfortunately, that will not be possible. You've just missed her."

My ears hammered with the roar of blood, as though oceans crashed within my skull. I spared Erix a glance, sensing his shared desire to flee the tent in chase of her.

"When?" I snapped.

"It has only been an hour since she left." Lady Kelsey clearly disliked Ailon, but she did her part to play demure around him.

"Then she can be recalled," I said, frantically looking to Erix, hoping he was already sending out word to his gryvern to locate Gyah and bring her back.

"And leave Althea to die? No, Robin."

"Cassial needs Althea. I hate to say this but she is far safer in his hands."

Lady Kelsey's lower lip trembled. "That is not a hope I can stand behind, Robin. I am sure you are already aware, my niece is currently being held by the Nephilim—"

"Fallen," I corrected. "They aren't who we have believed

them to be. There is so much you couldn't possibly begin to understand, nor do we have the chance or time."

"I am beginning to understand that." Lady Kelsey recoiled. "But we must not sit back and wait for something disastrous to befall Althea; the time to act is now, as per Gyah's request."

The ground fell out from beneath me.

"What did she say?" I leaned on the table for support, lungs aching.

"Gyah brought news to us regarding Althea's status," Lady Kelsey explained. "Although it was Eroan who spoke with her, he can best explain. We know he plans to use her, but how, we aren't sure. But whatever nefarious plans he has must not go forwards."

"Is this true?" I turned to Eroan.

If he confirmed, that meant that Duncan had given Gyah and Seraphine instruction to mobilise an army. But why give me the hope of trying to stop her, unless he knew we'd never catch up?

I looked to my advisor, recognising how he quickly looked to his feet and refused to look back up. "Gyah did visit me, yes."

"Alone?" I asked.

After a pause, he replied. I knew he lied the moment his eyes couldn't meet me. "Yes, Lady Eldrae was alone. Until she reached us, we all had believed she was the only monarch who did not perish alongside Elinor and you. All of you, actually. Of course, now we know this is not true, but advancements have been made. Gyah informed me about Althea and *how* Cassial wishes to use her. You must understand we only have acted as a means of necessity. We were under the impression that Althea was the last Wychwood royal still living–"

Eroan was lying about two things. One, that Gyah had arrived alone. And two, that he believed she was the only person to survive. I read it then, in his dramatic reaction when I entered the tent, the almost forced emotion. He knew I still lived, but the rest of the room didn't. And I seemed to be the only one to notice.

"Did any of you see her?" I asked, sweeping my gaze over the tent.

"Only Eroan," Lady Kelsey answered. "And per her requests, we have already sent a legion east of Cassial's lines, led by Gyah herself. She plans to attack Cassial from multiple sides, then we will be ready to strike."

Aiding Duncan's plans.

No, no, no.

I slammed my fist down on the table, knocking wooden figures onto their sides. "It is imperative that no attack is made."

"It is too late." Eroan refused to look at me. "Their goal is to free Althea with little bloodshed, but we are prepared in case more force is required."

"Send word to her. Draw her back. If she knows what awaits her, she will never act." I blinked and saw the humans, lined out like a shield, the innocent lives that would die. Althea wouldn't want it; I knew that in my soul. Gyah too.

"Impossible," Ailon answered. "We are prepared to march, as per the request of the Eldrae. We will not allow you to swan in at a convenient time and lay out demands. Your presence has already spoiled fey plans once before, I will not allow this to happen again."

Magic stirred beneath my skin, aching for release, pinned to the man who embodied the very people I hated. "Even if you knew that Cassial has put a wall of unarmed humans – children, innocent people – between us and him."

Ailon took in my question, chewed on it, and then spat out his answer. "As I said, a retreat is too late."

"If we attack, Gyah will not be met with the force of Nephilim, but the unexpecting terror of innocent lives. They will not survive it, and nor will she."

"The loss of life is inevitable in war," Ailon said with as

BEN ALDERSON 389

little emotion as his brother once had. "Something you should know by now."

"If you do not listen to me," I seethed, finger pointing at Ailon, poised as though it was a sword in my hand. "I will stop this army myself."

Ailon faltered, his expression morphing from enjoyment to shock. "Is that a threat, Robin Icethorn?"

"*King* Icethorn," I corrected. "And I don't waste my energy on idle threats, Ailon. Surely *you* have worked that out already."

I threw his statement back at him, delighting in the way his lips quirked downwards.

"We still have matters to confirm regarding our advancements," Lady Kelsey swept in, placing herself between us. Her expression was soft and deadly in equal measure. I caught the warning in her widening eyes, telling me to calm myself. "Sit with us, Robin. Your surprising presence may help."

"I have made my stance clear, Kelsey."

She gestured to a spare seat, then took her own, leaving the rest of the fey to stand. "And yet there may be time to alter ours."

"No–" Ailon was cut off as Erix took three strides toward him.

My blood fizzed in my veins, making my skin feel as though I was burning from the inside out. "We must *not* advance," I repeated. "No army is marching. No fey is going to engage in a fight. Withdraw our numbers, send word out to those who've already been sent. Do anything and everything you can to stop this. Attacking now will only cement that we are the demons Cassial is trying to paint us as. If we attack, it will not only ruin any hope of turning the tides, but any relations between our neighbouring realms. The future will not survive this... and nor will Wychwood once Cassial releases the power he holds."

"Cassial and his army are no match for us." Ailon was enjoying this, I read it in every smile line that spoiled his ugly face. "Every day reports show that they advance closer to our borders, they test us daily. We have the power to stop him."

"You may be right." An odd calm raced over me. "His *army* is nothing but innocent humans. You will lay them to waste in a matter of moments with the power you hold. But what happens after that, or do you not care?"

"As long as Cassial dies," Ailon said, gaze flickering down to the floor. "That is all that matters."

He was lying, I could read it in his lack of eye contact, the way his worn hands wrung together.

"I find it interesting that both you and Cassial actually want those humans to suffer," I said, narrowing my eyes on him. "You are only feeding our enemy what he wants. Then again, I suppose your brother petitioned for war no different to this before, what would make your desires so different?"

Ailon's silence confirmed that he knew. They all knew.

"Children, Kelsey." I fixed my eyes on her, pleading for her to see sense. "Cassial is using fucking children as a shield. You can give a person a sword and spear, that doesn't make them a fighter. And if my understanding is correct, Cassial hasn't provided even that to the humans. He is baiting you – using Althea as a means to start a conflict which he will end in seconds."

"You are quite wrong, Robin." Ailon grinned further at me, and for a moment I thought I was looking into the eyes of Doran Oakstorm again. "It is the hate within a person that makes them a weapon. And it is clear what the humans see us as. Monsters. Demons, as you put it."

"Ailon is not wrong, Robin," Kelsey said, eyes downcast. "They have taken my niece and use her as a pawn in this game. I will – *we* will – do anything to ensure another fey royal is not taken from us."

I couldn't believe what I was hearing. "You can't begin to understand what is happening."

"Gyah has updated us on Cassial's use of Duwar," Kelsey

said. "We are prepared for force. But one man is no match compared to an army of us."

"He *is* no man," I whispered, finding myself suddenly weak against this resistance.

"Nor is he a god," Ailon added, stepping around the table, coming to stop before me. "What matters is that we save Althea Cedarfall, and thus save the fey realms from Cassial. I will soon be following with Oakstorm warriors, once we know that Althea is no longer in Cassial's grasp."

My mind whirled like a maelstrom, but something in Ailon's words sparked a thought. "You would willingly put yourself in Cassial's line of sight, when he will be without a fey to host Duwar."

Again, Ailon looked away sharply. Before I could read further into his reaction, he seethed in his response. "This is an issue created by your hands, Robin. It was your names written in ink across the treaty between the humans. You signed Wychwood over to Cassial. We are simply trying to right the wrongs you have all—"

Ailon swallowed his next words as a bout of frozen winds shot through the tent. At my back, my power gathered, building into a force that would rival even the wings of a Nephilim.

"You want to offer yourself to Cassial, don't you?" I asked.

Ailon's sky-blue eyes flared wide. "How dare you. How very dare you, Robin Icethorn."

"Perhaps, but you have not told me I am wrong," I said, oddly calm, whilst the cold winds picked up my words and amplified them. "Duwar, the source of life and power, chaos and destruction. What an incredible tool for a man as weak and desperate as you."

I was no longer Robin Icethorn. I was a bundle of fury in flesh, ready to unleash it upon someone.

"You know, Elinor warned me about her advisors. She warned me about men like *you*. If you think for a moment that your presence is required, then you are wrong. I have returned, and as the final remaining fey royal this side of Wychwood, *I* will decide how we move. You can either listen peacefully in your chairs or face the wrath that has been building inside of me. So, Ailon, what will it be?"

"There is no need for this. Ailon will never give himself willingly to Cassial–" Kelsey stopped in her tracks as I snapped my eyes to her. "Fighting amongst ourselves when the enemy is outside these tent walls."

"No, not to Cassial. But he would willingly give himself to Duwar, which is exactly what the power requires for the transference."

Kelsey was shocked to silence. As was Ailon. The difference between them both, was Ailon simmered in his disdain for me, whereas I recognised hesitation in Kelsey.

Ailon's silence was incriminating.

Eroan spoke up, the gentle lilt of his voice a comfort. "Now, more so than ever, we must keep our fey relations aligned. Arguing will not solve the danger before us."

My voice darkened as magic still swirled around me. "Recall Gyah Eldrae. I will not ask again, nor is it up for a vote. It will be done."

Ailon glowered, taking an unsteady step closer to me. "No."

"I stand with Robin Icethorn," the Elmdew representative said. I hadn't caught her name yet, but I could see from the strength in her gaze that she, like me and Eroan, was keen not to encourage the unnecessary murder of innocent people. She was not the same woman I'd seen in Lockinge. She was likely held by Cassial still, alongside the Elmdew heir. But regardless of her unknown status, I was glad someone had finally stood beside me. "I expressed my concern when this was agreed, and it fell on ears who didn't wish to hear it. Our heir is in the hands of Cassial and his people, and yet no one mentions saving the child who will one day become King of Elmdew. I am with Robin. There is time to recall Gyah, before more mistakes are made."

I thanked her with a nod, feeling my power wane knowing I had someone else behind me.

"Sending our army in now will only jeopardise the success of our mission," I said.

"You and *what* army?" Ailon demanded, slapping an aged hand on the table. "Or are Doran's little pets the only people you have behind you?"

Erix snarled at that insult, baring the points of his teeth in Ailon's direction. "Careful."

"Yes, Ailon. Be careful. As you can imagine, *'Doran's little pets'* are an unruly bunch," I said, lip curling over teeth, matching the fury of Erix who simmered behind me. "If one deems it a requirement to tear you to shreds, there will be little I can do to stop them."

Ailon was appalled by the threat, which made a part of me rather happy. "Do you know who you are speaking to?"

I stepped closer to him, my shadow cast over the map of the realms. "I have an idea of who you *think* I'm speaking to, Ailon. But let me make this very clear, you are no one of importance. Without the passing of the Oakstorm key, there is no requirement for another Oakstorm king or queen. And if there was, I can assure you it wouldn't be you."

Ailon struck out, snatching my wrist like an adult punishing a disobedient child. "But I am the rightful–"

"Take your hands off him and sit *down*." Erix bellowed, his command coming out in cold mist before his lips. I had to withdraw my power before the entire tent was encased in ice, but with Erix unfurling beside me, he was the only power I required.

Ailon released me, then finally he sat. Erix grinned at his uncle, showing him the full mouth of teeth that would, in fact, rip him to shreds if the opportunity arose. "Now that's a good boy. Keep those lips sealed before King Icethorn sees fit to dismiss you."

"Thank you, Erix," I said, laying a careful hand on his arm. "To answer your question, Ailon, we do have an army."

And so I told them.

I revealed everything that had happened after the wedding and my supposed death. I revealed the story of Altar, the Creator and the power source of Duwar. How the Nephilim had split into two factions – Faithful and Fallen. I didn't miss a single detail – well, beside the mention of how Erix, Duncan and I celebrated after Duncan successfully passed The Transfiguration.

In the back of my mind, I wondered why Gyah hadn't mentioned any of this. Was the secrecy at the guidance of Seraphine, aiding in whatever game she was playing. No one had mentioned Gyah arriving with an Asp, but I had to believe Seraphine had been here.

I understood that Eroan had those answers. I just needed a moment with him to extract them.

"If Cassial is encouraged to use Duwar, it will weaken him?" Eroan repeated a question. "The risk of him using the full wrath of that power source is surely not what we want."

"Cassial will not waste himself," I replied. "Which is why you've not seen a display of power since the wedding. We must coax him. Make him feel as though he must use Duwar, because he has no other choice."

"I thought we were trying not to risk the lives of these humans you care so much about," Ailon reminded me, spittle flying past vile lips. "Or do your responsibilities change like the tides? How can we expect this half-human child to make decisions to benefit the fey, when his allegiance is split so clearly? Or, perhaps you are the one who wants Duwar for yourself, after all."

"I refused Duwar's offers for months," I spat. "My will is stronger than you think it is."

"And yet your will is what stopped Duncan Rackley from dying in the first place, saving us all this problem to deal with."

Ailon hadn't learned that his words could lead him into trouble. And he was old enough for me not to warn him again. I felt Erix stir, bristling like a hound behind me, teeth snapping, wings flaring.

I decided to ignore Ailon, speaking directly to the other three. My effort was better given to them. "Once Duncan has removed Althea from Cassial's grasp, that will remove the chance that she is the next host of the power source. That is why we believe she is being kept: as collateral."

"Why *not* let that power transfer?" Ailon asked. "If what you've said about Duwar's compatibility with the fey is correct, is it not best that we have access to the power? Althea can then use it."

"No," I said. "Our goal is to save Althea. If Duwar is transferred into her, she is at risk of being controlled. The monstrous acts she will be made to do would ruin her. And if not, it will only make her do the right thing. And if you wish to see Althea alive, long past Cassial's downfall, then she must not host Duwar."

"Then what are you suggesting we do?" Kelsey leaned forwards.

Eroan straightened in his chair, uncomfortable with the very clear outcome. "Robin means that Althea will need to die if we do not act."

I didn't tell him he was wrong. "There is much we don't know about Duwar. One clear way to remove the power from this playing board, is to ensure the host dies. There is no other known way of dealing with it." Although I had my suspicions, those were not confirmed. "If Althea takes Duwar into herself, she will soon sacrifice herself."

I could see from Lady Kelsey's shifting gaze that she'd worked out what I meant. "Althea will die either way, that is what you are saying."

"Exactly." We all knew Althea. Duwar was not a power that should've ever been at play in the realms. If Althea knew there was a real chance of returning Duwar to where Altar first stole it from, she would throw herself willingly into the oblivion. We couldn't let that happen.

"So, we have a plan then?" Lady Kelsey asked, between chewing her nails.

"Send word to Gyah, withdraw any planned attack. Give Duncan Rackley and the Faithful the time they need to slay Cassial without incitement of a war."

"Do you believe this will work?" Eroan asked.

"I can hope. It is our only option."

"There will be risks," Lady Kelsey reminded us.

"Anything worth something comes with risks. I've learned that along the way." I spared a glance at Erix, encouraged by his subtle nod and gentle smile. "Which is why we must show Durmain who the true monsters are. Between our retreat and the clashing of Faithful and Fallen, it will plant a seed of doubt in those who support Cassial."

Just as Duwar revealed themselves as a demon in the mirror, it was always about perspective. How power was only bad if used as such. If we could change the perspective of the humans – truly show them how Cassial was using the power source with evil intentions – then they would finally see the *real* demon. It would weaken Cassial's claim to be the prophesied saviour.

But it was important, before we acted, that we received word that Cassial had been killed.

"Eroan. How long will it take for the remaining occupants in Icethorn to evacuate?"

He pondered the question. "Not long. We've already requested that those who dwell close to the border shift northwards. Those who decided to leave have, but it will be impossible to move the rest. It is a lot to ask people who have spent years away from their home, to abandon it again after such a short period of time."

"I understand." And I did. "I want you to send as many of our soldiers as possible into Icethorn land. They will guard the populated areas, in case our plans go south. In the meantime, we offer the humans Cassial is using a path to take to safety. Getting them out of danger is our focus."

"I do not agree with these plans," Ailon said, as if his opinion mattered. "I have said it before, and I will reiterate it–"

"Shut up, Ailon," Lady Kelsey interrupted. "I thought we were done listening to that grating voice when Doran died, I do not want to have to survive you too. Robin." She turned to me after the dramatic roll of her eyes. "You have my support, as well as the support of the Cedarfall numbers. As long as Althea lives, and her life is not under threat, Cedarfall will follow."

"And me," Eroan added. "The Icethorn army is ready for you to command."

"If it required a vote, I would be with King Icethorn," the Elmdew Fey said. "But a vote isn't needed. As Robin has informed us, he is the last fey royal this side of Wychwood. We do as *he* commands."

"*My* army will not follow this pathetic human scum," Ailon hissed, palms slapping on the table as he stood. "Be it by my last breath, the Oakstorm court will advance and I will deal with this misbalance of power myself–"

Erix strode forwards so suddenly, Ailon choked on his words. With strong hands, Erix wrapped his fingers around Ailon's throat, nails pinching through skin, and hauled him from the chair. "Robin already told you, the Oakstorm Court does not belong to you."

"Then… who?" Ailon croaked, wincing as Erix drew his face inches from him.

"Me," Erix said, the single word as sharp as a knife. "It is mine, by birthright. You have not said it to our company yet, but we both know who Elinor Oakstorm has named as her successor, don't we, uncle?"

Erix released his neck, Ailon flopping forwards as he gasped to catch his breath. When he looked up, it was with a danger in his eyes that I hadn't seen since Doran died. "When I save this realm, and take Duwar for my own, you will all bow before me."

"At least you do not waste energy lying about your desires anymore," Erix said, wings flexing to his sides. "Although, I'm afraid honesty is not always as freeing as you think it would be. Bend the knee, uncle. Do not resist me."

"Over my dead–"

Erix flashed forwards, so quick I blinked, and it was over.

Snap. With the subtle but strong twist of Erix's wrist, Ailon's head bent at an ungodly angle. The light drained from his eyes, drawing back like a retreating tide. No one uttered a word, not as his death stretched out across the tent. Then Erix released the body, dropped him and stepped over the slumped body.

"Your wish is my command," Erix said to himself, glowering down at the corpse at his feet.

The tent was stunned into silence. Erix gathered himself and turned to the crowd, shoulders rolled back as he was aware everyone had just heard his admission.

"Before I'm accused of a war crime myself, Elinor Oakstorm informed me days ago that she named me as her heir to the summer court," Erix said, authority and command dripping from him in waves. "I am sure Ailon did not make this clear to you, just as I am sure you were not aware that Ailon has been sending letters to Cassial before the arrangement of Althea and Gyah's wedding. Between that, and his admission of his desires for Duwar, I trust he is a problem now dealt with."

When no one replied to him, Erix spoke one final statement aloud. "Oakstorm is mine."

Pride swelled within me, so poignant that I felt myself threaten to burst. Erix had finally accepted that half of him entirely. Not just the monster, the gryvern – but the bloodline that gave him that strength.

"King Oakstorm," I spoke the name for the first time, loving how it felt in my mouth. I dropped to my knee, not caring for anyone else that followed. But after a few beats, there was not a soul still standing. "As you can see, we all agree that you are rightful heir to the Oakstorm court."

No one refused Erix. No one offered objection. I spared Eroan a glance to see that he shared in my pride.

"Rise, please," Erix said, his voice firm and clear. "Bowing may be custom, but it isn't something I am ready to get comfortable with yet."

I made sure I was the last to do so. Erix put gentle fingers beneath my chin and lifted me up to face him. "You will never bow to me, not under such circumstances."

I swallowed hard, unable to look away from him. "If that is what you wish."

Erix dropped his finger from my chin, addressing the room. "I will visit our front lines, spread word that we are to retreat. Seeking out Gyah is our one focus now. The gryvern have been looking since this conversation even began. In the meantime, we will prepare for the Icethorn border to be unguarded, allowing for the necessary evacuation of as many humans as possible."

I nodded, longing to take his mouth and place it upon mine. But the time was not right for that.

"We shall all help where we can," Lady Kelsey said, gesturing to the other woman.

"And I'll be here waiting for you to return," I said, offering Erix an encouraging gaze.

Erix nodded, knelt to pick Ailon's body from the ground, and left the tent first. As the rest began to file out, I looked to Eroan and stopped him with a hand. "Will you stay with me? I have questions and need for council."

"As I expected you would," Eroan replied, dropping his eyes to the floor, hands fumbling with one another.

Eroan was never good at keeping secrets. I knew there was more to his visit with Gyah. He'd chosen not to mention Seraphine, so I believed there was a reason for that. I had to find out what that reason was, before I left for Icethorn.

"So," I started when we were the last left inside the tent, "are you going to tell me about what *really* happened when Gyah arrived, or shall we continue playing coy?"

Eroan took a deep breath in. I thought it was to give him the confidence to share his secrets, I didn't realise it was going to break our plans in two.

CHAPTER 31

I pinched my eyes closed, shaking my head as if I simply hadn't heard Eroan correctly, let alone understood him. My temple ached as I pushed fingers into it, trying to elevate the pressure building in my skull. "Eroan, what are you trying to tell me?"

"Seraphine made me believe it was the only way. She certainly knows how to plead a very convincing case, and at the time I believed her. Robin, this will work, I know it will."

My eyes flew wide, the anger unleashing in the tone as I interrupted him. "*Who* did Seraphine ask you to glamour her into?"

Eroan choked on his breath, trying to still his obvious panic. "Queen Althea Cedarfall."

"No," I exhaled, mind whirling. "No. No. No."

I looked around the room, desperately searching for something – anything, to face the brunt of my reaction. If I didn't release the power which had built inside of me, it would soon destroy me before I got the chance to fix this.

The table caught my eye, with its grooves and valleys as the oak had been carved into the map of the realms. In three strides, I stood before it, slamming my palms down into the wood. The pain was a pleasurable release, as was the wave of ice that exploded outwards. I watched, unblinking and numb, as my winter rolled across the map, devouring Wychwood and Durmain entirely in white.

My breath came out in clouds of frozen mist, the temperature dropping to new lows as the power continued to expel out of me.

I saw my reflection in the layer of fresh ice across the ruined map. Wide eyes, dishevelled hair and clear exhaustion. But it was the panic – the look of wild terror in my eyes – that made me feel like I was looking at a stranger.

"Who else knows of these plans?" I asked, finding it hard to manage my breathing. My chest ached with the vicious thump of my heart. If I'd eaten, the tide of sickness would've affected me.

The entire tent faded from view as Eroan's admission continued to repeat in my mind.

"No one else," Eroan answered, physically trembling on the spot. "Gyah was able to leave with Seraphine before she was noticed by anyone north of the Wychwood border."

"Why?" I whispered, more to myself than Eroan, but he answered anyway. "Why would she do this!"

"Seraphine told me it was under *your* order, Robin. I swear, you have to believe me. I wouldn't have done anything if I didn't think you had a hand in it."

"And you believed her?" I stumbled over the words, unable to fathom what I was hearing. "You believed I would freely send someone I cared about into the mouth of a monster?"

"No, actually, I didn't. That was until Gyah confirmed your alleged orders. I was but one against two, and they were adamant this was your request. They told me you still lived, and that alone was a shock. Between being blindsided by finding out a young man I admire and care for hadn't died, and understanding the horrifying prospects Cassial has for our dear Althea, I had to do something. I didn't question the plan. As Gyah said, glamouring someone had worked before, so it could work again."

Eroan referred to the time when he'd glamoured my face to look like Kayne – Duncan's oldest friend, who betrayed us from his poisonous jealousy and hate for the fey. Because of the glamour I was able to initiate an attack on Aldrick in Rinholm. But this was different. There was only one reason she'd ask Eroan to glamour her to look like Althea, and that was to trade places with the real Queen of Cedarfall.

Was this her way of paying penance for acting without us, or simply racing toward end of the game she'd been playing from the very beginning?

I thought of her husband and the child she'd accepted as her own. Pain was a constant in my gut knowing all the things she could leave behind if this went terribly wrong.

I turned and faced Eroan. He was locked in fear, chewing nails all whilst he could hardly look at me. I laid a hand on his shoulder, attempting to offer him comfort when I couldn't find any for myself. "You did what you thought was right, I cannot blame you for this or harbour any anger toward you. I'm only sorry you were manipulated into her game."

"So, you didn't know of this beforehand?" he asked.

"No. I didn't know of this plan. And it certainly wasn't given by me." A violent chill captured my skin, turning it to glass. One wrong move and I would shatter. "But I did know Seraphine was with her, and the fact you didn't mention the Asp only proved that secrets were brewing beneath the surface. I wouldn't have asked this of Seraphine. She – she has too much to lose by risking her life so willingly."

Another reply screamed inside of me. But I swallowed it down, refusing to lay blame on Eroan. He was simply doing what was asked of him. I shouldn't feel this anger toward him, and yet the emotion was a maelstrom within me.

"Seraphine was adamant this was the only way," Eroan confirmed. "I admit, the plan was solid. She shared in the desire for minimal bloodshed. A mission – quick in and out. I trusted in her chances because she was confident that all would be well."

I heard his words, but that didn't mean I wanted to believe them. "Did they mention any more of their plans?"

I saw the answer in Eroan's eyes, long before he spoke it aloud. "No. And I didn't ask further because Gyah told me not to. She made me vow secrecy, on the grounds that she'd tear my insides out if I told a living soul."

I bristled. "You told me."

"Because, until now, I thought they were *your* plans, Robin. In fact, they knew you would come. They told me to expect you."

It clicked, another piece of this puzzle. "Gyah is a woman of her word, which means she knew I'd likely follow. She wanted me to know they were doing this."

Gyah knew that I'd find out about her plans and chase after them. I'd bet she was banking on us following, for backup. Which meant we needed to leave for Cassial immediately.

"Tell me how to fix this," Eroan said. "I'm sorry, Robin. If you know of anything I can do to help fix this, I will. Just ask it of me. Anything..."

I felt the rush of blood in every vein and vessel. My ears rang with the echo of my heartbeat, driving me to the brink of madness. Standing here, wasting more time, was making the feeling worse. I had to act – to control the narrative, because this was the only way that we would win.

The realm didn't need King Robin, it needed a level-headed Robin Icethorn who loved his friends and wanted the potential of a tomorrow.

"Continue with my previous commands," I said, firm and swiftly. "See that those in Icethorn are protected and a path is made within the boundary for humans. If I can stop Seraphine before she makes this mistake, then we go back to our original plan. We lure the humans north, get them away from Cassial, and then attack... if Duncan has not been successful by then."

Eroan was silent, staring at me with a creased brow. Then he asked the question I wondered if he'd be brave enough to voice aloud. "But Robin, *why* do you need to stop Seraphine?

Clearly the Asp knows the price she is to pay. If she is taking this burden off you all, then let her. Sometimes you must understand that not everyone can be saved."

"No. I refuse to believe that. Seraphine's life is as important as Althea's. No one person trumps another, just because of the blood running through their veins."

It was Eroan's turn to lay a hand on me. "Seraphine made her intentions clear. A sacrifice she was happy to make if it required it. She knows what she is doing, Robin. Maybe we should allow one life to pass, if it means saving thousands more. Even you said that Cassial, if desperate, will transfer Duwar into Althea. This way, if that is the case, Seraphine will die to secure the Cedarfall name, and save the realms."

"That's just it, Eroan." I stared into his eyes, piercing him entirely with my gaze. "It isn't just one life. Seraphine has a family. A husband, and a child she has taken as her own. I can't believe she would do this, I won't believe it!"

"I didn't know." I could see the regret deepen within him, threatening to consume him. It took him a moment to gather himself, and when he blinked away the horror of my truth, he looked at me, brows rising in sudden realisation. "An Asp has no family but the serpents they nest with, everyone knows that."

I swallowed all my sadness and panic. "I have often said that Seraphine is, and will always be, an Asp. But it would seem that she shed her skin long ago and found something new beneath. I've underestimated her, but I also *need* her to survive this."

Eroan's eyes widened, as if remembering something. He reached into his pocket, rummaging around for something. I saw the moment he found what he was searching for as he released a soft 'ah', then withdrew a small wooden box. "Seraphine gave me this to pass on to you when you arrived. She said that when you came here, I was to make sure this reached you."

I took it, fingers shaking, unable to ignore that Seraphine had truly planned for this all along. Duncan must've known, because he was the one to give her the command to leave with Gyah.

So many threads where unravelling quicker than I could hold them together.

The box was no bigger than the palm of my hand. The rough edges had been hand-carved, a symbol of a snake etched into its face. Lifting the lid, I peered inside to find a single glass vial.

"What is it?" I asked.

"Seraphine didn't say." Eroan visibly shook. "But she made it clear that you would need it."

My heart lodged in my throat as I recognised the frayed yellow parchment that Seraphine had carried in her breast pocket. Unravelling it I knew what I'd find, but seeing it still took my breath away.

It was the sketch of her family, her found family.

My eyes caught on something the parchment had been hiding. Beneath it was a single vial, so small that I held it pinched between my forefinger and thumb. Inside, sloshing with my movement, was a liquid of pure gold.

Poison. The same she'd used on the ship to Irobel. My ears echoed with the sound of crunched glass, from when I stood over the broken vial.

Seraphine had said she only one of these left, and she'd given it to *me*.

I dropped it back in the box, disgusted and confused, then closed it. I held my breath until it was pocketed in my jacket, the weight of the poison and the picture of her family too heavy to bear. There was only one reason she gave me this vial of poison.

Because she knew a time would come when I'd need to use it. The question was, when?

"I didn't know about her family," Eroan said. "If I did, I would've refused her request. I believed Seraphine was the only one with nothing to lose, but I was wrong and I will regret that for the rest of my days."

"Seraphine is a woman of action, rather than her word," I said. "She would've done this, no matter what you said. She is, if anything, determined. I believe wholeheartedly that this outcome would've always been the same."

"What are you going to do, Robin?" Eroan asked, fear creasing his brow, and narrowing his eyes.

The answer was simple. "I'm going to continue playing this game of chase with her. Just as she wants. What she has left for me, she will want returned. That sketch is as important to her as the people made from the strokes of her pen."

Eroan swallowed a sob. I could see his desire to tell me not to go, but he knew that it would be wasted. "If that is what must be done, then so be it. But you must promise me *you* will be safe, Robin. It is important you come back. Icethorn needs you, and I need you. These days believing you died in the crossfire with the Nephilim have been some of the darkest. Your return has sparked a light in me, and I don't wish to see it extinguished."

I laid a hand on his shoulder and squeezed. "Kindle that light, Eroan for it is hope. Not of my return, but the reminder we have a chance to fix this. You're the best advisor in all the realms, remember that."

He scoffed, recognising the goodbye in my tone. Tears filled his eyes. "As if you've ever let me advise you, Robin. Like mother like son. She would've been so proud of you."

"I don't think so," I said, fighting the tears, understanding the possibility that this could be the last time I saw Eroan.

"Believe me, she would. And I am proud of you too."

"I haven't done anything yet."

Eroan refused to look away from me, his gaze fixing me to the spot. "You will. I know you will."

I almost turned to go when someone flooded my mind. "Jesibel, would you please see that she is safe. No matter what happens, I leave her for you to care for just as you have with me."

A single tear rolled down Eroan's cheek. "I will take that on board, even though you will be coming back, and you will see her yourself. Anyway…" he drew his loose sleeve across his face, drying his cheeks. "Jesi has something to show you upon her return. If that is enough to bring you back, then hold onto that."

I nodded, unable to say another word because of the lump of emotion clogging my throat.

It was difficult to leave Eroan. But as I turned, my limbs heavy as stone, I almost longed for him to call after me. But he didn't. Eroan didn't chase after me as I left the tent. My focus was strong – the need to find Erix the only thing that mattered. He had left a handful of gryvern behind to monitor my movements, which came in handy in a moment like now.

"I need to be taken to Erix, *immediately*." I made sure to remember my manners, even if my entire body was seconds from combusting. "Please."

The gryvern encased me in seconds, and I was airborne. I looked back in time to find Eroan – standing just beyond the tent, looking skywards, waving – who faded into the distance.

Erix took his time to dress me. I bit down on my tongue, choosing not to tell him about the vial of poison concealed within the wrappings of Seraphine's sketch. If he knew about it, there was a chance he'd try and stop me from going after Seraphine. Especially because I'd petitioned against that.

I hoped the gryvern would reach them first, and the poison and the sketch would be passed back into Seraphine's ownership. I couldn't risk this being the catalyst of a war.

I locked eyes with Erix in the reflection of the mirror. It had been propped up against the tent's main pole, large enough that I could see my entire body and Erix's every movement.

"You are going to be needing this," Erix said, brushing the hairs away from my forehead, flattening the strands of obsidian down. "Cassial will see you wearing your crown as a means to taunt him. Remind him who stands against him, not just the fey, but their protectors."

"I'll wear it with pride," I replied, cringing as the cool metal fell upon my brow. "Especially if it makes him sour at the sight of me."

A shiver passed over me, lingering across my skin which was currently hidden beneath layers of leather and armour. In the minimal light of late afternoon, it caught across the hard edges of armour, giving me the impression that I glowed. Every second that passed without news of Gyah and Seraphine's return was killing me from the inside.

"I understand why Seraphine would do this," I whispered, turning my back on the reflection and facing Erix. He'd been dressed in armour too, making his already broad shoulders seem as wide as mountains. His wings had been tipped with metal clasps, shaved to sharp points, turning his entire body into a weapon. "But that doesn't mean I can accept it."

"Little bird, we are all willing to do anything to save these realms. Seraphine is no different to you, or to Duncan. Even to me. We have a part to play, and she believes she has found hers."

He was right, but that still didn't make it easier to swallow. "I just hope we aren't too late."

Something in me told me we were, and what we would find when we arrived at Cassial's war camp was going to be the ruin of me.

"Should you not wear a crown?" I asked, looking up at Erix through my lashes. "King Oakstorm. If we are going to hope to get a rise out of Cassial, then he must see both Altar-chosen bloodlines rise against him."

He shook his head, silver eyes falling to our joined hands. "As much as you see that future for me, I think it is best to let the Oakstorm name die with Elinor. She was the best of them. I can play pretend until this is over, but I have no desire to be a king. I would not be a good one anyway. I am my father's son after all."

"You'd be better than good, Erix," I replied, running my hands down the smooth edges of his gauntlets. "If you gave yourself the chance. You have always told me about duty, and this is your greatest duty yet. Do not turn your back to it before you understand the potential for good you can offer Oakstorm."

"We shall see," Erix said, lifting fingers and using them to tuck a loose strand of dark hair behind my ear. "But, for now, let us focus on the issue at hand. Hopefully word has reached Duncan, and he has already been successful removing Althea from Cassial, before Seraphine needs to trade places. We have changed plans so many times, in such a short period of time, there is no doubt a lot of room for error. But we all have our focus, we all know what must be done."

I had hoped the same, but Duncan didn't know of these plans of Seraphine and Gyah. And I hardly believed our message containing the recent changes had reached him. If anything, his plans to save Althea only left a void in her place, perfect for Seraphine to slip in. I couldn't help but think that that was exactly what she hoped for.

Seraphine was always one step ahead.

"We focus and save as many innocent people as we can," I said, refusing to break Erix's line of sight. "Shifting the perspective of the humans, making them believe that Cassial is not the saviour he has sold himself as, that is our goal. We rip the roots of this fucking weed out with it. Cassial *will* perish, I believe that. But we must still fix the poison and scars he has left in his wake. That will be a battle unto itself."

Erix dropped my hands and turned me back to face the mirror. "It will work, little bird. Because it *has* to."

"I hope you are right." I sighed, the anxiety heavy in my spirit.

If my reaction didn't reveal just how I lacked the confidence in our plans, nothing else would.

"Are you ready?" Erix asked.

I held my chin high, rolling my shoulders back. Perhaps if I faked confidence, I could trick myself into believing in it. "I have no other choice *but* to be ready. Are you?"

"I am," Erix said with an air of truth. "Because this time, we fight beside each other."

"No fight, just saving humans," I reminded him.

"Well, hopefully a little fight after that."

"For our tomorrow," I said.

Erix squeezed my arms, soft lips tugging up at the corners. "For our tomorrow, little bird. And the tomorrow for everyone else. Human, fey, assassin, monster or angel. We will be given the chance of a new world, because we deserve it, and we will fight for it – together."

"Together," I said, blinking as the word settled over me.

I longed for Duncan to be here with us, sharing in his moment. But if anything, it made me ready to leave, to be reunited with him again. So the three of us could be whole once more.

Erix moved himself to stand before me, blocking out my reflection. I was forced to lock eyes with him, not that I cared to look anywhere else. He placed his hands on either side of my face, sharing the warmth of his gentle caress.

I closed my eyes and waited for his lips to touch mine. As they did, my body erupted in pleasure, my knees buckling – not from weakness, but the physical knowledge that I could rely on Erix to always prop me up. I hoped he felt the same, and I hoped that the poison in my pocket would never need to be touched by my hand until I was throwing it into the Sleeping Depths after Cassial's body.

Erix drew away, not completely, but enough that when he spoke his lips tickled a hair's breadth away from mine. "I love you, Robin Icethorn."

"Oh, we are using full names, are we?" My reply came out of me with ease and no hesitation. "If that is the case, I love you too, Erix Oakstorm."

"Ready to save the realm, once and for all?" he asked.

This time, when I straightened, my confidence was not forced or faked. I felt it in every fibre of my being, as if I was fuelled by the need to see this through. I would do anything to end this – *anything*.

I just hoped it didn't need to come to that.

I took Erix's hand in mine, overtly aware of how small he made me feel. "I'm ready to secure our future."

"That's the answer I was hoping–"

A horn blared out across the world, making the tent walls flutter against the sound. Our heads whipped around, ears ringing long after the horn silenced.

For a second, the aftermath of the sound was almost still. Quiet. As silent as death. I supposed it was an omen, because what followed was exactly that.

Death. But not ours. Not yet.

Shouts soon began to fill the silence. I felt my chest crack in two, my heart splintering as words trickled inside our tent.

A part of me died as they finally reached my ears.

"Queen Althea Cedarfall is dead," A keening cry split the camp, working its way deep into my bones. "Cedarfall has fallen!"

CHAPTER 32

I threw myself over the side of the armoured stag. My knees cracked against frozen earth, hands barely reaching in time to steady the fall. Then I vomited in my mouth. The wave of sickness caught in my cheeks, before erupting out of me. Pain ruptured across my chest, so viciously, I pinched my eyes closed and still I could see the image of Althea Cedarfall's head, pierced on the end of a pike.

We were too late. We failed Althea. Our hesitation, our wasted moments, all led to this. Her death.

Erix was behind me, encasing me in his arms, telling me that it was going to be okay, over and over. And yet, when I was brave enough to look back up, the pike was still there, the amber eyes of my friend staring down at me.

It had been a fey scout who had seen the Nephilim fly into the dead zone between the armies. They'd been alone, sent by Cassial as a harbinger of death. The scout – alongside countless of our soldiers, watched as the Nephilim planted the pike in dewy-wet ground. They'd withdrawn the severed head from a gore-soaked bag and sunk it on its tip.

I could hear the Nephilim's screams from here, as the fey tore into him. Maybe I should've stopped them, perhaps I should've turned my back on the severed head and called an end to the advancements.

But it was too late.

The damage was done. Cassial's message received loud and

clear. And, at my back, the shadow of the fey army proceeded forwards, their footsteps thundering across the ground.

"Stop looking at her, Robin," Erix said, voice breaking from strain. He then turned around and shouted at the top of his lungs. "Someone take her down. Now! Show the queen some fucking respect and take her head off that fucking spike!"

He couldn't be the one to touch Althea's head, nor could I. But I couldn't look away either. For hope that any moment this illusion would break, and it would be someone else's head on the pike, I kept looking. But it never changed, the vision never wavered.

I searched the details, locating proof of who the head actually belonged to. Was it the real Althea or Seraphine under her glamour? Either option was no better than the other. Both had the ability to ruin me entirely.

Althea's head looked down with endless eyes of amber-gold surrounded by the most beautiful freckles. Poppy-red curls hung limp and heavy from sodden blood. Her skin had turned a strange grey hue, the flayed torn bits of skin around her neck flapping against the subtle breeze.

"Cassial was never going to use her," I stammered as tears fell down my cheeks. "I was wrong."

I'd believed Cassial kept Althea alive to transfer Duwar into her, but that was never true. My hunch was what sent Seraphine on her own mission. And now I didn't know if she still lived, or if this was her glamoured face I looked at.

Althea was always going to be used as a catalyst for war... unless Cassial found out she was not the only living monarch of the fey realm...

Pain cramped in my stomach. If I had anything left inside of me, more vomit would've followed the feeling. Instead, I was empty. Completely, inconsolably void. Even my sadness didn't reveal itself in sobs, only silent tears that I had no control over.

"This is *not* your fault," Erix said, reading between the lines of what I said. "Do you hear me, Robin? Put aside your self-blame, it will not bring her back. Nothing will..."

Erix cried then, chest-cleaving sobs that broke his demeanor like the fragile shell of an egg, spilling out all the contents of his raw soul. Althea meant the world to us both, and Erix had known her far longer.

I clutched the sides of Erix's face, cold hands pushed on either side of his cheeks, keeping him facing me. "We will avenge her. Her death will *not* be meaningless."

Seeing Erix so broken was the reminder I needed to focus – to carry on and control the situation. I had to for him... and for Althea's memory.

"Another life lost," he spluttered.

"All because *I* didn't have it in me to destroy Duwar when I had the chance."

Erix shook his head, refusing to look away from me. "I refuse that statement. You have only ever done what you felt was right."

"Exactly," I spat, body aching, heart entirely shattered. "I was selfish then, and I am selfish now. But this needs to end."

"Stop it," Erix glowered. "Immediately. We have to trust that Duncan is acting according to our plans. You are not alone in solving these problems."

Duncan. I hadn't even thought about him since I was brought to see Althea's head. What had happened? What had he seen in the time we'd been apart?

"But Cassial needed Althea, he needs a fey royal to harbour Duwar successfully – so her death proves that he knows about me." Out the corner of my eye I caught sight of the fey soldiers removing the head from the pike, covering it in a red silken sheet before carrying Althea's remains away.

"If he knows that you still live," Erix said, voice trembling with unspent rage, "he is trying to bait you."

I knew, deep down, that Erix was right. "I know. And it will work."

"Now is not the time to react," Erix said, grappling a hold of me, fingers like iron against my skin. "Cassial is not going to get the chance to use you, I will not allow it."

As I stared into his silver eyes, drinking in the horror harboured within them, I realised something. "No, Erix. I'm not the only one at risk. He can also use you if he finds out."

Erix recoiled. I watched as the words sank in and realisation crept over his handsome face. It twisted into a mask of horror.

"Cassial couldn't know," Erix said, clasping a hand to his chest. "Before the wedding – Elinor promised me that no one else would know until my decision was made. Unless someone… Ailon Oakstorm added the information into his communications with Cassial."

"I don't believe your uncle would have done that," I said, mind whirling. "It would have weakened his claim. Ailon wanted Duwar for himself."

My throat ached with the fresh bite of bile.

"I'm at a loss for what to do," Erix admitted, standing tall as he looked at the advancing line of warriors. "I was never his second option for a host for Duwar. I think that the reason he has killed Althea, it means he has his hands on another option already…"

There was something in what Erix had just said that clicked in my mind. In a single moment my thoughts became frantic, but in the panic, I was piecing together the puzzle at efficient speed. "Who does he have?" Speaking it aloud tore apart the frail seams holding me together. "If he has used her death to spark the war, it is only because he is still a step ahead. I fear you are right, and he has another option already."

"The Elmdew baby," I gasped. "A host he can control."

His eyes locked with mine. Urgency overwhelmed any other emotion he felt.

"Regardless, he has made his move. Cassial has shown the world Althea is dead, it is to spark the war he has been desperately waiting for," Erix spoke aloud my very thoughts.

If that was the glamoured head of Seraphine on a spike, it would mean Althea was still alive.

Erix acted on instinct and called out to the soldiers taking Althea's head away. "See that the head is taken directly to Eroan. Make sure that he checks over it for any potential glamours or illusions." There was a hesitation from the solemn fey who looked as grief stricken as we felt. "Do it now, with haste!"

With my command, he rushed off, leaving us to wallow in the dark truth.

"Cassial must be desperate," Erix said finally. "That is what this move is. Using Seraphine to make us think Althea is dead."

That was if the head belonged to Seraphine, otherwise she was still out there, and her plans to sacrifice herself would be for nothing.

The box in my pocket grew heavy, reminding me it was one detail I'd not shared with Erix yet. And for good reason. Because Seraphine knew the risks when she infiltrated Cassial's camp, and she also knew I would follow.

"I *must* go to Cassial," I said, almost preparing for an argument or refusal. But Erix locked eyes with me, his lip curling over the slight point of his canines. And, as always with Erix, he was willingly to stand beside me, and never before me.

"It is not safe to make such decisions," Erix began.

I silenced him with a single look. "Our army is advancing. War is upon us. We can petition for them to stop if we can prove that it is not Althea's head that was just taken off that spike. But if they believe it was, they will move. If this is a ploy for Cassial to provoke us, it has worked. If not..." Then my closest friend was dead. "There is no other choice if we hope to save the slaughter of all those innocent humans he's using as a shield. But if I go, you can stop them. Put a halt to the army for as long as you can."

"Before you say it." I took his hands in mine. "*Please*, don't refuse me."

"You know I can't do that." Erix traced fingers down the side of my face, eyes brimming with tears. "And I will not, only if you tell me your plan and every step it entails. I can't let you go alone knowing there is nothing I can do."

"And I will. If we are wrong about the Elmdew child, then I am safe in Cassial's hands. He needs me, and he will not risk harming me if Althea is dead, or no longer in his possession. If I continue to hesitate, more people will die."

Erix swallowed hard, the muscles in his jaw feathering. "Then tell me what you need of me, and I will do it. Together, remember."

I looked up at him, recognising the slight hesitancy in Erix's lack of movement. His worry was written in every crease and line across his face. I wished I could tell him that this would all be okay in the end, but the severed head at my back was proof it wouldn't. Someone had died – I couldn't focus on who it really had been, for fear it would ruin me.

But I took it, harboured it in a chasm of vengeance in my chest, and knew it would be waiting and ready for me in time.

"Together," I repeated. "Whoever is left in this fight must all work as one, not separated. Not anymore."

Surprise broke over his face, lasting only a moment. "It would seem Robin Icethorn has learned the importance of trust."

"I just took a little while to recognise it," I admitted.

Too late to recognise, my inner thoughts added.

All my life, I had done things alone. No matter how people had offered their support, told me they'd work beside me. I'd always chosen the solitary path, hoping it would be the one with less pain and loss as I navigated it. But that wasn't true. I knew that now.

Regardless of the poison in my pocket, if Cassial became a threat, I knew what to do to use it against him. There were risks, but it would be worth it for the realms.

"Have your gryvern stall our army as long as they can," I said, aware how close they were to us now. It would take hours for them to reach Cassial, but he would be waiting. He'd be ready to show the humans that the fey are monsters.

So, we'd have to show them otherwise.

Cassial expected us to respond with a war, but that wasn't what he'd get.

At least, not yet.

"If I create a blockade between the fey, it *will* cause further tension between the courts," Erix reminded me. "So you must be sure this is what you want from me?"

"I am. Conflict in Wychwood will not matter if by dusk the courts have been completely eradicated from the map. Please, this is the only way. Block the army; you are king now, it is in your power to command as much. Whether you wear a crown or not, you must use the voice that Altar has blessed you with."

Erix closed his eyes for a moment, creases of concentration lining his brow. Then I heard them, the screeches and screams of gryvern. The sky broke with the noise, as bodies of grey flesh and leather wing cut out of dense clouds, spearing down toward the earth. Hundreds of them.

Monsters flocking to their master's call.

I watched in awe as their bodies thumped against the ground, one by one, forming a line of talon and claw between us and the advancing army.

I leaned into Erix, glad for his support, whilst hating that I would need to lie. I hoped for what was a final time. "There is one more thing I need to ask of you, Erix."

"Anything, little bird."

Magic unspooled beneath my hands like curling mists of winter's first frost. "Find Duncan when you can. And when you do, look out for my signal. You won't miss it. Only when my signal has been given do I permit you to lead a full assault on Cassial's camp, sparing as many as you can. I need death to be minimal. Any fey who harms someone without a weapon will be charged with crimes of war. Our focus is on the Fallen. Am I clear?"

"Crystal."

"Good." My blood thrummed through my veins, my muscles itching for action. "Then this is it. I need time to get ahead and reach Cassial. Ensure no one follows me. You must find Rafaela and Duncan; you must prepare them to act when the time is right."

Erix reached up, took my face in his hands and planted a kiss on my mouth. Although no more words were shared, the connection of our mouths told a thousand unspoken promises. When he pulled back, he fixed his gaze on mine, his expression set into a firm line.

"If Eroan can prove that it was Seraphine's head on that spike, it will hold off our armies."

I hated what I was about to say, hated that I even contemplated who I would've preferred to have died in that moment. Althea or Seraphine, they both deserved life and yet the truth was that one of them would never get to experience it again. Either option was terrible. "Then if it is Althea who is dead... you tell Eroan to lie. You make sure everyone knows the sacrifice of Seraphine, the Asp. Her story must mean something, and if she has died by his hand, the only way I can ensure that is by finishing the task. Tell Eroan that is a command from his king. Anything to hold back our army, Erix. *Anything*."

He winced, sharing my discomfort in discovering who Cassial had killed. "I will do it, for you, for the realms and for *tomorrow*."

"Thank you," I said, running my hand down his cheek.

"I love you." Erix said, sharp and sudden. "Go, before I see sense and change my mind."

I reached for the reins of the mount we'd ridden to get here, then Erix helped me into the saddle. There was so much I wanted to say, so much I wanted to do. But all I did was lay my hand on the vial in my pocket and look to the stretch of barren lands ahead of me. Erix patted his palm on the mount's behind, urging it forwards. And as it took me away, I didn't look back. Only forwards, focus ironclad, and will just as indestructible.

CHAPTER 33

A few miles outside the border of Wychwood, far from the shadows of the entangled forest, a sea of flesh and mortality stood waiting. Just as I had expected. Grand black tents took up old farmlands, stretching for as far as I could see. It encroached on fey lands, like spilled ink slowly spreading closer and closer. And yet there were no Nephilim amongst the camp, only unsuspecting humans.

A small part of me had hoped that we were wrong about Cassial's use of humans, but seeing them here, like this, only reinforced my conviction that we could *not* go to war. Enough innocence had been taken from the realms, I refused to allow another to be taken.

My mount cantered toward them, stopping when a Nephilim finally revealed themselves. Without warning, they dove down from the skies, tearing me out of the saddle. The ground fell away from me, as did my crown, which was knocked from my head. I watched it, as we flew higher, tumble to the sodden earth, landing in boot-trodden mud.

Humans raced for it like rats to food, clambering over my crown until I could no longer see it.

As my captor's shadow lingered across the patchwork of tents, humans looked up, pointing and shouting. They cheered for the Nephilim who held me – not knowing that the very being who held me was the monster – not the fey they held in their grasp.

Right in the heart of the encampment was a handful of larger tents. The material was a bright cream with gold stitching, standing out against the darker material on the outskirts of the camp.

Banners fluttered in a light breeze, the symbol of the Creator taunting me everywhere I looked.

And I had no doubt in my heart that the Nephilim was taking me directly to the man I needed to see.

Cassial.

Around me, a flock of Nephilim rose into the skies on feathered wings, brandishing weapons of gold. Did they wonder why I had come? Or had they been expecting me. The latter was more likely, considering I hadn't used my power against them yet. It was the flash of daylight, catching across glass, refracting beams of multicoloured light over the vicinity, that proved it.

I'd been so distracted with my welcome that I almost forgot the one important detail of why I'd come. So, I patted my hand over my jacket pocket, feeling for the small glass vial.

Seraphine felt as though the poison was important enough to leave with Eroan. She never acted without reason.

Never.

Had she known this would happen, that I would be forced to enter the heart of our enemy? Unless Althea was dead, and Seraphine was alive still, I would never get that answer.

My Nephilim captor nosedived to the ground so suddenly a scream tore out of my throat. The earth raced up toward me. I pinched my eyes closed, ready to meet my end, until everything settled.

I wasn't dead… yet.

We landed in the middle of a circle of armed Nephilim. The one holding me forced me out of his hands, pushing me to the ground. I stumbled over awkward feet, only for another Nephilim to push against me, knocking me backwards.

I hit the ground, to the amusement of those watching. Laughter erupted from every direction, as Nephilim delighted in watching a fey king squander in mud like a headless fowl.

They could not see me as a threat, so I made sure to stay on the ground.

"I come in peace," I said, sure I had read that exact saying in a fiction book I once read. To emphasise, I lifted my hands up in surrender, and offered the sweetest of smiles. Deep down, I wanted nothing more than to destroy each and every one of them. Slowly, I searched around the faces of the Nephilim for someone I'd recognise. Maybe Duncan, but that was only a hope.

"Look at the fey king on the ground!" A Nephilim shouted, brandishing a sword in my direction. "Where *it* belongs, fey scum."

"Incredibly original," I spluttered, dusting the grime from my trousers as if that mattered. "It's been a long time since I heard that one."

They sneered at me, teeth bared like rabid dogs.

"As much as I would enjoy hearing all the creative insults you've no doubt practiced six inches from a mirror, will one of you gracious angels do me the favour of taking me to your *Saviour*. I'd like to have a little chat with him, as you can imagine."

The title soured in my mouth, because I knew it belonged to another.

The Nephilim each looked at me as if I was mad. Crazed. Maybe I was. After all, I had come here alone. But for now, those feral desires had to be kept under control.

"*I knew you would come,*" came a voice belonging to the very prick I wanted to see. Except he wasn't here. Not physically. Cassial's voice came from within my head, piercing the veil of my mind. The pain that followed was so great, it brought me to my knees, hands smacking on either side of my head as if I could gouge him out with nails.

In seconds, rough hands were upon me. The cold kiss of iron encased my neck, clipping locked. The very same cuff that had been put on me when I was taken by Hunters months ago.

I'd expected a welcome like this. Mentally, I'd prepared for it. But still, as my power slipped away, falling through my grasp like sand through parted fingers, I felt a semblance of vulnerability rear its ugly head.

I looked up, not bothering to resist as the Nephilim reached for every concealed weapon they could find. But it didn't stop there. One by one, the plates of armour were removed, stripped off by careless hands, until the brush of cool air rippled over my bare skin. Even Seraphine's box was taken out of my pocket. My heart stopped as they opened it, tipped out Seraphine's sketch and discarded it on the floor. Out the corner of my eye I saw the slip of parchment flutter in the winds before landing in mud and being trodden by careless boots. The vial thudded into the mud, but before it was noticed I slipped a hand over it, fingers digging in the dirt for purchase, and picked it up.

With no time to clean it, I mocked a cough and slipped the vial into my mouth. I couldn't think about precautions as the glass tinkered against my molars, the vile taste of grit lathering my tongue and cheeks.

If they pried my lips open, they would find what had been missing from the box. Turned out, I was lucky they left my undershorts on, as a crowd of humans began to gather and watch. The hate in their watching stares was palpable. So strong it kept me to my knees, even if the Nephilim released me.

"*Do not fear, my dearest humans,*" Cassial's voice came again.

I continued to search for him, only to discover where it was coming from. Mirrors – the same I saw in hands during the procession to Althea and Gyah's wedding. They were propped up almost everywhere I could see: from grand, gilded designs to mundane mirrors in bland wooden frames. "*I will not allow such monsters to harm you. All is well, you are safe as long as you stay with me.*"

I strained against the harsh grasp of many arms, hoping that if Cassial was using this moment to converse with humans, showing them what was happening through Duwar's power, then I had to take my chance to ruin the picture he painted of the fey.

"Is that the excuse you used," I called out, a prominent lisp thanks to the small glass vial at the back of my teeth, "when you beheaded Queen Althea Cedarfall?"

Shock broke out around me, like the rush of a wave against the shore.

"*Lies*," Cassial's voice spat, hissing like water against hot coals. "*Never trust the tongue of a serpent who wishes to suffocate you with its coil.*"

"You *killed* her," I spat, sweeping my gaze around as much as I was allowed, trying to locate where Cassial was hiding. "You severed her head and planted it on a spike to taunt us—"

All around me, the disgruntled responses of humans began. It was clear they didn't believe me. Were they so blinded by Cassial's promises that they no longer could understand a truth from a lie?

Did they even expect the army that had been coming for them? I only hoped Erix's gryvern continued to hold them back.

Erix. I couldn't think about our last moments together. His touch, the brush of his caring gaze. Instead of faltering in my need of him, I placed all my hope that Erix would listen to my command and wouldn't come chasing after me until my signal was received.

"*Althea Cedarfall is not dead.*"

Fury ruptured through me at his bare-faced lie.

I was hoisted from the floor before the words could settle over me. "I saw her head. You can lie to those around you, but you can't lie to the ocean of fey who seek vengeance for her murder. I have seen the humans you store before you like shields, do you not care for their safety, or do you need them in their places to take the full brunt of the crossfire you so desire—"

"Enough of your deceptions, Robin Icethorn." Cassial's voice boomed over me, heavy with unseen power. I wondered the toll using Duwar's power had on him. *"You can perpetuate your mistruths about Althea Cedarfall. But every soul here watched as she was abducted from our care by that Eldrae woman. We have all bared witness as the Eldrae tore into the Creator's greatest warriors. You can spin your web to entrap us, but it is made from frayed thread."*

My reply failed me, words dying on my tongue. All I could think about was that Gyah had been here. If I was to believe Cassial, that meant Gyah *had* successfully saved Althea. But the relief of that revelation lasted but a second. Because it confirmed the one thing I had tried not to believe.

If that was not Althea's head on the spike, it meant that it belonged to Seraphine. Relief and grief melted through my mind.

When Eroan was successful at peeling back Seraphine's glamour, proving that it wasn't Althea's head presented on the spike, it would prevent the war that Cassial had hoped to spark.

"My Nephilim, see that Robin Icethorn is taken to my lodgings," Cassial's command rippled over the crowd. *"I wish to speak with him. It would seem that Robin here requires a reminder as to the peace accords he has signed."*

The circle of Nephilim parted enough to allow another figure to step through. I blinked against the glare of harsh light, lifting a muddied hand to my brow to get a better look.

My breath caught in my throat. From the top of my skull, down to my toes, a violent chill sliced down my spine, threatening to flay me open and reveal all my secrets.

"Up, fey scum," Duncan Rackley said as the chain at the end of my collar was handed to him.

I settled my disbelieving eyes on him – full snow-white wings, eyes as green as a forest in summer and a scowl I'd seen once before, when I was first captured by him.

Duncan. He was here. I barely had time to react as he pulled at the chain again, making me stumble to the ground. The skin around my neck ached as the cuff pulled. I felt a trickle of wet as fresh blood inched down my naked chest.

He had hurt me.

I locked eyes with Duncan, who'd not looked away from me all this time. "I said, get – *up*."

I did as he asked, unable to speak even if I wanted to. No one else seemed to notice that he didn't belong here. His act was so powerful, I too almost believed it.

Duncan's presence was yet more proof that Gyah had been successful. I had to believe it.

And I was safe with him, no matter the part he was playing.

I scrambled up before he tugged on my leash again, uncaring for the further discomfort he caused me.

Duncan led me through the gathered crowd, directly toward the structure of monstrous tents. As soon as we were out of ear shot, I readied myself to say something. But as the first word left my mouth, Duncan pulled hard on the leash, making me choke on the words.

"Not here," he hissed, turning casually around. I took it as a signal, following his gaze to the mirrors stationed all around the camp. Cassial was watching, no doubt. Duncan understood that. He had a part to play, as did I.

"Where's your Saviour?" I shouted, feigning panic and hate for the Nephilim before me, when the truth couldn't be more opposite.

"*Occupied*," Duncan replied, choosing his words carefully. "You will be *graced* with his presence soon. Once I ensure you do not pose a threat to him, that is."

Occupied. It could mean a few things, but the way Duncan said it, the tone he used, told me that there was only one fact behind his answer.

Cassial wasn't here.

A GAME OF MONSTERS

If not, then where was he? Had he already gone for Jordin Elmdew, ready to implant Duwar into the vessel of a child?

Duncan guided me into the shadowed archway of a tent. As I entered, the smell of blood slammed into me. It clogged in my throat, souring my tongue and making me gag. Duncan relaxed his pull on me as he rounded up to the back of another person.

A woman stood facing something on a table before her. Her form was hulking, with shoulders as broad as mountains and a stature tall and imposing. She wasn't a Nephilim – evident from the lack of wings – but that didn't take away from the aura of strength she emitted.

As she turned around, I caught a glimpse of another person, laid out across the metal table. She blocked their face from view, standing in front of me with hands clasped to a large, serrated knife, equally as bloodied as the black apron tied around her waist.

"Ah, so the famed Icethorn king has finally arrived, just as the Saviour knew he would." Her gravelly voice itched across my bare skin.

"Is this the welcome party?" I asked, hissing as Duncan tugged once again on my lead.

The woman ignored me as she lifted the bloodied knife and pointed in my direction. Down the jagged edges of the blade, she studied me with narrowed, hateful eyes.

"I knew that one day I'd get the chance to meet the boy who killed my brother. It's my honour to finally have you in my presence." She looked back to Duncan, excitement and pride swelling over her rosy-cheeked face. "Well done, initiate. You have proved yourself useful."

"This success has little to do with me," Duncan replied, fingers digging into my shoulder, anchoring me in place before the woman could snatch me away. "Robin Icethorn decided himself to come and pay us a visit."

"I came because you placed Althea's head on a spike and

lured me here," I snapped, wondering what game Duncan was playing, and how I could further it.

"Then it is fate that I get this meeting, oh how I have craved it for a long time." She refused to look anywhere but at me, and I saw the feral hunger for blood in her gaze, as potent as if she'd just used her words to tell me exactly what she wanted to do with me.

I chose not to hold her stare, instead searching for clues as to who she was. Apparently, I'd killed her brother, but that was like searching for a needle in a haystack these days.

"I was unconvinced your idea would work but using your *mistake* and turning the outcome to something positive will benefit you in the Saviour's grace," she said, voice rough from years of the pipe no doubt.

"I live to please." Duncan bowed. "Thank you for your praise."

She dismissed his bow with a wave of her blood-caked hand. "Now," she said, settling bulbous dark eyes on me once again. There were smudges across her skin, dark brown stains that could've been shit, if I didn't know better. It was blood, she was covered in it. "Hand him over. I will deal with the rest from here."

"Cassial has requested that the Icethorn is kept alive."

"I know that," the woman spat, rubbing the knife down her apron. It was then I noticed the faint outline of a symbol. A once-white imprint of a hand, now covered in blood and grime.

She was a Hunter. But I couldn't work out who her brother was, the one she'd referred to. The one whom I'd allegedly killed.

"Then there is no need for that knife," Duncan said, gesturing to the blade she waved around. "Robin is not to be killed, Cassial has use for him."

"Your Saviour also promised me I can have some *fun*," the Hunter said. "Who said anything about killing him? No, no. I will keep the Icethorn fey alive, but I cannot promise how many pieces he will be returned to you in. Hand him over. I've waited long enough for this day. I will not postpone it for another moment."

Duncan didn't move. Not even as the woman extended her hand, waggling fingers impatiently. I looked down his strained arm, to knuckles which had paled as he gripped the end of my leash.

His hesitation was seconds from giving him away. I had to do something. Already, I recognised the change in emotion on the woman's face as she watched Duncan lose himself to his inner thoughts.

She stepped forwards, head tilted. "What are you waiting for?"

It was then that I saw the root of Duncan's hesitance. As the woman stepped forwards, she gave me my first glance at the body on the table behind her.

Laying upon a metal slab was the *rest* of Seraphine's body. All that was missing was her beautiful face on her head, in its place was nothing but a pool of blackened blood and the jagged edges of a frayed neck.

"Seraphine." The name broke out of me. I sagged forwards, knees giving way.

What followed was a rush of agony that manifested in the desire to cause pain.

I knew she had died, but some part of me had refused to believe it. But seeing her corpse, headless and dull of colour, caused a dangerous venom to flood up from the deepest pit of my soul and spread. The pressure was so forceful that if I didn't act to expel it, I would combust.

As I stepped forwards on instinct, I felt the lack of hold. Duncan had dropped the leash, allowing me to act. So, I did. I snatched the chain before he could grapple for it again. He jolted sideways, shocked out of his stupor from my shout.

The Hunter, likely noticing her impending fate, snapped forwards, reaching for me, stumbling over sloppy feet. She was quick, but I was *far* quicker. I whipped the chain around, smashing the end into her face.

The crack was beautiful. Blood burst from the gash, blinding her as it smudged over her eyes.

I knew what I was going to do before I did it.

Without wasting another moment, I took my chance.

I spun around, threading my body behind the Hunter's back. Using the metal table as a prop, I pushed upwards, wrapping the chain around her neck three times. My foot wedged into her back, and I added force against her, whilst pulling the chain back.

"Fuck *you*," I seethed, spitting my hate into her ear. I used all my might, every ounce of power and strength I had left, and didn't release my hold.

"This," I hissed into her ear, "is for Seraphine."

The Hunter's knife had long since clattered to the floor. Now she used her spare hands to fumble with the chains, as if that would help free her. It was useless. Even after her fight died out with the last scraps of air from her lungs, I didn't let go. I couldn't. *Wouldn't.* Because the second I did, I would be free to turn around and face Seraphine, and the gaping hole her lack of life had presented to me.

I thought of Seraphine's husband, my knuckles paling as my grip tightened on the chain. Although I'd not seen the child she took on as her own in the flesh, the sketch of her heart-shaped face filled my mind. They had no idea that Seraphine was dead – that she'd died in a game of monsters that seemed to have no end.

But I would find an end, for them and Seraphine's memory.

My ears rang, my head throbbing from concentration and force. It was Duncan who eased me back to reality.

"Robin," his voice was cold and fearful. "It's done. She's... gone."

I heard Duncan, but that didn't mean I listened. In fact, my grip on the chain tightened until Duncan rested his hands on my arms, brushing a thumb over my skin.

"Let her go," he commanded, yet his voice was no more than a soft whisper. "You must conserve your energy for what else is to come, don't waste it on those who no longer require it."

Breathless, I released hold of my leash, letting the Hunter's body flop to the floor. A sob cracked out of my chest, but I had to hold it firm for fear I'd spit the vial out of my mouth or swallow it – then it wouldn't only be Seraphine's and this Hunter's bodies laid out dead in this tent.

Duncan wasted no time in embracing me, wrapping me in his arms, folding wings around me, so I was forced to not look anywhere but at him.

"They killed Seraphine," I spluttered into his chest. "She came to save the realms and died in the process. Duncan... she – she didn't deserve this end."

I had once thought Seraphine perished when Imeria Castle fell and crushed her nest of Asps. Turned out it was the weight of saving the realms that finally got her.

"Shh. It's going to be okay, Robin. Everything is going to work out just the way it needs to." Duncan brushed his hand down the back of my head, fingers tugging at my hair. "You must focus and calm down. We don't have long, and there is much you need to update me on. Starting with Erix Oakstorm, where is he?"

It was odd to hear Duncan refer to Erix with that last name. There must've been a time before we left Irobel that Duncan found out about Erix's lineage. Perhaps he knew because of his use of Duwar. Either way, it stopped me enough to focus.

I tried to steady my mind, understand what I had just uncovered.

"Robin," Duncan clasped my face in his hands, forcing me to look at him. Urgency widened his eyes, his frantic words proving he was deeply worried. "Tell me, where is Erix?"

I shook my head, wincing against the question. How did I tell Duncan what I'd done to Erix? "He has... he was going to look for you. To tell you I came here to prevent the war. We have managed to put a hold to the fey army, giving me some time to deal with the issue of Cassial. But now you are here, and we can do it together – once I give a signal Erix will come, but only then."

"Okay," Duncan said, nodding. His gaze lost to something pointless as his mind twisted with thoughts. "That's good, Robin. Really good. And what of this signal, can you give it now? It's important Erix comes as soon as possible, I – *we* – need him."

It took me a moment to realise that Duncan was hurting me. Once my emotions calmed enough, I felt the pinch of harsh nails into the skin of my arms. I tried to pull away, but it was no good.

"Where's Rafaela, Duncan?" I asked. "And the rest of the Nephilim? What about Althea and Gyah? Cassial said she was abducted..."

"None of that matters now." Out of all the questions I asked, Duncan refused to answer a single one of them. "What is important is that you listen to me, for we don't have long."

"Long until what?"

Duncan fixed his eyes back on me, and I felt myself buckle from the relief of seeing him. Voices sounded beyond the tent, deep rumbling tones. Duncan released me, looking frantically around. My arms ached from where he held me, so much that it took restraint not to reach up and rub them. He looked to the dead body of the Hunter, and then to me.

"Duncan, answer me." My heart lodged in my throat. "Until *what*?"

"Until Cassial comes for you. Before that I must understand everything that is happening in Wychwood: if you wish to save those innocent lives, we must re-plan our next moves carefully."

"What happened here, Duncan?" If he ignored this question, I would've asked it over and over. "How are you here and everyone else isn't?"

Clearly, he recognised my need for answers, because he gave them to me this time.

"Althea is alive, but she was taken away not long ago. When Gyah infiltrated the camp with the Asp, I was forced to act." Duncan's eyes settled on the decapitated body behind us. I dared not look. Pretending Seraphine wasn't dead was easier than facing the truth. "Gyah got Althea out, but Seraphine swapped places just as Cassial was going to use her to transfer Duwar. I had to–" Duncan paused, his face going pale. Regret lingered in his eyes, heavy as a physical burden.

"Had to what, Duncan?"

He dropped his eyes. "Kill her. It was the only way to stop Duwar looking for the *real* Althea."

"That was what the Hunter meant by you making a mistake," I said, unable to fathom that it was Duncan who took Seraphine's life. But the Hunter also praised Duncan, said he was successful in getting me here.

Dread crept over my skin, chilling me to the bone.

"Cassial is aware that the real Althea escaped, as is every Nephilim and human outside of these tent walls. He made sure everyone was aware, so that when the fey attack under the guise that Althea Cedarfall is dead, he had the motive and means to use Duwar against you, flattening the fey army in a matter of moments."

"He has the Elmdew heir," I said, grappling for his face to calm him, but Duncan pushed my attempt away. "Our focus must be on stopping that."

Duncan released a growl of contention, burying his face in his hands. "The Elmdew heir is the last resort. Cassial may store power inside of the baby, but it will not be used until the child is old enough to control it. It will leave Cassial weak and defenceless… he needs someone else… Erix, you must send him your signal."

Something dreadful clicked together in my mind. Duncan clocked it, finally reaching out for me again, sinking harsh fingers into my soft flesh.

"Why did you kill Seraphine, Duncan?" I asked, trying to step back but being unable to break out of his hold. If anything, his grasp was tighter than before, nails pinching until pain sang up my arms.

"Send the signal, Robin."

The harder I fought against him, the more pain I suffered. "Duncan, stop it. You're hurting me."

It was like he didn't hear me. Or perhaps he chose not to.

"*Good.* I want you to hate me," Duncan replied, as a slow creeping smile broke over his face.

Finally, he let me go. But I had nowhere to run. As I tried to step back, I was forced between Duncan and the table with Seraphine's decapitated body.

He began to laugh. As he did, he lifted a hand in a strange gesture. I refused to blink as I watched his skin melt from his body like smoke caught on a wind. Powerless and frozen in fear, there was nothing I could do but watch as the glamour before me dissipated, revealing the truth of who had been with me this entire time.

A gasp lodged in my throat, my feet stumbling back.

"Hello again, Robin," Cassial said, glowering down as the final dregs of his glamour dissipated. His eyes – so similar to Duncan's – glared at me, drinking me in. Except one was utterly ruined. The right side of his face had been gouged by something great, tearing through muscle, sinew and bone. Where his eye had been was now a gaping hole, dribbling unknown substances.

He truly was a monster. A walking corpse – a ruined body. And he had been masquerading as Duncan since I had arrived.

It was no wonder he hadn't shown his true self, there was no hiding what he had become from his followers.

Poison by the reflection of his own evil intentions.

"Do not be frightened, *little bird*," Cassial taunted. As he spoke, I could see his tongue move like a snake through the gap in his cheek. The wet sound of flesh on flesh, accompanied with the hot stench of rot and infection, made me want to vomit.

"You look like shit," I spat. "Had a hard time recently, have you?"

"Courtesy of your Asp," Cassial said, gesturing to his ruined face.

It was a miracle he was still alive – not a miracle, but the fact his body was a host for chaos itself.

She'd tried to kill him, that much was clear. A spark of joy simmered inside of me, knowing she had left her mark on Cassial.

"Half a job means a little less for me to do," I said. "Come closer and I will put you out of your misery."

"Misery?" Cassial cocked back his head and laughed, the sound grating and vile. I saw the workings of his inner body through the gouge marks, his tongue bulging like a bloated slug, strings of veins and sinew like threads holding his ruined face together. "My life is anything but, especially now you are here."

"You laugh at me, and yet your end is still inevitable." My tongue brushed over the glass vial hidden in the back of my teeth, making sure it was in place.

Cassial finally stopped laughing, and there wasn't a sign of humour on his face by the time he faced me again. "The Asp certainly gave it a good go, bless her. But in the end her luck had run dry. I took her life with a smile on my face, knowing that I may have lost the vessel required to use Duwar, but at least I could use her to *replace* what was taken from me. And look at you, here like a willing little lamb. I had hopes Erix would have followed after you, better to have two options than one. But I suppose now I know what I must do to send out a call for him."

"I never told you what type of signal Erix would expect," I said, holding on to that one hope. "Good luck prying it from me when I'm dead."

Cassial didn't bother to hide his displeasure. "You will not be dying yet, Robin Icethorn. I have a need for you. Starting with Duncan. Amazing, isn't it, this endless well of great power. I knew Duwar would provide me with possibilities beyond my imagination, but never did I think that any one thing can be achieved when using the source of power. Every power that a fey has – telepathy, illusion, glamouring, the conjuring of elements – it is *all* mine. Endless possibilities at my fingertips. It did not even cross my mind, until your little Asp came here and tried to mess with my plans. Imagine my surprise when I found out you all survived the journey to Irobel. Thank the Creator you did, because otherwise I would've been forced to put Duwar inside of that Elmdew babe and wait years until I could use it again. My weakness is my impatience."

Your weakness is your desire for power.

"You're wasting your breath on me, Cassial." My vision was red, my need for pain and fury a siren song too impossible to ignore. "It *is* over."

My eyes flickered down to the butcher's knife. It was only for a split second, but Cassial began tutting. "Now, now. Robin. I would suggest you do not make hasty decisions. The wrong move would not go well for you. So, let us sit, shall we? Talk about how we can help each other stop this war I know you will do anything to prevent. If you do, I have something of great importance I can return to you."

I couldn't get over the fact that Duncan had been standing before me one minute and was gone the next. My lips ached from the kiss he'd given me, the disgusting knowledge that it had never been Duncan.

"Where is *he*?" I seethed, my body trembling against unseen bounds.

"Oh, Duncan?" Cassial said the name as if there was even a possibility I'd spoken of someone else. "Well, he is here, of course. And if you behave, I may just let you see him."

That was how Cassial knew to glamour himself as Duncan, because he had come to Gyah's aid, but never left. That was why Rafaela wasn't here. Somewhere along the way, Duncan had been captured instead.

"If you harm him a single hair on his head–"

Cassial leaned in, his smile widening. It was only when he got closer that I noticed the cracks across his skin. The fissures, like scars in clay, revealed a glowing, fire-like light from beneath. "As long as you do as I ask, then I swear to you, no harm will befall Duncan Rackley. The same goes for Erix. So, shall we sit and discuss what it is I need from you, and then we can come to an agreement that will be mutually beneficial?"

"I have nothing to say to you." I rolled the glass vial of poison between my teeth. I got myself ready, poised to crack it and spit the poison over Cassial. Then this would finally be over. I had no antidote, no way of not meeting the same end as Cassial would.

But it would be worth it. The pain, the death, the suffering... it would mean something if I dragged Cassial to the afterlife with me.

"No, perhaps you do not. But I can tell you that I do not need to know what signal Erix Oakstorm waits to receive from you. To my luck, Erix is already on his way. Word has reached me that he is coming here, with a host of fey warriors at his heel. I think it has something to do with the return of Althea Cedarfall to Wychwood, and her orders to attack. But I would very much like to have this conversation with you first, before I must go and greet him. You never know, maybe we will come up with a way to stop the bloodshed that is... imminent."

I paused, letting the possibility of what he said sink in. "I don't believe you."

"Nor do I care if you do." Cassial tilted his head, like an inquiring mutt. "Time will show you that the war is now upon us. But I know what you desire, Robin. You truly would do anything to save those humans outside, no matter how they hate you, how they wish to see me destroy you. Then there is the matter of Erix. You are worried I may use him as Duwar's vessel if you are no longer an option. And I admit, you would be right to have those concerns. I also admit it would be ideal that he would be my second choice, considering he would willingly give himself up to save you. But you already knew that, which is why you came to me alone."

I could reply, but my silence was as much confirmation. "An educated guess."

"No, that was no guess. It does not take a scholar to see the ties between yourself and Erix Oakstorm. Not to mention how insightful Duncan Rackley has been. It has taken little of Duwar's power to crack into his mind and take out what I have needed–"

I leaned in, the glass vial aching between my teeth. "I will–"

"Listen to me, carefully." Cassial dug his fingers into my jaw, holding me in place. I could barely breathe, let alone move. All I was permitted to do was listen. "After all, that is why you came, because you *knew* I needed you. So, I think you would very much like to hear what I have to say. More importantly, what I have to *offer*. Starting with the fey army following in your wake. The sooner we speak, the quicker you can call an end to the death that awaits those souls outside this tent. Either you listen to me, or more innocent people will perish just like dearest Seraphine. Or, if you are unwilling to cooperate, we can have this conversation after the fey army soak the ground with the humans' blood. What will it be, Robin? Will you sit back and wait for the realms to tear each other apart, or will you do the right thing and see how we can stop it all – together?"

CHAPTER 34

Cassial was right, I had no choice but to comply.

He provided me with options of how this was going to end, each one leading to ruin. But if I didn't do as he asked, the fey army would come and trample the innocent humans within hours. His Fallen wouldn't stop them. We would become the demons he wished us to be.

If I accepted his offer, he'd use me as a puppet to destroy hundreds of lives.

With nothing but the wave of his gnarled fingers, Cassial had strung me up in the tent, arms and legs separated by chains, my back supported by a wooden beam. I fixed my stare on him, drinking in the not-so-subtle changes to his body. It was impossible not to see it now. How Duwar corrupted his body from the inside out, poisoning his already ruined soul.

Twin horns protruded from his skull. Where his skin had cracked in places, as though he was made from clay, he became the same monster I'd seen in Aldrick's mirrors.

It was no wonder Cassial had worn Duncan's skin as a glamour.

Perhaps those visions of Duwar I'd first seen in Aldrick's mirrors had always been prophetic. Duwar was showing the world the possibility of what the power could become, if used again. Cassial, the demon-god. That was who stood before me now.

Perspective, I reminded myself. However, I felt as though the reflections I had seen had always been showing the future... one I could not stop.

Duwar was destroying Cassial's body, as I had known it would. Except the truth was not as I had always believed. Cassial had been clever in his plans. He'd played the game of gods and shifted the board so he always would win. I thought he was a step ahead of us, but the truth was he simply adapted to the changing tide quicker than we could.

"All this for some land?" I asked, straining against my bindings. My words fumbled over my split lip, the frayed skin catching on my teeth. He likely put the slight lisp down to my split lip, and not the vial of poison still wedged between my back teeth. "Seems a little desperate, don't you think? You could have just tried asking nicely."

My sarcasm didn't faze Cassial, he was far too gone in the belief that he had won to care.

"No, this has nothing to do with land," Cassial said, standing far too still. "I am finishing the task the Creator set out to accomplish. As his Saviour, it is my duty to fix this world. To right the imbalance of power that was put into the hands of the fey. I do this to finally give that power to where it rightfully belonged. Long have the humans been lesser than your kind, small beings constantly at threat that the fey would one day decide to turn their sights on them and rule. And before you tell me I am wrong, even you know what Doran Oakstorm had planned. He wished to unleash a winter unlike any other across the world, devouring Durmain long enough for the fey to sweep in afterwards and lay claim. Power corrupts, it eats away at us, some slower than others. Even now, as Duwar floods my body, I sense this. I have come to ensure that this imbalance ends today. Humans have lived in fear that you would conquer–"

"Is that the power lying to you," I hissed. "Or your own deranged sense of grandeur?"

"We both know the answer to that." Cassial tilted his head, the cracks in his flesh stretching. "If you had not accepted your lineage, the human realm would have belonged to the fey seasons ago. Even you have seen the fey army that marches here and thought of the very same the first time you witnessed their might."

In the dark of my mind I recognised Cassial's accusation was right, but I wouldn't dare admit it aloud. "I stopped it once, and I will stop it again."

"Yes, you will. If you accept my offer." Cassial smiled, rot spilling out between decaying teeth. "Robin, you never put a stop to a war, it was simply postponed. But I am finally giving you the power that could stop it, for good. You accept and we right this imbalance, or you refuse, and we sit back and watch the army attack."

"They attack because of *you*," I said, blood leaking over split lips. "It has nothing to do with the need to rule or want for control. It's to stop the maniac behind it. Even the Nephilim are against you."

"Not all of them."

Cassial paced before me, fingers catching over his chin. Every slight movement – every step, and the feathers continued to fall from his wings. The skeletal frame of bone could be seen in places. No doubt, in time, as Duwar corrupted him more, he would truly look no different to the vision of Duwar I'd first seen.

"Do you think it wise to continue this disagreement, Robin Icethorn? Every second spared is another that your army draws closer. I have given you the chance to save the humans, yet you still hesitate. Why?"

I had too many reasons to begin to fully explain. "You ask me to choose which side of myself you wish me to save. Human or fey."

"Then you know we have come to a crossroads. You can see what Duwar is doing to me. I had plans, grand ideas of how this power could be used to get what I want–"

"A world without the fey."

"Ah," Cassial smiled, revealing the harsh points of monstrous teeth. "So, you do listen. Yes. A world without the fey. Do you know, when the Creator gave Altar life, it was out the kindness of his heart? Then Altar – selfish and proud – was not satisfised with his creation. So, he searched for it in the heart of the world, took the chaos and harnessed it. Made the realm's first monsters, parading them as great protectors. When the Creator longed for that power to give to his creations just to ensure they could protect themselves, Altar decided that he was the one in control. He locked Duwar away, keeping it from the Creator's grasp, and in doing so corrupted it. The humans were left powerless to defend themselves, whilst the fey bided their time to claim what was not theirs."

"Or maybe Altar knew what the Creator would do with access to power." I looked the Nephilim up and down. "Look in one of your mirrors, Cassial. You are the very thing Altar wished to prevent."

"Hearsay and speculation," Cassial snapped, his sickly grin unwavering. "All we know is Altar's treatment of Duwar spoiled the power. Ruined it. He broke Duwar apart and left it to deteriorate in the dark for far too long."

"Which is why you need me."

In a blink, Cassial was inches before me. He was so fast, the feathers that were ripped from his wings hadn't rested on the ground before his hands were wrapped around my throat. "I need you. Only a fey from Altar's direct lineage can handle such power. Your bodies were built in the very image of Duwar. You can withstand it. I know you can, because Duwar taunts me. Either you accept it, or I will give this offer to Erix Oakstorm. And we both know, if your life is on the line, he will accept without this pathetic hesitation you show me."

"He would never," I said.

"Are you trying to convince me, or yourself?" Cassial asked. "Say Erix refuses too, then this is not over. If you both refuse,

Duwar will go into Jordin Elmdew. Allow for that, and I will mould Jordin's beliefs the older he gets, until he is pleased with the chance to truly destroy Wychwood."

Cassial drew back, just as fast, leaving me gasping for air. He started slamming his knuckles into his temple. It was a surprise when he didn't begin cracking his skull into a wooden beam, just to rid himself of the inner voice.

"Time is running out, Robin! Quick, quick now."

"You are wrong about me," I said, grasping at straws. "I'm *half* fey. My body is part human. I will not be compatible with Duwar completely; if I take it from you, I will only die in the end."

"Which is exactly what I want," Cassial shouted, eyes glowing a violent red. "You are only the first step in my plans. Once Duwar ravages your body apart, there will be another who is willing to free you from the punishment of Duwar. At least you can die knowing the fey will not perish. History will look kindlier on the humans if it is a fey who banishes his own kind. You see, it must be you."

My heart sank deep into the pits of my stomach. "Erix will sooner die than help you."

As would I.

"Yes, you are right. But with you still living, he would give anything to ensure it!" Cassial refused to look away from me, his smile widening more, making the skin across his cheeks crack. "Erix Oakstorm. The berserker. King Oakstorm, whether he accepts it or not. He will do anything to fulfil his promise of giving you a... how did you call it? A tomorrow."

I swallowed the blood and bile, trying to steel my expression, but failing. Cassial knew he'd backed me into a corner. Because he was right. Erix *would* do anything to save me, he had proved that time and time again. I was being used to further Cassial's campaign, knowing that Cassial had contingency plan over contingency plan. There was not a single part of his path he'd not meticulously planned.

"I know Duwar taunted you too." Cassial began pacing again, wringing thick hands together, skin peeling back as soft as a butterfly's wing. "I hear it. It gave you the chance to host it, to save Duncan and thus save the world from ruin. And you did not believe it. Of course, I take responsibility for spreading the lies about a demon-god. No doubt every word and plea from Duwar was wasted on you. You would never for a moment see it for anything but evil. And yet the end is the same: you must *willingly* accept Duwar. Or you watch me die, then watch everyone else outside this tent meet the same fate. That, Robin Icethorn, is something even you will not survive. No one will."

Willingly. That was why Jordin Elmdew was not his option, because a child that young would never know what to consent to, or how. That was the beauty of youth. For now, it would save Jordin and give him a chance.

"You want me to save the humans?" I asked, urging Cassial closer to me.

"I want you to give balance to them," Cassial corrected.

The closer he came, the better my chance to crack the vial and spit the poison over him, killing him right here. But the Fallen would use him as a martyr. Seraphine sacrificed her life to give me this chance, and it was for nothing. Killing Cassial was not an option, not yet at least. If he died, Duwar would be released into the realms and there would be no hope of returning it to its eternal resting place. First, I had to show the world who he truly was – to rip back the curtain of lies and show them who the true monsters were.

I was left with only one path I could take, and Cassial knew it.

"If I accept Duwar, what is to say I will not go against you the second I get the chance?"

"I have thought long and hard about this outcome." Cassial came to a stop, coming oddly calm about his demeanour. "If you act against me, Duncan will be punished for as long as his new body can withstand. If you think my treatment of Rafaela was evil before, what will become of Duncan is far, *far* worse. You see, love is nothing but a weakness. A sin. It was what led to the Creator's downfall. His love for Altar, his trust, resulted in both gods perishing. And you, Robin Icethorn, are a sinner. Your heart has been split in two. It would have been more of a challenge to manipulate you if I only had access to one. But Erix will come for you, and so will your allies. One by one, I will see that they suffer pain until that alone kills you. They will not die; I will make sure of it. Instead, they will spend their long lives suffering, knowing that it is in your name. So long that they will learn to hate you. Every time they think of you their bodies will burn and scald until they are begging to forget you. Trust me when I say that my capabilities are vast and never ending. I will show Erix and Duncan how to hate you."

A growl built in my chest. No doubt, if the iron chains and cuff did not touch my skin, my power would have struck out.

I was helpless. Cassial knew that.

He used my life as leverage to everyone around me.

"There is something else I have done," Cassial added, a smile tugging at his ruined mouth. "Although I will not reveal what yet. But just know, if you think about killing me, ruin will still befall this world."

Every inch of my body prickled, skin itching with discomfort. "What have you done?"

Cassial smiled. "You will see, in time."

I didn't know what to think, but I believed there was a truth behind his threat. I couldn't place why or what.

"Do you really believe that I wouldn't forfeit Duncan's life, if it means saving the world?" Hate crashed within me like storm-gathered seas. I tried my best to steel my expression, but clearly it was a wasted effort. "No one life is more important than the realms."

Cassial could see right through my attempt to lie.

"Shall we test that theory, Robin?" He rolled his shoulders back, his posture reeking of his success. "Duwar has shown me what you were prepared to give up, just to save Duncan. Already, you've proved that the greater world and its occupants mean little to you. Having harboured Duwar for so long in secret, is only further proof of that. So, yes, I do trust that you will do as I ask, because you could not possibly live in a world in which Duncan or Erix no longer exist. Selfish, selfish Robin. You would give anything to have a… *tomorrow* with them. Am I right?"

He used that word against me for a second time, cutting deeper into my soul. My teeth shifted, the glass vial tinkling over the hard surface. Cassial wasn't wrong. I was selfish, but that was not always a weakness. It could be my greatest strength too. He just didn't see that yet.

I lifted my chin, trying not to show how Cassial's use of words had affected me. Fixing my eyes on his, I refused to look away as I asked my final question. "When I accept Duwar into me, what am I do to with the power?"

Cassial smiled, the corners of his lips splitting up through his cheeks, more brimstone and fire hissing in the cracks. "Finally, you have come round to the concept."

"Answer the question."

"What I require of you is to strip the access to chaos that Duwar gave the fey. Starting with the army heading our way. Draw out every ounce of magic in their blood, and transfer it over, just as the Creator first desired, to the humans." Cassial rubbed his hands together, his entire demeaner greedy.

"You do it."

"And kill myself in the process?" Cassial laughed. "No, we both know that will not happen. It has to be you. If you do it, the fey will be spared. We will strip them of their control, send them back into Wychwood and seal them away forever. That way you can continue in life knowing those you love will live.

But you must decide with haste. Time is running out. My offer only stands for as long as it takes for Erix to get here... then it will be presented to him once the ground is stained with innocent human blood."

My answer was simple. "I will not accept until I see Duncan for myself."

Cassial leaned in, washing the vile stench of decay over me. "Again, choosing Duncan over the lives you've sworn to protect, just as you tried to convince me otherwise. Further proof that I am right. If that is not confirmation enough of how selfish you are, Robin, I do not know what is."

"That is my counteroffer," I sneered, breath coming out ragged.

Cassial offered me a grin so wide, his crumbling face cracked like broken glass. "Would you like to know what the Asp said before I tore her head from her shoulders?"

I didn't want to do it, but my eyes trailed over to the headless body to my side. Cassial had made sure I didn't stop looking at it, as if the reminder of what could happen would make me act in his favour.

In truth, it was working. "I don't care."

"Oh, but you will." Cassial was so close I felt the rotting flesh emanating from him. "The Asp said, 'be selfish, Robin'. It was a message for you, proving to me that you would always be chasing after her. I knew, in that moment, you would come. Odd words to waste your final breath saying, but those were it. I could not help but believe she wanted you to hear them. You see, even she knew you were a selfish person. No doubt everyone who follows you does too. And I promised her I would tell you, before her pretty little head fell from those pretty little shoulders. Although by the point I finished agreeing, she could no longer hear me."

Be selfish. Those were Seraphine's last words. *Robin.* Meant for me.

Her last command.

I pinched my eyes closed, remembering what she had told me back on the ship to Irobel. *"An Asp is trained to use their last words as a means to guide the next onwards... Not a breath is wasted, not a word is worthless."*

I drew back my disdain, knowing Cassial was right. I was selfish, and Seraphine knew it. But her reasons for saying it were not what Cassial hoped for.

This was what Seraphine wanted. Everything she'd done was to get me here, in this place, with this choice. I had to believe that she'd put herself in Althea's position, knowing her imminent death would start the war we all tried to stop. Because she needed me to accept Duwar *before* acting.

I had to ensure her death was not wasted.

Be selfish, Robin.

I fixed my eyes on Cassial as a rush of calm came over me. With the sweep of my tongue, I pushed the vial back between my teeth, ready for another time. "I will do it."

His eyes widened, red hot like the churning fires of the sun. "You will?"

"I willingly accept Duwar." I made sure my voice had no room for anything but confidence. "You are right, it is the only way."

"Then we begin—"

"No," I answered. "First, you take me to *him*. Prove to me that you are a man of your word, and I will then do the same."

Be selfish, Robin. My request to see Duncan was only further proving the point, which was exactly what I needed.

"Then the Asp was right," Cassial said. "You truly are selfish, Robin Icethorn."

Cassial's impatience had little to do with the impending army. He too was selfish – using the humans as a shield proved that. His impatience was born from a place of knowing that everything he planned for rested on my cooperation.

"Shall we?" I asked, itching to get out of these chains. "As you said, time is not our ally."

Cassial nodded, before waving a hand. He changed before my eyes. His skin rippled, his face morphing back into another. Cassial used Duwar to build an illusion around him, fixing Duncan's face where his hand been.

At first, I thought he had been tricking me all along, until the chains shattered apart, and I slumped forwards.

Cassial wouldn't allow himself to be seen by the world outside this tent. Because if they saw the truth of what he'd become, then his illusion that the fey were monsters would be ruined.

"I trust you will not do anything stupid, Robin?" Cassial asked as he took the leash connecting to my cuff and guided me toward the tent's entrance. "Remember, I have preparations if you do."

"Of course not," I replied, "I know who is at risk."

"Good boy," Cassial praised, making me wish to tear my ears off my head.

As we stepped out into the glare of daylight, I winced, hiding my smile. A plan formed in the back of my mind, in a place Cassial couldn't touch.

Cassial was just as desperate to survive Duwar's corruption as I was to stop this war. I would use that to my benefit. But for that to work, I needed to give my signal. I had to hope that Erix would still not act until he saw it, army or no. When the time came, it would take Rafaela, and the full power of the Faithful to save the realms.

With every step toward my destiny, I could practically hear the ghost of Seraphine whisper in my ear. *"Be selfish, Robin."*

"Always, Seraphine." I thought. *"As if I haven't been all this time."*

Cassial had to believe I was hesitant. He had to believe I was unsure of how to act, when the truth was, I knew it was going to end like this. From the beginning. Cassial didn't know it yet, but this was all working to *my* plan after all.

CHAPTER 35

Dark storm clouds rolled over the sky, blanketing it in a heavy, oppressive darkness. My bare skin itched against the charged air, as though I could feel unseen fingers offering me a sense of calm in a moment of complete lack of control.

Magic was everywhere, but it didn't come from Cassial or his warriors. It came from the distance, like a song caught on the breeze, whose tune promised war and ruin.

The fey were close; my time was running out.

I lifted my hand to shield my eyes, giving myself a better view of the hell before me. Beneath the darkening storm, an army – *my* army, stood waiting. A shiver ran over my skin as I took in the distant vision of the stain of fey. The sun caught off plates of metal armour which refracted the light back over the league of humans behind me. Banners danced in the winds, showing the humans a united front as the full might of four fey courts stood as one, ready to fight back against them.

Cassial – wearing Duncan's skin – was at my side, the leash connecting to my iron cuff held firm in his hand. He hadn't given me the option to put clothes on, instead parading me in nothing but my bare skin and undershorts. His attempts to demoralise me wouldn't work. I had other focuses now.

Fallen warriors waited behind him, poised and ready. Not to fight, but to stand back and watch as they sent their human shield forwards to face death.

I felt the tension in the air, so palpable that I could taste the sweat and anxiety on my tongue.

"Bring forwards the *Defiler*," Cassial commanded in Duncan's voice. He didn't necessarily shout, but his voice carried on the winds, no doubt amplified by Duwar's power.

I turned back as the rustle of bodies sounded. Even though I knew what I was going to find, it still took the wind from my lungs.

Duncan – cast in the illusion of Cassial's form – was guided through the crowd. His skin had broken in parts, his left eye swollen shut, lip split and a web of dark bruising mapped out over his naked torso. A gag had been forced into his mouth, muffling the grunts he expelled with every painful movement.

Cassial had done this, to keep Duncan silent. To keep him from spoiling this glamour and telling the world that he was not Cassial, but someone under his guise.

"The fate of his life will be in your hands, Robin," Cassial warned at my side, speaking with a voice that never belonged to him. He'd stolen it from Duncan. Snatched it from his throat and kept it for himself. It sickened me, but I couldn't react – I wouldn't.

Not yet.

"Let me speak to him," I pleaded, unable to conceal the bite of hate in my voice. "If you want me to do as you will, then I will need to hear him one last time."

"We both know that wouldn't be wise." Cassial leaned into my side, turning his back on the fey army, whilst bringing his mouth down to my ear. "You've been given a simple choice. Aid me, and Duncan will live. The Nephilim will find it in their hearts to forgive him for his sins. Work against me, try and dismantle my hard work, and I will personally see that his throat is split from ear to ear."

"Don't you get tired of threats?" I asked, body trembling with the need to lash out and cause pain.

"Yes, actually, I do," Cassial replied, drawing back. "Duncan may not be able to speak, but he *can* listen. If you have got anything to say to him, this would be your moment."

There was so much I wanted to say, but a goodbye was the only thing that I could offer. I needed Duncan to know how I felt, and what I required of him moving forwards. I didn't want our last moments to be cursed.

With a wave of Cassial's hand, Duncan was brought to kneel before me. As he hit the ground, fingers digging into the dirt, I noticed the flash of an iron cuff bound around his wrist.

I knew exactly how this would look to the fey.

They would see Cassial – broken and bloodied – on the ground. They'd think we'd already won. That was why they glamoured Duncan to look like Cassial. More proof that the real Cassial was always a step ahead – constantly painting pictures to those around him, tricking us with lies. He mentioned a contingency plan if I tried to kill him, and I knew now that this was it.

At least that was what I hoped.

It was the real Cassial's attempt to disarm us, weaken us, just in time for Duwar to be used against them with little effort.

I took a deep inhalation, sucking in the horrid scent of blood. Slowly, the real Duncan lifted his eyes and locked them onto me. It took great restraint not to crack with a sob. I didn't dare move a muscle.

There was so much I longed to say. Words that lodged in my throat, promising to choke me. So, holding Duncan's strange stare, I did the one thing that I could. An action that would show him – not tell him – that I loved him.

I lifted a hand to my eye, lowered it shakingly to rest above my heart and then pointed toward him.

I love you.

I waited, with bated breath, for Duncan to complete our sign. To lift his hand and gesture toward me, proving to me that he had some strength left him in.

But he didn't.

The only way he reacted was as his lip drew back in a hateful snarl.

Realisation hit in so suddenly, I couldn't hide it from my face.

Cassial noticed, offering me a winning smirk, thinking my pain was a result of Duncan's refusal of me. But he would never refuse me that answer – not when he was dying, not when he was possessed and not when he survived judgement all to come back to me.

"What will it be, Robin?" Cassial glowered. "You wanted this moment, and yet you waste it with simple gestures. The fey approach like the swift storm of promised death."

There was no replying to Cassial without giving away the detail I'd just figured out. I looked up, ears ringing, the glass vial tickling over my molars as I positioned it. "I accept your proposal, willingly. I will take the burden you wish to give me and do with it as you desire."

Cassial's eyes widened. Did he expect more of a fight? Not wanting to disappoint, I silently told him that the fight would come. "You surprise me."

"I surprise myself." My blood ran cold; even with the iron limiting my magic, I felt powerful. Because I knew now what Seraphine meant. Everything she'd done, all her sacrifices and lies, led to this moment. And I wouldn't waste it.

Because I was in control, whether Cassial figured that out or not.

"I will give you Duwar, and with it, you will draw the source of magic out of every fey before you." Cassial loosed his hold on my leash. The chain dropped to the ground with a thud, splattering in boot-trodden mud. "Once the fey have been whittled down to husks, you will complete Aldrick's wishes, and transfer those gifts to the humans behind you. Am I clear?"

"Very." I clenched my fingers tight, refusing to look at the fake Cassial. Even as the real Cassial lifted him from the ground and held the limp male to his chest with a broad arm hooked around his waist.

"You promised me you wouldn't hurt him," I gasped, forcing out the emotion, trying to show some semblance of worry. When in truth, I wanted to laugh. I had no care for the weak, limp person in Cassial's grasp.

Cassial didn't reply. He was using the fake Cassial as a way to control me. Even as he gave his Nephilim the order to remove my iron cuff, it was all a test of boundaries and trust. I could've unleashed the sudden rush of my magic at him, but that would have ruined everything.

Patience was never a virtue I had. My father once told me it would take a firm hand to teach me the lesson. He was right – almost. It took two hands from two different men to teach me the importance.

Which was exactly the game Erix was playing. I could almost feel his eyes on me, scoring through my skin, telling me it was all going to be okay. If I had it in me, I could've searched the surrounding area and found him.

He was waiting for his signal – as I commanded – so I would give it to him.

"Use Duwar to sever the magic in the fey, give it to the humans. Is that all you require of me?" I asked, mouth drawn into a tight line.

"Let us first see if you survive that," Cassial grinned, lifting a mouth that didn't belong to him. His foot was tapping, his fingers drumming over the fake Cassial's body.

He was nervous.

And he should be.

"I'm ready," I said, chin jutting forwards.

The beat of fey traipsing closer toward the camp had grown louder in the passing moments. I felt the vibration up my feet, followed by the distant screams of Cassial's human shield, likely scrambling to get out of the soldiers' path before complete annihilation.

Cassial nodded, tongue lapping his lower lip. There was certainly trepidation in his eyes as he lifted his hand toward me. I thought back to what Erix said he'd seen in Duwar's realm. How the physical embodiment of Duwar had laid a hand on Duncan's chest, imbuing him with power.

Power that was not inherently good or bad.

Power, the morality of which was determined by the person who wielded it.

I strode forwards, stopping just shy of Cassial's fingers. The fake Cassial was between us, snivelling at me, eyes drinking me in. I barely looked at him. Cassial would think it was because it hurt me to see what had been done to the love of my life – the truth couldn't have been more different.

"Remember," the real Cassial hissed through clenched teeth. "One wrong move, and he dies."

"I heard you the first time," I replied, knowing these would be the last words I could physically speak. Part of me wanted to say something grand – some inspiring speech that told Cassial he had failed just so I could watch the shock morph to horror, and then to defeat.

But my actions would be enough. They had to be enough.

Cassial's lip curled upwards, his smile one I'd looked into many times before. The expression tugged at the scar down the side of Duncan's face. I fixed my gaze on it, letting a tear fall down my cheek. It wasn't sadness born from a place of fear or grief.

But relief – relief that this was all going to be over soon.

Cassial laid a hand over my chest, his touch abnormally warm. I looked down, watching the hand cover the burn scars Althea's hand had left on me when she saved me from dying the first time.

Funny, how one saved me, and the other would lead to my demise.

I didn't know what I needed to do. Nor what to expect. I simply allowed myself to be open to the power, accepting it like a gift – the last I'd receive.

Cassial closed his eyes and exhaled. He uttered no words of power or conjuration, he simply let go, and I accepted.

What followed was a rush of pure, blinding light as it filled me. It bloomed in my chest, spreading from beneath Cassial's palm, filling every vein, sparking my blood into an inferno, melting my bones and reforming them into something stronger – *older*.

My mind conjured an image of a thread. Something tying me and Cassial together. It unspooled into me, knotting within my gut as I gathered the thread into mental hands. I pulled at it, drinking it in with vigour until it abruptly stopped.

"It is done," Cassial exhaled, a tinge of sadness in his voice as he had to give up this power. He withdrew, shaking hand falling to his side, fingers flexing. But that thread inside of me pulled taut, as if I was separated, but still bound to Cassial.

Because he hadn't given it all to me. I couldn't explain the sensation, except the new power inside of me was drawn – stretched as it searched for the missing part of it. I felt it tug inside of me, like a rope pulled taut, fraying in the centre. Panic rose inside of me – because Cassial revealed his final attempt to trick me. He'd not given me all of Duwar. That was how he kept his glamour up. He'd saved a sliver of power, and now we warred for it. My initial instinct was to grapple with Duwar, forging unseen hands to ice, doing my best to keep hold.

We fought for Duwar like two starved mutts for a bone.

I didn't speak, but my shock told Cassial that I had worked out his final deception.

Cassial fixed Duncan's verdant eyes upon me, refusing to look away as his smile darkened. "You know… what needs to be done. Consider my hesitation as insurance if you go against me."

I would've replied, but the vial was forced between my teeth, the glass aching beneath their tension. My silence drew out, and lips curled over my teeth.

Duwar was in part within me, and the remaining part left inside of Cassial. And it was wrong – the separation of a corrupted power.

"Make the right decision, Robin," Cassial warned, quickly drawing the false Duncan back to his chest, sinking nails into his shoulder like the claws of some great bird of prey. "Do not be blinded by the power. Do as I command, or he will die—"

I leaned in toward them both, gathered the moisture in the air around my hand and conjured a shard of pure ice. Cassial's eyes widened a second too late, because he couldn't move. Not that it would matter if he had, because my blade of ice was never meant for him.

I thrust it directly through the fake Cassial's chest. Piercing through flesh, chipping bone and goring muscle, not stopping until the ice spear came out the other side of him.

Blood spluttered over the gag, choking the fake Cassial on their own gore, their death slow and torturous. The real-Cassial attempted to stagger back, but the end of the spike had caught his side. His gasp roused the Nephilim around us into action, weapons drawn from hilts, the song of metal against leather splitting the air.

"You fool!" Cassial cried, pushing the body away from him, which tore the blade from his side.

I smiled, vial straining between my teeth, as a thought speared through my mind. I hoped, between the odd connection of a separated Duwar, that Cassial heard it.

No, you're the fool.

It had never been Duncan under that glamour.

Duncan would never have not finished our signal. Even as he was dying, he did it. And this was no different. Except the person Cassial wished for me to believe was Duncan looked at me with the very same hate of the Nephilim around me. It was an expression I had grown used to, so much so that I almost found it comforting.

His inability to gesture at me, finishing the 'I love you' had been the first giveaway. Cassial's nervous energy was the next.

The sky broke with lightning. Everyone who looked skyward would've seen the countless outlines of winged figures illuminated against the glare. There were thousands of them, the Faithful hidden within storm clouds, waiting for the right moment to attack.

And that was when I heard it. The beat of wings sounded a moment before the *real* Duncan Rackley and his army of Nephilim exploded out from dark grey clouds.

I should've known that my Duncan was here, from the way charged air rippled over my skin. I didn't notice it when Cassial first brought me out of the tent, but the more the storm built, the more the undeniable presence of Duncan's magic called to me. I had put it down to the building of fey magic in the distance but hadn't clocked onto the fact that it was Duncan calling to me all this time.

Like called to like, after all.

I wanted nothing more than to look up and find him – *my* Duncan, one final time. But I couldn't. I had one more thing to do.

For Wychwood.

For Durmain.

For Seraphine and the *tomorrow* she'd never get to experience.

Cassial jolted toward me, clasping the sides of my arms with firm hands. I let him. I needed him close after all. The second he touched me, the seed of Duwar inside of him began to war with the part which lingered inside of me.

But I wasn't going to give it up so easily.

The Fallen around us jolted forwards, unknowing that their deaths would follow. I smiled, lips curling over teeth, flashing the glass vial. Cassial noticed, his eyes widening. I forged my ice to his skin, preventing him from pulling away from my touch. He was a fly, willingly entering my web, one he would not break free from. Then I clamped my teeth, shattering glass, releasing the noxious cloud of poison. But instead of spitting it out, I sealed my lips and swallowed it down.

Every last bit.

Be selfish, Robin.

"No," Cassial gasped, feral eyes wide, as he attempted to skin his hold onto Duwar and wrench it back into himself.

Satisfised the gas had successfully threaded down my throat, infiltrating my lungs, I gathered the shards of glass and spat them directly into Cassial's face. He pinched his eyes closed a second too late. Beneath the thundering war cry of the Faithful, and the keening screams of Cassial, my mind imagined the sound of his flesh slicing apart against the broken shards.

It was a pleasant thought. One I'd gladly take to my grave.

"It was your mistake not to understand the meaning behind Seraphine's last command," I said, blood running down past my sliced lips. Although I felt no pain, only the euphoria of Duwar. "I *am* selfish. But not in the sense you first thought."

I couldn't feel the tips of my fingers. As the poison spread throughout me, suffocating Duwar and my control over my body, I relished in my one final battle.

Taking as much of the power as I could from Cassial, so it would perish alongside me.

"You've doomed the realms," Cassial spat, dark eyes flaring wide. Between the blood streaking down his face and the few shards of glass embedded in his cheek and nose which glittered every time lightning cut the sky, he looked the part of the monster he truly was.

"I have saved them," I managed. "From *you*. But I must first show them the real threat, so they never forget who started this game, and then who ended it."

There was something delightful about controlling Duwar – even as my mind was failing alongside my body. I didn't need to gesture with a hand or visualise what I desired. It simply did what I wanted. Using the shard of Duwar I had hold of, I stripped Cassial of his glamour. Before the fey, the humans and every soul who watched – they saw the truth he hid from the world. I showed them the *true* monster.

I revealed to them exactly who Cassial had become.

"No," Cassial stammered as his horns grew larger, his skin cracked, the skeletal wings of a monster stretched wide at his back. Cassial tried to withdraw from me, but I refused.

We would both die today, one way or another.

Cassial took a jolting step back before thrusting his clawed hands out for my throat. He could kill me himself, but it would be wasted effort. The poison was already destroying me, taking Duwar's power to the void. But I didn't have it, not completely. Duwar stretched between us, pulling between two conflicting consciences. The good and the bad – and yet no one would win.

"I warned you not to go against me," Cassial shouted as the winds began to roar and a force built up inside of me. It was the chaotic beat of war drums, and yet no instruments were being played. "I will destroy everything you love before letting this go to waste. There will be no peace in the void for you, Robin Icethorn."

The world was so loud. Between the distant cries of battle and the clashing of magic, I only hoped that the humans had been spared. My eyes closed, growing heavier by the second. "Maybe not. But at least it will be quiet. It is... *over*, Cassial."

"You are right, Robin Icethorn," Cassial snarled, skin falling away like ash, revealing the monster which hid beneath his skin. "It is over, for you."

The tether binding us together frayed and snapped.

I felt it shatter, like a fragile thing, instead of an ancient power. Perhaps Altar and the Creator's previous fight had corrupted Duwar to the point of fragility – but I sensed the moment it finally broke.

A force tore me from my feet, casting me backwards through the air. My heavy limbs splayed, tangling in the fabric of a tent as my body broke through it. I'm sure a bone snapped, as did the wooden skeleton of the tent I'd just smashed through.

The world was howling. I managed to lift my neck enough to watch as a dark stain broke out across the view ahead. It crackled and spat, like dried kindling on a newly lit hearth. And yet the sky not only burned but turned into an obsidian storm.

It echoed within me, deep in the pits of my soul, where the shard of Duwar was left to whimper.

I blinked, watching in slow motion, as Cassial parted from the scar of shadows. He reached for me, spitting and snarling as the mass of power built and built into a wall at his back. "Now you will die knowing that final part of Duwar kept from you will ravage the world."

I had been wrong all along. Cassial wasn't using the part of Duwar he kept back, but he'd *released* it. Because he knew he'd lost, and in Cassial's desperation, he would take the realms with him.

Cassial had released the last part of Duwar I fought for into the world. "Die knowing you have failed. The realms are doomed, Robin. Take that into your quiet peace and hold it close. Because every soul left behind will soon follow you and haunt you for your failure forever."

I opened my mouth and cried out a single name. "Erix!"

The word was swallowed by the realms screaming in terror. The ground shuddered with the advancing army. The sky sang with Nephilim and gryvern. And all the while, that mass of ruin and chaos gathered into a pillar so great, I couldn't see anything beyond it.

"Will die, Duncan will die, they all will die," Cassial shouted over the song of destruction he'd unleashed. "And it will all be your doing."

"No," I gasped, trying to grasp for the released power. With enough, maybe I could use it to cleanse my body of the poison. Regardless of my hopes and wishes, I was weak, the power ravaging the world was no match for my failing body.

What have I done?

"Erix…" I choked, my throat closing up. "Please."

"Erix Oakstorm cannot hear you." Cassial stumbled forwards, looking no better than I felt. Limp skeletal wings dragged through the earth behind him. He had his clawed, twisted hands reaching out for me, so close now I could smell the rot emanating from his broken skin. "As I said, it is over. *You* are over. Duwar or no, the fey will fall today. Be it by my hand, or yours. The will of the Creator is strong, as am I. Watch now, Robin... witness what your actions have–"

Before Cassial could score his talon through my flesh, a bright bolt of lightning shot between us. I closed my eyes against the glare, smiling as the feeling of magic itched over my skin. Vaguely, I was aware of the scorch of flesh, and the howl as the lightning bolt ate down to the bone on Cassial's arm. What was left behind was nothing but torn flesh and ichor.

My consciousness gave out for a moment. I fell back onto the bundle of collapsed tent, just as a familiar voice worked through into my subconscious.

"No one dares touch Robin and gets to see another day." Duncan's voice filled my world, violent and demanding as the Hunter I'd first met. I couldn't see him because my eyes would not open. But I heard him – felt his presence close. A simmering mass of light, a guiding force, even when I couldn't open my eyes to see him, I could follow.

"Duncan... Rackley," came a broken, weak voice.

"Hello, *father*. Is it okay that I call you that? As you can imagine, I have wondered all my life about my parentage, and longed for the day to use that title."

"You are too late!" Cassial bellowed, pain creasing his voice, and yet he crumbled into a fit of laughter. "Duwar is free. My intention woven into the threads of the power. You can kill me, and the outcome does not change, *son*."

I wished I had the energy to keep my eyes open, but the darkness was gaining. I fought against it, trying everything to gather the loosed part of Duwar back into myself. But there was a resistance – something keeping me from it.

"Desperation has blinded you," Duncan called back, lightning cast around his angelic body in a wreath of purple-white flame. He looked the painting of the saviour he had become. "Faith has destroyed you. You know nothing of the Creator, because you know little of love. And it was love that started this war over Duwar, and it will also be love that ends it. Love will see us through to another day, as it always will."

"I do not need another day, traitor." Cassial howled like the wounded creature he was. "The end is upon you now. Love will not save you now, just as it didn't save your filthy mother—"

Another voice rose, a husk of silver steel that I would recognise even in death. "Spit more poison out your serpent mouth, and I will tear the tongue from your skull."

"Erix Oakstorm, you can gladly take my tongue, but you will not have anything else of merit when this is done."

"Famous last words, Cassial?" Erix asked as a growl worked out of the depths of him. "Perhaps I will make sure they engrave it on your tombstone. Or maybe I will smear the words with shit instead."

My head slumped back, my body no longer able to hold itself up. I faced the darkened sky, watching a vicious power thrash against the world and devour it.

"Kill me," Cassial screamed out, an edge of begging in his tone. "Do it!"

Silence followed, and I couldn't begin to imagine why.

I had thought the noise of Cassial's skin ripping against the glass shards was the most beautiful thing in the world. But I had been wrong.

It was the voices of the two men I loved that took that mantle.

"I would normally correct someone on their manners, but I will make an exception this one time."

"Do the honours, he is your father after all."

Duncan hefted a great sword above his head and swung down before him with all his might. Steel through the air, Cassial lifted powerless hands up to shield himself. His attempt was wasted.

Duncan's sword carved clean through Cassial's neck, severing head from shoulders, taking part of his hands with one strike of the blade.

As if time slowed to an almost stop, the severed head tumbled onto the ground where it bounced over mud and grime, before rolling to a stop.

Once the dead, lifeless eyes of my enemy stared at me, I no longer had the strength to resist the poison. I gasped out the names of Erix and Duncan, aware that they were shouting for me, searching the rubble for where I had fallen.

They were too late. By the time they found my body, leaving Cassial's corpse framed by the stain that the released portion of Duwar had become, I was fading.

Hands grasped me. Voices shouted demands. But this time, when my eyes closed, I was unable to open them again. My mind latched onto Erix's and Duncan's cries, filling my exhausted thoughts, refusing to let go as they called for me. They were the last things I heard, my name painted on their beautiful lips.

All I could think about was how I had failed.

My end came swiftly for me.

CHAPTER 36

At least I wasn't alone in death.

On both of my sides, warmth radiated from the bodies of two men. I didn't need to see them to know they were with me. Nothing could keep us apart, not even the endless abyss of the beyond.

I luxuriated between the heat of Erix's and Duncan's forms. They filled my senses, their touch something so familiar that even in this strange place of shadow, I couldn't help but imagine their flesh against mine.

Even if I'd failed the world, they would never leave me.

In this strange state, I wasn't confident I had hands, but I imagined reaching out with them, only to feel the physical wall of flesh as if I could physically hold it–

"Robin." Two voices sang from beyond the dark, blending seamlessly together.

"He's awake, Altar, he is going to be okay!"

I felt the firm grip of fingers wrapping around mine. It was odd, to have death react as though it was as much a living thing as this illusion it awarded me. Then the caress of a hand brushed over my chin, inching into my hairline where it was laid flat.

"Slowly, little bird. Don't rush yourself," Erix's voice called through the haze. He was here. But how? Panic seized me, making me believe he had somehow died as well. How else was he here, in this strange place?

I longed to roll toward his voice and forge my body with his, just to stop this illusion from ever ending.

"Take your time, darling. We're here. And we're waiting for you."

I longed to call for them, to locate them and never let go.

What had Cassial done? Had he followed through with his promise of destroying the realms, and both of them had found me in death?

This was not the peace I expected, and certainly didn't deserve.

Or was this Duwar, in death with me, tricking and punishing me with eternal torture?

Splitting pain scorched through the nerves in my brain. I must've groaned against it, because I was aware of another voice, one that belonged to me, interrupting the gentle hush of Duncan's encouragement.

Pain and punishment – weapons used against me for my final act.

I deserved it.

The suffering came again, thick and fast, penetrating my skull, turning my bones to sodden parchment. I ached against it, crying out again. And just like that, the touch of the men I loved faded away. I was no longer a corporeal thing – but a mass of the same darkness that surrounded me.

Paradise never lasted long – not for someone who didn't deserve it. Not for someone like me. I clawed at the remaining scraps of warmth, feeling them fade away like a receding tide. Then, just as the final touch of it disappeared, so did I, down into the belly of the beast that was death.

Jesibel was there to welcome me in the dark. She smiled, clutching not one rose, but a bunch of them, overspilling and red, beautiful as life had been. I knew this was no dream, because when she opened her mouth, I wasn't greeted with silence. Instead, she offered me words. Words she had long lost to the suffering at Aldrick's hands.

"Wake up, Robin. The world needs you. Your family need you."

Voices. *More* voices, coaxing me out of nothing. I was surrounded by all the people who had perished because of my failure. They'd found me in this afterlife to taunt me. I strained to make them out, or who spoke.

"His heart beats stronger today."

"It has been two days," Duncan replied to the mysterious speaker. I knew it was him, even in death I'd recognise his voice. Although he was panicked, his words rushed and chaotic, I imagined myself smiling just at the pleasure of hearing him again. "If any more days pass, we will lose him for good."

"I'm doing my best–"

"Work faster." Erix growled – my Erix, with his voice of commanding iron – interrupting the unfamiliar voice. "Harder. Just do not fucking stop until you fix him. Please."

"He isn't broken. Robin is fighting. But it's up to him to determine how strong he is."

"But what of the antidote? You told us there was an antidote, if that is what we need then that is what you must retrieve." Duncan was calmer, but even beneath his voice I could hear the undercurrent of pure anger, born from fear. His was frightened about something, his voice lifting in pitch on his final word.

"There hasn't exactly been the time to locate one, not with half the realm being covered by Duwar's ruin."

All noise stopped as though a great hand grabbed my head and dumped me in water. The only thing I heard was the long hiss in my ear. Then, as if that same hand tore me back out the water, the voices returned.

I couldn't work out who spoke, but I listened like a scholar learning the secrets of the universe, clinging onto every little scrap of knowledge.

"We cannot afford to move him until he improves, and yet we also must understand that there will come a time that the option to wait here will be taken from us."

The voices were becoming muddled, as if my mind was no longer able to determine who said what.

"And you think staying here will help? The ruin is growing by the minute. There is no saying when it will reach here."

"Robin's in a too fragile state to risk travel."

"What about the realms? What about everyone else outside these walls. The world needs us still."

"My world means nothing without him—"

Crash. I was back beneath the waves of impenetrable dark, limbs helpless and lungs aching for breath. I couldn't make sense of reality. This twisted hellscape where I could hear the voices of those I loved but couldn't reach them.

It was like I was dreaming – so deep, and yet my consciousness fought to hold on. This time Jesibel wasn't here to greet me, and yet I still heard her voice as clear as day, and cold as Icethorn's winter snow.

Your family needs you.

I exploded back from the dark waters, out into open air as I grasped hold of a sense of my reality.

"Althea, we must not leave. Robin is our only hope of saving the realms."

My awareness snapped at the name. Althea. Althea Cedarfall. I imagined fire-red hair, wide eyes, a fierce mentality that could go against a gryvern and a Nephilim.

"I'm with Duncan on this," Erix replied, although it was barely a whisper. I could almost picture him slumped over me, grief stricken and pale.

Althea's sharp, burden-heavy voice rose up. "We can't just sit around and wait – what good are our attempts if we are consumed by the ruin."

"There has to be something which can bring him back to us."

"Not something, but someone," Althea replied, sombre as the atmosphere. "In fact, both of you. Guide him back to us. If you want to fight for him, then do it. Remind Robin what he is going to leave behind if he gives up."

Fight for who? I was hearing them but couldn't make sense as to what they spoke about. How could they possibly fight for me? I was dead – gone. If only I could tell them that I was okay, and they could move on. If only I could voice the words aloud, but alas, I couldn't. Because I was dead. The poison made sure of that.

"Little bird," Erix pleaded, my nickname echoing in the dark.

"Darling," came the other voice – Duncan. The lilt of his tone sinking into my bones and etching itself upon them. "Fight the shadows. You are so much stronger than they are, so fucking strong. Come back to us. I'm begging you – *we're* begging you. We need you, and so do the realms."

I felt a strange shuffling beside me, as if I was physical in matter but just couldn't see it. What else was the dark hiding?

"Do you hear Duncan?" Erix whispered, and I could almost feel the soft brush of lips against my ear. I imagined his hand running down my head, brushing strands of hair away from damp skin. "Don't you *dare* leave us. You will not do that to us, would you Robin?" He took a deep trembling breath in before continuing. "Come on. I know you can hear me. Follow my voice. Come back. Come back… little bird, do you hear me? Come… back…"

Your family needs you.

Bright blue-white light carved apart the dark, brandishing away the grasp of death. It wasn't that I'd opened my eyes exactly, but the hot, white light seared through me, snatching me out of nothingness, back to a sense of awareness.

"More, Duncan! More."

"I'll kill him – this isn't working."

"He will die anyway if you don't try. Do it again, don't stop until his heart is stronger."

More hot light speared through me, burning away flesh and blood, vein and sinew. I felt my body arch against it, spine bending as the bolt of life was passed into me, gathering in my bones, sparking dead limbs to life.

When the pause came, I relished in it. The dark returned, creeping in at the corners of the cosmos of stars around me. Every time death believed it would swallow me whole, there was more light – more boiling heat. It filled me. I glowed from the inside out, like a star against the obsidian sky. And yet I knew death was winning. That was why stars glowed, wasn't it? It is a strange fact to think of, but I could almost hear my dad telling it to me as we lay on our backs in the middle of a cornfield, staring up at the sky.

He pointed to one star amongst many. I found it with ease, because it blazed so bright it was impossible not to see it.

"When a star reaches the end of its life, it burns, in signal to its brothers and sisters."

"Why?" I heard my young self ask.

"To say goodbye, perhaps. Or maybe the star wishes to use its last moments to light the way for those who will come after him."

"That's so sad, father."

I could almost hear him sigh as another bolt of hot light shot through me, fighting back shadows – banishing death, keeping it at bay.

"We all grieve death, but like that star, do you see how beautiful its final moments are? Even in our final moments, we have a purpose. When we die, our life might end, but for those we leave behind, we gift them a purpose."

"What's will be my purpose in life?"

"That is yet to be determined, son. I hope it is a long time until you have to find out."

* * *

I opened my eyes, slowly peeking through one at a time. What greeted me was a dark room, the sounds around me muffled and strange. All I could think about is how terribly my body hurt. Every muscle burned, every bone throbbed and vein stung as though they'd been plucked by something sharp. The pain was close to unbearable, and yet it was fading.

My first instinct was to figure out where I was. The room was small and shadowed by midnight, the walls leaning inwards, the ceiling stout and low. There was something overtly familiar about the smell of the place, but my tired mind could not place it.

But one thing I understood for a fact was I was alive. For a brief moment I had the feeling of relief and amazement.

It was a fleeting feeling, one I didn't deserve.

It was the terrible taste in my mouth that reminded me of what had happened, the moments that led up to this. It was similar to the taste of rotten meat. The skin inside my cheeks was tender as I ran my tongue over it, aware of the jagged marks left from broken glass.

All this feeling, all this awareness... and not an ounce of kindness to it.

Reality slammed into me, almost knocking out the little wind from my lungs. I felt everything. Not only the ache in my body, and the residual pain housed within my skull – but the bed sheets against my damp skin, the brush of cool wind from the open window in the distance, the press of the mattress beneath me.

Most of all, I caught the gentle snores of two other bodies beside me. I didn't notice them at first, but as my sensations became mine again, I used the little energy I had and turned to look.

To my left, Duncan slept on a reading chair placed beside my bed. His proud white wings were wrapped around him, his chest rising and falling, his hand stretched out between us, fingers gently laid on the blanket at my side.

To my right, Erix waited for me. His body was stretched out on the side of the bed, curled on his side, his soft breath brushing against the side of my face. His features, although smooth, were still etched from deep exhaustion. Shadows clung beneath his eyes, his forehead creased in perpetual worry lines.

They had never left my side. I knew that fact without question. And yet their joint presence sparked a horror within me, curdling next to something else in my soul that didn't belong.

A part of me longed to wake them both, but something stopped me.

I recognised a seed of sudden realisation deep in my gut. Like the uncaring teeth of a starved wolf, it sank its maw into my consciousness and locked its jaws in place, refusing to let go.

I was alive, but that wasn't the only realisation that filled my exhausted mind.

My gaze fixed on the curtainless window at the end of the bed and looked to the night sky beyond, the glittering of stars. Some burned brighter than others, reminding me of the story my dad had told me.

I took a deep breath in, my lungs aching, a slight rasp in my throat. I filled my body with fresh air, banishing the cobwebs that filled me. My throat was dry as stone, my body tired and heavy. It took great effort to sit up, careful not to disturb the men at my side.

There would be a time for rejoicing, just not yet.

Pushing my awareness down my limbs, I didn't stop moving until I felt the very tips of my fingers. They too were heavy and stiff, but I forced my awareness to make them wiggle. One finger at a time, my body came alive.

Alive.

The words had such sudden meaning, I sat up, feeling the ache across my chest. I sank my teeth into my lip, stopping the cry of pain from leaving me.

My initial instinct was to reach down, running tingling fingers over my torso, feeling the tender burn of recently charred skin. Even in the dull light of evening, I recognised the outline of a hand. A new scar above an old one – fingers splayed larger than the mark Althea had left long ago.

It didn't belong to my hand, but to another. Small scars spread outwards across pale flesh like serpents... like lightning.

As I brushed my finger over the tender skin, my mind was filled with a bright bolt of light. Duncan's magic lingered. Had it been his light that guided me back? Re-sparked my struggling heart, as he refused to let me go?

I moved my hands atop the outline of my new scar, no longer caring about the pain. Instead, I was full of wonder, looking at just how large the familiar outline was. The skin was coated in a thick salve that made my fingers stick together, webbing as though sap had been plastered across the new wound.

Questions thrummed through me, most notably: what had happened?

I should be dead, but here I was, alive and breathing – not completely well but alive nonetheless.

I scooted to the end of the bed. My body was mine, and yet I felt some disconnect. As though it was not my consciousness that filled my limbs, but something else, belonging to another.

I used the final dregs of strength to push off the edge, wobbling on weak legs. I used the wall to steady myself as I came into view of the window. And in it, I saw my reflection.

I knew what I'd find before I saw it.

Duwar – looking back at me through its eyes. Except it wasn't a demon, but my face just... different. Bright with power, features sharp and otherworldly. A light encased my skin, haloing my reflection as though I was imprinted in glass like the windows of Abbot Nathanial's church.

The horror of it, the reality that I had somehow survived the poison that was meant to kill me, came flooding in. Unable to look at myself, I tore the metal handle of the window from its clasp and pushed it open. With unnatural force, the window slammed into the wall outside, shattering glass.

"Robin!"

I didn't care who called after me, which one of my loves shouted my name.

Not when I got my first look of the world outside, a familiar street with close-knit homes, narrow streets and a view of patchwork fields now full of pitched white tents. I didn't get a chance to truly understand where I was, before a panicked gasp sounded at my back.

"Little bird, you're—"

"Alive," I said, skull thundering, lungs aching for proper breath, I looked behind me to see both Duncan and Erix were alert.

Erix was pale as the sheets he lay upon, looking as if he'd seen a ghost. Duncan's verdant eyes glittered with tears, his brow pinched but his lips curved in a smile of pure relief.

Disbelief rang in every crease and line across their handsome faces.

To them, I'd survived. The truth of the fact was far worse. Because I was not the only one to defy death.

The shard of Duwar had survived alongside me.

Both men looked at me as if I were an apparition, seconds from fading from view. I wished that was true. Knowing what I had survived, and kept with me, was enough to shatter my soul.

"I… just needed some fresh air," I said, sagging back onto the bed as my limbs gave up on me.

In seconds, Erix's arms were around me, gathering me to his chest. Duncan joined, the bedframe bowing beneath his added weight as he forged his arms around me.

I pinched my eyes closed, wishing to enjoy their touch – whilst suffering inside, knowing what I continued to harbour.

"Not everyone can face death and survive. And yet you have. Robin, you must not rush this," Duncan said, longing to reach for me, to lay fingers on me and prove that I was real. "Take your time, do not give your body any more of a shock than it has had."

"What matters" – Erix leaned his forehead onto my shoulder, gasping out his words – "is you came back to us. You fought hard, and for that I will be forever thankful."

I couldn't speak. Words failed me. Even if I wanted to say something, there was a lump of iron in my throat, keeping me from uttering a sound.

Duncan shifted until he knelt before me, Erix still at my back. His eyes roamed over me, settling on the new wound on my chest, then back to my face. I could see he was looking for proof that this was not real – but then his expression softened as he came up empty handed.

"Did I... Did I hurt you?" Duncan asked, eyes flicking back down to my chest.

"No." I lifted shaking fingers and pressed them to my tender skin. "I saw your light and followed it back to you."

Duncan practically melted at my words. Then he gathered me up, soft wings wrapping around me, whilst Erix's folded in from the back. I was encased in them both, unable to think of anything but their touch, their scent – the very real pressure of two bodies.

"Cassial?" I said the name in question, feeling as though I had to hold my breath as I waited for my answer.

"Dead," Erix confirmed. "Four days ago, now."

Relief was short lived. I knew he was dead; I'd seen his head part from his shoulders, no one could survive that.

"I've missed four days?"

I couldn't believe how much time had passed. All I knew was that I had survived, and so had Duwar. Whatever state the world was in, it was forever going to be under threat.

"Duwar–" the name got stuck in the back of my throat. "Is still a problem, isn't it?"

Those voices I had heard beyond the dark were not illusions or punishment. It was my subconscious listening in to a world that I was slowly vacating.

A world Duncan and Erix had given me a second chance to experience.

"That's not for you to worry about right now," Duncan said, doe eyes wide with concern. "What matters is that you have survived, we haven't lost you."

Right now – but still a problem. That was enough to answer my concerns.

Duncan was undoubtedly burdened by something. Erix shared in his feeling. Both men believed Cassial, but they did not rejoice. They did not tell me everything was okay.

Because we all knew it wasn't.

"I took the poison... I should have died."

"Seraphine tricked you," Erix explained, silver tears falling from silver eyes. "But most of all, she tricked us too. Robin, if I'd known what you had on you, I wouldn't have agreed to leave you... I would've fought tooth and nail at your side..."

"Erix, don't." I grasped his hand, squeezing. Mine was steady, evident against the violent tremble of his. "Please, you don't need to hold onto guilt or regret."

Those were emotions for me to wear proudly.

Mouth dry, I managed a final question as the exhaustion built to new heights within me. "How did she do it?"

"There will be time for us to catch you up, darling." Duncan ran his hands over my face, still utilising his touch to prove I was real, and not some figment of his deepest wishes. "For now, you *must* rest. You've flirted with death and survived it. Your body is going to take some time to heal from what you've endured."

That wasn't true. Every second, I could feel myself gaining in strength. It was Duwar, filling me with power and possibility, stitching together the frayed threads that had weakened me.

"No," I pleaded, pinching my eyes closed, wishing I could rejoice in this moment instead of fear it. "You must tell me what I've missed – please. I need to know everything."

Duncan shared a look with Erix. I caught Erix's subtle nod out the corner of my eye.

"Just time, darling. That is all that you have missed," Duncan said, offering a smile that was void of any sadness. There was only relief across his face, disbelief and reprieve.

I didn't believe him, and one look in my eyes told Duncan as much, so he continued.

"Cassial is dead. The Fallen have been stopped and the Game of Monsters prevented – all because of you, darling," Duncan said.

"You… you knew this was going to happen," I accused, drawing back as much as my body allowed. "Everything you told Gyah to do, the instructions you gave Seraphine… you knew."

Duncan gritted his teeth, regret darkening his gaze, which refused to leave me. "I did. The Creator showed me an outcome, and the threads to pull to make it happen."

"Seraphine died…" I choked, an image of her headless body flashing through my mind.

"Seraphine sacrificed herself to save Althea," Duncan corrected. "However, those were not my orders. I would never have told her to do what she did… not knowing the outcome. Trust me."

I did, one look in his eyes and I knew that Duncan was telling me the truth. He, like me, toyed with guilt as if it was an old friend.

"The realms are safe from Cassial," Erix added. "That's what matters. Seraphine did not die for nothing."

How could the world be saved, when the crux of the danger lurked within me?

I didn't know I was crying until Erix leaned over and swept a thumb across my cheek. "Eroan told us about the vial Seraphine left you. He was confused as to why she would leave you a store of Gardineum, so didn't question it."

Gardineum. Impossible.

"But it was gold," I stammered, knowing neither Duncan nor Erix had seen the poison Seraphine used on the ship to Irobel. "It should've killed me."

Both men shared a look, brows furrowed over confused eyes. "It was an intense dose, yes."

It was never the poison I had expected. I ran my tongue over my lips, no longer feeling the torn skin that the broken vial had torn apart. "Seraphine tricked me over and over."

Then I began to laugh, the sound rupturing from my belly and out of my dried lips. I told them both of the poison Seraphine had used in the ship, how she put the small vial between her teeth and spat out the gas-like liquid across the Nephilim. They listened in shock, reality sinking in that I really was prepared to end myself to save the world.

"Once an Asp, always an Asp. But her deceit saved you, and has given the realms a second chance," Erix added as I lifted fingers to my ear, half expecting brain matter to have leaked out of them.

"I saw the path ahead," Duncan echoed his earlier sentiment. "And you lived in it. *We* lived in it."

Reality was not kind or careful – it hit me with the force of an exploding star. "She tricked me into believing I would take the poison. She knew I would do it–"

"She *saved* you," Erix answered before laying a kiss upon my crown. "Seraphine knew, on the chance that you ingested the poison, you'd not suffer. If you used it against Cassial, it would give us the chance required to end him–"

So that is what they believed had happened? I didn't have it in me to tell them the truth, not yet.

Be selfish.

I couldn't ruin this moment, not for them and not for me. In time I would have to tell them both how wrong they were. But that would come, just not yet.

"I heard you, both of you, calling for me," I admitted, taking my time to look them both in the eyes.

"And you came back to us," Duncan said, catching yet another tear as it spilled down my cheek. "Just in time."

"We knew you would, little bird."

I couldn't fathom what had become of the world outside this door, but just for now, I wanted to forget it. To push to the back of my mind the knowledge of what I still had to do.

"Would you lie down with me," I said, pleading edging my tone. Not that I needed to, because the moment the request left my lips, Erix and Duncan obeyed.

"Of course, we have some time to spare," Duncan said, sharing a look with Erix that suggested a silent conversation between them both.

It took little effort for them to get me back under the sheets. Erix to my right, Duncan to my left. It was a miracle I was alive – and a miracle the bed did not crack beneath our conjoined weight.

I didn't speak until we were nestled against one another, sharing heat. I began to shiver, not from the cold, but from the reality that of what would happen when I finally was brave enough to get out of bed.

"How long do we have?" I asked.

There was something great and unspoken between us, and yet I knew we all could not ignore it for much longer. It was a gaping yawn of truth and burden that was keeping us away from truly celebrating the tomorrow we'd wanted.

Peace wasn't here yet, and we knew it.

"Forever, gods willing," Duncan replied, laying his arm over my stomach, anchoring himself to me. And still I sensed something in his voice, a truth that he was holding back, the same that I refused to voice aloud. Or was that seed of doubt Duwar, poisoning me from the inside, making me distrust the world around me?

"We *will* have our tomorrow, Robin. And every tomorrow that follows after the next. You… have given the realms the final chance it needs, and there will come a time to enjoy the bounty of your actions. But for now, you should rest."

I didn't argue with that. I couldn't, because if I opened my mouth to speak, I feared I'd only ruin the moment for them both. For now, I would be selfish and enjoy the peace of their lack of knowledge.

I would afford them some time to revel in their relief before destroying it.

But first, I had to ensure their tomorrow *was* secure, before leaving them all to enjoy it. Seraphine may have tricked me into thinking I would destroy Duwar. What she didn't account for, was that I was a man of my word.

Neither Duncan nor Erix had told me of the danger lurking outside this room, but the shard within me shared whispers about it.

Taking what I thought was poison had simply postponed my ultimate task.

The outcome, no matter how my mind screamed for me to pretend otherwise, was inevitable.

A part of Duwar still lingered within me, and from the faint tugging in my gut, drawing my attention to the window ahead of us, I knew that the other half was out there somewhere, waiting for me. Needing me.

Calling for *me*.

CHAPTER 37

Erix and Duncan took turns soaking my body, but not even their hands could distract me from the oddity surrounding us. Something was wrong, I could read it in the tension-heavy air and the silence of the world beyond my childhood home. There were moments of unspoken words shared between Erix and Duncan – stiffening postures and weighing heavy on their shoulders.

Most of all, the strangest detail was that I was home. Not in Imeria, but back in Grove, where my story began.

I'd recognised that was where we were – back in the rickety house which was now a burial site for lives lost. Perhaps that was the cause of the sombre mood, and yet I knew it was not.

As Duncan ran careful hands down the curve of my back, not speaking a word, I gazed out the narrow window. Even the sky was heavy with darkness. Whispers of strange-coloured clouds swallowed any daylight. Neither Erix nor Duncan paid much mind. Or, perhaps, they simply wished to ignore it.

Whereas I found it impossible.

"Your bruising is fading quicker than I thought it would," Duncan said as he drew the soft sponge down my spine. I shivered against the warmed water. It hadn't long been filled by Erix, and yet it was already losing its heat, tainted by the unusual air infiltrating the room from the open window. "I imagine, in a matter of days, the mark on your chest will heal too."

I curled my legs up to my chin, sparing a quick glance to Erix who sat on the lip of the tub. He barely took his eyes off me. That was the thing about Erix, he had an inability to lie, but when he held something back, he just kept quiet.

And his silence was loud.

"Are we going to talk about it, or carry on pretending like everything is normal?" I asked, bringing the conversation back to the passing comment Erix had said when we woke earlier.

In the reflection of murky water, I caught Erix shooting a glare at Duncan. His circular motions stilled on my back, Duncan's hesitation screaming in the pause.

Still neither of them replied. Instead, Duncan offered a hand to Erix, who quickly placed a stiff towel into it. "Let's get you changed and then we can talk."

"I'm capable of changing myself," I said, snatching the towel, hands shaking. "You don't need to treat me like a baby needing coddling."

"I can speak for us both when I say that we are just wanting to take things slow, you nearly–"

"I'm alive, Duncan." In turn, I looked them both dead in the eyes. "Can't you see? My body is healing with every passing minute, and yet you still treat me like broken glass. But I can see in the way you look at me that you know. We all know what is happening, and yet it has not been mentioned."

How dare I feel so displeased that they kept secrets from me, when I was keeping the biggest secret possible. Perhaps it was my own lies that made me distrustful. But I also recognised my intuition, and there was no denying something was wrong.

"We can talk about it on the journey back to Icethorn," Duncan persisted, dismissing me.

Erix's jaw flexed, the muscles feathering in his cheeks. I locked eyes with him – hating myself for using his weakness against him. But needs must.

I was his weakness.

"I. Am. Alive." I forced each word out, really hammering the truth home. "Whatever is happening, it is time to face it. *Please*. No more secrets, if anything will kill me it will be that."

It was my pleading that made Erix wince.

Duncan sagged, wings damp from the moisture-heavy air. "Fine. We can talk."

"There *is* a problem," Erix said next, eyes fighting to glance out the window. "One that has not yet been dealt with, but something that we are constantly working at resolving."

"We?" I replied. "We are doing nothing but playing house, Erix. Who is we?"

"The realms," he said, chin jutting out, gaze hardening. "Fey, humans. Icethorn has become a haven for human refugees, just as you wanted. Our numbers, alongside Duncan's Faithful."

My skin shivered at his words, the discomfort working down to my bones. "Is it the Fallen who persist as a problem?"

"No," Duncan answered, hesitantly. "Rafaela and the Faithful are currently passing judgement on the Fallen who survived. They will be given an opportunity to change their ways, and if not, they'll be reunited with the Creator."

His answer was rehearsed. As if he'd stood before a mirror and practiced. I could tell from how quickly he replied, and how precise his words were.

"And you are sure Cassial is dead?" I had asked the question, in a variety of ways, about six times since I'd come around from Seraphine's poison.

"He is," Duncan glowered, fists squeezing the sponge so tight that water spilled over his white knuckles. "I made sure of it."

Then where was the celebration? The joy? If this was the tomorrow we fought hard for, it felt as though I was still hanging from tenterhooks, struggling for sense like a fish out of water.

Erix looked down to his hands, picking at the skin around slightly pointed nails.

I reached over and laid a hand on his, stopping him before he broke skin. "This isn't the tomorrow we wanted together. So, tell me what we have to do to ensure it."

"You have faced enough, little bird." Erix dropped my gaze, pinching his eyes closed.

"Erix is right," Duncan added. "We hesitate to tell you because we know what you will do."

I snapped my head between them, frustration boiling hotter than ever before.

Had they worked out that I still had a scrap of Duwar in me? Was this why they kept me at a distance, keeping the truth from me? Or did they believe I was just too broken to handle what they had to say?

Erix took a hulking breath, lips parting, readying himself to speak. But he was interrupted by a thunderous knock on my home's front door. For a split second I was transported to another time, when it was my father knocking on the door to wake me if I'd overslept.

Duncan peered to the hallway beyond the cramped bathroom. "We really should get you changed, darling. Our convoy to Wychwood has arrived."

The water sloshed as he made a move to lift me out of it, but I held firm. As my anger spiked, so did Duwar. I gasped, having to choke back the power or it would threaten to reveal my secrets. Darkness and light thrashed like dancing waves behind my closed eyes, so potent I could almost taste the potential on my tongue.

Then a shout sounded from the door downstairs. "Duncan, Erix – we need to leave. *Now.* And I will not hear your refusal otherwise I will personally drag you out of this house by the short and fucking curlies."

Althea. I'd recognise her voice in any life, in any time. Even spoiled with panic and urgency, there was a joy in hearing her, when there had been a time I believed it was never possible.

"Come on, you heard her," Duncan commanded. "Help me, Erix."

Both men hoisted me from the tub, standing me bare in the centre of the room. I wrapped the towel around myself just a second before the poppy-red-haired fey came barrelling into the room.

Wide eyed, pale taut lips, Althea scanned the condensation-heavy room before settling on me. Her brow creased as a small chirp left her mouth. Disbelief melted to relief, then her mask quickly crumbled as we crashed into one another, tangling arms and holding firm.

"You are awake," Althea said, wide eyes fixed on me, holding me out at arm's length as she took me in from head to foot.

"Do you mean alive?" I asked, words muffled as she dragged me back into her strong embrace.

"Well, yes," Althea sobbed, laying her chin atop the damp strands of my hair. "Actually, that is exactly what I mean. Gods, Robin. I really thought we were going to lose you for a second."

"Surprise," I replied, voice muffled in her embrace.

Althea smelled faintly of char and burning. The scent clung to her skin, her armour and hair.

She took turns holding me close, then pushing me at a distance so she could get a better look at me. Althea shot the men behind me a look of pure annoyance, accusation rushing out of her mouth. "Why did not you send word for me? I thought I made myself clear that the moment you saw any improvement in Robin's fate, you would call for me. And yet here he stands, bathed and fed, and not even so much as a fucking word."

Fire sparked on her tongue, shifting the room to an uncomfortable heat.

"Robin deserved a moment of peace after what he has been through," Duncan said, bristling his white wings. "We made the call that he could have a few hours of normalcy, before we ruin it."

"Ruin it?" I barked, looking between my three closest friends. There was one person missing. Gyah. But there was no time to contemplate where she was.

I had no peace to ruin, not since I woke still harbouring a part of the problem in me. A part of Duwar.

"You have not told him, have you?" Althea raged, eyes widening a fraction until I noticed the whites of them were bloodshot. "Of course you have not!"

Their joint silence was answer enough.

"What did you possibly think would happen by keeping this from him," Althea continued, her skin growing uncomfortably warm as magic seeped from her pores.

"To protect him," Erix said, silver eyes narrowing. "That is all we have wanted to do."

"From what!" It was my turn to shout, and as I did, a rush of winter ice flashed through the room. Glass cracked; the water in the tub froze solid. It was an uncontrollable power, a level which I shouldn't have been able to do.

If anyone noticed, no one said it with words.

Except Erix had noticed, of course he had. His eyes barely left me for a second, playing into his never-ending duty to protect me. I expected him to voice his worries, but he forged his lips together.

"From. What?"

"Yourself," Duncan sighed. "We are protecting you from making the decision we know you are going to make."

Duwar unfurled within me like a serpent in a fragile box. I closed my eyes, wincing against the sensation. And then, whispering into my ear, Duwar told me the truth. In truth, I think I knew it from the moment I came around from the Gardineum. I just didn't want to admit it to myself.

I saw flashes of the moments before Cassial was killed. How we warred for Duwar, only for him to unleash the power in a storm at his back.

Cassial's final act. The reveal of his plan if I attempted to go against him.

"It is Duwar, isn't it?" I asked, eyes opening to see a room locked in tension. "Cassial is dead, but the seed of chaos he released in the realms is still a problem."

"Yes, Robin. Cassial has left his mark on the world, a mark that we are struggling to scrub clean," Althea said, and for the first time I noticed just how exhausted she really was. Slumped posture, the dark circles beneath bloodshot eyes. This was the appearance of a woman who had not stopped fighting an enemy, whilst I had luxuriated in a bath, giving into this pretend illusion of a tomorrow with the men I loved.

My hands balled to fists at my sides.

Althea released me, moving back toward the door, which she gripped for support. "Cassial may be gone, but his final act has truly put the realms under threat. And it is growing. Nothing we have done so far has been able to stop it, no power held by any of the fey can dispel it. If anything it feeds this shadow of Duwar, giving it more power, encouraging it to spread faster."

"Tell me *everything*," I demanded, still dripping water onto the panelled floor, body simmering with distant aches. And yet I stood tall. "I need to know it all."

Althea nodded. "Get changed first. We must leave Grove immediately, as the storm Cassial unleashed is spreading in this direction fast. Gyah is waiting for us outside with a handful of mounts for the journey. Once we are safe in Wychwood, we can further discuss all that we have learned in the days you've been unconscious, and then we can plan how to fix this, once and for all."

Safe? I shook my head, pinching my eyes closed as a sudden spear of pain shot through my skull. "It sounds an awful lot like we are running from the problem."

"I hate to admit it, Robin, but running from Duwar is the only option we have. Nothing can stand against it, no power is strong enough to quell its thirst for devouring," Althea replied.

Except, I was alive, and with that, there was a part of Duwar still lingering inside of me. This was why Duncan and Erix didn't speak. Why they had a hesitation to tell me what was happening. Because they had worked out what lingered inside of me, and what I would do with it.

"I can fix this," I said, more to myself than anyone else.

"No, darling," Duncan said. "What this power is capable of outside a mortal or immortal body is unlike anything you can imagine. There have been Faithful I have sent to attempt to accept it into their bodies, but the power tore them apart. Fey too. Cassial has released a power back into the realms, poison with his intention for destruction."

"The same goes for one of my gryvern," Erix added, regret darkening his silver eyes. "And they met the same fate. Fey, human – brave souls have attempted to take the loosed power of Duwar into them, and they all perished. It is not just ruin that spreads, but death itself."

And yet Duwar was more than death. It was life too – it gave the fey power, it gave the world a purpose before it was banished to its dark void. Duncan had shown me that, spreading vines and flowers over the crumbled remains of Imeria castle. "And yet the issue still persists, and I still have part of that power inside of me."

I clutched at my chest as if my nails could sink through flesh and drag it out of me just to prove what I was saying.

"What?" Althea gasped. "You what, Robin?"

"I took that vial after Cassial expelled Duwar inside of me," I said. "He didn't trust me with all of it and kept a part for himself. We can run, but it will continue to spread, I don't need to be a scholar to know that."

Althea asked Duncan and Erix the question that I knew was pointless. "How long have you known?"

Duncan straightened, inhaling a sharp breath before replying. "I would recognise the echo of that power in any life."

Because he had shared it, Duncan knew on a deeper level. Or maybe, the path he saw this ending in, the one the Creator showed him, meant he always knew I would accept the power.

Either way, that didn't matter now. What mattered was using the second chance Seraphine had given me. Doing something worthy for the realms.

There was something in the way Erix looked at me that revealed his thoughts were in line with mine. That was why he hesitated to speak before, that was why he could barely look at me without it seeming like he was looking at someone already lost.

Because he knew what I had to do.

"Robin," Duncan said, shivering with unspent power, fingers flexing beside him as if he wanted to reach for me and never let me go. "I know what must be done, but that doesn't mean I want to accept it."

"Then you will not refuse me when I ask you to take me to it, will you?" I asked.

Duncan's eyes downturned to the floor, Erix stepping in and laying a comforting hand on his shoulder.

Their silence was answer enough.

I walked past them, toward the narrow window set into the far-off wall. Setting my gaze out across slanted rooftops and farm lands, I found what I was looking for. Or it found me.

A mass of darkness, a wall of pure power that swallowed the sky and the land behind it.

I clutched onto the window frame, sodden wood snapping beneath my hands.

"It's moving toward us," I said, watching the mass of darkness roll over fields, shadow-made talons gouging earth before swallowing it whole.

"And it has, for days now. Countless miles it has consumed, and yet as of this morning it changed its course to this direction," Althea said. At some point she'd come to stand beside me, a comforting hand laid on my shoulder. "Rafaela believed it is searching for something, a replacement for Cassial. Now I know why."

Tears filled Althea's eyes as she realised what had to be done.

Turning my back on the view outside, I looked to Duncan, who would understand my next words better than anyone. "Me."

"Yes, darling. Like calls to like." Duncan stepped out of Erix's embrace. "Give it to me. I brought it to the realms, let me be the one to fix it."

I shook my head, smiling at his ease of putting himself before me. "No, Duncan. And I am not scared of it."

There wasn't an ounce of a lie in my words.

I looked back out the window, drinking in the rolling clouds of pure darkness. "Duwar is broken. Two parts of a whole. And it is no different to my own desperation of searching the realms for you if you were taken from me. If you take me to Wychwood, Duwar will follow. This is not something I can run from."

"I can't just accept that you are the heart of its desire, Robin," Duncan gasped.

It was in that moment I understood that the reason no one had given me answers was not because they knew I couldn't handle them. But because they knew what I would do when I found out.

"*I* can save us," I said, not needing to further explain myself.

It was as if Erix was ready for me to say those four words, because he broke, pain etched in the single word that came out of him. "I hate the world for making it so, but I trust in your strength, Robin. I believe in you."

I dared not move. My body was trembling, my power barely containable. Except it wasn't my power that was responding to the conversation. It belonged to another, the broken part of Duwar, left to wallow inside of me.

"I must go to it," I said, glad Althea was holding me up. "I can at least try."

"Please," Duncan said, this time shouting it, spittle flying out of his mouth. "Give it... to me."

The time for others sacrificing themselves for me was over.

Closing the space between us, I entered the bubble of affection that me, Erix and Duncan created just from our proximity. "Duncan, I must do it. And for that, I need your support. Remember what you showed me Duwar was capable of, spreading new life across the ruins of Imeria Castle? I can do it again, I can – I must at least try."

Duncan blinked heavily, releasing a breath full of tension. Then he looked from me to Erix. "It is our duty to support him, to stop him from putting himself in any further unnecessary danger."

"Even I must learn that we can't always do that, Duncan," Erix said, drawing a soft hand over Duncan's forehead. "Stand by him, not against him."

"Robin is not your broken little bird, Erix. And he is certainly not your incapable fey boy bound in chains, Duncan." Althea straightened, growing taller, shoulders rolling back. She did not wear a crown on her forehead, but she stood as if she bore one made of pure fire. "He is a king. And above that, he has already proven he would give his life for these realms. Aid him in this decision. He will need our belief in him to succeed."

Duncan looked up at me again, tears brimming in those eyes that I loved so much. And when he spoke again, it was with words that sang of his acceptance. "It is not our belief that matters. Robin trusts in himself, so I must accept that. I believe in him, but he too believes in himself. That is enough."

My heart swelled in my chest. I clung to the feeling, refusing to let it go. I mouthed my thanks, knowing how much this was hurting Duncan.

"Then the fate of the realms is in the best hands, little bird," Erix said. "You have my support."

Duncan lowered his head in defeat, chin to chest, leaning into Erix's side for support. "I could never stop you, Robin. You know that–"

The ground rumbled, shaking the foundations of my home. Dust fell from the rafters, furniture toppled over, glass smashed. Althea was in the door frame in seconds, breathless and panicked.

"Time to go?" Althea said, the glint in her amber eyes singing of her worry, but she too believed in me. After all, it was all their love and support, their patience in me, that moulded this very moment.

"How close is it?" I asked, sensing the tugging inside of me.

Althea's panicked eyes flared with fire. "Duwar's practically knocking on the front door for you."

CHAPTER 38

The mass of swirling, destructive power that was Duwar had spread like spilled ink across Durmain's landscape. It was a scar upon the world, a shadow demanding all light. Within it, flashing with flames amongst thick unnatural smoke, a monster roamed, but not one made from flesh and bone – one crafted from the twisted will of a person's final wish.

Ash coated the air, spoiling each inhalation, lathering my tongue with the taste of… death.

This was a disease on the realms – a physical reflection of Cassial's intent and promise.

Duncan had been the one to fly me toward it, with Erix following not far behind. Even from my distance, I couldn't fathom just how far the disease had spread. Miles. Leagues. Where human towns and villages had once been, was now swallowed whole by the gaping maw of this beast. It had almost reached past Wychwood's borders, creeping closer toward those who dwelled in the fey land. Whatever it had touched was left drained of life. Trees bowed, limbs frail and colourless. Even the air it touched seemed poisoned with the promise of more ruin.

We'd left Grove just as the mass of power overcame it, swallowing everything I had ever known in darkness.

And it wasn't going to stop. Devouring, destroying – but also something else.

It was searching. A broken lover, searching for the other part of them. The shard inside of me. I knew it like a deep

494

keening cry as the part of Duwar inside of me rose its head like a serpent from its nest.

"Where are the humans who lived in the affected areas?" It was the first question I asked after we landed. "Tell me they are safe…"

Gyah had not long transformed back into her fey form, smoke still slithering off her shoulders as though like called to like within the wall of storm half a mile ahead of us. We hadn't shared a moment of relief at seeing one another, because there hadn't been the chance. But we did share a look, one that spoke a thousand words. I had questions for Gyah, relating to Seraphine and her layers of plans. In time, if we survived this, we would discuss them.

"They have been evacuated into fey lands, as many as we could manage," Gyah said, voice thick with tension. "I believe those were your orders, to get them into Icethorn."

Relief swelled thick within me. "They were."

"Any we could not reach in time are currently on their way toward Lockinge," Gyah added. "We are trying to get as many people as possible away from this ruin, in hopes it gives us time to find a solution to this. Rafaela has promised haven in Irobel for children, women and the weak. But that blessing will only last until this rot turns its attentions to the seas and passes over them."

"Which is looking to be soon," Althea added. Her brow had furrowed as flame-filled eyes settled on the rolling mass of darkness. It swallowed up the sun, spoiling the sky in clouds of dark grey. "There is no power strong enough to battle this back. This is chaos incarnate. I have tried with my own magic, and the wall only seems to feed on it. But you, Robin – you *will* succeed."

Gyah stiffened, placing a hand on Althea's arm. "He has no choice but to beat this. We are all relying on you, friend."

I rolled my shoulders. "Thanks for the reminder." I flashed a pathetic grin at Gyah, one she gave me back, whereas her golden eyes revealed the concern she harboured inside for me.

I felt Erix's and Duncan's eyes bore into my skin. If I was brave enough, I would've looked at them in return, but I couldn't take my eyes off the ruin as it raced toward us. Billowing clouds spat out of the mass, roaring and spitting, devouring fields. As it touched the earth, it leached the colour, draining the very ground of the life it held.

No, not draining.

It was taking the power back.

It was Duwar who made this world, and it would be Duwar who'd destroy it.

"Althea and Gyah, you should leave now for Wychwood," Duncan said, voice raised above the sky-shattering roar of Duwar. "Gather a council, perhaps for any outcome. If Robin is unsuccessful, the doom falls back into our hands. We cannot waste time in searching other avenues."

"It won't be good enough," Gyah snapped. "There is nowhere we can hide from this."

"I will fix this," I said, turning my back on the ruin to face my allies.

I took my turn drinking them in, smiling naturally, as if death didn't race toward us. Althea, the fierce warrior. Gyah, the loyal protector. Erix, the guardian of my heart. And Duncan, the man who had hunted me down and captured my love. Four of the most important people in my life. People I'd give my life for, over and over.

"Robin, ready?" Erix asked, speaking for the first time since we arrived here. He was haunted by the possibility of his greatest fears but daring to admit them aloud.

"I am," I said to him, then swept my gaze over the small group. "And it's all going to be okay, I promise."

Duncan's eyes filled with tears, but this time he held them back, showing me the strength that I willed him to have. "You've got this, darling. Show that fucker exactly who you are, and what you are capable of."

The sky roared louder as the storm of ruin closed in. I

could see Gyah's urgency to leave in her inability to stand still. Althea too. "Althea, let's go."

"Yes," I agreed. "You need to leave. Get as far away as you can. Remember... I will see you soon."

Gyah's jaw tensed, lips pursing as she regarded me. "You better, Robin."

I nodded, smiling through the prick of tears behind my eyes. "I will."

"I don't want to leave you," Althea said, looking at me like I was crazed. She waved a hand, gesturing for us to make a move. "If you are to face this, you do it with all of us behind you."

"Oh, Althea," I said, grasping her hands and squeezing. "We both know that Gyah is never going to let you put yourself in any more danger than you've already faced."

"The princeling is right," Gyah said, tears spilling over her lips and curling down her chin. "But may I remind his lordship that if he doesn't come out of this alive, I will personally find his corpse and punch him in the dead face."

"If anything is enough motivation to beat this, that would be it," I laughed, sweeping my eyes over them all. "I won't fail because I know what I am fighting for – *who* I am fighting for."

"Comforting words, Robin," Gyah said, clutching Althea, who'd paled rapidly, colour draining from her face. "But if you survive this, I'm *still* going to beat the shit out of you."

"What for this time?"

"Scaring me," Gyah replied. "Always scaring me."

Gyah embraced me, holding me as if it was the final time. Which it might be. She brought her lips to my ear and whispered words meant only for me. "Before you go, Seraphine wanted me to remind you to be selfish."

"Seemed that she wanted a couple of people to remind me." A warm rush of shivers passed down my spine. "Well, you know me. It's one thing I'm good at."

"You deserve to live, just remember that. I think that is what she meant."

I took Gyah's reminder, storing it away in the chambers of my heart.

I turned next to Erix and Duncan, who stood side by side, equal in height, power and determination. For the first time, taking steps toward them was hard. But I did it, because I reminded myself that this was for them.

For the men who held my heart.

For the men who showed me the world I wanted to be a part of.

I'd do this for them – over and over, if given the choice. Because that was what love was, perseverance. Choice. And most importantly, power.

The ground shook as the mass of chaos and power raced closer. My core tensed, just to keep me standing steady, my boots sinking into mud-trodden earth. The more time that passed, the heavier the taste of ash and decay became. It lathered my tongue, tainting each inhalation and making the exhalation no more pleasurable.

I didn't turn to watch it arrive.

Althea took me in her arms a final time and wished me luck. From the shake of her voice alone, I knew she had little faith I was going to survive this.

But I would. I had too. I would survive, because we had finally achieved our tomorrow, and I wasn't going to give up on it.

Not yet.

"If there is anyone as stubborn enough to survive this, it is you." Althea's words warmed me from the inside out. Her stare was determined, and yet there was no denying the quiver in each word and what that meant. "Beat it."

"I'm not going to let a little storm cloud ruin my day, Althea."

She sniffed, drying her face with the back of her hand. "You better not. We deserve peace. All of us. That includes you."

"Something we can agree on."

She knocked my shoulder with her fist, stepping back before her body betrayed her. "It's a possibility. I just wish it was not you who had to deal with it."

"We all have a purpose, perhaps this is mine."

Fire lit within Althea's eyes, and then it was the Queen of Cedarfall who stood before me. "It better be, Robin Icethorn."

Gyah gathered Althea back, otherwise she would've never left me. "We love you, friend. Remember that."

"How could I ever forget?" I replied, offering her a sympathetic smile. "Is your promise of punching me still on the table?"

"Of course it is," Gyah snapped, her forced anger melting back into trepidation that they all faced me with. "If you die and upset Althea any more than she has already been, I'll find a way to strangle your ghost. Just *live*, Robin."

"That's the plan." I squeezed her fingers back. "Now, get Althea out of here."

As Gyah drew back, her skin melted to shadow and revealed the Eldrae lurking beneath. When she replied, it was half in words and the other half a tempered growl. "Already on it."

Watching Althea and Gyah leave was the most painful part. It solidified their goodbye into a physical thing, rather than words. There was so much that could've been said, but we didn't have time.

When I turned to Erix and Duncan – my strength incarnate – I found my knees weakening. I had to pretend I was okay, but looking at them, taking in the horror plastered across each of their faces, ruined me.

"Look after each other," I said before gritting my teeth to stop the sob from breaking free. "Promise me that at least."

Duncan steeled his expression, the scar down the side of his face deepening. He nodded, because clearly forging a word was impossible. I could sense it, in a way, his need to demand we all leave and find another way to solve this. But he knew, just as I did, that this was the only option.

"We will not be far, little bird," Erix said, stepping in and taking my hands. He was cold to the touch, as though the worry he held for me leached the warmth from his skin and soul. He had a haunted look about him, his pupils far too dilated for normal. "This is not a goodbye. It is only a see you soon."

"We will be reunited with you on the other side," Duncan added.

These could be my final words to them, I wouldn't part with a lie.

I lifted a hand, placing it carefully on the side of Erix's face. The second I touched him, Erix melted into my hold, leaning into my palm and releasing a groan. "I need you to say it, Robin. Tell me this is not a goodbye."

"Robin?" I spluttered feigned surprise to lighten the tension. "Is this really the time for using my actual name?"

His silver eyes pooled with tears. "You've always been Robin. My Robin, my little bird. The man who inspires me, the man who changed me and the man who saved me."

"I haven't saved you yet," I reminded him, the lump in my throat becoming unbearable.

Erix closed his famously silver eyes. "You know exactly what I mean."

"I know." A pain shuddered in my chest, part from emotion and the rest from the chasing storm of chaos at my back. It was gaining. Quickly. "This isn't over. We promised each other a tomorrow, and I am far too selfish to not see it through."

"Being selfish is not a bad thing," Erix added, staring deep into my soul. "You have always punished yourself for making decisions on your own, when all your life that is what you have relied on yourself to do."

"It has taken a long time to work that out, but I see it now. Because of you, because of your patience and guidance."

"It *is* my honour."

"As my personal guard?" I said, with a smirk that was seconds from breaking into a chest-breaking cry.

"No, little bird. As the man who loves you, without bounds and limitations."

I trailed my hand down his cheek, brushing my thumb over his lips. "I love you too, Erix." My eyes lifted over Erix's shoulder, coming to rest on Duncan, who had not stopped smiling toward us. "And you, Duncan Rackley. Come here."

Duncan lifted a finger to his eye, lowered to his heart and then slowly pointed toward me. Those actions spoke more than words. Duncan took confident steps, closing the space between us. Erix took the moment to step back, allowing room for Duncan, respecting that we all needed equal time.

As much as we pretended this was not a goodbye, it certainly felt like it. But I wouldn't leave until I had given them both their final command.

"You're the bravest person I know," Duncan said, running his hands up my arms as though using his last moments to memorise me. "I saw it in your eyes the first time we met, and I see it now. You'll do anything for the people you love, and that is an admirable trait."

Duncan leaned in and placed a kiss on my cheek. His lips brushed the corner of my mouth, and I fought the urge to back out of my decision. Which was why he did it – careful not to touch my lips completely. He knew I needed to do this, and no matter if both men hated that truth, neither one would stop me.

I steeled my expression, growing taller and broader, just at his confidence alone. "You're not going to try and stop me this time, are you?"

Duncan shook his head. "It would be a waste of breath, darling. I've tried that before and learned the hard way."

"Learned that I always do what I want?"

"No. I learned that you do what is necessary to secure the lives of those around you. When you took that vial, believing it was poison, it was to save the realms. That is the most *selfless* act of anyone I have ever known."

"I thought the whole point of this was that I was being selfish," I said, allowing myself to be wrapped up in his arms. His grasp was firm, his newly formed wings folding over me, encapsulating me in heat.

"To be selfish for selfless means is one of a thousand reasons why I admire you."

"Do we have time for you to share your list with me?" I scoffed, desperately wanting to draw out the moment, but knowing I couldn't.

The rumbling of thunder at my back told me I was right.

Duncan planted a kiss on my crown, exhaling a hard breath that spoke of a million unsaid things. "How about we make a deal. You go and save the realms, collect that lost part of Duwar, and then I will gladly sit and list every single one of the reasons why I love you."

"I like the sound of that," I replied, knowing this moment was coming to an end. But in my last grasp to enjoy this, I shot out a final command for Duncan, perhaps the most important. I made sure to keep my voice to a whisper, something only he could hear.

"Look after Erix," I whispered.

"He will be fine–"

"No," I stuttered. "I need to hear you say it. I need you to tell me you will care for him, look after him just as you have with me. He is going to need you – Altar, you'll need each other."

"Focus," Duncan choked. "Then return to us and be the one who completes that task."

"Duncan," I warned, the panic bubbling inside of me. "Please, say it."

He grasped my face, peering down at me. This close, I could see every pore and scar, and what I'd give to kiss each and every one of them one final time. "Okay, darling. It will be done."

I mouthed my thanks, unable to form the words aloud.

A bout of confidence raced through me as I took in both of my men. Before it faded, I turned my back on them and walked away. I didn't wait and watch to see them fly away. I didn't want to see them leave. Instead, I pretended like they were watching me as I walked over the trodden field, toward the moving wall of destruction and chaos.

Silently, with my fading focus, I opened myself up to the whimpering shard of Duwar in my chest. I coaxed it free, encouraging the broken power to rise to the surface. It came with ease, with bright wings of a white dove. I felt it rise in me, just like the ice I housed in my blood, except this was potent... ancient.

I faced the wall of power and sensed it the same moment it sensed me. I felt its course change in a heartbeat, as the rolling clouds of decay shifted in my direction and picked up speed.

The part of Duwar that had lingered in that storm found what it was looking for. Just as I hoped it would. And as the power demanded, it made toward me with haste.

In the face of danger, my mind lingered back to a moment many months ago.

Locked in a Hunter's cage, surrounded by frightened fey expecting to meet their end, I had comforted a child. The technique I used was one my father had taught me, over and over, as I grew up and discovered new fears. It was strange, because in that moment, I found myself reverting back to it.

So, I began to count.

"One."

The air scorched with power, making the hairs on my body stand to attention.

"Two."

I pictured two men in my mind, one with eyes of silver, the other with jewelled eyes of green. They stood, watching and proud, with nothing but the confidence that I would survive this. I had to believe them, otherwise I'd never make it through.

"Three."

I wondered if my mother and her family had the time to prepare when the monsters came to kill them. Was it better to meet death unsuspecting, or with the time to prepare for the unpreparable?

"Four," I screamed, finding my confidence wavering as the wall chased closer, tearing up earth, leaving nothing but char in its wake.

"Five."

I laid a hand over my chest, as if that would prevent it from splitting through bone, muscle and flesh.

"Six."

There were no more tears to cry. I knew why I was doing this. For me, for Erix, for Duncan and for every life that also waited for this doom to come and claim them.

"Seven."

Breathe, Robin. Breathe.

"Eight."

Duwar – or what remained of its corruption – was so close that I felt my skin singe. The violent clouds spat and hissed, like a beast loose from its cage, ready to wreak punishment on a world that had only ever used and abused it.

"Nine."

Power licked at my skin. I pinched my eyes closed as my name rang out at my back.

"Ten–"

Chaos engulfed me.

CHAPTER 39

Duwar gathered me into the heart of its storm. Vicious clouds of white-cored flames billowed around me, ripping my skin and snatching the hair from my face. My skin did not burn, my flesh resisting the licking tongues as though they enjoyed the taste but didn't want to devour me.

At least, not yet.

I fought against the tension, lifting a hand to shield my eyes, squinting to make sense of this hellscape.

Decay was everywhere. Ruined earth shattered beneath my feet, cracking to dry plates of mud. There was no life. Not a speck of it.

I supposed it was fitting, considering Duwar gave life, and yet it could take it away.

And that was exactly what the power did. Duwar took from the realms, just as Cassial's intended.

I wondered when it would finally take me.

Unlike the grass of the field that had been beneath me moments ago, I stood tall. My body had not yet shrivelled, the air in my lungs scorching but constant.

Duwar screamed like a dying animal both around me, and *inside* of me. It unleashed its fury around me, smashing power and debris into my body. An instinct told me to release more of the power lingering within me, to prove myself worthy of surviving this final trial. But I wouldn't give it what it wanted.

I refused the lure, instead I began to draw Duwar in. I offered the broken part of Duwar's vengeance a home inside of me, whilst securing one for my own if I succeeded.

A home, with Erix and Duncan, with my friends and those they loved.

And it worked. Duwar's power pierced me from either side. Thread upon thread of hot, angry power speared through my chest. The vacuous place in my chest began to fill, like a well in a storm, catching the rain and preventing the flood that would destroy the world.

The cost was yet to be made clear.

Pain. Pure, undulating agony exploded inside of me. I imagined that was what a star felt like when it died. Beautiful, no doubt, but the beauty was rooted in pure agony.

The clouds rolled over me, the darkness taking up my offer, the power sinking into my fucking bones. But it was too much. The more power that entered my body, the more I felt it press against my boundaries.

As suddenly as my own intentions worked in my favour, they began to slip.

"No," I groaned as my feet left the floor, the strain against my skin becoming all-consuming.

Rip-roaring winds lifted me up, catching me in the swirling mass of fury that was Duwar. I kicked against it. The air, in the belly of the storm, was poisonous. Each breath burned. At first it welcomed me, but it was as if Duwar itself was refusing my body – begging for me *not* to steal him.

I pinched my eyes closed, trying to focus on the battle, not on the fact that my skin felt like it was cracking apart as brimstone and the fire of ruin replaced my blood.

"Duwar," I screamed, choking on the name as though I wasn't worthy of it. And I wasn't. No one had been. Not even Altar as he used the chaos of the world and made the fey. Not the Creator who went to war for the unequal balance of power. "Please. Let. Me. *Help*."

If the power heard me, it didn't listen.

The shard inside of me shifted. Not moving to make room for Duwar, but it began to slip from its place. It stirred, as if Duwar was a serpent draining it from my flesh with fangs.

Panic seized me as I grappled, for the second time, to keep Duwar under my control. But like sand through splayed fingers, it left me.

I focused on my magic, mentally freezing the power in place until I could regain control. But it wasn't working. I felt the power of the storm around me triple in strength.

As Duwar began to leave me, that was when the real agony began.

I shrieked, but no sound left me. Tendrils of power held my mouth open, spreading down into my throat, searching for purchase to the power within. No matter how I tried, I couldn't close my mouth. My cry of desperation continued out of me without control, until my throat bled and the vessels in my skull popped one by one. Vaguely I was aware of the warm trickle of blood slipping out of my nose, down each ear and laying tear tracks down my cheeks. Even if I wanted to wipe my skin clean, my body was no longer my own.

I was a puppet on the strings of power, the puppeteer moments from destroying me.

It was just as the final thread of Duwar slipped down my mental fingers, I heard my name. It carried out across the wild storm, so poignant that even Duwar seemed to ease. I imagined the power turning its attention in the direction of the noise, surprised by the presence.

"Robin Icethorn."

My energy waned quickly.

I had enough to crack my eyes open and find out who called for me. My tired eyes found them, amongst the raging maelstrom of ruin and decay, stood two men.

An angel and a demon, side by side. Duncan and Erix.

"Robin, I command you to beat this!" Duncan bellowed, although his command sounded more like a whisper beneath a clamour of thunder. "Do you hear me? You will win this for *us*."

A single clear thought came to mind. *Why were they here?* They should've been so far away that nothing could harm them, and yet they stood amongst the destruction with little care for their own sakes.

Amidst the shield of purple lightning which kept most of the ruin away, Duncan and Erix had found me.

Spears of dark power lashed against Duncan's shield, looking for chinks in his armour, longing to devour them both – Duwar's last punishment for his misuse.

"Fight it, little bird!" Erix screamed, his words carrying over to me. "I believe in you! Duncan believes in you. But most importantly, you believe in yourself."

I blinked, vision blurring. "Go. Away."

"Never." Duncan fixed verdant eyes on me, boring through my weak, tired skin. "Fight it."

Seeing them both, knowing the pain they would suffer, reignited the last scrap of energy I had.

A war of intention and will, I grappled for the power leaking out of me, trying to afford the men I loved enough time to get far away from this destruction.

"Go." I could barely speak the word. It tore up my sensitive throat, burning like acid on the way up.

But neither man listened to me.

Instead, they proved themselves as stubborn as I was.

Without taking his eyes off me, Erix reached beside him and took Duncan's hand in his. They forged a link of flesh and bone, sending me a signal that they were never going to leave me – not in this life, and certainly not in the next.

This time, as the warmth slipped down my cheek, it was not blood but an honest tear. Seeing Duncan and Erix – facing the reality of danger they'd put themselves in – had forced me to not give up.

I had no choice but to fight for them. No doubt that was exactly the motivation they wanted to inspire in me.

"Life is not worth living without you," Erix shouted, his body rigid as the power battled against the shield Duncan held up. They waged forwards, light battling against darkness, life against death. "Use us. Take this as a reminder of why you cannot give up."

"That's why we are here," Duncan shouted. "Are you going to beat this, or give up?"

"I'm… trying," I sobbed, words barely a whisper, more to myself than anyone else.

Erix tore his harrowing gaze off me, laying it upon Duncan. It was a signal, a plan that only they knew.

"Then try harder, darling." Duncan lowered his outstretched hand, and the lightning around them simmered. Magic severed, the shield popped like a bubble, letting Duwar in.

This was their last-ditch effort to motivate me. Joined as one, eyes boring into me, Duncan severed the ties to his power.

It was going to kill them. Duwar would tear them apart the moment this decay got the chance. And they didn't have Duwar inside of them to protect them.

But I did.

Watching death race toward them was what my mind needed, just as Duncan knew would be the case.

I shouted at the power, sinking my talons into unseen flesh. Then, with the force of determination Erix and Duncan's presence awarded me, I clawed it back. I didn't coax it into me, but dragged it, like a fearful animal in a trap. I grappled and pulled, refusing to allow the power to reach them.

And slowly, second by second, it rescinded. Not without friction, not without a fight – but Duwar was mine, and so were the men I loved with every fibre of my being.

Saving the world was one thing and saving my own was another. And yet, both of those facts were hand in hand before me, waiting for death to claim them.

I wouldn't let it happen. I wouldn't allow Duwar to harm another. Not any more of the realms, and certainly not the two men who occupied my heart.

I'd had enough. Sinking my teeth into my lower lip, I focused on my task. Not once did I take my eyes off Erix and Duncan as they huddled together. The storm sensed their fear, as did I. Because I controlled it. It belonged to me.

The power was mine, so, I took it.

Every last bastard scrap.

I stopped only when the final whisp of decay slipped into my body, and the skies above were blue once more. Slowly, the raging winds died down, enough for me to lower myself to the ground.

Erix and Duncan tried to reach me before I hit the ground, but it was too late. I met it with force, slamming my hands and knees into ruined earth. Breathless, my mind detached and my body not completely my own, I could barely move.

The war may have been over, but the fight had just begun. It found a new battlefield, one inside of me. A war of wills, as Duwar's corruption and my control clashed.

"Robin," Duncan breathed, coming to kneel beside me. "You did it. My darling, you really did it!"

"I am so proud of you." Erix stood over me, his shadow casting a cool relief over me. My skin felt like it was on fire, my blood sizzling. I had no doubt he hated what he saw, the blood down my face, the pain evident in every crease across it. "You've proved, once again, that you can do anything–"

"I. Can't. Hold. It." I forced out my words, knowing time was limited.

Both their eyes widened, their touches becoming hesitant as they finally noticed the cracks forming across my flesh. Duwar could free themselves at any moment, shattering out of my body as though it was made of cracked glass.

I looked down to my arm, only to find the skin parting, allowing the decay to glow like lava through cracks of earth.

Duncan jolted toward me, laying a hand on my shoulder, ready to scoop me in his arms. His touch lasted but a second. I looked up to see smoke slithering off his palm as he clutched it to his chest.

My eyes widened as panic simmered beneath the battle inside of me. "I'm sorry–"

Erix tried next, cautiously reaching for me, only to find the tips of his fingers scorched. "What is happening?"

Their relief at the success they believed I held faded in seconds. The silence stretched on. I attempted to keep it bound inside of me, but the cost was going to kill me.

I was not fey – not completely. And Duwar knew that.

"Give it to me," Erix said, quietly at first. It took him but a second to realise why I suffered. Then he fixed his wide silver eyes on me, repeating himself but louder, with more vigour. "Give Duwar to me. I *willingly* take the burden."

I turned my head, gritting my teeth, blood spoiling the insides of my cheeks. "No. I can't – I won't put you through this."

"Robin," Erix demanded, using my name as a weapon. "It will destroy you. Remember, the power is not inherently bad or good. It is what we do with it. I can survive it. I know the cost."

Something about Erix's words sparked a solution within me. Duwar was continuing their campaign for release, but Erix was right. Duwar wasn't good or bad – not by choice.

It was what Duwar was used for that determined that.

I sank my fingers into the cracked, blackened earth. Erix didn't stop begging me to give the power to him, all whilst Duncan watched in shocked silence. I looked up, recognising just how far Duwar's power had devoured and destroyed. A blackened scar stretched out as far as I could see. In the distance, the sentinel barrier of Wychwood forest was charred, the trees skeletal. Behind me, farmer's fields were void of life. I could only imagine how far this destruction stretched, and how much more it would've taken.

A plague had swept the realms, and it required a cure.

I could be that cure, Duwar could be – if only it heeded my next command.

"Duwar demands release," I exhaled, breathless and suffering. "I need to let it go."

"Then give it to Erix," Duncan said finally. His tone was pleading, his words trembling with emotion. "If that is the only way for it not to claim you, then so be it. You must, Robin. Please, do it for us. Give up the–"

"No, Duncan," I seethed, focusing on him, finding that my eyesight faltered as his features blurred before me. "You showed me what Duwar could be used for. I didn't listen to you then – I should've listened."

Realisation lit Duncan's eyes, as though a beacon of hope sparked in the depths of his soul. "It's destroying you, there isn't time for talking, Robin."

"Life," I spat, ignoring his plea. "Duwar is not solely destruction and ruin, but it once was used for beautiful means. For life."

Duncan's eyes widened, realisation setting in. "It's not worth the risk."

I nodded, every passing moment leading to more pain, more suffering. "Yes, it is. You are. I can do it, Duncan – I can give Duwar new purpose."

Duncan pondered my words, knowing exactly what I referred to. It was Erix who replied, silver eyes sinking through me, piercing my soul and holding on. "Remind Duwar of the good it can award. I believe in you. I trust you. And I stand by you with this decision. Your intentions for the realm are, and always have been, good."

Even if I wanted to hesitate, there was no time left to. Duwar banged against the bars of its cage, shattering my flesh until strings of light and dark could be seen in place of muscle and vein.

I had to focus. If this was to work, my mind had to be clear of anything but the single intention I wanted from my next act.

I focused my intent and did the one thing I'd fought against. Then I released Duwar. But unlike Cassial and every soul who wished to use the power for bad, I focused on the possibilities of *good*. The healing, the life, the flourishment and love. I reminded Duwar what it had been before the corruption.

Fingers sinking into life-drained earth, I focused my desires and liberated Duwar.

Inside of me, it was no longer broken, no longer shattered into pieces. Closing my eyes, I focused on the two men before me. I pictured a life we could have, one together, no longer under threat.

I gathered that image in my mind, something solid and so tangible I could almost touch it.

Erix and Duncan stood in the kitchen in my home, laughing at something one of them said whilst washing dirtied dishes. I could smell the aroma of food they cooked, feel the warmth awarded by their happiness. The picture built in my thoughts, in full colour, heightening every one of my senses.

"For our tomorrow," I stammered the promise we'd made to one another. And then I released the power back into the realms, just as Cassial had before he was killed.

Fresh shards of grass sprouted through the cracked earth between my fingers. Where the ground had been solid under my palm, it now softened with life as flowers grew. It spread in a wave, flooding out of me with the desperation of a bird fleeing a cage. I simply reminded Duwar what it could be.

Duncan laid a hand on me again, and this time he didn't burn to the touch. "And for all our tomorrows after that."

Erix followed suit, gathering me up in his arms, whilst I continued to pour Duwar into the ground, offering it life, guiding it.

"Until so many years pass that we forget about our tomorrow and focus on nothing but the now," Erix encouraged. "Together, at last, with nothing but joy to separate us."

Power had been what the gods had fought over. It had split the courts in Wychwood, turning allies to enemies, leading to my mother's death. The realms had warred over it.

But for once, it would be power that brought us together.

"No more suffering," I said.

"Spread those wings, little bird." Erix pressed his mouth to my temple, holding the kiss there as I continued to free Duwar, but not from a place of hate and ruin. I was engulfed in love, and I made sure to expose Duwar to the same concept.

"No more wondering about the possibilities of what would happen if the world was in our favour," I said as the rush of life fed the earth, imagining it spread for miles, fixing the destruction Duwar had left in its wake. "It is about our *today*. That is what matters. Not what came before, or what will come after. We enjoy the present, because that is what we fought hard for."

"Today sounds beautiful," Duncan said, running his hands in circles around my back, whilst wrapping the other over Erix's neck.

"Today, yes," Erix repeated, laying his forehead on mine. "For today."

Gathered in the arms of the men who held my heart equally, my fingers buried in the dirt, the last scrap of Duwar left me. I felt relief bloom inside of me, instead of the hollow, empty void. There was room for it now.

"For us," I said, rocking back into the arms of the men I loved. Something cool and damp slipped over my knees, soddening my trousers. I looked down, not sure what I'd find. But what I did shocked me to my core.

Where we knelt, water spouted upwards. It was crystal clear, and fresh. It welled up, building until it soaked through our trousers, not stopping until we were waist deep.

Duwar had been freed, and so had I.

We watched as more water rose out of the earth, relishing in the cold kiss as it worked at my sore skin, washing away my worries and anxieties.

My head spun as exhaustion rocked through me. I forced to keep my eyes open, not wanting to miss a moment of the miracle that occurred before us. As light spread beneath blackened earth, life sprung forth and spread like a wildfire across the ruined landscape.

"It is time to go home."

I wasn't sure which one of them said it, but I revelled in the promise of the words.

"Home," I repeated, tasting the joy of that single word across my parched tongue.

Arms wrapped around me, wings beat, and we were airborne. My tired eyes opened enough to look down at the earth. Stretched out for as far as I could see, was a lake – sunlight glittering across its surface, sparkling like a million diamonds.

Where Duwar had drained and destroyed, new life was given. I watched rivers spread like searching fingers, revitalising trees and fields, returning colour to a world that had been leached of it.

My mind was slow, at the cusp of collapse, and yet I fought against it, not wanting to miss a single detail. Duwar had found a new home, just as I had secured my own. It was over – the realms saved – and even in my tired state, I knew that life had only just begun.

CHAPTER 40
SIX MONTHS LATER

My ears rang with the cheers of the fey procession. I imagined it would take days more for my eardrums to settle, and the thundering beat of footsteps to stop reverberating in my bones. Not that I cared. Because seeing Erix take the mantle of King of the Oakstorm Court, was one of the greatest days of my life.

It had been six months since I released Duwar into the world, and the lake it created glistened before me. Summer sun beat down onto the body of water which separated Wychwood from Durmain. A place that had become a meeting point for the humans and fey in the months past.

It represented peace: Duwar's waters signifying life and hope.

The fields around it flourished with life, the forests and woods fed from the well of pure power. Villages and hamlets that the chaos had ruined had been reclaimed – and with the help of the fey, we'd begun to rebuild homes for those who'd been displaced.

Aptly named the Waking Shallows, in conjunction with the Sleeping Depths – the lake had become a symbol, for the fey and humans, as to what price was paid to secure the future.

And there hadn't been a day in the past six months that had been wasted.

I peered over the edge of wooden slats, catching my reflection in the azure lake. Wide black eyes set in a fuller face, with skin glowing with vitality. Seeing the man in the water made it impossible to imagine the terror and pain that had come before. Sometimes it was easier to hide from reminders, but every time I laid eyes on the Waking Shallows, I felt a sense of clarity to the past.

Over the far side of the lake, the humans stood, flanked by the Faithful. Rafaela was at their helm, her wings grown back in place, speckled with a multitude of greys, whites and browns. In her arms she carried a rather plump looking child – the human heir to Durmain, Princess Eugena.

I tipped my head in Rafaela's direction, our eyes locking, and silently promised to speak with her tonight during the celebrations. The slight tip she returned confirmed it.

The Waking Shallows' water was so clear I could see the bottom, where fish of the most vibrant colours swam amongst reeds and breathtaking purple flowers. Swans with elegant necks and prowess jetted over calm waters, dancing for all to see.

I wasn't the only one who sensed the magic oozing from the lake's surface. In the past weeks we had heard of humans with aliments who bathed within the lake, climbing out revitalised. Crops once afflicted with diseases had been cured.

This was what power should have always been used for.

I looked out across the wooden jetty, gaze fixing to where Erix stood, his broad outline reflected on the water behind him. A crown of gold, inset with the cut-out emblem of the summer court, literally glowed on his head. It refracted the light across the planes of his face, making him glisten as though he too was made from the same luscious metal.

"He needs to stand up straighter," Duncan commented from my side. His attention was fixed on Erix too, pride evident in every smile line, hands nervously wringing before him. "I told him that before we left, and yet he still slouches."

"Keep your voice down," I said out the corner of my smiling mouth. "You and I both know it is Erix's impressive wingspan that affects his stance. No one can blame him for that."

"You and the obsession with wingspan." Duncan flashed me a mischievous grin, his white wings coming to fold around my shoulder. He lifted his left hand, flashing the band of silver wrapped around his ring finger. "Any more mentions of it and I might start to get a complex."

I leaned into his side, delighting in the strength of his constant presence. "Remember what I said last time?"

Duncan's tongue traced his lower lip, before replying. "It's not the size, but what you do with it?"

I giggled into my fingers, a blush creeping over my cheeks. "I thought we were talking about wings, Duncan?"

He laughed too, the sound melodic and as beautiful as the lake of life stretched out before us. "Oh, were we?"

"No more nitpicking the Oakstorm king, Duncan. You might find yourself getting in trouble," I said.

"Trouble is my middle name. Even if I wasn't under the protection of two kings, I welcome it. Although, I hardly imagine my head is under any threat – unless you are talking about a different head than I'm thinking about, darling?"

"Does everything that comes out your mouth need to be so filthy?" I asked.

I scrunched my nose up, leaning on my tiptoes to lay a kiss on his cheek. His beard had grown out, the coarse hairs tickling the soft of my lips. Duncan knew how much I enjoyed that very tickle – especially in-between my thighs – so it became his personal mission to continue growing it out.

"No," Duncan replied. "Sometimes the things going in my mouth are just as naughty."

My cheeks flushed with heat, staining them a deeper scarlet. The crowd around us erupted in cheers once again, distracting me from the budding heat in my groin. "Best we save this conversation for later I think."

"I bloody hope so," Duncan replied out the corner of his mouth as he began to clap his hands, joining in with the crowd around us. "It will certainly get me through the next couple of hours."

Across the distance between us, I locked eyes with Erix for a fleeting moment. Elation and pride swelled in my chest. Seeing him finally accept his own truth made me breathless, just as he had the first day I laid eyes on him. Garbed in silver-plated armour, he glowed beneath the sun, his skin dusted in gold leaf that Althea Cedarfall had supplied.

Erix ignored the Elmdew dignitary he was speaking with, focusing only on me.

"Hello, little bird," he mouthed.

I fought the awkward urge to raise a hand and wave at him. Instead, I mouthed back. "My king."

My eyes fell to the silver band on Erix's ring finger, matching the one Duncan wore and the same I also had on mine. It was an engagement – a promise to one another. Although marriage was never something I imagined possible for me, nor coveted, seeing the band on his hand made me buzz from the inside out.

It had been close to two weeks since I'd last seen Erix, and my body was practically trembling from the need to touch him. He'd been kept busy in Oakstorm, gathering his support, solidifying a new council whilst I was doing the same on Icethorn lands.

Keeping myself distracted from our separation, I'd thrown myself into helping the many humans who took up residence in my court, alongside aiding the fey who had chosen to move into Durmain. There'd been so much paperwork I was surprised my fingers hadn't fallen off. Bless Eroan, he'd done anything he could to make my life easier. Even learning to forge my signature, which was something Duncan wasn't too pleased about.

I had to force myself to look away from Erix before a fire started in my groin. Two weeks without him – his touch, his kiss, his taste – had turned me into something feral. This must've been how Althea and Gyah felt the night before their wedding ceremony a month back. I had put down Althea's constant downing of sparkling wine to nerves, but now I know it was because she was simply filling the void of the woman she loved with alcohol.

Altar, hand me a glass or *four*. I would drink the barrel dry just to stop myself from imagining how I would be celebrating our reunion tonight.

"Regardless of his hunched shoulders, Erix looks perfect, don't you think?" I asked.

"He does indeed," Duncan said as Erix continued the procession down the jetty toward us. He had to stop at every court member– the names of whom I'd still not memorised. "Erix was born for this, and it suits him well. Just perfect."

That it did.

I was jealous of every moment he gave to another person. By the time he was halfway down the line, I was practically trembling with the need to stand inches before him.

"Ethereal," I replied. "Perfect seems like not enough of a word to describe him."

"Not long left, darling." Duncan leaned in, lips brushing my ear. It was his turn to kiss my cheek, his tempered breath tickling over my skin. "We will be reunited soon enough. I don't know about you, but I certainly have some interesting suggestions of what we can do when the sun sets, and we are all alone together."

"Careful, Duncan." I winked. "Keep those ideas you have as a surprise."

"You always did like a surprise," Duncan growled, his eyes burning with pent-up lust.

With so many eyes on me, it would've been improper to grab the – no doubt hardening – bulge in Duncan's trousers, especially during the coronation of a king.

"I'm seconds from burning up."

"Are you, darling?" Duncan's eyes drank me in from head to toe. "I can practically see the thoughts swimming behind those eyes of yours. Say the *right* thing and I might just take you here and now."

"As much as I would like that," I replied, rubbing my now sweating palms down my silken trousers. "I can cope for another hour or so."

"I'm rather enjoying the direction this conversation is going," Duncan encouraged.

"I can tell. Perhaps we can talk about something else?" I pleaded, wiggling to get comfortable in my almost-too-tight trousers. "Something that's going to *calm* me down?"

"Of course, Your Majesty." Duncan settled his eyes back on Erix, copying me as we waited for him to make his way down the line. "How about the topic of the impending potato harvesting and how we are still going to be short to feed a court full of people. If anything can make me limp, it's the discussion of vegetables."

I choked on a laugh, catching myself with fingers placed over my lips. "And then I will remind you, for the umpteenth time, that trade routes have opened between Durmain and Wychwood. We no longer need to rely on our own supplies, or those of our neighbouring courts, to help us. And who are you kidding, Duncan? Remember what you wanted to do with the carrot–"

"Okay, okay," Duncan hushed, turning his back to the crowd so he peered down at me, eyes alight with equal excitement. "Who would've thought a discussion of food supplies was going to go in *that* direction?"

"I mean, I'm all down for trying something new for once."

Duncan knew I was joking, but only in part. So, to stop myself doing or saying anything else incriminating, he captured my jaw in his large hand and laid his lips on my mouth. I melted into him, tongues mixing, teeth grazing. I was starved, so much so that I almost longed for the world to fade away, so we could turn this kiss into the storm it wanted to be.

He came away breathless, all whilst my body still leaned into him, seeking more.

"How am I going to cope without you for the next few days?" Duncan asked, laying his forehead on mine, a taint of sadness lingering across his tone.

"You'll be fine," I said, although I thought the same. "We have managed it before; we can survive it again."

"Speak for yourself," Duncan replied, hardening in every sense of the word. "It is not the time apart, but the distance that will be between us. That will be the hardest part."

I shook my head. "I think we will survive, even though the bed is going to feel rather empty. It is only a few days; you will be far too busy in Irobel to think of me–"

"Lies, darling. There isn't a moment of the day that passes without you occupying my thoughts."

"Say that again and I will refuse you permission to leave me."

"Then tell me to stay," Duncan whispered as the crowd rose in yet another cheer. "Please."

I couldn't see Erix; he was blocked from view behind Duncan's frame. But I imagined he was close to reaching us, and that made my heart leap in my chest.

Reaching up, I laid a hand on the side of Duncan's face. He leaned into it, releasing a low groan. "Duncan, you *must* go. The Faithful need you. Just be quick about it, bring back the books, any knowledge you have and..." I stopped myself before my tongue got me in trouble.

"And?" he echoed.

"Just make sure there's not a single Fallen left, okay?"

I hated how easy it was to talk about the demise of the twisted Nephilim who, even after Cassial's death, persisted in their desires to rule the realms. Six months, and hardly a percent of them had retracted their dark desires and changed their ways. Because of that we were left with only one choice to deal with them. A choice that would protect the peace that we had finally achieved across the realms.

A creeping sadness filled Duncan's eyes but lasted but a moment. "Do you think I should give them more time?"

The ice-cold, ruthless side to me came out in full swing. It took effort to hold the majority of my bite back. "You've given the Fallen half the turn of a year to change their ways, to repent. And they haven't. We all have had to make decisions and choices we aren't happy about. This is one of them."

I knew that the idea of putting the Fallen through the Binding ceremony displeased Duncan, but it was the only way. And it wasn't to say that they wouldn't get a chance to change their ways, in the future. Duncan would return after some time, free them, offer them a new life, and it was up to them to decide what they wanted.

Anyway, a little solitary confinement never hurt anyone.

"It's a better option than death," I reminded him. "They have some alone time, hopefully a good old think, and then they will be given a choice. You can't do any more."

Duncan dropped his chin to his chest. "You're right. I know you are."

"Of course I am," I muttered, patting him on the shoulder. "I'm *always* right."

"Even about the carrot conversation?" Duncan raised a single brow, the right side of his mouth turning upward, flexing the scar down the side of his face.

Before he could reply, another voice spoke. It was made of silk, a soft purr that sent a shiver straight into the centre of my core.

"I have been gone for two weeks, and you are discussing replacing me with a carrot?" King Erix Oakstorm scoffed, his intense gaze making my skin tingle with burning need for him. "It would have to be a rather impressive carrot if that was the case."

"My king," I breathed his title, just as Duncan stepped aside, revealing the summer court king before me.

"*My* king?" he replied, soft lips curved into a smile, silver eyes glistening. "I could get used to that."

Erix turned to Duncan, clasped his hand and brought him in for an embrace. It was not like the way Erix held me, but the intimacy between them had built to new levels. I enjoyed the soft moments they shared, even the light kiss Erix planted on either side of Duncan's cheeks. It warmed my soul to witness – and other parts of me. As Erix withdrew, Duncan lifted Erix's knuckles to his mouth and offered the same kiss in return.

"Your Majesty," Duncan purred. "I can speak for us both when I say you have been sorely missed these past couple of weeks."

"The feeling is mutual, Duncan Rackley," Erix replied, sweeping his eyes between us, making my clothes feel tight and skin far too hot for normal. "But I'm back now. With no plans to leave you for the foreseeable."

If I wasn't so enamoured by his presence, perhaps I would've said something. Instead, I drank Erix in, leaving no inch of his body spared.

"Promise?" I asked.

Erix's steel gaze narrowed, his crown refracting light across where I stood. "With my soul."

"Erix, I admit you've done well today." Duncan stepped back, and I swear my heart exploded like a dying star. Seeing them both, side by side, was an image I'd want immortalised. If I could stop time, and paint them together, I would have. "It is no easy feat to stand before two realms and accept yourself as a king."

"You would know that, Duncan?" Erix nudged his side, nose scrunching up endearingly.

"Take the compliment," Duncan said.

"Oh, I will," Erix replied. "Although, when they tried dressing me in in reds and burgundies, I *had* to refuse. The Oakstorm court has been given a new lease of life, and I refuse to lead it in the colours of my... of Doran Oakstorm."

Duncan mocked a gasp. "How dare they! You need an Eroan in your life."

"Or a flock of gryvern at my back," Erix replied, eyes constantly flickering to me. "It was high time the Oakstorm Court had a change anyway. I thought it was easier to start with the colours of my clothes, before moving onto more politic matters."

"Such as?" I asked, worried that he had already faced resistance to his claim.

"Like taking away the land given to Doran's favoured supporters. Turns out a lot of them aren't too happy about a gryvern becoming king. The same group who didn't want Elinor as queen either. It would seem it takes a lot to please them, and luckily, I have a lot in me to give."

Erix lifted long fingers and placed them to the metal clasp holding his cloak over his shoulders. It was the brooch that Elinor had given him all those months ago. Seeing it over his heart made mine shiver, reminding me of the woman who had not made it to today.

"She would be so happy to see you today," I said, offering the little comfort those words could conjure. "This was the future Elinor foresaw for the Oakstorm Court. You'd make her proud."

Shared blood or not, Elinor accepted Erix as her own. She had lost two sons and had space within her heart for more. I was overwhelmed with the belief that she would be looking down on us, pride overspilling, just to see us enjoy a future that was taken from her.

"I hope so," Erix said, his voice heavy with emotion. "I do this to make her proud."

"I know," I replied, offering him a gentle smile.

We held each other's eyes, and the world seemed to fall away.

"On that sombre note," Duncan announced. "I should go and speak with Rafaela before tomorrow's journey to Irobel. I'll leave you both to... reacquaint, although I ask that your refrain from exploring that concept *too* deeply. Save it for my return in a matter of hours."

"I can't make any promises," Erix said, unable to take his attention off me. I felt so small beneath him, so fragile. In his hands, I'd let him break me and put me back together, just to be broken again. "Although, as king, you have my word that I will try my very *fucking* best."

"Language, Erix," I said, wide eyed as a few fey nobles gasped at their new king's use of curses. "It's unbecoming of the new Oakstorm king."

He leaned in, cool breath working against my cheek as he lowered his lips to my ear. "What *is* unbecoming are the thoughts currently racing through my head."

"And on that note, let me get my duties over with so we can explore those thoughts." Duncan chuckled, patted Erix on the back and offered me a wink. "See you shortly."

I nodded, fighting the urge to tell Duncan not to leave.

With the swift beat of his snow-white wings, Duncan flew across the Waking Shallows, directly toward Rafaela.

Erix beamed down at me, drinking me in with eyes that devoured me whole. "I have missed you very much, little bird. Saying that seems like the right thing, when the truth is the words barely scrape the sides of what I really have felt in the past two weeks."

His words encouraged a long groan to escape my lips. "Gods, and I've missed you, too."

Erix offered me the crook of his arm. "Grove is only a short flight away from here. Duncan will know where to find us. How about we get out of here before I'm thrown into yet more dull conversations about Oakstorm's treasury and agriculture?"

"But... this is your day. No doubt your council have you scheduled for meetings and conversations aplenty, before tonight's celebrations. I have waited for your return up until now, and I can manage a few more hours–"

"It would seem that your patience is far greater than mine. There is only one way I would like to celebrate my coronation, and that is with you, at home, with my face buried between your thighs. However, I would gladly settle for just the company if that is what you are suggesting?"

Home. Grove. The little house I had grown up in, which had become a meeting point for when our duties separated us. It had been ravaged when Duwar's power devoured the village – but what remained had been rebuilt, something both Erix and Duncan had arranged in secret for me.

"Trust me," I whispered, "I want nothing more than to spend the next few hours with you away from so many prying eyes."

"Then it is decided. Let's go before I can't hold back anymore and bend you over for all the realms to see."

"Erix," I gasped, enjoying the way his true name rolled off my tongue. "What a wicked tongue you have."

"Want me to put it to the test?" He nudged his offered arm again, and this time I took it.

"I do," I said, stomach flipping, my groin burning like a furnace in my trousers. "In fact, it is all I want."

"Then it is my duty, as your most loyal ally, to make sure you are satisfied." With one dramatic shift, Erix snatched me from standing, laid me out across his arms and lowered his face to mine. "Hold on tight, little bird."

I wrapped my arms around the back of his neck, mouth salivating so much that I couldn't reply for fear I'd dribble down myself. Disgruntled mumbles sounded around us as the star of the celebrations leapt into the air, stealing me away, leaving the pompous affair behind.

I looked back, just in time to see flaming-red hair. Althea was laughing at something Gyah was whispering into her ear, whilst both their eyes were locked on me. In a gesture that spoke a million words, Althea lifted a hand to her forehead and saluted me.

Ever the ally, ever my most loyal supporter. Althea always celebrated the moments when I broke the mould, and this was no different.

* * *

My back arched from the bed, my scream of pleasure so powerful the glass in my window frames shuddered. With one hand I reached backwards, grasping the headboard, whilst my other hand was tangled in Erix's hair, keeping pace as he devoured my cock with his desperate tongue.

I had to pinch my eyes closed, because if I looked at him – saw his enjoyment and the attention he paid to me – I would've reached my end before the fun truly began.

"You taste divine, little bird," Erix gasped, taking a moment to catch his breath. "Nothing in all the realms could ever be as sweet as you are."

As Erix righted himself and crawled atop me, every single muscle across his stomach rippled. I didn't need to count them to know all eight mounds were there, far more prominent than they had been the first time we shared a bed.

"If that is the case, why have you stopped?" I pouted, only for Erix to catch my lower lip between his teeth.

He released it, and I tasted the hint of blood. It excited me no end. "Because any more and you would have burst. And I am a man of my word. A promise to Duncan is important. We can finish this when he returns."

We'd been waiting for Duncan for hours now. Which meant hours of edging each other, existing on this bed as if the world beyond didn't matter. Not that the time had dragged at all. In fact, I only knew the day had passed because outside, the sky was black, with the occasional glow of fire displays in the distance, courtesy of Althea.

"So *I* deserve the punishment for *his* tardiness?" I asked, running my tongue over my lip as it already began to heal. "You would really deny me my pleasure?"

"That is one way to look at it." Erix spun me around so quickly my eyes blurred. One minute I was on our bed beneath him, the next I was straddled over his waist. I sat back, rocking myself on his impressive, hard length – coaxing his need to fuck me away from the guidelines of 'promises made to Duncan'. It was becoming harder and harder to wait for the release.

"Whatever ideas of pleasure you think you are about to experience, little bird, you can't possibly imagine even half the truth of it. When our beloved walks back into this room, only then will you truly understand that word for all it encompasses."

My heart leaped in my throat, choking me like hands around my throat – which was turning out to be something I enjoyed as of late. "I like the sound of that."

"I like the sound of your groaning when I'm inside of you."

"Fuck me, Erix," I said, running my finger down his sharp nose.

"Oh, I intend to." Erix reached up, placing both hands behind his head. His wings were splayed out like a sheet beneath us. I ran my finger down their edges, enjoying the sensitive purr he released. "In the meantime, you *could* make yourself useful."

Mischievous hope glittered in his eyes, evident from the way he waggled his brows at me.

"Useful?" I gawped, reaching back and cupping his balls. I squeezed, not too tight, but enough that it elicited a snarl of excitement from him and, more importantly, want. "Care to expand?"

"Are you going to make me beg?" Erix asked. "You know what I want."

"I mean, seeing you beg for it wouldn't go amiss."

Erix lifted his hips, pressing his cock harder into the soft of my ass. "Please, oh mighty world-saver, oh favourite king of mine. Suck my cock. Show me exactly how wicked that mouth can be."

Pinching my fingers around his nipple, I conjured a little ice to encapsulate the tip. "How could I say no to someone with *such* impressive manners?"

Erix reached over and tangled his fingers in my hair. With his gentle but guiding push, I repositioned myself, crawling like a cat on all fours, until I faced his cock.

Taking the base in my hand, I brought it to the pad of my tongue and slapped it upon it, three times.

"In," Erix growled, practically dribbling with anticipation.

Not needing more encouragement, I took his length as far down my throat as I could manage. Erix Oakstorm, ever the challenge. With every ache of my jaw, it only forced me to work harder. Tongue wrapping around his shaft, I sheathed him inside until the gag forced me to stop.

Tears of pleasure filled my eyes, pouring down my cheeks, soaking my skin. Erix reached up and cleared them away. Knotting his fingers in my hair once again, he guided me back to my task.

With my lips and starved tongue, I showed him just how much I missed him.

"Good boy," Erix purred. "My good, *good* boy."

I didn't notice the door to the bedroom open, or the footsteps, until the cool brush of a breeze dusted across my parted arse. "Well, isn't *this* a welcoming sight."

"Finally, the Saviour arrives," Erix said, leaning up on his haunches. "Better late than never."

I looked behind me, Erix's hard cock gripped in my hand. Duncan's gaze darkened as he took me in, on my knees, arse positioned up. Unable to take his eyes off my sex, Duncan's hands rushed to fumble with the belt at his waist.

"Join us," I encouraged.

His trousers slipped over powerful legs, before he stepped free of them. "Oh, I certainly intend too."

The way Duncan looked at me set a rushing blaze within my chest.

"I hope you've been so busy that you've built up an appetite?" I asked. "Because a feast awaits you."

I already knew his answer.

"I'm famished," Duncan replied, confirming my thoughts. "Utterly, desperately *famished*."

Working Erix's cock with my hand, I looked back to watch Duncan shed the rest of his clothes on the bedroom floor. His eyes were lost to my entrance, completely engrossed with it

I delighted in the way his tongue lapped over his lip, a glistening line of spit left in its wake.

"Get back to work, darling," Duncan said as he came to kneel at the end of the bed. "Don't stop on my account. You know I enjoy watching."

Smiling to myself, I did as he asked, knowing exactly what was coming next. Duncan spread my arse apart, lowered his tongue to my entrance, and began the feast he'd finally arrived in time for.

We were a tangle of perfectly poised bodies. Erix was content with having his cock in my mouth, so he carefully leaned over my back to pass the vial of lubrication to Duncan. There was always a supply in the bedside drawer, where once had been books and miscellaneous items. I didn't ask which of them supplied it, but there was always plenty to spare.

Just as stores of milk, bread and soap were necessities in life, so was lubrication in our case.

As one, Erix and Duncan turned me on my back. The care that they put into every move was obvious. Erix placed a pillow beneath the bottom of my spine, propping my hips up. He helped place my legs over Duncan's shoulders, laying kisses up my thighs and over my shins.

Duncan busied himself with drawing a couple of my toes into his mouth. There was never a chance he missed to wrap his tongue around each digit, hungry eyes fixed to me, then to Erix.

"Now these are exactly the type of celebrations I had in mind for today," Erix said as he knelt at my side, turned my head with a careful hand and placed his rock-hard length back into my mouth.

"I always knew you had good taste, Erix." Duncan's fingers worked to touch every inch of me, memorising me with his touch as if he didn't already know me to the finest detail.

"Something we share in common," Erix added.

"Then would you both get to work," I begged, mouth salivating for what was to come. The pleasure, the enjoyment – existing with them in the same moment was life's greatest joy. "I can't wait another second for this."

"I'm going to make you enjoy every fucking moment." Duncan simmered as he righted himself, lathered his cock and then proceeded to guide the thick head to my entrance.

The warm spread of pleasure and pain echoed up my spine. The feeling only intensified as Duncan eased himself into me.

Duncan's strokes started off slow, then built as he recognised my body growing used to him. Two weeks without sex, and I felt like it was the first time again.

"Take your time, Duncan," Erix warned, reaching over and brushing soft, encouraging fingers down his hard jaw. "He is all yours tonight. Only fair since I've got him to myself for the next few days. Do not be surprised if when you return from Irobel, you will find us here, in the same place you left us."

"I don't – blame you – *Erix*." Duncan could barely get his words out as he fucked me. Pleasure creased his face, made him breathless. Sweat glistened over his brow, making the strands of dark brown hair gather at his temples. "Robin, you feel... incredible." At his praise, I forced my arse to tighten, making Duncan throw his head back and moan to the darkened ceiling. "*Gods*."

"Am I that good that you thank the gods for me?" I asked as Erix continued stroking his cock over my face, toying with my desperate, reaching tongue. My mouth was full of his taste, my body screaming with the welcome tension of Duncan's cock. I smiled up at the dark, closing my eyes, enjoying every exploding sensation as if it was the first and last time.

"Yes," Duncan cried out. "I thank them for you – *both* of you."

We existed like this for as long as we could hold off. But like all good things, we found our end soon enough.

Erix reached his climax first. I took his seed in my throat, swallowing it down deep. He then got to work on me, with the aid of Duncan's hand on Erix's head, he sucked me in, encouraging me to swell in my pleasure.

It was bliss. It was everything – this moment. The three of us, as one, sharing moments no one else could understand.

And I felt worthy of it.

Duncan finished a few seconds after I did. He withdrew from me slowly, chest heaving with each breath.

Yes, the sex was incredible, but it was the moments afterwards that I craved the most. The constant praise, the touches and tired kisses. Sometimes we would go rounds, and other times we'd finish each other off before the penetration could begin. But it *always* ended the same. With both their bodies next to me, hands laid out on my stomach, or fingers grasping my thighs. If I closed my eyes, I wouldn't know who touched what, and which hands belonged to whom.

That was exactly how I liked it – how I liked *us*.

"Well, that certainly was worth the wait," I said, filling the silence, breathless as if I had just run across the realm and back again. In truth, all I'd done was lie on my back. "If I could feel my legs, I would demand we go again."

"Indeed it was, little bird," Erix cooed, brushing soft fingers over my lower stomach, painting circles against my damp skin. "More than words could possibly describe."

He nestled into my side, the pillow shifting as he added his weight to it.

Duncan did the same. "I would suggest that we should go back outside and join the party. But I think we've missed most of it by now."

"How unfortunate," Erix mocked.

"Oh well," I echoed. "I am exactly where I want to be. Duties can wait, but my love for you both will never."

"My sentiment exactly," Erix said, giggling softly into my ear, tired mouth pressing soft butterfly kisses to every bit of skin he could reach.

"Life would be even better," Duncan began, leaning up to catch his eyes, "if only we could exist like this without duty getting in the way."

"Took the words right out of my mouth, Duncan," Erix said, offering him a lazy smile in return. "But at least there is always a reason to rush back to each other. A purpose that will never diminish, thanks to the incredible man between us."

"I attempted to fight off the yawn, but my mind was as exhausted as my body. And I couldn't help but recognise that the sooner we slept, the sooner we could wake and do this all again. Duncan wasn't leaving for Irobel until tomorrow, so we had the time. Time – such a precious thing. Something I would never waste again.

"No more talks about duties tonight. Just do me a favour, and don't let go of me, either of you, okay?" I asked, closing my eyes and giving in to the rush.

"Never," Duncan replied, running soft fingers up my torso.

"Never *ever*," Erix said, always attempting to one-up Duncan. A little healthy competition certainly didn't go amiss.

We fell swiftly into silence, allowing our laboured breathing to intermingle, playing a symphony around our bedroom. With nothing but their warm flesh and proud wings to cover me, I closed my eyes and focused on the joy that I was full of when existing between the men I loved.

I was the last of us to find sleep. When I did, it was with the warm kiss of two mouths lingering inches from my throat. And in those last moments of clarity, I felt whole: utterly, completely and *entirely* whole.

ACKNOWLEDGEMENTS

To my readers. Without you supporting me and my books, this entire book, series, career... would never have been possible. I want to acknowledge that your on going love and encouragement has meant the world to me. This series has been one of the hardest to write, but your messages, comments and DMs have really inspired me to keep going.

To my husband, for being the best research partner. I love you very much. You have always been my number one fan, encouraging me to take scary steps in this wild career. Without you, I would have stopped trying to chase my dream of being an author many years ago.

It takes a village to turn an idea into a book, and since working with Angry Robot, I have had an amazing team behind me. I want to give my thanks to every person who has worked on the Realm of Fey series. It has been a learning curve, a journey that I am so thankful to have been given the chance to take:

Eleanor Teasdale
Caroline Lambe
Antonia Desola Coker
Amy Portsmouth
April Northall
Shona Kinsella
Dom McDermott
Paris Ferguson
Sarah O'Flaherty

Hannah, my wonderful agent. In the short time we have been working together, we have already achieved so much. Thank you for being the best person to have in my corner. I appreciate everything you've done for me, and this series.

A special thanks to my friends, Jasmine Andrady, Kirsty Bonnick, Laura R. Samotin and Merlin, who have championed this series from the day it was all but an idea in my mind. Without your encouragement, this would never have been possible. Thank you for the endless texts and calls of me throwing ideas at you. You've each had such a firm part in this journey for me. If not for you, I likely would never have even finished this series.

To Ben of 2019: thank you for ignoring those negative comments, and writing this series. They told you no one would want a 'gay fae fantasy' book, that it would never do well in a market led by straight fae romances. If you hadn't blocked out the noise, you would have never been able to write this acknowledgement in the first place.

Lots of love,

Ben Alderson

xo

We are Angry Robot, your favourite independent, genre-fluid publisher, bringing you the very best in sci-fi, fantasy, horror and everything in between!
Check out our website at www.angryrobotbooks.com to see our entire catalogue.
Follow us on social media:
Twitter @angryrobotbooks
Instagram @angryrobotbooks
TikTok @angryrobotbooks

Sign up to our mailing list now: